THE
Colonial Countess
TRILOGY

ROBIN BELL

BALBOA.PRESS
A DIVISION OF HAY HOUSE

Balboa Press books may be ordered through booksellers or by contacting:

Balboa Press
A Division of Hay House
1663 Liberty Drive
Bloomington, IN 47403
www.balboapress.com.au
AU TFN: 1 800 844 925 (Toll Free inside Australia)
AU Local: (02) 8310 7086 (+61 2 8310 7086 from outside Australia)

Print information available on the last page.

ISBN: 978-1-9822-9268-3 (sc)
ISBN: 978-1-9822-9267-6 (e)

Balboa Press rev. date: 11/22/2021

CONTENTS

The Colonial Countess

The Compassionate Countess

The Countess Connections

The Colonial Countess

CHAPTER 1

Despite the need to get home for the evening milking, seventeen year old Mary Evans couldn't resist pausing at the top of the hill, to gaze out over the view she loved so dearly. The rolling hills, bathed in sunlight, and the flats, with dairy and beef cattle grazing in the paddocks, stretching down to the sea sparkling on the horizon. After a couple of minutes, she sighed and turned her horse, knowing that she had a busy afternoon and evening ahead of her before she could relax for a short time after dinner prior to going to bed.

As Trixie cantered slowly along the drive to the farmyard, Mary thought of the letter in her pocket. They rarely received letters these days, let alone ones from overseas. Stratford, Synbeck and Lyons, Solicitors, sounded very formal, and she wondered '*why is a solicitor from England writing to mother?*'

After leaving the groceries and mail in the kitchen, and checking that her mother was comfortable on the couch beside the fire in the living room, Mary went out to the dairy to assist her step brother Graham milk the small herd of cows that they still owned, following their father's tragic death fighting a bushfire two years ago.

They chatted as they milked, then, while Graham shut the cows in their night paddock, Mary fed the chooks and locked them in their shed, shut the pigs in their sty, then fed and chained the dogs to their kennels before heading to the kitchen for dinner.

1

Aunt Clara, their father's sister, lived on the farm with them, doing the bulk of the house work and cooking now, while Mary and Graham did the farm work. She also nursed Mary's mother Patricia, who was virtually bedridden these days, following a severe bout of influenza three months ago that had left her with a severe cough and muscle weakness.

When Patricia read the solicitor's letter after dinner she went very pale, and took some time to regain her breath before she looked up at Mary. 'Please help me back to bed Mary, then bring me the large yellow envelope that's in the top drawer of my desk.'

Patricia lay back against her pillow with a sigh of relief. 'That letter was from my mother's solicitor Mary, asking me to return to England as soon as possible. My brother David has been killed in a riding accident, and my mother is desperate to see me again.'

Mary was astounded to hear this news, as she had no idea that she had a grandmother and, until recently, an uncle in England. Her mother had always been very reticent to discuss her life before she arrived in Australia and met her husband Tom, a widower with Graham his two year old son.

Imagine Mary's astonishment when she saw that the solicitor had addressed her mother as Lady Patricia! 'Why does the solicitor call you Lady Patricia Mother?'

Before Patricia could answer she was overcome by a severe bout of coughing, and took some time before she could speak. 'Mary my love, you will have to go to England in my place to see your grandmother. There is no way that I could undertake a three month sailing voyage in my state of health.'

When Mary opened her mouth to reply, Patricia squeezed her hand gently. 'Mary, the contents of the yellow envelope, plus the key taped to the desk drawer, must be taken to the solicitor Mr Lyons, at his office in Lewes in southern England as quickly as possible. I will explain all about our family in England after you get me a cup of tea.'

While Mary was in the kitchen making the tea, she heard her mother coughing again, so hurried back to her bedroom. To her horror, when she entered the bedroom, she found her mother lying motionless on the bed, eyes staring sightlessly at the ceiling.

Three days later, on the first day of the New Year, Patricia was laid to rest beside her beloved Tom in the local cemetery. Mary was the sole beneficiary of Patricia's will, her worldly wealth appearing to consist mainly of a few pieces of jewellery and a small amount of money. The farm was now Graham's, so Mary was at a loss as to what the future might hold for her.

As the days passed, Mary began to think more about the mystery of her mother's family in England, and re read the solicitor's letter. He stated that a solicitor in Melbourne had been instructed to arrange and pay for Patricia's passage to England, and this led Mary to wonder if those instructions might now apply to herself, if she decided to go to England. Following much discussion with Graham and Aunt Clara about the pros and cons of such a trip, it was decided that Mary should at least take the train to Melbourne and speak to the solicitor Mr Mee.

So, on a hot January day a fortnight following her mother's death, and two days after her eighteenth birthday, Mary arrived at Flinders Street Station in Melbourne, feeling stiff and sore after sitting on a hard wooden seat for the three hour duration of her first train journey.

After a refreshing cup of tea at the station, Mary hired a cab to the solicitor's address in King Street. Walking up the stairs to the office on the third floor, she began to have serious doubts regarding what she was about to do, but then decided that she was being pathetic, and before she could change her mind she knocked on the door with Mr Mee's name on it, opening the door when she heard a voice call, 'Come in.'

A young lady sitting at the desk smiled as she looked up from her typewriter. 'Good morning Miss. How may I help you?'

Mary handed her the letter and Patricia's will. 'My name is Mary Evans. Could I please see Mr Mee about this letter to my mother?'

The letter was taken through to another office, and soon after a middle-aged man appeared and ushered Mary into in the inner office, where he pointed to a chair in front of his desk.

'Please take a seat Miss Evans. I'm Charles Mee, the solicitor referred to in this letter to your mother. May I ask why your mother has not accompanied you to speak to me?'

Mary took a deep breath. 'My mother died not long after she read that letter she received just after Christmas.'

'I'm so sorry to hear your tragic news Miss Evans. How may I help you?'

'Thank you Mr Mee. Before my mother died, she told me that she was too unwell to travel to England, and wanted me to go to meet her mother in her stead. I must tell you, Mr Mee, I had no idea I had relatives in England.'

'Did your mother never speak to you of her life before coming to Australia Miss Evans?'

'Please call me Mary, Mr Mee. Mother never spoke of her life before she met and married my father in Melbourne, and I'm very puzzled to see my mother being referred to as Lady Patricia.'

'I'm sorry Mary I can't help you, and like you I know nothing of your mother's history.'

'Mr Mee, as the sole beneficiary of my mother's will, could the reference to 'arrangement and payment for Mother's passage to England' be transferred to me?'

The solicitor quickly reread Patricia's will then smiled. 'I see no reason why not Mary. The sooner you leave the better. Would you like a cup of tea while you think seriously about what a trip to England would entail?'

While Mary drank the tea brought in by Mr Mee's receptionist, he took a folder from the top drawer of his desk. 'I will start looking into booking your passage on the next steam ship bound for England straight away Mary. Do you have somewhere to stay in Melbourne while these arrangements are being made?'

Mary shook her head in dismay. 'No Mr Mee. I came to your office straight from the station, and was expecting to travel home this afternoon. I'm afraid that I don't have enough money with me to stay one night in Melbourne, let alone more.'

'As your mother's sole beneficiary, all of your expenses from today on will be covered by her estate.'

Mr Mee stood up and opened his office door. 'Carol, please take Miss Evans to the Winsor Hotel, and book her a suite for the rest of the week.'

As Mary and Carol were leaving the office, Mr Mee handed Mary a heavy leather purse. 'This should cover your personal expenses while you wait to hear about your passage to England Mary. Make sure that you leave this purse in the hotel safe whenever you leave the hotel.'

The next three days were a blur of totally new experiences for Mary. She had never seen such splendour as the foyer of the hotel, the rooms of her suite that would have housed a family at home; and the dining room and food were beyond her belief!

When she tentatively asked how she was to pay for all this luxury, she was told that everything was taken care of. '*By whom*' she wondered '*and why?*'

The crowded streets, and the shop windows fascinated Mary, though she was careful not to wander too far from the hotel on her own. Mr Mee called to see her just after lunch on the third day, to inform her that she was booked on a ship sailing for England in two days' time. He introduced her to his Aunt Felicity, who was also booked to travel to England on the same ship, and was seeking a female companion for the trip. Like Mary, Felicity had never travelled abroad, and was rather apprehensive of being on her own.

Felicity had a list of clothing and other articles required for the three month journey, so the next day they went shopping together for all the necessary items. Felicity had been left very comfortably well off by her deceased husband, and Mary had been assured that her family in England would pay all her costs. Mary however was still very careful not to go overboard with her spending, never having been in the habit of spending money on things she really didn't need.

CHAPTER 2

On Board ship
Mid January 1886

The following day, all their luggage was transferred to the ship, and just before they too were taken to board, Mary posted a long letter to Graham and Aunt Clara, explaining that she was about to sail for England, and apologising for not getting back to say goodbye in person.

The ship towered above them as they stood on the dock, and it seemed just as huge when they climbed the gang plank, and stood on the upper deck, waiting to be taken to their cabins. Mary was delighted, but rather stunned to find that she had been allocated a first class cabin all to herself, while Felicity was in a similar cabin a little further down the passageway. Both ladies went back out onto the deck to watch as the ship left the dock and sailed down Port Phillip Bay, and out through the Heads to Bass Strait, each of them wondering if they would ever return.

Thankfully, both Mary and Felicity were good sailors, and were two of the few passengers who regularly met in the dining room for meals during the first three days of the journey, when the weather was extremely windy and the huge waves seemed to toss the large ship around like a cork.

Following their first stop at Albany, on the southern tip of West Australia, the ship headed north into the Indian Ocean, on route to the next stop at Galle, a port on the island of Ceylon. Apart from a couple of rather violent storms, the voyage was uneventful. Both women enjoyed the journey immensely, filling their time with the many activities on the ship, reading books from the ship's library and chatted as they wandered the decks or sat in the passengers' lounge. Soon the weather became quite hot as they crossed the equator, and neither of them ignored the stewardess's suggestion to divest themselves of as much of their heavy under garments as possible, and to wear cotton dresses, if they had them.

Felicity and Mary both enjoyed getting off the ship at Galle, keen to stretch their legs and see some of the sites near the port, before the ship headed to Suez, where they began the much anticipated journey through the Suez Canal to Port Said on the Mediterranean Sea. The canal was quite narrow, the banks seemingly quite close to the sides of the big steam ship as it slowly made its way towards Port Said. There were a couple of lakes where ships could pass, so their progress was unimpeded.

The Mediterranean Sea was calm and the weather fine for most of the journey to Marseille, the southern French port where some of the passengers disembarked, before the final leg through the Straits of Gibraltar into the Atlantic Ocean, then the English Channel and finally, just after breakfast on an early April morning, the ship sailed up the River Thames and berthed at the Royal Albert Dock, London. The journey had taken two and a half months, the Suez Canal cutting the voyage time by a couple of weeks.

While Mary and Felicity were a little sad that they were to go their separate ways when they docked, they were also relieved to be at the end of their sea voyage, and were looking forward to having solid ground under their feet once again.

CHAPTER 3

England
Mid-April 1886

The purser met Mary before she left the ship. 'An employee of the solicitor Mr Lyons is waiting for you at the foot of the gangplank Miss Evans. He will collect your luggage and arrange transport for you.'

When Mary walked down the gangplank, a young man with a broad smile stepped forward and touched the brim of his bowler hat. 'Would you by chance be Miss Mary Evans?'

'Yes I am.'

He continued in an accent that she found hard to understand. 'My name is Ben, and I have been sent to take you to meet Mr Lyons. Please wait in this cab while I collect your luggage.'

Ben handed Mary into a waiting hansom cab, then proceeded to instruct porters to gather all of Mary's luggage and stow it in a second cab. When all was ready, Ben climbed into the cab with Mary and tapped the roof with his umbrella. 'We are going to Paddington Station Miss Evans, where we will catch the afternoon train to Lewes, a town in Sussex about sixty five miles south of London. We should arrive there late in the afternoon.'

After lunch at Paddington Station, Mary and Ben were taken to the front of the train, where Mary found herself seated in a well-appointed first class carriage with padded leather seats, a far cry from the hard wooden seat she had endured when travelling to Melbourne. Mary was apprehensive, yet excited about her unknown future as they travelled through countryside, so unlike the country she was accustomed to. The trees were different in shape and colour to the gum trees that she was so fond of at home.

When the train arrived at Lewes later in the afternoon, Ben escorted Mary to the White Hart Hotel, where a middle-aged gentleman, dressed in a black suit and holding a bowler hat met them in the foyer. Ben introduced them. 'Mr Lyons, this is Miss Mary Evans. Miss Evans, may I introduce Mr Lyons?'

While the introduction was being made, Mr Lyons stared at Mary with a puzzled frown before he eventually spoke. 'It is a pleasure to meet you Miss Evans.' A little shaken by his cool reception, Mary seriously wondered what had possessed her to travel to the other side of the world, with no knowledge of what awaited her. However, after his apparent surprise at seeing her – '*he was after all expecting my mother*' she supposed – Mr Lyons booked her a room at the hotel.

Over a much needed cup of tea in the hotel dining room, Mr Lyons enquired about her trip, and her first impressions of the countryside that she had seen on the train journey. 'The scenery is very different from what I'm used to in Australia.' Mr Lyons spent a lot of time watching Mary as she spoke, then excused himself for his rudeness. 'I'm so sorry Miss Evans. You look so much like your mother when I knew her nearly twenty years ago that I am quite lost for words. I was devastated to receive Mr Mee's telegram informing me of dear Lady Patricia's passing. Do you feel up to telling me a little of her life in Australia?'

Mary once again found herself telling the story of the arrival of his letter, and the subsequent events leading to her arrival in Lewes. She also informed him of her total lack of knowledge of her mother's English background, and her anxiety regarding the money being spent on her behalf, without knowing why, or how she was to pay it back.

Mr Lyons noticed Mary stifling a yawn, as fatigue from her travels caught up with her. 'Why don't you retire to your room for a rest my dear, while I read through the contents of the envelope that your mother sent with you?' Before she went to her room, Mary gave Mr Lyons the key that she wore on a chain around her neck. 'Thank you Mary, this is the key for your mother's bank security box.'

That evening, Mary, Mr Lyons, and his wife Celia had dinner at the hotel. Mrs Lyons was keen to hear about Mary's life in Australia, and was amazed to hear of the native animals that Mary spoke about, especially the kangaroos. Before they parted at the end of the meal, arrangements were made for Mary to meet Mr Lyons at his offices across the road, at 9.00 the next morning, where he would explain everything.

The next morning, following her first night on solid ground after the two and a half months on board ship, Mary was ushered into Mr Lyons office, where she and Mr Lyons sat in the two lounge chairs near a glowing coal fire. Mr Lyons looked at Mary and took a deep breath. 'Mary, I must warn you to prepare yourself for some rather surprising information that might take some time to adjust to.

Your maternal grandmother, Lady Emma Everton was a Countess who it turns out, sadly died just a week before your mother. This meant that her daughter Lady Patricia inherited her title, and was unknowingly a Countess for just a week. Mary, as your mother's only child, on her death you inherited her title.'

On saying this, Mr Lyons stood in front of Mary and bowed. 'It gives me great pleasure to be the first person to greet you with your full title – Lady Mary Emma Evans, Countess of Longmire and Oakdale Estates.'

Mary sat stunned for a moment, then started to laugh, much to the chagrin of Mr Lyons. It took a while for her to realise he was being very serious, and that maybe she should listen to the full story. Mr Lyons smiled at her, then sat down. 'As the elder of two children, Lady Patricia was the heir to her mother's heraldic title, a fact bitterly resented by her younger brother David. He tormented Patricia throughout their childhood and into their teenage years whenever he was home from boarding school until the day after her eighteenth birthday when Lady Patricia suddenly disappeared.

David told everyone that his sister had slipped and fallen into the river and had been swept away, but they never found any trace of her body or her clothing, and there was always some doubt of her death. Her mother, the Countess, was grief stricken, but was finally forced to concede that, in Patricia's continued absence, David would become her heir when he was twenty one.

David was the total antithesis to Lady Patricia. She was of a sunny disposition, always helping others, and wonderful with children and animals, while David was surly and cruel, to people and animals alike.

Although the Countess was forced to name David as her heir, she didn't trust him, so had a codicil added to her will, stating that should she die by accident or misadventure, David would not inherit the title, nor the fortune and lands that went with it. Consequently, he spent most of his time living in the family residence in London, spending his allowance as quickly as he received it, gambling and drinking to excess, and growing more bitter and unpleasant as the years passed.

Unfortunately for David, lack of concern for his horse and judgement clouded by a bad hangover caused him to be ejected from his saddle when he tried to make his horse jump a large hedge on a frosty morning. He was found barely alive with a broken back, and taken to the local doctor's surgery, where he died later that afternoon.

Apparently, he made a deathbed confession to the doctor, admitting that he had arranged and paid for his sister to be kidnapped, drugged, and put on a ship sailing to Melbourne, Australia. The couple paid to accompany Patricia, virtually as her gaolers, were told that she was a thief and escapee from the asylum, and was to be kept locked in a cabin for the entire voyage.

As soon as the Countess was informed of this confession, she sent people to Australia to search for any information about her beloved daughter. As Patricia had similar features to her mother, a sketch of the Countess was sent with the private detectives.

Finally, after nine months of searching, word arrived of a woman married to a Victorian farmer, who might be the lady being sort. A detective from Melbourne thought he had spoken to your mother when he called at a farm to ask for directions to the next town.

Unfortunately, letters from the colony take months to arrive, so it was a further seven months before my letter to your mother arrived just prior to her death. Unbeknown to Patricia, her mother had caught a chill and died just a week before her own untimely death. The wording of Patricia's will, which I'm sure didn't make much sense to you at the time Mary, verifies your ascension to the title, and to all it pertains.'

Poor Mary was totally confused and unsure what all this meant to her. 'I will have some tea and cake sent in, and will give you time to digest the information I have just given to you, before we discuss how this will affect your future.'

Half an hour later, Mr Lyons returned. 'Mary, you are now a Peer of the Realm, an extremely rich young lady, and owner of thousands of acres of land, with stewardship over many thousands more. Also, you are the owner of numerous businesses in England and overseas.'

He paused while Mary looked at him in horror. 'The family residence, Longmire Hall, is about six miles from Lewes, with three farms and Longmire village within the vast Longmire Estate. An equally large acreage, the Oakdale Estate, is up north in Yorkshire, and there is also the family residence in London.'

Head reeling, Mary agreed to go out to lunch, then to visit the bank to have the estate accounts changed to her name. However, when Mr Lyons asked if she would like to move into Longmire Hall that afternoon Mary shook her head. 'I would prefer to spend tonight at the hotel, if you don't mind Mr Lyons, to try to get my head around all of this incredible information before I take on the next challenge.'

CHAPTER 4

Sussex, England
April 1886

T he next morning, Mary was astounded when people addressed her as My Lady, or as it sounded m'lady, the women curtseying and men bowing their heads to her as she made her way to the breakfast room with Mr Lyons and Celia.

Celia was amused at Mary's confusion. 'As you are now a Countess Mary, people speaking to you will refer to you as My Lady or Your Ladyship, not Mary as you are used to, and you will be referred to as Lady Mary when being spoken about. Your full title will be used when you are introduced to new acquaintances, or at formal occasions.'

Soon afterwards, Mary and Mr Lyons left Lewes in a hansom cab, Mr Lyons patiently explaining what Mary was likely to be confronted with when they arrived at Longmire Hall. A messenger had been sent ahead to advise the Longmire Hall servants of the new Countess's impending arrival.

While Mary was trying to take all this in, she was also observing the countryside they were travelling through. So different to the scenery she was used to in Australia, yet quite appealing in a way she couldn't quite fathom.

At first this confused Mary, then she remembered she was now on the other side of the world, and although it was summer when she left Melbourne in January it was now spring in England.

About half an hour after leaving Lewes, the cab passed through two imposing wrought iron gates, opened by an elderly gateman who doffed his hat and bowed at the waist as they passed.

The wide driveway passed through a dense woodland of trees, of a type Mary had never seen before, many just beginning to burst into leaf. The woodland changed to open parkland, with grass so short Mary thought it had been freshly mown, until she noticed some black faced sheep grazing a little way from the driveway.

Mary had lived her entire life in a small, single storey, wooden farm house in Australia, and was totally unprepared for her first sight of her new home, Longmire Hall.

As the cab rounded a curve in the drive, before her at the end of the long, straight, tree lined driveway stood an imposing white, multi storied stone building, with elegant steps leading up to an impressive portico and stout wooden front door. Windows seemed to cover the entire facade of the building, with numerous dormer attic windows under a high pitched roof with countless chimneys. The grand building was set on a slight slope of immaculate lawn, with a small lake to the side. The whole setting seemed like a fairy tale to Mary.

As the cab stopped at the marble steps, a man appeared to hold the horse's head, and another man held out his hand to help Mary down from the cab. The front door opened and a tall, thin lady, dressed in a long black dress appeared, and waited as they ascended the six steps.

'My Lady, may I introduce you to Mrs Howard, the Longmire Hall housekeeper. Mrs Howard, your new Countess, Lady Mary Emma Evans, Countess of Longmire and Oakdale'.

Mrs Howard gave a brief curtsey, and said curtly 'Welcome to Longmire Hall My Lady,' then stood aside when Mr Lyons stepped forward to lead Mary through the open doorway into a huge, high ceilinged hallway, with a black and white tiled floor. There was a wide, beautifully carved staircase, dividing to lead to landings on the left and right of the hall, with a large framed landscape painting adorning the wall at the top of the stairs.

Mary was guided through a door into an imposing sitting room, with a fire blazing in the large ornate fireplace, and a magnificent view through French doors of the manicured green lawns leading down to the lake.

Mr Lyons turned to the housekeeper. 'Mrs Howard, please have all the indoor staff here in five minutes.' When the housekeeper turned abruptly and strode out of the room Mr Lyons frowned, then turned to Mary, who he knew would be feeling very intimidated. 'Don't worry my dear, all will be well. Just be polite and formal with the staff.'

Mrs Howard returned, followed by two women and a teenage girl. 'Your Ladyship, this is Mrs Smith the cook, Polly the parlour maid and Jane the kitchen maid.' All three curtsied and said 'Good morning My Lady' in unison. 'The groom, stable hand, gardener and his assistant, are outside and will be introduced to you later. There is also an estate steward, who is at the moment away from the estate.'

Following lunch with just Mr Lyons and herself sitting at a dining table large enough to seat twenty four, Mr Lyons had to leave to go back to his office in Lewes. 'Don't worry too much Mary. I will keep in touch. I suggest that when I leave Mrs Howard shows you some of the house.'

He glared at the housekeeper as she said 'I'm very busy at the moment, but I will make time to show you to your room m'lady.'

Half an hour later, Mary was happy to retire to her room, staggered at the size and number of rooms she had eventually been shown, and she had yet to see many of the bedrooms, the nursery wing, and the servants' rooms in the attics, plus two more wings. But her relief was more due to the fact that she was away from Mrs Howard's barely disguised contempt and ill feeling towards her.

Mary's bedroom on the first floor was immense, seeming to be about half the size of their house at home. There was a large four poster bed with curtains tied back, a charming fireplace with a glowing coal fire, two lounge chairs, and window seats under the two large windows overlooking the lake. There was also a dressing room, a bathroom with the largest bath Mary had ever seen, and an indoor water closet.

In fact, everything in Longmire Hall appeared to be of huge proportions. Next to her bathroom was a smaller bedroom (still larger than her bedroom at home) that Mary assumed had been used by her grandmother's maid.

Not sure how to spend the rest of the afternoon, Mary went back down to the sitting room, taking with her a book from her luggage that had been taken up to her room and unpacked while she was at lunch.

She didn't like the idea of someone else going through her personal things, but decided not to say anything until she had a better understanding of what was expected of her, and what she could, or should and shouldn't do. Everything seemed to be run extremely formally.

Dinner that night was a lonely affair for Mary, sitting at the head of the long empty dining table. Although the meal was delicious, there was far too much food for her to eat – she just hoped it wouldn't be wasted.

Polly stood silently near the table, serving the various courses, and removing dishes as Mary finished first the soup, then the main course and dessert. Not sure should she speak to Polly, Mary stayed silent, other than to thank her for serving her meal.

Again, at a loss as to what should be done when the meal was completed, Mary excused herself and went up to her bedroom. As she entered the room, she felt so miserable, the homesickness she had managed to control throughout most of her journey, swept over her, and she lay on the bed and sobbed into her pillow.

Sometime later, she heard a gentle tap on the door and Polly's anxious voice. 'Are you alright m'lady? May I come in?'

'Come in Polly. I'm fine, just exhausted from travelling. By the way Polly, who unpacked my luggage?'

'I did m'lady. It is part of my job. I hope I put everything in the right place. I will be looking after your rooms, and will be at your service should you require anything.' She pointed to a bell pull near the fireplace. 'Just pull that cord whenever you want me m'lady. I will come up to your bedroom after dinner each night to close the curtains, turn down your bed and, if it is cold, I will warm the sheets with a bed warmer before you come up to bed.'

Mary felt encouraged by this short conversation with the maid. 'What time should I go down for breakfast in the morning Polly?'

Surprised, Polly looked at Mary. 'Breakfast will be served at whatever time you ask for it to be served m'lady.'

'Polly, being in a household this large with servants is all very new and strange to me. What time does Mrs Smith usually start work in the kitchen each morning?'

Polly could see that the young lady in front of her appeared to be very unsure of herself. 'Since the passing of your grandmother the Countess, Jane has been going down to the kitchen at 6.00 each morning, to stoke up the range and put the kettle on, while I follow soon after to set the fires in the breakfast and sitting rooms.

Mrs Smith is in the kitchen by 6.30, where we all have a cup of tea before breakfast is prepared for the indoor and outdoor staff. However, now that our new Countess is in residence, we are awaiting your directions as to what our morning schedule will be.'

Mary took a deep breath before issuing her first direct instruction to a servant. 'In that case Polly, I would like to have my breakfast at 7.30 in the morning.'

Polly smiled. 'I will let Mrs Smith know m'lady, so your breakfast will be served in the breakfast room at 7.30 in the morning. Would Your Ladyship like a cup of tea brought up to your room before you dress?'

Mary felt uncomfortable having someone her own age being subservient to her. 'Thank you Polly that would be lovely.'

Polly's gentle tap on her door roused Mary the next morning. She entered, carrying a tray bearing a china teapot, milk jug, cup and saucer all with the same delicate floral pattern, a red rose in a vase and a small white card with a hand written message 'Welcome Your Ladyship.

Polly opened the curtains, then turned to face Mary. 'Your Ladyship, we servants are very happy to have a mistress in the house again. The past months, since your grandmother's death have been very unsettling, as we didn't know what the future held for us.'

Mary drank her tea, dressed in a skirt, blouse and jacket – she wasn't at all interested in the ladies' fashions that she'd seen in London and Lewes, but supposed she would have to have some for formal occasions. She carefully tucked the card in her bag, then went downstairs, hoping that she could remember where the breakfast room was.

Mrs Howard was waiting for her at the bottom of the stairs and after a sharp 'Good morning m'lady' led Mary to the breakfast room.

At the doorway she stopped. 'My Lady, you should speak to me first before talking to the servants, as I am the only one to instruct them.'

Stung by this rebuke, Mary poured herself a cup of coffee from the silver coffee pot sitting on the sideboard laden with steaming dishes, and sat beside the fire, wondering how she was going to deal with this situation. Mary had the feeling that Mrs Howard didn't approve of her being there; why she wasn't sure. Wherever Mary went in the house after breakfast, the housekeeper seemed to be present, and always intervened if Mary tried to speak to any of the servants. It appeared that Mrs Howard was a hard task master to the indoor servants, and Mary was horrified at the way she constantly berated them for what seemed to be very trivial issues.

During the next few days Mary was extremely miserable, feeling very alone, and at a total loss as to what she could or couldn't do in the house. Mrs Howard made no effort to help, seeming to take great delight in her growing misery. Neither Polly, Jane nor Mrs Smith were permitted to speak alone to Mary, and Mrs Howard demanded that they stood with their heads bowed if Mary was nearby, and to only respond with either 'yes or no m'lady' if Mary spoke to them.

At first, Polly tried to talk to Mary when they were alone in Mary's bedroom, but the poor girl was severely reprimanded when the housekeeper found out. From then on she was forced to enter and leave Mary's rooms with the barest acknowledgment to Mary. Both thought that Mrs Howard must listen at the keyhole while they were together.

As a naturally active, independent young lady, used to working hard from dawn to dusk, there was no way that Mary could live the sedentary, empty life it appeared she was expected to endure at Longmire Hall, thanks to the title of Countess that had so suddenly been thrust upon her.

Mary's only release during those boring, lonely days of her first week at Longmire Hall, was to go for long walks in the parkland, or to visit the stables, where Mrs Howard had minimal influence. A keen rider and horse lover, Mary took great delight in meeting the half dozen horses in the paddock – or as she was told 'the field.' The four black horses were coach horses, while the two bays, Rusty and Tiger, were usually used to pull the cart and buggy, though they had been broken to ride.

'Where are the saddle horses, Robert?'

The older groom frowned. 'All the hunters were sold following Mr David's death, m'lady.'

Mary decided that she would buy herself a new horse, so sought Robert's advice. 'I wish to purchase a horse suitable for my personal use Robert. Will you please help me choose one?'

Robert was thrilled to discover that their new mistress was interested in the horses, and was happy to discuss them with her. Mrs Howard, on the other hand, was furious and barely disguised her disdain. 'Your Ladyship, it is not correct for a person of your status to visit the stables alone, and certainly not to talk to the groom.'

However, despite Mrs Howard's orders not to do so, Robert encouraged Mary to talk about her life in Australia when she visited the stables. During their discussions, Robert realised that their new Countess, although young and struggling with the strangeness of her new life, was a lady with a mind of her own, and a strong belief in right and wrong. Quite the opposite to the uneducated, unskilled peasant from the colonies that Mrs Howard kept implying Mary must be, during the staff meals in the kitchen. She was sure that the young upstart wouldn't last a fortnight at Longmire Hall. Robert didn't agree, but made no comment.

CHAPTER 5

Longmire Estate,
Sussex, England
April 1886

After breakfast on her first Sunday at Longmire Hall, Robert drove Mary to the Longmire village church half a mile away, while the rest of the servants walked. Several people were waiting outside the church, no doubt to see the new Countess, but no one moved until the Vicar introduced himself, and led Mary to the family pew at the front of the church, where she sat in solitary isolation throughout the service.

When everyone followed Mary and the Vicar outside after the service a couple of ladies introduced themselves, and told Mary that they remembered Lady Patricia well, and were very sorry to hear of her sudden death. However, everyone else quickly left the church yard, but not before Mary heard words like 'upstart, too young and won't last' muttered from a group surrounding Mrs Howard.

Back at the Hall, Mary went into the sitting room to await lunch, and sat staring into the fire, wondering what in the world she should do. Suddenly she felt as though her mother was in the room speaking to her. '*You are the mistress in your own home now Mary. Mrs Howard is obligated to carry out you wishes, if she is to stay on in your employ.*'

Mary knew that there was a servants' hierarchy, according to position and length of tenure, but she was after all their employer, and had ultimate authority, even over Mrs Howard!

During lunch, Mary decided that if she was to assert her authority it was best not to procrastinate, so as she left the dining room she turned to Polly who was clearing the table. 'Polly, please tell Mrs Howard that I wish to see her in the sitting room immediately.'

After waiting five minutes for Mrs Howard to appear Mary went to the kitchen, to find the housekeeper sitting at the table with a glass of wine in her hand, talking to the embarrassed servants. 'That young upstart can just wait. Who does she think she is?'

Furious at such blatant insubordination, Mary quickly removed the glass from Mrs Howard's hand, and firmly placed it on the table. 'You will go to the sitting room *immediately* Mrs Howard.'

Before she left the kitchen, Mary turned to Polly. 'Did you say 'immediately' when you passed on the message Polly?'

'Yes, I did m'lady. Mrs Howard just laughed, poured herself a glass of wine, and said that she would go when she was good and ready.'

When Mary entered the sitting room she walked past Mrs Howard, who was standing in the middle of the room, and stood looking out at the lake for a moment before turning slowly to face the housekeeper. Mrs Howard suddenly appeared to realise that she had overstepped the mark, and showed signs of apprehension as Mary stared at her.

'Mrs Howard, I am not prepared to put up with your discourteous behaviour towards me any longer. Unless you accept the fact that I am your employer, and am to be given due respect at all times, your employment will be terminated immediately, without a reference.'

Mrs Howard was speechless, staring at Mary as though she couldn't believe what she was hearing. Without a word, she turned abruptly and stormed out of the room, slamming the door behind her.

Mary decided to give the housekeeper time to calm down, and went out through the French windows into the garden. She had only been out there for a short while, when she heard a loud scream. Running back inside she was met by Polly. 'Please come quickly m'lady. Mrs Howard has collapsed in the hall.'

The housekeeper was lying unconscious near the front door, a large carpet bag clutched in her left hand. Her breathing was very shallow, and as Mary knelt beside her, she gave a slight shudder and stopped breathing. Looking up at Polly, Mary could see that the maid understood what had just occurred, and appeared to be accepting the housekeeper's death without undue fuss.

'Polly, please find Robert, and ask him to send James for the doctor and then come back inside with you.'

As Polly ran towards the back door, Mary went into the housekeeper's room to collect a sheet to put over the body. She was amazed to see the mess that Mrs Howard had left behind, and had no doubt that the housekeeper was leaving when she collapsed.

Robert followed Polly into the hall, and he prized the carpet bag handles from Mrs Howard's grasp. They were all shocked to see that in addition to a few articles of clothing, the bag was full of silverware. There was also a purse that Polly told Mary held the house keeping money for each month, and sure enough there was quite a sum of money inside. There was also the housekeeping bank book, to which Mrs Howard was a signatory.

'Polly and Robert, please don't mention this bag or its contents to anyone else.' Mary took the bag back into the untidy room, and locked the door behind her, then she, Polly and Robert went to the kitchen for a much needed cup of tea.

Mrs Smith was very upset when she heard what had happened, but was even more concerned at having Mary sitting at the kitchen table, drinking tea from a mug!

Mary looked at her shocked servants sitting in the kitchen. 'Could you all please try to ignore my title for the moment, while we discuss the current situation?' Despite some initial embarrassment of sitting at the same table with their young mistress, everyone eventually relaxed to a point that they felt comfortable enough to join in the conversation.

Polly recalled 'I was in the dining room when I heard Mrs Howard groan, then I heard the crash.' Mrs Smith added 'Mrs Howard complained to me before church that she had a headache.'

Mary tried to take their minds off the tragedy by explaining her background. 'I'm sure that you all realise by now that when I landed in England I had absolutely no idea of my family title, and all that it entails. I really am struggling to come to grips with all the formality that I now have to deal with, as well as trying to understand the whole servant system, which is as strange to me, as is the title I now possess. I'm going to be relying on all of you to help me cope.'

Dr Wilson arrived mid-afternoon to sign the death certificate. 'Mrs Howard appears to have suffered a massive seizure Lady Mary. I will arrange for the undertaker to remove the body, and will also ask Mr Lyons to arrange the funeral and contact any relations that he can find.'

Mary spent the rest of the day in the sitting room, thinking that maybe this tragedy might give her the chance to become more involved in running the house, at least until a new housekeeper was employed. She just wanted the servants to accept her, without the abject servility that she had encountered so far. Even Mrs Smith relaxed more as the day wore on, so Mary asked her to just prepare sandwiches for dinner. She told the servants that they could have light duties for the rest of the day, while they dealt with the shock of the housekeeper's sudden death.

Mr Lyons arrived the next morning, James having told Mrs Lyons the news when he passed their house on the way back to the Hall. Mary took Mr Lyons for a walk through the rose garden to explain what had occurred the day before. When they turned to return to the sitting room Mary asked 'Mr Lyons, would it be possible for me to run the household until we employ a new housekeeper? I really need something to do while I come to grips with this massive change in my life. Before I left Australia, I helped my aunt run the house, and I also did the milking and other farm work with my step brother. Now I'm going mad with boredom.'

Mr Lyons began to realise just how hard it must be for such a young lady, with no previous training for the formal role that she was being forced to undertake. 'I know of no laws stopping a Countess running the household m'lady. As to the formal role that you will be expected to undertake in the community, I will try to find someone who can help you learn what will be expected of you by your peers. I will also endeavour to find Mrs Howard's next of kin, and will arrange the funeral accordingly. Also, I'm sure Celia will know of women who might be suitable to employ as your housekeeper.'

Before Mr Lyons left they decided not to make a fuss of Mrs Howard's apparent attempt to abscond with the silver and housekeeping money.

Following Mr Lyon's departure, Mary called all the servants into the servants' hall at the end of the kitchen to tell them her plans. 'From today, you will all be referred to as staff not servants, and while I recognise and plan to keep the servant hierarchy, I will expect everyone to work together and respect each other. Mrs Smith, you will be in charge of the kitchen, and you and I will consult daily to plan meals and the kitchen budget. Jane, you will assist Mrs Smith and Polly, you will take instructions from me. The outside staff will work as usual for the moment.'

Her new 'staff' couldn't hide their surprise at her radical suggestion. 'While I'm keen for you to show respect to my title, and I'm happy to be called m'lady or Lady Mary, I hope that you will all soon feel comfortable enough to speak to me when we meet in the house or outside. I'm sure that you can all be respectful without being servile.'

Mary then astounded everyone further. 'I would prefer to eat most of my meals in the servants' hall with you. I realise that you may be self-conscious with this change to start with, but it makes sense when I'm the only 'above stairs' resident. Apart from the fact that it will save Mrs Smith and Jane from preparing, cooking, and clearing up after two different and separate meals, there will be a big saving in the kitchen budget; and I won't feel so lonely, being waited on and eating alone in that vast dining room.

Another plus will be a greater variety of meals for you, as Mrs Smith and I will be organising one menu for the staff dinners, not just mine.' This brought a murmur of approval from the group. 'Of course, if there are visitors, roles will have to become more formal, with meals being served with the required protocol. However, I can't see this being a big problem, as I have no other family that I know of in England, nor friends who might visit regularly, if at all.'

Leaving her staff to discuss her proposal, Mary went out to the garden, then decided to walk around the lake. Fascinated by the numerous birds on the water, she walked to the far end of the lake. As she paused to look back at the Hall, Mary thought she heard a whimper. She couldn't see a dog anywhere nearby, so started to walk off, but again she heard the whimper, louder this time.

Looking more closely at the water's edge, she noticed a brown sack half submerged at the edge of the lake. Quickly she pulled it out of the water and discovered to her horror that the sack contained a small, very wet grey puppy. He felt so cold and lifeless, but as Mary cuddled him inside her jacket and rubbed him hard, he began to revive, to the point that he looked at her with big trusting brown eyes, then promptly went to sleep.

Mary hurried back to the house with her precious cargo, and met Polly in the hall. 'Polly, please find me an old towel, and ask Mrs Smith for some warm milk to give to this poor little pup.' She then went into the sitting room and proceeded to rub the puppy hard in front of the fire. Slowly he warmed up and dried off to the point that he could sit up and gulp down the warm milk that Jane put in front of him. After a couple of licks to the hands patting him he curled up beside the fire and went back to sleep.

While Jane went to the laundry to find an old laundry basket and blanket to make a dog bed, Mary wondered who in the world would tie a helpless little pup in a bag, and throw it into the lake. At first she pondered whether she would be able to keep the puppy, and where would he live – in the house or in the outhouse? Then she remembered; it was her decision what happened to the pup.

With Mrs Smith's consent, Jane was given the job of keeping an eye on the pup, while Mary and Mrs Smith consulted on the following week's menu. Both felt that it would help take the young girl's mind off the recent tragedy. Mrs Smith stood up as Mary was about to leave the kitchen. 'Lady, after you left the kitchen earlier, everyone agreed to give your proposal a trial run. We are all very pleased to be called staff instead of servants, and are keen to work hard at our jobs without the rigid formality that has always been imposed on us throughout our working lives.'

Ben arrived mid-afternoon, and was surprised to find Mary helping James brush two of the large carriage horses. 'Good afternoon Your Ladyship. I have a message for you from Mr Lyons. He has contacted Mrs Howard's brother, who lives in Wales. They have arranged for her funeral to take place in the village church at the end of the week. Mr

Jones said that he and his wife will attend the funeral, then will take Mrs Howards possessions back to Wales with them.'

As Mary and Polly had already packed all of Mrs Howard's clothes and possessions into a chest, Mary was able to show Ben what needed to be removed. 'Ben, please ask Mr Lyons to issue an invitation to Mr and Mrs Jones to stay at the Hall, should they desire.'

'I will do that m'lady. Also, Mrs Lyons has offered to take you shopping for suitable funeral clothes tomorrow morning.'

'Thank you Ben. Please tell Mrs Lyons that I accept her offer, and will meet her at their house in the morning.'

That night, the staff and Mary, who conceded to sit at the head of the servant's dining table, were served with a three course meal of soup, roast beef with all the trimmings and finally, a large apple pie with cream. 'This meal is in honour of our new working and dining arrangements. Just don't expect every dinner from now to be like this one!' Mrs Smith reminded the staff as they left the table.

When she went up to bed that night, Mary felt the happiest she had been since her mother's death. She truly felt that she could live at Longmire Hall, with the support of her new staff. Also, she now had some company in her room. Scruffy, as the pup had been named, was curled up in his basket beside the fire. Mary had always had farm dogs for company in Australia, and had longed to have one of her own that she could have in the house with her. But her mother had been adamant that dogs must stay outside. Mary and Scruffy had other ideas.

Mary was woken early the next morning by Scruffy scrabbling at the door. Taking him down to the back courtyard, he happily obliged to do his business, then trotted straight back inside, up the stairs to her bedroom and onto the bed. Mary concluded that any fleas that he may have had would have drowned in the lake, so she allowed him to cuddle up to her and went back to sleep.

Breakfast was quite relaxed as the staff discussed their plans for the day. Mary had asked them the night before if they would mind using breakfast time as a semi-formal staff meeting, when they could all keep each other abreast with jobs needing to be done, if extra help was required etc. Everyone was quite enthusiastic at this new approach to their work.

Robert and Mary set off for Lewes in the buggy straight after breakfast, the horse setting a good pace, covering the six miles in just over half an hour. Celia Lyons greeted Mary with such a big smile and friendly approach that Mary instantly felt at ease in her company. 'I hope you don't mind that Mr Lyons discussed your unexpected elevation into the aristocracy with no formal training, with me Lady Mary. I am only too happy to help you, whenever you wish.'

'Celia, does this title mean that I can no longer be called Mary by my friends? At least in private?'

Seeing the anguish on Mary's face Celia smiled 'I can see no reason why not Mary! A less formal title for others maybe Lady Mary if you prefer.'

Robert drove Mary and Celia to a large clothing emporium in the town. There, the two women spent the next few hours purchasing the type of fashionable clothes that Mary would be expected to wear, not only to the funeral, but also when socialising in her role as Countess. Mary was pleased to discover that Celia had a modern approach to fashions for younger women, and could select designs that Mary felt reasonably comfortable wearing, but were still fashionable. Thankfully for Mary, she had a figure that allowed her to escape the use of corsets and stays!

At first, Mary was concerned about the amount of money being spent on all the shopping, which also included shoes, hats, under garments and accessories. 'Celia, all of these purchases are far too expensive. I won't be able to pay when we leave the shop.'

'I can see that my husband hasn't explained your new financial situation to you yet Mary. For the moment, just rest assured that you can afford this new wardrobe, and much, much more. An account has been set up at the Emporium in your name, which will be paid with the estate accounts at the end of each month. Relax and enjoy the experience.'

All the boxes were to be delivered to the Hall later that afternoon, so Mary and Celia retired exhausted to a nearby tea room for a late lunch, where once again it appeared that she had an account. Celia chuckled at Mary's response to this revelation. 'Your title of Countess is high up in the aristocratic hierarchy Mary, so any business you choose to deal with will be only too happy to open an account for you.'

'What will be expected of me if Mr Jones and his wife stay overnight at the Hall Celia?'

'Make sure that the servants know what is expected of them, and you entertain your guests. Don't chatter, let them lead the conversation. You would be wise not to disclose your family history or your lack of training. As there is no housekeeper at the moment, I suggest that you hire a couple more maids, and promote Polly to a more senior maid's role; to answer the front door, monitor the new maids etc. If you think Jane is up to the job, maybe she could assist as a parlour maid. I'm sure that there would be some young girls in the village willing to work at the Hall, even for just a short period.'

The drive back to the Hall was more leisurely than the morning's drive, and Mary was quite embarrassed to wake up with her head on Robert's shoulder when the buggy came to a halt at the front steps. Polly opened the door for Mary as she walked up the steps, and she was greeted by a grey furry ball tumbling down the steps to meet her. Scooping him up, Mary gave Scruffy a big hug and was rewarded with a lick on the nose. *'He sure doesn't treat me like a Countess'* she thought as he wriggled in her arms.

There was great excitement when the Emporium cart delivered the myriad of parcels soon after Mary's arrival home. They were stacked in the hallway, from where Polly and Jane took them up to Mary's dressing room. Conscious of the necessity to consult with Mrs Smith, partially in recognition of her more senior position, and also because she was becoming fond of her cook, Mary went to the kitchen to discuss the possibility of hiring two more maids while they had visitors.

'I know of two sisters in the Village who could help me in the kitchen m'lady, and I'm sure that Jane would be delighted to be allowed 'upstairs' and out from under my feet all day.'

Polly and Jane were called down to the sitting room where they were told of the proposed rearrangement of staff. 'You will also be getting new, more modern uniforms as soon as possible.' Both Polly and Jane found it very hard to contain their excitement as they went upstairs to continue to unpack the parcels and to put the new clothes away.

CHAPTER 6

Longmire Estate
Sussex, England
Late April 1886

The morning before the funeral, all the staff had breakfast as usual, and Mary explained that they would all have to resort to a more formal attitude when Mr Jones and his wife arrived later in the morning. Menus had been arranged, food purchased and a bedroom prepared for the guests. Mary was probably the most apprehensive of them all regarding the formality required throughout the visit, whereas all the present staff were familiar with the protocol. They assured Mary that they would perform as required, and maybe if needed, would as unobtrusively as possible assist Mary if she was at a loss as to what was required in certain circumstances.

The two new maids from the village, fourteen year old twins Sissy and Julie, were to arrive just after breakfast, so the staff suggested that they go formal from then on, to practice before the guests arrived. When the two young teenage girls entered the Hall, a very formal Polly introduced Mary, using her full title before escorting them off to the kitchen. It was all Mary could do to keep a straight face until the door shut behind them, then she buried her face in a cushion to muffle her laughter, thinking '*maybe the practice period isn't such a bad idea after all.*'

Polly greeted the Jones family when they arrived in the afternoon, announcing them to Mary in the sitting room. Jane brought in a trolley with tea and cake, very self-conscious as she carried out her first official 'upstairs' duty. As Jane was leaving the room Mary thanked her, then turned to Mr and Mrs Jones. 'May I offer my condolences on your loss Mr & Mrs Jones?'

'Thank you Your Ladyship. I'm afraid I haven't seen my sister for many years, but we felt that we should attend her funeral. Was she in your service for long?'

'I only arrived at Longmire Hall a few days before your sister's death Mr Jones, so I'm afraid I didn't really have time to get to know her.'

Mary was relieved when Mrs Jones covered a yawn. 'Would you mind if we retire to our room for a rest before dinner Your Ladyship? We had to catch the early train before dawn to arrive at Lewes today.'

'Not at all. Jane will knock on your door to allow you time to dress for dinner.' Mary was happy to be saved, for a time, from having to explain her new position.

When her visitors retired upstairs it suddenly dawned on Mary that she had only been at the Hall for just over two weeks. So much had happened in that time, she had seen little of the estate, other than her walk to the end of the lake. Mary knew that there were three farms and a village attached to Longmire Estate, but so far she had only met the two new maids and a couple of people at church. She must remedy that following the funeral.

Dressed in one of her more sombre new dresses, Mary led Mr and Mrs Jones in to dinner, where Polly and Jane served a magnificent four course meal, with a solemn Polly keeping an eagle eye on Jane, as she carried dishes to and from the table, prompting her softly when required.

After dinner, Mary and her guests retired to the sitting room. 'Polly, please thank Mrs Smith for the wonderful meal. Jane, you can feed some of the left overs to Scruffy; but not the bones.'

Polly smiled and closed the dining room door behind her as Mrs Jones looked at Mary. 'Who is Scruffy Your Ladyship?' Which led to said puppy being allowed into the sitting room to spend the rest of the evening lying near the fire. Mary hadn't really considered what breed Scruffy was, but Mr Jones thought he knew. 'He looks awfully like our neighbour's Lurcher pup. He will grow up to be a bit like a long haired greyhound.' Thanks to Scruffy, the evening passed quickly, with the conversation being mainly about dogs and other family pets.

The next morning Polly brought a cup of tea up to Mary, prior to her breakfast in the breakfast room with her guests. 'All the staff will be attending the funeral m'lady, except for Tom and Sam, who will remain to keep an eye on the Hall in your absence.'

Later that morning, resplendent in his formal coachman's uniform, Robert brought the coach with the Countess's insignia on the door to the front steps. As Mary and the Jones family set off down the drive in the coach, Mrs Smith, Polly, Jane, and the maids were helped into the older coach by James, also dressed in his best groom's uniform.

Much to Mary's surprise, there were a number of people waiting outside the village church. Ushered to the front pew by the vicar, Mary asked Mr and Mrs Jones to join her. Her staff, she noted, sat near the back of the church. Following the internment in the graveyard next to the church, the mourners were invited to the Hall for refreshments, so quite a large procession followed the coach back to the Hall.

James had taken Mrs Smith, Polly, Jane, and the new maids back to the hall immediately after the service, to give them time to put out the plates of food prepared earlier in the morning. He then very capably stepped up to the roll of footman, serving drinks to those who preferred an alcoholic drink rather than a cup of tea.

Mary was very proud of her staff's versatility, and told them so when she met them in the kitchen after Mr and Mrs Jones had retired to their room for the night.

The next morning, when saying goodbye to Mary, Mrs Jones remarked 'None of the gentry that I know treat their servants with such respect as you do Your Ladyship. I found it most refreshing.' A wink from Polly behind Mrs Jones back was nearly Mary's undoing. Following their departure, Mary turned to Mrs Smith. 'Could you please join me in the morning room Mrs Smith?' This was a delightful, smaller room facing east, warmed by the morning sun that streamed in through the French windows leading out into a rose garden.

'Please sit down Mrs Smith.' Mary indicated a lounge chair near the windows. 'I want to thank you for the wonderful meals that you have provided, especially over the past two days.'

Mary waited until Jane left after pouring them each a cup of tea before asking 'How long have you been at the Hall Mrs Smith?'

'I have been employed at the Hall since I was a twelve year old scullery maid forty years ago m'lady, and worked my way up to be the cook here fifteen years ago.'

'So, you would have known my mother, Lady Patricia, Mrs Smith?'

'Oh yes m'lady. All the staff loved Lady Patricia, and we were devastated when she disappeared. We all had to be very careful when Mr David was home from school though, because it wasn't just Lady Patricia he was cruel and vindictive to. Everyone was shocked when he died, but not particularly sorry.'

'Do you have family living nearby Mrs Smith?'

'As far as I know, I have no family left m'lady. I now consider the staff at the Hall to be my family.'

Mary knew that Mrs Smith was happy as the cook and ruler of the kitchen, so decided to divulge an idea that she had been mulling over since Mrs Howard's death. 'Mrs Smith, I understand that most aristocratic residences have a butler, footmen and housekeeper, plus a cook and many maids of various seniority. However, despite this being the Countess's residence, I don't see the need, nor can I justify the expense, of employing a butler and footmen for just my service most of the time.'

Becoming a little more comfortable with Mary's 'ideas', Mrs Smith nodded her head. 'Might I ask what you have in mind m'lady?'

'Initially, I thought that I could take over some of the housekeeping, but I now realise that I need to get out to meet people on the estate and further afield, and also I know that I wouldn't be happy to be kept in the house for days on end.'

Mrs Smith smiled, then Mary continued. 'I have been wondering, and need your thoughts on this Mrs Smith. Would it be acceptable to have a combined butler/housekeeper position for front door duties, overseeing the maids not under your management, and general housekeeping? This role would be carried out in consultation with both you and myself for financial and budgeting decisions.'

'I suppose it might work m'lady. You can arrange the household however you wish. If you don't mind me asking, who do you think would take on a role like that?'

Mary paused for a moment. 'Do you think Polly would be up for such a role, with our support of course?'

Without pausing to think the matter over further, Mrs Smith smiled. 'I could think of no one better m'lady. Of course, she would need support, but while we are in our 'informal mode', there wouldn't be too much extra to do to start with.'

Over another cup of tea, they then discussed Jane's possible elevation to parlour maid, with the twins being offered permanent live in positions as kitchen and scullery maids with Mrs Smith. Mary could see that Mrs Smith was thrilled to be involved in such a conversation with her. 'Do you know m'lady, this is the first time I have ever had my opinion sort by the Countess, other than for menu planning?'

When Polly was asked would she be interested in the new proposed duel butler/housekeeper role, she was speechless and begging her lady's pardon she sat in the nearest armchair. After a few minutes she stood up and faced Mary. 'I would love to give it a try m'lady.' Jane was similarly thrilled with her promotion.

Mary then went out to the stables to tell Robert, James, and the gardeners of the new indoor staff roles. 'Robert, you will be my head groom/coachman, while James will from now on be the groom. A new stable hand will be employed when more horses are purchased. Tom, you are the head gardener, and Sam, you are his assistant. As before, the outdoor staff will still be involved in the breakfast staff meetings.'

CHAPTER 7

Longmire Estate
Sussex, England
Late April 1886

Deciding to follow up her plans to buy herself a horse, the next morning at breakfast Mary looked across the table at Robert. 'Where could I buy myself a suitable horse Robert?'

'There are a number of stables in the area selling horses broken to side-saddle m'lady. I will start making enquiries immediately.'

Everyone at the table was shocked when Mary shook her head. 'I have never ridden side-saddle in my life. I learnt to ride astride in Australia, and I have no intention of riding any other way!'

Listening to Mary confirmed Robert's growing opinion that their young Countess had a mind of her own, and was prepared to flout some of the traditional standards it was just assumed that she would adjust to. 'Would you like me to saddle up the two bays to go for a ride this morning m'lady?' Robert thought this would give him an opportunity to assess her riding ability.

'That is a wonderful idea Robert. I have so missed being on a horse since I left Australia. I will go up to change into my riding habit straight away.'

Mary was thankful that she had bought a split riding skirt, jacket, and riding boots when she was shopping with Celia. Dressing quickly, she almost ran back to the stables, so keen was she to sit on a horse again.

After a quiet greeting with Rusty, the horse that James had saddled for her, Mary accepted his offer of a leg up; though normally she had no trouble mounting a horse by herself. Gathering the reins, she took Rusty for a quiet walk around the courtyard to get the feel of his mouth, and to allow him to adjust to her weight in the saddle.

When Robert mounted Tiger, they walked side by side until they were at the edge of the park, where Robert pointed to a large oak tree in the distance. 'We will ride to that oak tree first m'lady.' Urging Rusty into a gentle canter, Mary found his gait to be quite comfortable, so let him have his head to allow him to keep pace with Tiger. Mary felt exhilarated as the wind whistled past her, and at the joy of being on a horse again. When they pulled their horses up at the oak tree Robert smiled. 'I'm most impressed with your riding m'lady. Rusty hasn't responded so well with others who have ridden him.'

Turning the horses for home, after allowing them time to regain their breath, they rode at a more leisurely pace, discussing where they might find a suitable horse for sale.

Mary decided to have a long hot bath when she returned to the house, knowing that she would probably be stiff after being out of the saddle for such a long time. Once she convinced Scruffy that the bath was not for him, she lay soaking until the water started to cool. As she was about to get out of the bath, Polly tapped on the door. 'Excuse me m'lady, I have some warm towels for you.' Towelling herself dry with the thick warm towels, Mary began to admit that she could easily get used to this life of luxury!

After church the next day, Robert spoke to Mary about buying a horse. 'M'lady, I have spoken to Mr Grant, a local farmer on the other side of the village, who has some horses for sale. He would be honoured if you chose to look at them. He is well known for breeding good hunters, though you won't have to hunt if you buy one of his horses.'

The following day Robert took Mary in the buggy to Mr Grant's farm, about a mile from the village. It had a neat, double storied farm house, large barn, out houses and an impressive stable block. Both Mr and Mrs Grant came out to greet Mary, and she was invited into the house for a cup of tea. Mrs Grant was so nervous serving a Countess she nearly dropped the tea pot, but eventually calmed down so that they could enjoy her lovely scones and cake.

Half an hour later, Mary and Robert were taken to the stables and five horses were paraded before Mary. All were geldings of about sixteen hands, which didn't worry Mary, as she had often ridden larger horses. However, none of them made her feel *'that's the one for me.'* As she and Robert were discussing each of the horses they had been shown, there was a commotion in the stables; a horse neighing loudly and men yelling.

Rushing into the stables, Mary saw two men with pitch forks advancing on a dappled grey filly, who was rearing as she was forced into a vacant stall. Mary shuddered as she heard the horse crash backwards into the stall and the door slammed shut.

Mr Grant was dismayed that the Countess had witnessed the drama. 'I'm sorry about that Your Ladyship. She's a rogue horse that I was given to break, but as no one can get near her I'm going to have to shoot her.'

Mary smiled at the upset farmer. 'Mr Grant, could I please have a closer look at her in the stall?'

Watching the young filly trembling at the back of the stall, with blood trickling down her chest from a pitch fork prod, Mary's heart went out to the poor animal. Softly she started to sing to her, soothing words with no real meaning, but they appeared to settle the trembling horse. After a while when Mary softly called to her, the filly began to take hesitant steps towards the stall door.

Everyone watching held their breath as Mary began to fondle the muzzle extended towards her, because the horse was known to have a vicious bite. In a dream like state, the filly allowed Mary to move her hand all over her head, behind her ears and onto her neck. Then, much to everyone's surprise, she stood still to allow Mary to put the halter hanging near the door on her.

Mary turned to the watching men. 'Please could everyone leave the stable and shut the door. I'm going to open the stall door, and don't want the filly to escape if she decides to bolt.'

When they had done as she asked, Mary clipped a lead to the halter, then slowly opened the stall door, talking quietly as she did so. The filly hesitantly walked out into the central passage, then with a long sigh put her head on Marys shoulder, almost like saying *'at last, someone who is going to look after me'*.

Mary decided there and then this was to be her horse, even if she wasn't ready to be ridden yet. In Australia Mary had taught horses to let her ride them, without using the usual method of domination and breaking the horse's spirit. She felt confident that she could do the same with this little gem. And that was what she would call her – Gem

About ten minutes later, Mary called for the door to be opened, and she went out with Gem walking calmly beside her on a lead.

'I would like to buy this horse Mr Grant,'

'Take her immediately Your Ladyship. I'm only too happy to be rid of her.'

So Mary left the farmyard walking beside the buggy leading Gem, who was looking around with ears pricked, alert to all that was going on about her, gently nickering as Mary spoke to her. Robert couldn't believe what he was watching, after having seen the crazed horse of an hour ago. Mary didn't want to scare Gem by tying her to the buggy. 'Robert, do you think Rusty would let me ride him while he is in the buggy shafts, while I also lead Gem?'

'I'm not sure m'lady, but I think it is worth trying. If anyone can do it, I'm sure that you can m'lady.'

As Robert held Gem's lead and Rusty's bridle, Mary explained to Rusty what was going to happen, then sprang onto his back. After a startled look behind him, he stood still while Robert handed Mary Gem's lead and climbed back onto the buggy. They started at a walk, then soon Rusty was trotting briskly towards home, with Gem trotting beside him. Mary found that she could use the shafts like stirrups, making the bare back trot more comfortable.

When they arrived back at the Hall, everyone was amazed to see their young mistress riding Rusty in the shafts of the buggy, leading a beautiful young grey horse. At Mary's quiet command, they all stood back as she dismounted, still holding onto the new horse's lead. Rusty was released from the buggy, then both horses were led into the stables and placed in adjoining stalls. Mary gently brushed Gem, while James rubbed Rusty down. Both horses were fed and watered, then left contentedly standing close to each other in their stalls.

Early the next morning, Mary went out to the stables to find both Robert and James quietly talking to Gem, who was standing at the back of her stall. Apparently she had had a settled night, but had become frightened when the two men came downstairs from their quarters above the stables. However, when she saw Mary, Gem walked to the stall door, and stood quietly to have her head rubbed. 'Robert, come and stand next to me.' Taking his hand, she held it for Gem to sniff, then with Mary's soft voice encouraging her, she allowed Robert to gently rub her cheek, then her ears.

Mary then called James over and introduced him to the nervous horse. Both men were experienced horse handlers, but were amazed at the way the horse responded to Mary, and how she was prepared to accept them so quickly following her quiet introduction. With Mary still near her head, Gem allowed James to enter her stall to place feed in her feed bin.

Robert shook his head in amazement. 'Lady Mary, how do you calm her like that?'

'I'm not really sure Robert, but a lot depends on trust. The horse has to trust me, and I have to trust that the horse won't hurt me. I have always had a special rapport with horses, and people at home jokingly called me a horse whisperer. I'm sure that Gem will learn to trust both you and James if she doesn't feel threatened, like she felt at the Grant's farm. I would be happy to come to the stables for the morning and night feeds, until you feel confident that Gem trusts you to go into her stall.'

As Mary and the two men walked through the back door on their way to the kitchen, Mary noticed a door partially hidden by a small cupboard. Neither men knew where it led. When they reached the kitchen, Mary looked at her cook. 'Do you know where the door behind the cupboard near the back door leads to Mrs Smith?'

'That is the indoor entrance to the estate office m'lady, but it has been blocked off since Mr David's death.'

Curiosity aroused, Mary decided to have a closer look at the door after breakfast. Everyone was talking about the new horse, but Mary asked them not to go near her until she had settled into her new home.

Excusing herself as the staff chatted, Mary walked around the outside of the house until she came to a heavy wooden door with a big metal door knob. Turning it, she found the door to be locked. Standing on tiptoes, Mary peered through the small window recessed into the wall, and could see a large desk with some papers and a book on it, plus cupboards on one wall and a large safe beside a door that she presumed was the one that she had seen in the passage.

With Polly's help, Mary pulled the cupboard away from the door but found that it too was locked. 'There are some keys in Mr David's study m'lady.' This was a room that Mary had not been shown by Mrs Howard.

The study was very dusty. 'Mr David never allowed us to go into his study, and no one wanted to go in following his death.' Mary had no such qualms and walked in, gazing around at the bookcase on one wall, a well-stocked gun cabinet on the other, and a large window looking out over the long driveway behind the ornate flat topped desk. A couple of sheets of paper and an inkwell were the only items on the desk.

Sitting in the high backed leather chair, Mary tried to open the drawers on either side of her knees, but found that they were all locked. Frustrated, she turned to look out of the window, and saw Robert walk across the drive. The sun glinted on his watch chain, and she had a sudden memory of her father's watch chain with some keys on it. Mary turned to Polly, still standing at the doorway. 'Polly, do you know what happened to my Uncle David's personal possessions?'

'As far as I'm aware, everything is still in his room m'lady. The Countess ordered that his room was to be left undisturbed.'

David's watch chain, with his watch and two keys attached, was on the dressing table next to his brush set, and a wooden box containing studs, some rings and cravat pins. Taking the keys back to the study, Mary was relieved to find that the first key she tried opened the drawers in the desk. A metal box in a top drawer contained a number of keys, all conveniently labelled with yellow tags. Laying them on the desktop, Mary discovered a key for each of the estate office doors, plus another larger one labelled Office Safe.

Mary and Polly could hardly contain their excitement as they hurried back to the inside door and inserted the key. With little pressure it turned, and when Mary turned the door knob the door opened into the small room. The office was tidy, with a less ornate but larger flat topped desk and a leather office chair. The book on the desk was a ledger of rents, collected quarterly from the farms and village tenants. By the dates, it looked like the next payments were due in a few days.

Mary had enjoyed doing the bookwork and budgeting on the farm at home, and hoped that she might be able to be involved in the estate bookkeeping. She had yet to meet the estate steward, who was still away from the estate. The gong sounded for lunch before they could look much further, so everything was left as they found it, and the door was locked behind them as they left.

Deciding to spend some time with Gem after lunch, Mary took her to the small field behind the stables. At first a little hesitant, she followed Mary around the field, occasionally taking a bite of grass as she went. Eventually, she felt comfortable enough to move a little way from Mary, who stood in the middle of the field talking quietly to her. When she felt that Gem had relaxed enough, Mary asked Robert to let Rusty loose in the field.

Mary walked to the gate, where she and Robert watched the two horses canter around the field, obviously enjoying the freedom, but keeping close to each other. As they watched, a buggy with a woman at the reins entered the courtyard.

'That is Tess Telford from Home Farm m'lady.' Robert went over to assist the lady alight, prior to introducing her to Mary.

Mary remembered seeing Mrs Telford and her husband at the funeral. She led her into the house, on the way meeting Jane. 'Please bring some tea and cake to the sitting room Jane.'

When they were seated near the window in the sitting room, Mrs Telford turned to Mary. 'I do apologise for calling unannounced My Lady, but I didn't know what else to do. Our family is in utter turmoil at the moment, with the quarterly rent due at the end of the week. I'm afraid that we will not be able to pay the increased amount that Mr Morris insists we must pay. He has threatened us with instant eviction from Home Farm, if the amount isn't paid in full this rent day.'

Tess broke down sobbing, then continued. 'My husband is currently arranging to sell some of the dairy herd to try to meet the higher rent, and I know that Old Tom on Farm Two is planning to sell all of his cattle and leave. Mr Morris has threatened eviction to any tenants who don't pay the increased rent.'

Mary was appalled to hear that all of her tenants on the three farms, and in the village, had had their rents raised to an extortionate level since her grandmother's death, and were all under a similar threat of eviction.

When told how much the Telfords were expected to pay, Mary excused herself to go to the office to check the rent ledger that she had seen on the desk earlier. As she thought, the amount that Mrs Telford had told her that they were expected to pay was nearly double the amount listed in the ledger. All the rents listed were of varying amounts for different tenants, but as far as Mary could see, everyone's quarterly payment had not changed for the past few years. What was going on?

Hurrying back to the sitting room, Mary was pleased to see that Mrs Telford had composed herself, and Jane had placed the tea and cakes on the table. As Jane poured the tea, Mary sat beside Mrs Telford. 'Do you mind telling me about your family and the Home Farm Mrs Telford?'

'Please call me Tess m'lady. My husband Bob and I took over running Home Farm from Bob's father, who had lived there from the time Bob's grandfather took on the tenancy of Home Farm. We have three sons, two in their early twenties, and our youngest son is sixteen. We hope that Will, our eldest son, will take over from us when he is older. We own the dairy herd, some sheep, pigs and cattle, and supply the Hall with meat, milk, butter, cheese and eggs, our rent being adjusted to cover payment for these supplies.'

Finishing her tea, Mary turned to Tess. 'I will look into the matter Tess, and I assure you, you will not be evicted from Home Farm by Mr Morris.'

When Tess left, Mary went back to the office to look through the desk drawers and the cupboards on the wall, finding nothing that she considered untoward. Just Agricultural books, leaflets, bank receipts for money paid into the estate bank account, and invoices from the numerous vendors with whom the estate dealt with.

However, when she opened the safe, Mary discovered a newer ledger with all the tenants listed, all with higher rental amounts next to their names. These figures were for quarterly payments dated from before David died, the amounts increasing each quarter. Money paid and upcoming rent was listed, plus there was an additional listing of payments for an address in London. It appeared that each tenant's rent would have more than doubled by the time the next rents were paid. There was also a cash box containing a large sum of money, and pushed right to the back of the safe was a bank book in the name of Anthony Morris, with some large deposits listed.

Sitting at the desk comparing the amounts in both ledgers, Mary began to suspect that the deposits in the bank book were similar to the difference between the amounts listed in the ledgers. It looked very much as though Mr Morris was embezzling the extra money that he was collecting in rents each quarter.

During dinner that evening Mary asked her staff 'Have any of you heard of increased rents in the village?'

The twins looked at each other. 'Our parents' rent has gone way up m'lady, and they are really worried about Mr Morris's next visit, and so are our neighbours.'

Robert added 'I have heard that a number of your tenants in the village are concerned about possible evictions m'lady.'

Mary decided that she needed to speak to Mr Lyons about these revelations. 'Robert, I wish to leave for Lewes immediately after breakfast tomorrow morning. James, do you feel comfortable spending some time with Gem by yourself?'

'I would be happy to m'lady. I'm becoming very fond of Gem, and she seems quite happy when I'm near her.'

Chapter 8

Longmire Estate
Sussex England
Late April 1886

When Robert dropped Mary off at the solicitors' offices early the next morning, she was ushered straight in to see Mr Lyons, where she showed him the two ledgers and bank book, and told him of her suspicions. He was horrified at what appeared to be embezzlement of funds, not from the estate but from the tenants. 'Mr Morris was a friend of David's, who appointed him as estate steward, but I haven't seen him much since David's funeral.

So long as he collects, registers, and pays the collected amounts into the estate account, Mr Morris is pretty much a free agent, travelling between the three properties, arranging for repairs as required. At no time has he informed my office of the increased rents. Not long ago, I heard that Mr Morris has been spending quite a lot of time at the London residence, instead of at his cottage on the estate, but that didn't unduly give me cause for concern.'

'*What are these sums of money from the London residence?*' Mr Lyons wondered as he looked through the ledgers. The butler and his wife had a set budget for keeping the house ready, should her Ladyship wish to visit London, and they sent their accounts to Mr Lyon's office to be paid monthly, so there should be no additional money going into anyone's bank account.

'Mary, may I have your permission to keep the ledgers and bankbook to spend more time comparing them with the estate accounts, and to also possibly show them to the police?'

'I'm sorry Mr Lyons, I don't think I can leave them, as I'm concerned that should Mr Morris return before I put everything back, he will be alerted that someone has been in the office.'

Mr Lyons immediately set three of his office staff to copying all relevant pages from the ledgers, so that Mary and Robert could return to the estate after they had had a short lunch.

'Mary, I will come out to the Hall later tomorrow morning to report on progress, and maybe to offer some plans of action.'

Mary was relieved to get everything back into the office when they arrived home, then she went out to spend the rest of the afternoon in the field with Gem, getting her used to being handled out of her stall, and gently introducing her to the lunge rope. At feed time Gem trotted over to James, who was watching near the gate, and followed him into the stable.

The following morning, Mr Lyons arrived and told Mary of his visit to the police, the estate's bank manager, and the manager of Mr Morris's bank account. 'The police suggest that we supply Bob Telford with the bank notes to pay his rent on rent day. I have arranged to record the note numbers before we give them to him. When the final tenant leaves the office, the police will go in and check the ledgers and the safe. I suggest that we both go to Home Farm straight away to discuss this plan with Bob and Tess.'

The Telfords were thrilled, and very relieved that Mary and Mr Lyons were putting a plan into place to stop them from being evicted from their farm. Mary and Mr Lyons were invited to lunch, and it was a very jovial meal. Mary was introduced to the three sons Will, Matthew, and John. Both younger boys were currently working part time next door, helping Old Joe with his cattle. Mary found it a little disconcerting having boys about her own age, all being so subservient towards her.

On their way back to the Hall, Mary and Mr Lyons called to see Old Joe to tell him that he would not be required to sell his herd to pay his rent. 'I'm relieved to hear this, and promise not to spread the news, m'lady. However, I'm sorry to tell you Lady Mary that I'm finding the farm too much work with my arthritis, and will soon have to sell my cattle, to allow me to move closer to my daughter near Brighton.'

This started Mary thinking on the way back to the Hall. 'Mr Lyons, would it be possible for me to buy Old Joe's cattle, and employ men to work his farm, rather than leasing the farm to another tenant?'

Mr Lyons was becoming used to Mary's interesting approach to her new role, and only paused briefly before he replied. 'It could be possible Mary. Do you have anyone in mind?'

From her earlier conversation with Tess, Mary knew that her two younger sons were looking for more work, as there wasn't really a living for them working for Old Joe on Farm Two. 'Matthew and John Telford already do most of the work for Old Joe, so I was thinking of offering them positions as fulltime paid employees to run Farm Two.'

When Mr Lyons returned to Lewes, Mary had James saddle Rusty, and she rode over to Home Farm to discuss her plans with Bob and Tess. Bob smiled at Mary. 'That would be the answer to our prayers to keep both boys employed near home, m'lady. I'm sure they will do a good job.'

When Will was consulted, he agreed with his parents. 'It will be good for the two lads to work for themselves, but they would still be near enough for us to help each other when needed.'

Matt and John were ecstatic when told of Mary's plan, though she had to restrain their enthusiasm. 'Don't forget Matthew and John, I still have to discuss this proposition with Joe, and get his agreement before you can start on your own.'

As Mary rode next door she thought '*this is work the estate steward should be doing, certainly not someone in my new position.*' However, she shrugged her shoulders and decided that she would do what she wanted to, within reason of course. It was a lovely day for a ride, and she was thoroughly enjoying the sun on her back.

Old Joe was overjoyed at her proposition, and was pleased to hear that Matt and John would be taking over the farm he had loved and tendered for nearly all of his working life. 'Joe, could you please find out at the market what would be a fair price for your cattle? I will consult Bob Telford about the prices that he would offer if he was buying your other goods and chattels. Also, Joe you won't be expected to pay any more rent.'

Chapter 9

Longmire Estate
Sussex, England
First week May

As rent day approached, everyone was on tenterhooks, awaiting Mr Morris's arrival. Usually he was on the estate well before rent day, but he had been away for so long, no one knew when he would arrive. They thought that Mr Morris must know by now that a new Countess had been found, and wondered whether that would make him stay away, or would he dare come back and bluff his way through, collecting the rents then take the contents of the safe and run, Mary and Mr Lyons weren't sure.

He would be aware though, that this rent day would probably be his last chance to make a lot of extra money, and might gamble on the fact that the new Countess was not yet in residence, or at least would not deign to be involved with the tenants.

Mr Lyons had a suggestion. 'I don't think you should be introduced to Mr Morris when he arrives Mary. Let him think that you aren't in residence yet, and see what he does.' All the staff were keen to play along with the plan to keep Mary's arrival a secret when the agent arrived.

Mid-afternoon the day before rent day, Mary was in the hall talking to Polly, when they heard a horse galloping down the drive. Looking through the front window, they saw a large man whipping his lathered horse, which made Mary's blood boil. As she went to open the front door to yell at him, Polly grabbed her arm. 'Begging your pardon m'lady, that is Mr Morris. Please go upstairs before he sees you.'

Still seething at the ill treatment of the horse, Mary ran upstairs to her bedroom as had been decided, while Polly went to warn Jane and the kitchen staff. Not long afterwards, the back door burst open and Mr Morris barged into the kitchen, pushing Sissy against the wall as he strode past. He was a big man, with a bald head and a shaggy beard, which Polly later told Mary, looked like his hair had slipped down his head. He bellowed for a cup of tea and something to eat, and slapped at Julie as she moved past him to pour water into the tea pot.

From past experience, Mrs Smith knew that there was little use trying to stop him being so rough with the girls, as he had knocked her over a couple of times in the past, when no one was watching. He had always been a bad tempered bully, so she wasn't surprised at his ill humour today, as she was sure there would have been some heckling as he rode through the village.

Mr Morris lived in one of the cottages near the stables, and there was great relief when he informed Mrs Smith that he would not be requiring dinner or breakfast, as he had brought some food with him. He took fresh milk, cheese, and tea from the kitchen over to his cottage, and was later seen entering the estate office with his saddlebags over his shoulder.

Dinner that night was a sombre affair, with Mary eating in her room and James in the stables, keeping a watch on the office door. Robert had set up a roster to keep an eye on the cottage all night, and he would make sure that no horse could be taken from the stables during the night, should Mr Morris decide to bolt. The gate keeper had also been warned not to open the gates for anyone, and to stay out of sight, opening the gates only when Robert told him to do so in the morning.

Rent day dawned as an overcast, drizzly day, in keeping with the mood of the tenants as they gathered in the courtyard to pay their rent. Mr Morris walked across to unlock the estate office five minutes before the first tenant was summonsed to enter. Each tenant's time in the office was just long enough for Mr Morris to count the money handed to him, check it off against the tenant's name and have them sign the ledger, or as in most cases, to make their mark, before they were curtly told to leave. The next person had to wait some time before he was called in to go through the same process.

Mrs Smith kept the waiting men supplied with hot tea and scones, though some grumbled that the Countess should do more than just hand out scones. All the tenants assumed that Mary would allow things to just carry on as they had since Mr David had become more involved in running the estate as his mother grew older. They therefore held her responsible for the higher rents, and the suffering that they now had to endure to try to scrape together the money demanded. Only the Telfords and Old Joe knew of the fraudulent rise in rents, and what was to happen later that day.

Two men who hadn't managed to produce the higher rent came out of the estate office looking stunned, having been told that they were to be out of their cottages by the end of the week. Mary had earlier instructed Robert to quietly move any tenants threatened with eviction away from the waiting men as quickly as possible, to stop more unrest, and to take them home, after explaining that the Countess would not allow any evictions to be carried out.

Bob Telford was one of the last to enter the office. When he emerged, he went over to where Mary and Mr Lyons were waiting in the stables. 'Mr Morris appeared quite disappointed when I handed him the full rent he demanded. It was as though he had been looking forward to telling me to leave Home Farm.'

When the last tenant left the estate office Mr Morris locked the door, and spent the next half hour in there alone, before coming out with his saddlebags hung over his shoulder. As he locked the door behind him the two police constables, who had been waiting in the stables, walked up to Mr Morris and pushed him up against the door. While one policeman removed the saddlebags from the steward's shoulder, and the key from his hand, the other burly policeman snapped a pair of handcuffs on Mr Morris's left wrist. When the door was unlocked they pushed him inside, where he was shackled to a chair to await Mary's and Mr Lyon's arrival.

Mary and Mr Lyons entered the office together, in time to hear Mr Morris proclaiming 'I'm innocent of whatever you fools think I've done. Wait till I see your sergeant.' He barely gave Mary a glance as he glared at Mr Lyons. 'What the hell is going on Mr Lyons? I demand that these handcuffs be removed immediately.'

Without answering the furious man, Mr Lyons opened the ledger on the desk to the latest entries for the current rent day, each showing the lower rents with the tenants' signature or mark in the column beside their name and the amount paid. While he scanned the ledger, Mary opened the safe and found the cashbox with the money to go into the estate account, tallied to the amount that the lower rents added up to, with a bank payment form filled out to go to the bank the next day, as was the usual practice.

Emptying the contents of the saddlebags onto the desk, Mr Lyons showed the policemen the newer ledger with the higher rents, as paid that day and signed by each tenant. A leather pouch contained the excess money paid by each tenant, some of the notes being those paid by Bob Telford. There was also a payment form made out to Mr Morris's bank account, for the money in the pouch, plus an additional amount in another purse tallied with a new notation against the London address. The bank book, and the amount of money that Mary and Mr Lyons had earlier seen in the safe, was found in Mr Morris's jacket pocket.

The sullen steward was bundled unceremoniously onto the cart that Robert had waiting in the courtyard, and was driven off to the Lewes police cells. Mr Lyons accepted Mary's offer to stay overnight, Robert being asked to inform Mrs Lyons and to collect an overnight case for him before returning from Lewes.

Mary was amazed at how easily the staff snapped into formal mode, much better than she felt she did, when they were informed that Mr Lyons would be staying the night. He was quite amused at the transformation, knowing of Mary's usual informality with her staff. After the evening meal, served in the dining room by Polly and Jane, he sat back in his chair and drank the wine left in his glass. 'Mary, I must apologise. I truly believed that your less formal approach with your servants would have led to less care in their work, and possible disrespect towards you and your visitors. However, I'm beginning to see that your staff, as you call them, appear to be happier in their work, and are trying hard to do their best to please you. I believe that they have the utmost respect for you, even after such a short period.'

Mary was thrilled to hear such praise, and was pleased that her changes were working at the Hall. However, she was well aware of the simmering resentment many of the villagers felt towards her, due to the higher rents that they had been forced to pay to her family. This money, Mr Lyons assured Mary, would be put into the estate account after Mr Morris was tried for fraud and robbery. The rest of the evening Mr Lyons and Mary spent discussing how best to deal with the excess rent and the money in Mr Morris's bank account, which appeared to be the exact amount collected since David's death.

'Mary, I have heard from the private detective I sent to the London residence, after I saw the additional money listed in the ledger accredited to that residence. Apparently Mr Morris, the butler and his wife have been leasing out rooms to younger sons of the aristocracy who needed a London address for short periods of time. They provided breakfast, but all other meals were sort elsewhere. It was quite a lucrative business, with a long waiting list. I'm prepared to go to London to dismiss the butler and his wife if you agree.'

That night, Mary lay in bed thinking about the illegal business being carried out at the London residence, which she had yet to visit. She wondered what would be required to make the business legal, and make the residence a profitable business for the estate, rather than a drain on its finances.

CHAPTER 10

Longmire Estate
Sussex, England
May 1886

The Sunday following rent day, Mary asked the Vicar if she could speak to the congregation before they left the church. Although a little nervous when the Vicar announced that the Countess had an announcement to make, Mary stood up and faced the congregation.

'Ladies and gentlemen, I wish to apologise for the way you have been treated over the past two years, with your rents increased and the threat of possible eviction being held over your heads.'

Mary paused when there was a low growl of displeasure, then continued. 'I'm also very sorry that I was unable to ease your fears before the recent rent day, knowing that some of you were going hungry to scrape together the demanded amount. The police needed to catch Mr Morris red-handed with your money, to enable them to arrest him and seize the money that he had in his possession.

I plan to return the excess rent collected by my Uncle David and Mr Morris to all of my tenants, after Mr Morris's trial. In addition, this week there will be a bag of flour delivered to each tenant's household, plus the estate will pay up to £12/household to the village butcher and up to £10/household to the grocer, to be rationed on a weekly basis for the next quarter, according to the size and also to the earning capacity of each family. Also, a load of coal will be delivered to each household for the winter.'

There had initially been murmurs of disbelief about her plan to return their money, then everyone stood up and cheered when she told them of her additional proposal. The entire congregation continued to clap and cheer as Mary and the Vicar led them out of the church. Once outside in the sunshine, every man and woman bowed or curtsied to Mary, and thanked her for her generous offer.

Finally, when Mary was able to make her way out of the churchyard, she decided to walk back to the Hall with the staff, who were basking in the goodwill now being bestowed on their mistress. The twins in particular were ecstatic, as they knew how much Mary's offer would mean to their own family.

A couple of mornings later while Mary lay in bed, she realised that she still hadn't seen the rooms on the floors above hers, nor had she been to the village, other than to the church. It was time to slow down and get her bearings, and meet more of the people on the estate.

After working Gem for an hour that morning, Mary decided to try putting a bridle on her. As she had hoped, Gem accepted it without any show of irritation or discomfort. She even allowed Mary to lie across her back, much to the disbelief of Robert who held the bridle. He had never seen a horse trained to take a rider this way, and wouldn't have believed it if he hadn't seen it with his own eyes.

Mary was thrilled with Gem's progress, and felt that she might soon be ready to allow her to sit on her back. However, she didn't want to push her too fast. Scruffy seemed to sense her elation when she went into the house, racing backwards and forwards, attacking her feet as she walked, then racing off to get a toy for her to throw.

He had grown in the short time since she'd found him, and was becoming a much loved member of the household. He adored Mary and followed her everywhere. He was a quick learner, and knew that he wasn't to go near the horses. When Mary was with Gem, Scruffy lay patiently outside the fence, not moving until Mary called him.

Before lunch Mary met Polly in the hall. 'Polly, would you like to move to the housekeeper's rooms today?'

'Oh, m'lady. That would be wonderful. Thank you.'

Polly and Jane spent the afternoon cleaning Polly's new rooms, while Mary and Scruffy set off to explore the upstairs rooms. She was surprised to find an additional five large bedrooms, as well as the nursery, which consisted of the school room, a small sitting room, nursery maid's bedroom, governess's bedroom and sitting room, plus five smaller children's' bedrooms around the corner, each with a large single bed, chest of drawers, wardrobe, and desk.

There were steep, narrow stairs going up to the attics, and down to the kitchen at one end of the nursery, next to a bathroom that Mary assumed must be for the staff who slept in the attic rooms, while the bathroom at the other end of that wing would be for the children and nursery/ school staff.

On a lower shelf of the bookshelf in the nursery Scruffy found a toy pig, which he gently took in his mouth and pranced around Mary, before galloping down the stairs to show it to everyone else.

Mary followed more slowly, and met Polly and Jane leaving Polly's new rooms. 'Polly, could you please show me the attic rooms when you go up to collect your possessions and clean your room?'

Sounds of singing were drifting up from the kitchen, and Mary thought how much happier the staff were, smiling as they worked and often helping each other with their jobs, whereas a few weeks ago they weren't even allowed to speak to each other when they were working, and were constantly in fear of suffering the wrath of the housekeeper.

The twins were a breath of fresh air in the kitchen, sharing the roles of kitchen and scullery maids, amid peals of laughter, and quite often somewhat tuneless duets. Mrs Smith was revelling in their company, as well as in her daily chats with Mary when they planned the dinner menus. The entire staff were thrilled with the variety of evening meals being served, and all were enjoying the less formal approach to their work and to each other, although they were always polite and respectful to Mary when in her company.

When Mary and the two maids made their way up to the attics, she was surprised at the number of doors along the passage. However, when she saw the size of the rooms she understood how there could be so many rooms on that floor. Most were used as storerooms, and five were currently the bedrooms of the female staff. Each room had a sloping ceiling and a small window, and there was only just enough room for a single bed and a wash stand with a jug and basin, plus a small set of drawers.

Polly saw Mary's expression change when she looked at the attic bedrooms. 'In summer these rooms are very hot and airless m'lady, as many of the windows don't open; while in winter the rooms are freezing and damp. Mrs Smith told us that she had ice on her blanket one winter, before some much needed roof repairs were finally carried out.' Compared to the proportions of all the other rooms and staircases that she had seen in the house, Mary was appalled at the basic sleeping quarters for her staff, who after long hours of hard work were expected to climb up the very steep, narrow, wooden staircase to the top of the multi storied house.

She was beginning to realise just how much women and men in service were seen and treated as chattels by their employers, with little to no thought to their comfort and wellbeing, other than that they carry out the duties set for them. If they couldn't, they were quickly replaced.

Later that evening, Mary had a drink of cocoa in the kitchen with Mrs Smith. 'Is there was any ruling that live in staff, other than the butler and housekeeper, have to sleep in the attics, Mrs Smith?'

'No m'lady. It is just a cheap, convenient way to keep staff apart from, and out of sight of the family living in the house.'

Mary thought about this reply while she finished her drink. 'Mrs Smith, would you like to move down to the governess's bedroom and sitting room?' The incredulous look on the cook's face surprised Mary, until she realised that having a larger room with a fireplace 'downstairs' to herself, was beyond Mrs Smith's wildest dreams.

'Jane, Sissy and Julie can move to the children's rooms, which are larger and more insulated than the attic rooms, and each has a small fireplace. You can all move tomorrow, after the rooms have been prepared.'

The next morning, while the excited women cleaned their new rooms, Mary and Robert took Gem out into the small field for some lunging work. There, much to everyone's surprise, Gem not only allowed Mary to lie across her back as she had the day before, but stood still while Mary slowly swung her right leg over her back and sat up. All the time, Mary spoke softly to the young horse, whose ears flicked backwards and forwards as she listened intently. Gem looked around as Mary sat up, then walked quietly around the field with Robert walking near her head, his hand lightly resting on her neck.

After about ten minutes of walking and trotting, Mary dismounted and hugged Gem, as Robert shook his head in disbelief. Never had he seen an unbroken horse allow a rider on its back without bucking and trying to throw the rider off.

The following days were spent much more quietly than the previous few, the staff settling into their new quarters, and happily going about their duties. Mary spent a lot of time riding Gem, who didn't appear to be worried by the light saddle she now wore when being ridden. In fact, she seemed to revel in their rides around the park. Scruffy had been accepted as a riding companion, provided he stayed away from her hooves, and the three of them spent many pleasant hours together out in the fresh air and sunshine. Gem and Rusty still spent time together, but Gem appeared to be happiest when she was near Mary.

Two weeks later, the trial of Anthony Morris was held at the Lewes court of assizes, where he was charged with embezzlement and fraud. Mary was called as a witness, and was treated with great deference when she entered the court house. It took a very short time for Mr Morris to be found guilty on both charges, and he was sentenced to twelve years imprisonment at Reading Prison. All bank accounts in his name were confiscated by the court, and the misappropriated money was ordered to be returned to the Countess to do with as she wished.

Following the trial, Mary was invited to lunch in the judge's chambers, where she was introduced to several members of the local legal fraternity. All professed their gratitude for her speed in notifying Mr Lyons of her suspicions, which had led to Mr Morris being apprehended; an act that they sadly often found lacking when dealing with many of the aristocracy.

After lunch, Judge Stephens took Mary out into the back garden. 'Your Ladyship, are you aware that, as a Peer of the Realm, you are entitled and expected to become a local magistrate?' He chuckled at the shocked look on Mary's face. 'You won't be required to take up your full duties until you are twenty one, which I gather is in a couple of years. I would be honoured to coach you in the duties that you will be expected to undertake as a local magistrate, and to instruct you in English law. I can assure you that you will not be expected to sit in court alone until you feel confident to do so.' A very bewildered Mary travelled back to Longmire in the carriage, wondering what else was in store for her.

As life settled into a more regular pattern for Mary, she had more time to survey her new domain. She spent time with Polly, going through each floor and wing of the Hall, discussing how best to deal with the vast number of unused rooms. They decided to close the unused bedrooms, as well as the ballroom and two of the reception rooms, to minimise cleaning, until they were required for future formal occasions. Mary also chose to only use the dining and sitting rooms when visitors called, and to refurbish the study for her personal use. Although a smaller room in the Hall, it was still larger than the living room back on the farm in Australia. Once the study had been thoroughly cleaned, two comfortable lounge chairs were placed on either side of the fireplace. The desk, bookcase and gun cabinet remained in place, cleaned, and polished.

In the absence of an estate steward, Mary began to keep the books, checking invoices, and sending them to Mr Lyon's office for payment. At first she worked in the estate office, but once the study was available, she completed most of the bookwork at the study desk. If tenants called to discuss issues, they met her in the estate office.

Mary finally managed to visit Glendale, the third farm on the Longmire Estate, after the tenant Thomas Grey called to ask for help to repair storm damage to his barn. Glendale was larger than the other two farms closer to the Hall, and was situated in the higher country of the Longmire Estate. Thomas and his brother Paul, with the help of four shepherds, ran large flocks of Suffolk and Border Leicester sheep in the hills.

Robert accompanied Mary when she rode to Glendale. 'The shepherds sleep in small huts dotted around the hills m'lady, following their flocks as they graze the hillsides for about nine months of the year, then they move down nearer to the house in the winter, when the hills are covered with snow.'

Mary had never seen snow, so had little concept of the hardship it caused for hill farmers like Thomas and Paul. However, she listened carefully to Robert's explanation, and was quick to ask questions if she didn't understand. By the time they reached the valley where the house was situated, Mary felt that she understood most of what Robert had told her, but was totally unprepared for the sight she beheld as they topped the rise overlooking the farmyard below them.

The small thatched cottage was built up against a large boulder in the side of the hill. Attached to the side of the cottage was a large barn, and several out buildings bounded the small farm yard. The end of the barn furthest from the cottage had been crushed by a large boulder that had rolled down the hill during the storm. Luckily, the cottage had not been damaged.

Both Thomas and Paul were in the yard when Mary and Robert rode in. As they dismounted, two large, shaggy black and white sheepdogs raced into the yard, barking furiously. At Mary's quiet command they sat quietly in front of her, leaving Thomas and Paul staring in amazement. Thomas bowed his head in embarrassment. 'I am so sorry m'lady. We normally tie the dogs up when we know visitors are coming, but we didn't realise that Your Ladyship was riding up to see us.'

Mary smiled. 'In the current absence of a steward, I'm dealing with the estate affairs, and am keen to familiarise myself with as much of the estate as I can. Coming up to Glendale is more easily accomplished riding Gem, rather than being shaken about in a carriage.'

Paul took the horses into the stable, leaving his brother with Mary and Robert. 'Thomas, may I please look around the barn and out buildings before going inside?' Poor Thomas could only nod his head, as he had never known a lady, let alone a Countess, interested in being in a messy farm yard and its buildings. Taking pity on him, Mary told him a little of her farming experiences in Australia, and her desire to learn a lot more about farming in England.

Mary was fascinated to see that more than half the barn was divided into many small pens. Seeing Mary's obvious interest, Thomas slowly overcame his embarrassment. 'All the pregnant ewes are brought into the barn to lamb when it is snowing, m'lady. Paul and I take it in turns to sleep in the barn during lambing, to assist ewes if required. The other sheep are kept in sheltered fields near the farmyard during the winter, to make it easier to feed them, and to monitor the new lambs.'

Hay and grain were stored in the far end of the barn, where the roof gaped open. Obviously, repairs needed to be carried out as quickly as possible, to stop rain ruining the stored feed so essential for later in the year.

'Thomas, what needs to be done to repair the barn, and to protect the fodder in the interim?' With Thomas's requests written in her notebook, Mary had a quick look at the other buildings, noting that as they walked closer to the cottage that both Thomas and Paul were becoming more and more anxious.

As they neared the cottage, Mary began to wonder if they were embarrassed for her to enter their cottage. 'Would you mind if we sit outside on the bench beside your cottage, and have a cool drink of water while enjoying the sunshine?' She had to smother a smile at the look of relief on their faces.

Both dogs lay at Mary's feet, having walked beside her on the tour of the farm buildings, often with their muzzles pressed into her hand when she stopped to look at something. Paul was quite bemused at their antics. 'We've never seen them be so friendly, even to you or me, have we Thomas?'

Before riding away from Glendale, Mary told the Grey brothers 'I will get work started on the barn as quickly as possible. In the meantime, I will have a large tarpaulin sent up to cover the fodder, as a short term protection from rain.'

On the way back to the Hall, Mary called in at Home Farm, while Robert went back to the stables. Mary sought Bob's advice on potential workers in the village, who would be capable of carrying out the repairs, and where she might source the materials needed. 'I'm going to Lewes market tomorrow m'lady, and will speak to a couple of tradesmen who I'm sure will be pleased to give you an assessment and quote for the materials needed.'

The next morning, Mary walked to the village, where she was now a very welcome visitor. As she walked along the street, she received a cheerful greeting from all she met, and she stopped many times to enquire after the welfare of family members. Eventually, Mary spoke to the four men Bob had mentioned, and offered them the job of repairing the Glendale barn. All accepted immediately, declaring that they would be happy to start as soon as the materials were delivered. Mary knew that several of her tenants in the village were struggling to find lasting work in the district, and she was determined to help them as much as she could.

She was pleased to hear that the two Telford boys who she now employed were working hard on Old Joe's farm, sowing new crops, and repairing fences and buildings and preparing to purchase more cattle to run on the property. '*Maybe they will need some extra help soon,*' she mused as she made her way back to the Hall.

CHAPTER 11

On a cool, late June morning Mary, Gem and Scruffy were returning from a ride on the estate when Scruffy suddenly dived into a dense bush and began to bark. Thinking that he had bailed up a fox, Mary whistled to him, and was about to ride on, when a small boy ran out of the bush screaming. Jumping off Gem, Mary grabbed the boy before he could run away, and held him to her until he stopped struggling. 'Help, my brother is being eaten by a wolf!'

'Scruffy, come here immediately.' When he reluctantly emerged from the bush, he stood whimpering while staring at the bush. 'Be quiet Scruffy!' When he stopped whimpering, she could hear sobbing.

Letting go of the boy, Mary pushed her way through the low branches, to find a younger boy curled up with one arm wrapped around his head, sobbing uncontrollably. His thin grubby shirt was bloody on the back, and he was shaking, from cold or fright Mary wasn't sure which. Probably both. Struggling out of her coat she placed it over the sobbing boy and backed out of the bush, saying 'I will be back as quickly as I can.'

She wrapped her riding jacket around the other boy, and lifted him up onto Gem's back before he realised what was happening, then swiftly mounted behind him. Gem turned her head in surprise, but with gentle encouragement from Mary she stood still. Scruffy was ordered to stay guard, Mary praying that he wouldn't follow as she turned Gem towards home, hugging the young boy to her as she urged Gem into a gallop.

Robert and James ran out of the stables, and Tom and Sam appeared in the courtyard when they heard Gem galloping towards the Hall. Mary handed the boy down to Tom. 'Please take this lad straight to the kitchen to warm him up Tom, and don't let him out of your sight until I return. There's another younger boy injured, and lying under a bush near the old oak tree. James, please ride to Lewes immediately to get Dr Wilson. Robert I need you to follow me with the cart.'

While Robert quickly harnessed Tiger to the cart, Mary grabbed an old coat from the tack room, then set off on Gem back to where she had left Scruffy and the second boy. Scruffy was very pleased to see her, and enjoyed her praise for staying when she had ridden off. There was no sound from the bush, but a quick look showed her that the boy had not moved.

He was barely conscious when Robert arrived and crawled in, and gently slid him onto Mary's coat. Together, he and Mary slowly pulled the boy out through the low lying branches, wrapped him in the coat, and then laid him in the cart. Gem followed close to the side of the cart, where Mary sat holding the boy as they made their way to the Hall. All the staff, except Tom, were waiting at the back door when they arrived back in the courtyard.

While Mary took Tiger and Gem into the stables, Robert carefully carried the boy into the kitchen and placed him on a small mattress that Mrs Smith had placed near the stove, to help warm him up and reunite him with his brother, who was almost asleep on Tom's lap as he sat in Mrs Smith's armchair.

When Mary entered the kitchen, Tom turned his head. 'This lad on my lap is Alfie m'lady, and his brother on the mattress is Jack. All Alfie will tell us is that Jack was whipped and hurt his arm.' Mrs Smith had given Alfie a drink of hot chocolate, and he had also eaten a bowl of bread and warm milk before sitting with Tom near the fire. As Jack lay unconscious, wrapped in a blanket on the mattress, Alfie scrambled down and cuddled up to him; and so they stayed until the doctor arrived.

In the meantime, Mrs Smith turned her attention to Mary, who was obviously chilled to the bone after riding in the cold without a jacket or warm coat. Ordering her to sit in the other chair near the stove, Mrs Smith wrapped a blanket around Mary's shoulders, and gave her a hot mug of tea, with some brandy in it. As her mistress gratefully sipped the hot tea, Mrs Smith smiled and thought '*Who would ever have thought I would order the Countess to sit in my kitchen, and give her a mug of tea!*'

About half an hour later Dr Wilson arrived, James having met him on his way home from a visit to a patient the other side of the estate. He was horrified to see Jack's back when the bloodied shirt had been gently removed. His back and buttocks were criss-crossed with angry red welts, many of them still seeping blood.

Dr Wilson gently bathed the wounds with warm water, mixed with some antiseptic from his bag, then added some salve and covered the boy's back with a piece of clean sheet. He then straightened the obviously broken arm, thankful that his young patient was unconscious, and bound it with a splint and bandages. After checking Alfie, and announcing that he would be fine after a hot bath and some good nourishing food, Dr Wilson took Mary aside. 'Your Ladyship, I have been informed that two young boys are missing from the town workhouse.'

'Dr Wilson, please don't report the boys' whereabouts until we have found out how Jack received his injuries.'

Agreeing to wait until he returned the next day, Dr Wilson left, with instructions that Jack would need to be watched throughout the night, even after he regained consciousness. He was put to bed in the room next to Mary's, and Polly agreed to sit with him, while Alfie was given a long hot bath and a bowl of vegetable soup, with a chunk of bread and cheese. Clad in one of Robert's old shirts that came down below his knees, he climbed into bed beside Jack, and immediately fell asleep. Scruffy would have happily joined them, but was ordered out to his bed downstairs.

Jack recovered consciousness later in the afternoon, and after a small serving of soup, and a dose of the laudanum that Dr Wilson had left, he fell asleep. Both boys woke in the evening, ate some stew, and then went straight back to sleep, cuddled together in the thick feather mattress. So far, nothing more had been said about who they were, or where they had come from.

Polly, Jane and the twins took it in turns to sit with the boys throughout the night, having convinced Mary that she should have a good night's sleep, following her chilly experience in the morning. 'We are sorry to order you about m'lady, but we can't look after you too, if you catch a chill.' Despite her reluctance to leave the work to her indoor staff, Mary was secretly thrilled that they were genuinely concerned for her wellbeing, and more so that they were prepared to ignore her title, and treat her as someone they respected and cared for.

Alfie came down to breakfast the next morning, wrapped in Polly's dressing gown, and ate a bowl of porridge and some toast. He looked at Mary and hesitantly began to speak. 'I'm almost ten and Jack is eight m'lady. We were sent to the workhouse when I was six, after both our parents died from typhoid. The supervisor and his wife, the matron, were kind to us, and they made sure that we weren't picked on too much, so we settled in quite well. However, a few months ago the supervisor died, and a new man and his wife took over.

They were really strict, and beat us for no real reason. They cut our meals to two a day, and fed us as little as possible, to the point that we were soon starving. For some reason, the new supervisor picked on poor little Jack a lot more than the others, and took great delight in keeping us apart.

Last week, Jack accidently bumped into the matron in the corridor at breakfast time, and he was dragged into the supervisor's office, where he was whipped with the horse whip kept in the cupboard. When Jack didn't cry out or beg for mercy, he was hit even harder, then thrown against the wall, and hurt his arm. The supervisor stormed out, leaving Jack lying on the floor. Eventually, he managed to drag himself out of the office and was found by another boy who brought him to me.'

Alfie paused to drink some milk. 'I'd been planning to run away for a while, and decided that it was time to go. I hid Jack in a laundry basket due to be collected that morning, and hid in another just before the laundry cart rumbled into the yard. Once outside the gates, when the cart stopped to pick up more laundry further along the road, I quickly climbed out of my basket, helped Jack out of his, then we ran and hid.

We left town that night, and walked into the country, sleeping under hay ricks or in barns, eating whatever we could find. We managed to hide on a number of carts going along the road, which helped us get further from Lewes. Unfortunately, Jack's back and arm became more and more painful, and we were forced to hide under the bush where Scruffy found us, and Jack couldn't go any further.'

Dr Wilson arrived later in the morning, and after checking Jack's back and changing the dressing, he asked Alfie to repeat his story. As one of the Lewes Workhouse Board of Guardians, he was stunned to hear of the recent ill treatment of the children by the new supervisor and matron. The regular reports sent to their meetings had been quite positive, and there had been no hint of mistreatment or cutting back on food. Though he had to admit, none of the Board members had visited the workhouse following the new appointments, as planned visits by the Board members had been postponed at the last minute. As the boys appeared happy to remain at the Hall, Dr Wilson was prepared to leave them in the Countess's care, until he could investigate the accusations further.

During the following days, Jack's back slowly healed, and he gradually regained his strength and desire to move downstairs and spend time in the kitchen with Mrs Smith. Alfie was often to be found out in the garden with Tom and Sam, helping them weed and dig the various flower and vegetable beds. Both boys were eating prodigiously, and slowly gaining weight. Tess Telford sent over a range of boy's clothing that she had stored in their attic, so both boys would be warmly clad when the days became cooler.

Scruffy was friendly with both boys, and was often seen racing from the house to be with Alfie for a while, then back to the house to be with Jack. He seemed quite relieved at meal times, when both boys were in the house together.

Mary began to think about the boys' future as they settled into life at the Hall. She knew that they were both terrified of being sent back to the workhouse, but they were still too young to be sent out to work. She was becoming very fond of the youngsters, who still slept in the room next to hers, and they loved to have her tell them bed side stories of bushrangers or farm life in Australia, before being given a big hug and a kiss goodnight.

At one of the breakfast staff meetings Mary made an announcement to the staff. 'I'm thinking seriously of applying to become Alfie's and Jack's guardian as soon as possible, so that they can remain here at the Hall.' Everyone was pleased, as they too had become fond of the two lads. 'It is lovely to have youngsters in the Hall again m'lady.' Both Tom and Robert agreed that they were happy to have the two boys in the garden and the stables at any time.

Dr Wilson had spoken to his fellow Board of Guardians about Jack's beating, and after some discreet investigation had brought to light the appalling treatment administered to the children in the workhouse, the supervisor and matron were summarily sacked.

Mary was asked to meet with the Workhouse Board of Guardians, initially to give an account of finding the boys, and of their behaviour during their stay at the Hall, and also to invite her to become a member of the Board of Guardians. Her first reaction was to say no, but then she thought that maybe in her privileged position in the community, if on the Workhouse Board she might be able to bring about some changes for the better for the Workhouse inmates, especially the children.

Mary's request to be taken on a tour of the facility horrified many of the guardians, but on her insistence, arrangements were made for all of them to be shown through the facility. Only Dr Wilson and one other guardian had actually seen inside the grim walls, and all the men were visibly shaken when they returned to the Board Room. While they were still in a state of shock, and calming their nerves with several glasses of brandy, Mary asked for, and was granted, access to all the recent financial paperwork for the Workhouse. Mary's request to have permanent guardianship of Alfie and Jack was also quickly granted, much to her relief.

Jack's wounds healed quickly, and both boys were soon gallivanting around outside with Scruffy, or were in the kitchen with Mrs Smith, helping her roll out pastry or peel potatoes, actions they knew would be rewarded with a scone or piece of cake. Both boys were devoted to Mary, who was enjoying their company in the huge Hall, and beginning to look on them as she would two younger brothers. She realised however, that if they were to grow up on the estate, they would need to continue their education.

Mary discussed this with Celia. 'I know of a young lady, Sarah Green, the twenty four year old daughter of an old friend of Mr Lyons, who is seeking a new governess position.

Sarah's father was a banker in the City of London, and the family lived in a large house in Notting Hill, where they employed a number of servants, in keeping with their upper class lifestyle. Sarah attended a private finishing school in France, learning the accomplishments such as music, sewing and dancing required to equip young ladies for marriage.

Sadly, when Sarah was nineteen, her parents were drowned when the ship in which they were sailing, struck rocks near the Isle of Wight and sank. Regrettably for Sarah, her father had been renting the house, and living way beyond his means, leaving his daughter in a precarious financial state, with no home or income. Forced to seek work and lodgings, Sarah applied for a live-in position as governess to a family with two young boys in Kent. Sarah held this position for five years until the boys were sent to boarding school.'

Celia paused, then continued. 'I thought that as well as being governess to Alfie and Jack, maybe Sarah could be a companion and mentor for you Mary, to assist you in developing the social skills appropriate for your position.'

Mary and Sarah were first introduced at a luncheon held by Celia, and after an afternoon chatting in the garden, both young ladies felt comfortable enough to give Celia's proposal a try.

At first the boys weren't at all pleased having to go up to the school room each week day morning, to learn to read and write. However, when Mary explained that it was a condition of their being able to live at the Hall, they stopped complaining and settled down to their lessons.

Rather than becoming a live in staff member, Sarah accepted Mary's offer to live in one of the three cottages across the courtyard from the Hall. The two bedroomed cottage had a kitchen (to be supplied weekly with provisions from the Hall kitchen) a small sitting room and bathroom. Sarah had dinner with the staff, but prepared her own breakfasts and lunches. This way she wasn't crowding the boys, and had some independence in her off duty time.

Mary was beginning to understand that her title overrode existing social prejudices regarding her age and being a woman; and few men or women were prepared to dispute her decisions or requests. Such power she realised could easily be abused, and was determined not to allow that to happen. She found Mr Lyons to be a great confidant, who listened to her opinions, and he was prepared to offer her guidance when required.

Another person Mary was becoming very fond of was Tess Telford, who recognised the lonely young girl still grieving for her lost mother, while trying to cope with the enormous responsibility landed so unexpectedly on her shoulders.

Mary often rode Gem over to Home Farm early in the morning, with Scruffy loping along beside them. His legs seemed to be growing longer every day, and he was beginning to look rather like the shaggy greyhound Mr Jones had predicted. Scruffy and the farm dogs had developed a pact to leave each other alone, but if at any time he felt threatened when Mary was inside with Tess, Scruffy kept close to Gem.

Mary and Tess would sit and chat, or she would help her in the kitchen, and some mornings, if early enough, would help with the milking. At first the Telford family were self-conscious in her presence, but quickly relaxed when they saw the pleasure that Mary gained by helping with jobs around the farm, and in discussing the farm work with them. It wasn't long before Mary asked Bob and Tess to call her Mary.

Like Mr Lyons, Bob and Tess would listen to Mary's thoughts and plans, and would go through the pros and cons with her, reminding her not to buck the system too much, too quickly.

Chapter 12

London
July 1886

Early in July, Mary was stunned to receive an invitation from Buckingham Palace, to attend a garden party that Queen Victoria was holding at the end of the month to meet her new Peers of the Realm. Terrified at the prospect, Mary wanted to decline the invitation, but was promptly informed by her horrified staff that one did not refuse an invitation to meet the Queen!

Every spare moment for the rest of the month was taken up with lessons on etiquette, how to address the queen, appropriate responses to questions etc. So much so, by the time Mary, Sarah, Celia, and Mr Lyons travelled to London a week before the garden party, Mary's head was spinning. They all stayed in the family residence in Mayfair, now staffed with a new butler, cook and parlourmaid. Again, Mary couldn't believe the size of the residence, with so many rooms of all descriptions.

To take Mary's mind off her visit to the palace, Mr Lyons arranged for her to visit some of the businesses she owned, to meet the executives and senior staff. Celia and Sarah also took her shopping, which didn't really do much to calm her nerves.

One evening after dinner, Mary started a discussion on what should be done with the London residence, as she had no intention of spending more time than necessary in London. Sarah and Celia both tried to convince Mary that she would be expected to be in London for the season, but she was adamant that she wouldn't stay. 'I'm not the least bit interested in spending any more time in London than is absolutely necessary to socialise with the aristocracy I have met so far. I find both the men and ladies to be incredibly self-centred, ostentatious, and decadent. As far as I'm concerned, most of them are just empty headed fops!'

Seeing the shock on her companions' faces, Mary adroitly shifted the conversation back to the future of the residence. 'I've been wondering if it would be possible to turn this residence into a private hotel or boarding house.' This caused an interesting debate lasting well into the night and the next morning at breakfast. Finally, everyone agreed that it might be well worth pursuing; much better than selling the building, as Mary had intimated at one stage in their discussion.

Mr Lyons sighed. 'I will look into the feasibility of the plan, possible development costs and expected return for the expenditure Mary, then we can discuss the matter further.'

The day of the garden party dawned fine and sunny, much to Mary's relief. Mr Lyons escorted her to Buckingham Palace, where she was met by a liveried footman who took her to a small reception room to wait, for what or who she wasn't sure. Imagine Mary's astonishment when the door opened a few minutes later, and Queen Victoria walked in. Standing, Mary curtsied and greeted her monarch as she had been coached. Not sure what to do next, she waited for the Queen to sit, then sat when gestured to do so.

'Mary, your grandmother Emma and I were good friends from childhood, and I have been looking forward to meeting you. I was very sad to hear how your mother, Lady Patricia, was treated by her despicable brother, and of her early death.

I was delighted to hear that her daughter was to be the new Countess of Longmire and Oakdale, but I had no idea that you would be so young to take on such a high ranking position, especially with no training in the ways of the aristocracy. I'm interested to hear how you are coping.'

Mary spent almost ten minutes talking alone with Queen Victoria, before an aide entered to inform the Queen that the other guests had arrived. To Mary's amazement, as they left the room the Queen instructed 'Walk with me to the garden Mary. You will be more readily accepted by your older peers if you are seen entering with me.' It appeared that the Queen had already heard some derogative comments about Mary's age and colonial upbringing. The rest of the afternoon passed in a blur for Mary, as she was introduced to many men and women, all of whom were extremely polite, following Mary's entrance with the monarch.

Mr Lyons was waiting at the palace gates to accompany Mary back to the residence, where she spent the evening telling Celia and Sarah all about the afternoon.

Despite Mary's sudden favour with the aristocracy, who were now keen to be seen with her, she was relieved to leave the city and return to Longmire Hall a couple of days after her visit to the palace.

Several of the local gentry, hearing of Mary's visit to Buckingham Palace, called at Longmire Hall to meet their young colonial Countess, fully expecting her to be totally lacking in the social proficiencies expected of one of her status in their society. They were pleasantly surprised by her demeanour, range of conversation, all be it in a strange accent, and her genuine interest in the local community.

Many had heard of Mary's different approach to her servants, and were amazed at Polly's and Jane's competent dealing with all requests, whilst being respectful but not subservient. Both smiled while working, and appeared to enjoy their work; not usually condoned behaviour in servants.

Realising that it was expected of her to entertain at times at Longmire Hall Mary, Mrs Smith, and Polly set about planning some dinners for the local gentry. They decided that four couples at a sitting would be a comfortable number to cater for, and planned to have three dinners over a three week period in August.

With the growing number of occupants in the Hall now eating meals in the servants' hall, dinner was served in the breakfast room, with everyone seated around the large table. Everyone generally served themselves from dishes on the table or sideboard, but occasionally these meals were used to help train all the maids in the duties and skills required for serving at table. James was also given training in the duties of preparing and serving wine at dinner.

Mary's neat, hand written invitations sent to a variety of local gentry were accepted with alacrity. Those invited lived within easy carriage driving distance, to allow for a safe drive home in the evening after dinner. As yet, Mary was not prepared to have strangers staying overnight at the Hall.

Mrs Smith was in her element, once again preparing a variety of courses for a number of guests, as she had when Mary's grandparents were both alive. Two extra women from the village were employed to help prepare the drawing and dining rooms, and to clean all the cutlery, silver, and dinnerware.

Mary, Polly, and James ventured into the cellars to take stock of the wines stored there. Mary had little knowledge of wines, but helped Polly and James list all contents of the large underground wine cellar. Mr Lyons was a great help, with suggestions for the wines it would be advisable to have on hand, and he arranged for additional wines and spirits to be sent out to the Hall.

The first two dinners went without a hitch. As couples arrived, they were ushered into the drawing room, and offered a sherry and hors d'oeuvres. At the appointed time dinner was served, and the guests thoroughly enjoyed the meal, and to their surprise, Mary's vivacious personality, which led to lively conversation around the table.

She didn't like the way many of the so called upper-class men treated their wives and daughters as chattels, assuming that they were incapable of rational thought or conversation. So, while at the dinner table she took great delight in discussing farming and business with the men, whilst also including the women in more general conversation, though at first they were rather hesitant to speak in front of the men.

Aware that at the end of a meal it was customary for the men to stay at the table to drink port with their host, while the women retired to the drawing room with the hostess, Mary decided to flout convention and asked all her guests to withdraw to the sitting room. Her excuse was that, as the hostess, she couldn't be in both rooms at the same time.

Before they withdrew, Mary thanked Polly, Jane, and James for their excellent service, which thrilled her staff and caused a few raised eyebrows from her guests. Mary knew how hard the three had worked to make the evenings run smoothly, and was extremely proud of them.

CHAPTER 13

Longmire Estate
Sussex, England
August 1886

Regrettably, the third dinner didn't run as smoothly. Ronald Hawkins, a stout, surly, middle aged man, arrived for dinner already under the influence of alcohol. He constantly belittled his younger wife in front of the other guests, and he was barely civil to Mary, much to the embarrassment of the other guests. At the dinner table Ronald drank profusely, to the point that he became raucous, demanding more wine from James, and trying to grab Jane when she was serving the dessert.

Disgusted with this loutish behaviour, Mary glared at Mr Hawkins. 'There will be no more wine served for the rest of the meal, as I don't want my guests to become so inebriated that they won't be able to appreciate Mrs Smith's excellent dessert. There is water on the table, should anyone need further liquid refreshment.'

When Ronald started to curse and swear at Mary, his wife pleaded with him to be quiet. Turning to her he punched her in the face, knocking her off her chair, to lie unconscious in a crumpled heap on the floor.

Mary was horrified and stood up. 'Mr Hawkins, how dare you! Leave this room immediately!' When he made no effort to rise, Mary quickly walked to where he sat, grabbed hold of the collar of his jacket and yanked him off his chair onto the floor. As he staggered to his feet,

Ronald swung his fist at Mary's head, but was totally unprepared for her to duck and deftly grab his fist, swinging him around and twisting his arm so far up his back he screamed in agony.

Mary forced the bewildered man towards the door, looking over her shoulder as she went. 'Polly please see to Mrs Hawkins; James tell the Hawkins' groom to get his carriage to the front door as quickly as possible and Jane, please open the front door.'

Mary forced Ronald into the hall, out through the front door and down the steps. There she pushed him forward as she let go of his arm, and was pleased to see him lose his balance and sprawl on to the gravel drive. Standing on the steps, Mary watched the poor groom try to drag his cursing employer into the carriage. 'You are no longer welcome on the Longmire Estate Mr Hawkins. Your wife will remain here tonight, and will be taken home when she is fit to travel.'

When Mary returned to the dining room, she was pleased to see that Jane had covered Mrs Hawkins with a blanket, and was carefully bathing her bloodied face with water. Polly, in Mary's absence, had asked the remaining guests to be seated, and had given them each a small glass of brandy.

Kneeling beside Mrs Hawkins, who was beginning to regain consciousness, Mary thought her nose was possibly broken and her right eye was rapidly swelling shut. Assuring her that her husband had left, and that she was welcome to stay the night, Mary asked James and one of her male guests to carry the poor woman up to the guest room, and for Polly to put her to bed.

As no one felt like eating dessert, Mary took the remaining guests to the sitting room, offering a further brandy or port to anyone who wished it. She began to apologise for the abrupt ending to the dinner, but was politely interrupted by one of her neighbours. 'We applaud your actions Lady Mary. Ronald Hawkins has been throwing his weight around since his arrival in the district two years ago. Requests to tone down his boorish behaviour have been rudely rejected. We are astounded that a young woman has not only stood up to him, but has physically thrown him out of the Hall!'

As they left, all three couples told Mary that they felt privileged to have her as their Countess, and would be honoured if she would visit their homes at some time.

When everyone had driven away, Mary went into the kitchen and collapsed into Mrs Smith's chair beside the fire. Handed a restorative mug of tea, Mary thanked all the staff for their efforts, in what had turned out to be a very trying evening.

Polly was sitting beside Mrs Hawkins when Mary went upstairs to see her unexpected guest, who was sobbing into a handkerchief. 'I must get back home, or my husband will kill me Your Ladyship.' Shocked by such a statement Mary stared at the battered face. 'You should stay the night and wait till the doctor has seen you Mrs Hawkins.'

It being quite late in the evening, Mary decided to send James to Lewes at day break to summons Doctor Wilson, and informed her staff that she would stay with Mrs Hawkins throughout the night.

With her guest tucked up in bed, wearing one of Mary's nightgowns, Mary listened to the sad tale of Lilly's forced marriage to Ronald Hawkins. 'My widowed father owned a prosperous cutlery factory in Sheffield, South Yorkshire. Ronald somehow worked his way into my father's favour, and convinced him that he would be a good husband for his only daughter. I had no say in the matter, and found myself at twenty married against my wishes to a brute of a man twenty five years my senior. In early 1884, six months after our marriage, my father suddenly died from a mysterious illness, and I inherited his factory and fortune. Unfortunately, as a married woman, my entire inheritance belonged to Ronald, and I have never had access to any of it.

Ronald immediately sold the factory, and bought our current house, where I'm kept more as a prisoner than as his wife. I'm regularly subjected to brutal beatings for the most minor transgressions, and I'm rarely allowed outside the manor grounds. The only reason I was allowed to accompany Ronald tonight was because the invitation to Mr and Mrs Hawkins was from you, the Countess.'

Mary stayed with Lilly until just before dawn, when Polly brought her a cup of tea. As Lilly had finally settled into a more relaxed sleep Mary followed Polly down to the kitchen, where she had a short nap in the chair beside the fire after Polly informed her that James had just left to get the doctor.

Doctor Wilson arrived after breakfast, and was shown up to the guest room where Lilly was slowly waking. He confirmed that her nose was broken, and possibly her cheekbone as well. 'I will return tomorrow, better prepared to set Mrs Hawkins' nose, Your Ladyship.'

'Thank you Dr Wilson. Please call me Lady Mary as I find Your Ladyship rather intimidating!'

Once outside the bedroom he turned to Mary. 'Lady Mary, Mrs Hawkins should stay in bed for at least a fortnight, following such a blow to her head. I don't think she is fit to travel back to her home at the moment, and I'm worried about the bruising I saw on her back, arms, and legs. Would it be possible for her to stay at Longmire Hall for a few days?'

'Dr Wilson, Mrs Hawkins told me last night that her husband regularly beats her. She is welcome to stay at Longmire Hall for as long as is necessary.'

That afternoon Mary rode Gem into Lewes to speak to Mr Lyons about Lilly's situation. She was staggered at Mr Lyon's reply. 'I'm sorry to inform you Mary, but by law, not only does Ronald Hawkins have absolute control of his wife's money, but it is also his right, as her husband, to keep her under control, however he feels fit.'

'Do you mean to say that thug won't be charged for the assault on Lilly last night?'

Mr Lyons shook his head sadly. 'Unfortunately no Mary. Not only will Ronald Hawkins not be charged for assault, he is quite within his rights to demand his wife's immediate return to his house.'

Furious at this callous treatment of a young woman, Mary stood up. 'Mr Lyons, I wish to lay charges against Ronald Hawkins for verbally assaulting me, and for attempting to physically assault me. As a guest in my house, he attempted to punch me, swore at me in front of numerous witnesses and verbally and physically abused my staff.'

Had Mary not been the Countess, Mr Lyons may not have taken her accusation seriously, but seeing her determination to follow it through, he sent a clerk for the police sergeant. Hearing Mary's charge, the sergeant grinned. 'I will go out to Mr Hawkins' immediately Your

Ladyship. We have had a number of complaints recently from his workers about his brutality, but I haven't been able to charge the man without more proof.'

Mary arrived back at the Longmire Estate gatehouse just before sunset, to be stopped by the gatekeeper. 'Lady Mary, please be careful. Mr Hawkins has just pushed his way past me and is riding up to the Hall. He looks awfully angry.' Forewarned, Mary rode Gem in a roundabout way to the field behind the stables, leaving her there to graze while she ran to the back door.

A fact that Mary had not made known since her arrival in England, was that she carried her father's Colt.45 revolver in a discreet holster sewn into the pocket of her riding skirt whenever she went out riding. Polly was the only one who knew of the gun, as she had unpacked Mary's cases on her arrival at Longmire Hall. However she didn't know that Mary was a crack shot, having been taught well by her father.

Slipping in through the back door, gun in hand, Mary could hear Ronald shouting at someone in the front hall to get his wife immediately. Quietly entering the hall, Mary saw Ronald hit Jane across the shoulders with his riding whip, then throw her to the ground and raise his foot to kick the poor girl.

'Stop that you brute!'

Ronald whirled around to see who had called out. Seeing Mary he grinned, raised his whip and took a few steps towards her, only to pull up short when he saw the revolver pointing straight at him. 'Turn around and leave this premises immediately Mr Hawkins!'

After a moment of uncertainty he smirked, and told her in the crudest fashion what he would do when he caught hold of her. Disregarding Mary's sharp warning 'If you come any closer I will shoot,' he laughed and took another step towards her. Before he took a second step Mary pulled the trigger, sending a bullet through Mr Hawkins' right knee. As he lay writhing on the floor clutching his leg, the police sergeant and his constable ran in through the open front door. The sergeant bowed to Mary. 'Your Ladyship, I heard Mr Hawkins' threats and your warnings before you fired the gun, as I ran up the front steps.'

Once Ronald had been handcuffed, and an old sheet was torn up to roughly bind his wound, the sergeant was fascinated to hold Mary's gun, as he had never seen a six cylinder revolver before. 'My father gave me the gun after I had demonstrated to him that I was capable of handling such a weapon, whereas my brother Graham wouldn't even hold it.'

Lilly remained at Longmire Hall for a month while her face healed, during which time her husband Ronald was held in custody awaiting the next court of assize. When his day in court arrived he was led into the court leaning on a crutch, looking very contrite when the charges were read out.

However, the moment Mary was called to give evidence, Ronald flew into a murderous rage, ranting and raving, screaming that he would kill her, then he turned his abuse on the judge who had called him to order. When Ronald refused to quieten down and stop struggling with the two constables who were trying to hold him, the Judge wasted no time in sentencing him to be confined in the Oxford County Pauper Lunatic Asylum.

Ordered to take the prisoner back to the cells, the constables had to drag the struggling man towards the steep stairs down to the cells. As they reached the top of the stairs, Ronald turned to shout further abuse at the judge, his foot slipped off the top step, and he pitched head first down the stairway. The horrified occupants in the court room were later informed by a court official that sadly the prisoner had died from a broken neck.

On Mr Lyons advice Lilly immediately applied for, and was granted, control of all of her husband's accounts and assets. While all this was being finalised, she moved into the empty cottage next to Sarah's at Longmire Hall, where the two young ladies with similar social upbringing and interests soon became friends.

Sarah continued to teach the boys each morning, but her initial duties as lady's maid and social coach for Mary had been reduced considerably, as Mary developed her own way of dealing with her title. She had discovered that, providing she was polite and not too radical, most people attributed her different approach to the way things were done to her colonial upbringing.

Mary didn't adhere to the practise of being dressed daily by a lady's maid. Only for the more formal occasions did Sarah assist her to dress and 'dress' her hair. Most days Mary wore a long skirt, blouse, and jacket, changing into her riding outfit when she went out on Gem. Consequently, Sarah had more time to herself, and was pleased to have Lilly move into the cottage beside hers.

Both young ladies were accomplished seamstresses. Lilly, while not having actually being apprenticed to a well-known fashion house in Sheffield, had worked there for four years before her marriage. Mary bought them one of the new Singer sewing machines, and employed both ladies to make staff uniforms and clothes for the boys. They also took over mending the linen as required. Both were very happy to be fully occupied, as well as having convivial company.

Chapter 14

Longmire Estate
Sussex, England
September–October 1886

The next rent day, which fell at the end of the week following Ronald's death, was a much different event from the previous rent day. Women and children were invited to attend with their menfolk, as Mary had arranged with the Grey brothers and the village butcher for a lamb to be spit roasted near the stables. Mrs Smith had also prepared a vast array of salad dishes and cooked vegetables, so food was provided for all who could attend.

Mr Lyons helped Mary collect the rent from each tenant, recording the amount and their signature or mark in the ledger. Tenants came and went with smiles on their faces, a far cry from the previous rent day.

A message had arrived a few days before from the tenant of Mary's other estate, Oakdale in Yorkshire, enquiring when the estate steward would be visiting. Mary had totally forgotten of its existence, and felt bad that she had never visited or acknowledged them. She replied that she would visit the Oakdale Estate later in the month, if it was convenient for the family.

During her visits to the village, Mary had noticed two empty buildings next to the church hall, and asked Tess why they were empty. 'They were the schoolhouse and village school until the day, for reasons unknown to anyone, Mr David closed the school and sent the schoolteacher packing.

A couple of years before his death, Mr David took over managing the estate for your grandmother, who by then had little contact with anyone, other than her servants. As far as I'm aware, the Countess had no idea that Mr David was making such radical changes to the running of the estate, nor of his callous treatment to the tenants and servants.'

Mary thought that there could be up to twenty village children, including Alfie and Jack, who would benefit from the reopening of the village school. 'Sarah, if I was to reopen the village school, would you be interested in being their teacher? Lilly could be your assistant when required.'

Sarah thought for a moment. 'I would love to m'lady.'

Keys for both buildings were found in the study desk, and Mary was surprised to discover that the schoolroom was still furnished with all the desks, books, slates, and stationery required to commence teaching when the room had been cleaned. It appeared that the school door had been locked when the teacher left, and nobody had been in the building since. The small schoolhouse next door had also been left fully furnished.

Mary called a meeting of her tenants with children aged between five and fourteen, to inform them of her decision. 'I plan to reopen the school, as soon as both the school and schoolhouse have been thoroughly cleaned. All boys and girls between the age of five and fourteen will be expected to attend.

Those women interested in earning some extra money by doing the cleaning, please see me after the meeting. All children who go to school will be given a free midday meal each day that they attend. Food for these meals will be provided by the estate, but I would like you women to make up a roster for serving the food each school day. All women will also be fed on their rostered serving day.'

Despite much of the family rations being supplied by the estate for the quarter, Mary was well aware that more than half the village families still struggled to have regular meals, as most of the men were poorly paid farm labourers. Consequently, the roster was filled very quickly.

The Longmire Estate owned all the buildings in the village, which included the church, vicarage and church hall, the schoolroom and empty schoolhouse, plus residences and working facilities for the blacksmith, wheelwright, baker, butcher, and grocer. The publican lived onsite at the local pub. The remaining dozen cottages were rented, mainly by local farm labourers and their families. The buildings had become rundown through lack of maintenance, and the majority of the villagers were struggling just to survive.

Now the tenants had someone at the Hall who not only had the money to make improvements, but was also prepared to listen to them, and wanted to help, encouraging them to take pride in their village once more. They soon forgave Mary for sometimes hounding them into doing things for themselves, often finding a basket of groceries or something they needed left at the back door when they had carried out the required task. No words were said, just an acknowledgement that the job had been done.

For the next couple of weeks following rent day, Mary spent a lot of time riding around the estate, checking on the barn repairs at Glendale, spending time on Farm Two discussing prospective cattle sales and purchases with Matthew and John, and talking to Bob and Tess about her plans for the estate and village.

Life was finally settling into a sort of routine, between riding around the estate, spending time with the boys, overseeing the preparations to open the school, and spending time with the villagers. They were becoming used to their young Countess's regular visits to the village, and were constantly thankful for her desire to improve their lot in life. She chatted to everyone, and helped with odd jobs when needed. Some even overcame their initial embarrassment to invite Mary in to their homes for a cup of tea.

A far cry from the past few years, when they never saw or heard from the previous Countess, and had been happy to see as little as possible of Mr David, when he was managing the estate.

Following a meeting with the Vicar's wife to discuss the main issues besetting the village, Mary invited a small group of women to form a welfare committee. Their role was to inform Mary of those villagers genuinely struggling to cope. At Mary's request, Dr Wilson and his assistant agreed to run regular fortnightly clinics in the church hall, at rates subsidised by the estate.

Alfie and Jack were thrilled at the idea of going to school, and playing with the village lads. Both boys were showing the benefits of regular healthy meals and plenty of exercise in the fresh air and sunshine. They loved being outside with Mary and Scruffy, and their biggest disappointment was not being able to go with Mary when she rode Gem around the estate. Unbeknown to them, Mary and Robert were keeping a look out for a couple of suitable ponies for the boys for early Christmas presents.

Once the boys went up to bed, Mary spent most of her evenings in the study doing the estate bookwork. While she enjoyed doing this, she knew that she should start looking for a suitable replacement for Mr Morris, although after discussions with Bob and Will Telford, she was beginning to think that she should employ someone who could also advise and assist the farmers on more modern farming techniques, to help to increase the profitability of their farms.

Mr Lyons had been organising the trip to Yorkshire to visit the Oakdale Estate and it was decided that he would accompany Mary on the trip, as it would be a long, tedious journey, with a number of train changes and a couple of overnight stays before they arrived at the Oakdale Estate. Also, he wanted to check on the contract with the current incumbent Mr John Watson, who was actually managing the Oakdale Estate, not leasing it as a tenant farmer.

Mary had written to the Watsons to give them the expected arrival time, and also to explain that she would be travelling as Lady Mary Evans, not using her full title, as she would like her visit to the area to be as informal as possible. It was unfortunate that Mary's visit to Yorkshire would clash with the planned opening of the school, but she felt sure that Sarah, with Lilly's support, would cope admirably, so left it to Sarah to start teaching when everything was ready. They weren't planning to have a fancy opening ceremony before opening the doors to the students.

Sarah and Lilly decided to move into the school house once it had been thoroughly cleaned, as being next door to the school would give them more time to prepare for the expected students.

CHAPTER 15

Mary spent the night with the Lyons prior to Mr Lyons and her departure on the morning train to London, where they stayed overnight in a hotel, as the London residence was being renovated. Early the next morning, they caught the train to York. Train travel was still a novel experience for Mary, but once she grew accustomed to the speed at which they were travelling, she thoroughly enjoyed the trip. Amazed at the change of scenery as they travelled north, Mary again had to adjust to the change of seasons in the northern hemisphere, where it was now autumn and the foliage of most trees was changing colour.

At York they changed trains to Pocklington, which was the closest town to the Oakdale Estate. As it was late afternoon by the time they arrived in Pocklington, they booked into the Railway Inn for the night, and sent a messenger to the Oakdale Estate to notify the Watsons of their arrival.

The next morning, as Mary was leaving the hotel restaurant after breakfast, a tall, grey haired man mistook her for one of the hotel staff. 'Miss, please bring me a pot of tea while I wait for my visitors to arrive.' Mary smiled, and passed the message on to a maid, then went up to her room to prepare for the last leg of her journey. Imagine Mr Watson's embarrassment ten minutes later when Mr Lyons introduced Mary to him. Mary smiled at her embarrassed manager. 'I'm pleased that you have so readily embraced my request for informality Mr Watson!'

'Please call me John, My Lady. I apologise that my wife Elizabeth can't be here to meet you, but our cook sprained her ankle a few days ago and has gone to stay with her sister in a nearby village. Our daughter Angela, who is married to a Pocklington policeman, would normally have helped her mother, but she has just had a baby, so Josie our maid has gone to look after the other two young children, to allow Elizabeth to remain at home to be with our guests.'

'I hope our visit isn't going to put too much pressure on your wife John.'

'Oh no Your Ladyship, she is over the moon about your visit.'

When Mary, Mr Lyons, and Mr Watson boarded the waiting coach, the coachman set off on the half hour journey to the Oakdale Estate.

'How long have you worked at the Oakdale Estate John?'

'My grandfather worked for your great grandparent's m'lady, and he was promoted to manager of the Oakdale Estate when they left to live at Longmire Estate, prior to the birth of their first child, your grandmother I believe. As far as I'm aware m'lady, you are the first member of your family to visit the Oakdale Estate since that day. My father took over as manager when his father died, and I followed my father in the role.

Due to this unbroken family succession, and lack of connection with the Countess's family, few, if any of the local people know that I'm the manager, not the owner of the Oakdale Estate, which is by far the largest land holding in the district. The locals called my father 'Squire', and the name passed to me when I took over. I assure you m'lady, I take the token title of Squire seriously, and am heavily involved in the local community, helping the needy when possible. Profits from the estate are kept in an account to be used for the upkeep of the estate, and also for some community support.

My wife and I have two sons, as well as our daughter Angela; Paul is twenty six and lives with us on the estate. He works with me, and hopes to take over the management of the estate when I retire. Hugh, our younger son, is twenty one, and has just completed his studies at the Royal Agricultural College, in Gloucestershire, and he is expected home presently.'

Soon the coach passed through an imposing set of gates, with Mary's family crest on each gate post. A large country manor house stood at the end of a long avenue of large oak trees. As they drew closer, Mary saw a rambling, grey stone, double storied house covered in ivy, with a pitched slate roof. The front door was protected by a portico, to shelter passengers at the doorway from the Yorkshire weather.

A small, grey haired lady stood in the open doorway beside a tall young man with brown curly hair, as the coach pulled up. When the groom handed Mary down from the coach, the lady glanced at her, then stood looking towards the coach until John called to get her attention. Like John, Elizabeth had been expecting to meet an older woman, possibly dressed in the fine travelling clothes often worn by those flaunting their position.

Following John's introduction, Elizabeth was about to curtsey when Mary took her hand. 'It is a pleasure to meet you Mrs Watson. Please may this visit be as informal as possible.' The young man introduced himself as Paul, then greeted Mr Lyons, who had followed Mary and was being introduced.

As John led the way inside to the sitting room, Elizabeth excused herself to get the tea and scones that she had prepared earlier. While Mary and Mr Lyons were chatting to Paul, John left the room to help his wife wheel in the trolley. While in the kitchen, he reminded Elizabeth of Mary's desire to be as informal as possible, and reassured her that their livelihood was secure.

A more cheerful Elizabeth entered the sitting room, and was soon telling Mary of their new grandson, who was only two weeks old. Mary was happy to see Elizabeth relax as she chatted, and was pleased when she accepted her offer of assistance to take the trolley back to the kitchen. Mary told Elizabeth that she felt more comfortable in the kitchen than in the more formal rooms, and explained a little of how she and her staff ran Longmire Hall.

'John has explained about your lack of staff here at Oakdale Elizabeth, and I'm hoping that you will try to treat me as one of the family, to save the extra work guests create. I'm sure that Mr Lyons, who is only staying the night will agree.'

Soon after Mr Lyons and Mary had been shown to their rooms, Mr Lyons and John retired to the estate office to go through the Oakdale Estate books, and Mary helped Elizabeth prepare lunch.

After lunch Elizabeth turned to Mary. 'I have a roast ready to put on for dinner m'lady, sorry Mary, so would you like to go for a ride around the estate with Paul?'

Mary thought that this was a wonderful idea after sitting in coaches and train carriages for so long, and went up to her room to change into her riding outfit. When they met at the stables Paul was surprised to see her riding habit. 'We still have mother's side-saddle Mary, but her horse is quite elderly now, and hasn't been ridden for years.'

'That's no problem Paul, because I ride astride.'

Mounted on a striking bay mare, Mary spent a wonderful couple of hours, riding through the fields where Shorthorn cattle were grazing, and going through copses of various types of trees, mostly bare of leaves. Several of the fields were bare, and Paul explained that they grew various crops to be harvested to feed the cattle that lived for many months of the year in the barns.

Back at the house, Mary met with Mr Lyons when Paul and his father left to milk the cows. 'John keeps the books well, both for the estate and his personal income and costs. However, there are some things I need to discuss with you Mary when we have more time in the morning.'

The following morning, after a large hot breakfast in the cosy country kitchen, Mr Lyons and Mary retired to the estate office, while John and Paul went out to clean the cow barn. As Mr Lyons. went through the books with Mary, she realised that, while Oakdale Estate was a profitable property, the Watson's appeared to be only just making ends meet.

'John told me that Mr Morris made extensive changes to his contract when he called early last year. He told John that he was increasing the percentage of profit to go to the Countess's account. He informed John that the Oakdale Estate would no longer pay wages for their cook, maid, and the dairy maid, who made the butter and cheese that they sold each week. He also instructed that as their children were now grown up, Elizabeth was to carry out those jobs.

Two of the estate workers were dismissed, Mr Morris insisting that John and his two sons should be able to cope. He wouldn't allow John to put Paul on the payroll, and told him that his contract would be revoked if he argued. John has been using his own savings to pay the cook and maid to help Elizabeth, who spends many unpaid hours in the dairy, and he also pays Paul a small wage from his own wage. They haven't seen Mr Morris since that visit, and had no knowledge of his dismissal and imprisonment.'

When Mary saw the small amount of money that John withdrew as wages from the estate each month she raised her eyebrows. 'What would be a fair wage for a manager of a large estate like Oakdale, with a number of employees on the payroll Mr Lyons?'

'John is being severely underpaid Mary. His wage seemingly has not increased much from what his father was paid thirty years ago. To be expected to pay the Oakdale Estate employees as well is absurd.'

Knowing what they did of Mr Morris's greedy, uncaring dealings at the Longmire Estate, neither Mary nor Mr Lyons were surprised to see what he had demanded of the Oakdale Estate manager. For the rest of the morning, they worked on new contracts for both John and Paul, plus they reinstated the two estate workers, the cook, maid and dairymaid to the payroll. A much smaller percentage of the profits was allocated to Mary's account, the remainder to be used for estate maintenance and community assistance.

Mary wondered where Mr Morris had banked the additional percentage that he had removed from the estate account, and where he had kept the books for the Oakdale Estate.

Mr Lyons was catching the late afternoon train to York, as he couldn't stay away from his office for too long. 'Mary, we need to visit the bank in Pocklington this afternoon before my train leaves, to check if Mr Morris has an account there, and also we need to have your details put on the estate account.'

John accompanied them to Pocklington, and introduced Mary to the bank manager, using her full title with her permission. The bank manager was thrilled to meet the Countess, and they quickly completed the Oakdale Estate account paperwork, and cancelled Mr Morris's authority to withdraw funds from the estate. Mr Lyons gave the bank manager a brief account of Mr Morris's fraudulent dealings and consequent imprisonment. 'Does Mr Morris have an account in his name at this bank, and if so, may we please look at his statements?'

'Mr Morris does have an account here, and he also has a safety deposit box. Unfortunately, I can't give you access to either the account or deposit box this afternoon. However Your Ladyship will be able to see both if you obtain a signed order from the Judge who presided over Mr Morris's court case and sentencing.'

Mary was determined to find out if the bank held more of Mr Morris's embezzled money, so decided to extend her stay in Yorkshire to give Mr Lyons time to send up the relevant information.

Mary and John went to the station with Mr Lyons, and waited until he could board the train to York. Mary waved as the train slowly began to move. 'Goodbye Mr Lyons. Please send a message to Longmire Hall to let them know that I will be away longer than planned.'

After seeing Mr Lyons on his way to York, Mary and John walked back to the hotel, where they were to stay the night, it being considered unsafe to travel back to the Oakdale Estate in the dark. As they walked into the hotel foyer, a young man who looked remarkably like John, greeted him with an enthusiastic hug. 'Hello Father. What are you doing in town at this time of the afternoon? I've just arrived in Pocklington and planned to stay the night at the hotel, before hiring a horse in the morning to ride home to Oakdale.'

Disentangling himself from his son's embrace, John introduced his younger son Hugh to a rather startled Mary, then suggested that they all go into the dining room for dinner. At first Hugh found it hard to believe that Mary could be a Peer of the Realm, as she had none of the fancy airs and graces that so put him off many of the daughters of the aristocracy, who he was forced to mingle with at social functions near his College. Also, she was younger than he was, and seemed just like a friendly country girl, with a funny accent.

The next morning when they had returned to the Oakdale Estate, Mary told John and Elizabeth of the proposed changes to his contract, the estate staffing and running costs. At first they were speechless, then thanked Mary profusely. To allow the family time to discuss their new circumstances Mary excused herself and went for a walk in the garden.

Ten minutes later Hugh found her sitting on a bench with one of the farm cats curled up on her lap. 'Thank you for setting my parent's minds at rest about their future Mary. Would you be interested in accompanying me while I check the cows in the barn, and the pigs in their enclosure?'

Both put on their wellingtons and thick coats before heading to the pig-sties. 'While our cows spend a lot of time in the barns, our pigs spend the nights in their pens, but free range in selected fields during the days, except when the snow becomes too deep.'

When they entered the barn Mary was intrigued to see the large red and white Ayrshire cows all tied in separate stalls, placidly eating from feed bins in front of them. 'I lived on a dairy farm in Australia Hugh, where we milked the smaller Jersey cows. They spent every day and night of the year out in the paddocks eating grass, only coming to the dairy to be milked.'

Mary and Hugh spent the rest of the morning discussing their shared interest in farming. Mary wanted to hear more about Hugh's agricultural studies, while he was fascinated to hear of her own farming experiences in Australia.

After lunch, Mary spent time with John and Paul, explaining in more detail the new contract that Mr Lyons would be drawing up for John, including Paul as assistant manager. 'All of your workers, both inside and out, will have their wages increased to be on par with those at the Longmire Estate down south. Elizabeth will also be recompensed for the long hours she has worked in the dairy over the past year, producing the butter and cheese sold for the estate.'

John was thrilled with Mary's news, but still looked worried. 'I'm concerned about Elizabeth's health Mary. Usually she's an energetic, cheerful person, but lately she has become withdrawn and lethargic.'

Mary wondered if the additional work in the dairy and house, combined with the worry about their financial situation may have led to these changes. 'John, why don't you convince Elizabeth to spend some time with Angela and your grandchildren. Maybe not exactly the rest she needs, but a break from her normal work. Mrs Turner is due back tomorrow morning and Emma could return to Oakdale, plus I would love to help where possible. I know that I'm your employer John, but my visit has been extended to wait for the letter for the bank, and I find it very hard to sit around being 'a lady' all day.'

At first John was reluctant to even consider the proposition, but he finally relented, and went to speak to his wife. The next morning Paul set off to Pocklington, with Elizabeth sitting on the carriage seat beside him, not looking happy at leaving such a titled guest, but accepting that it just had to be. As Paul was bringing Emma back with him and would also collect Mrs Turner from her sister's, Elizabeth thought that Mary wouldn't have much to do.

Little did she know that Mary and Hugh would take over the butter and cheese making, before a new dairy maid was employed. Also, Mary helped with the milking and other jobs around the farm. She found the Ayrshire cows, with the longer teats, easier to milk than the Jerseys that she had milked at home, and was often in the barn at dawn to assist with the morning milking.

Some afternoons, she and Hugh rode around the Oakdale Estate, and he told her more about his agricultural studies. During the evenings after dinner Mary was quite happy to sit back and listen to Hugh discussing with his father and brother how they could increase the productivity of their pastures and crops, and improve the breeding of their cattle. As she listened, the germ of an idea began to form. Although only twenty one, Hugh might be an ideal estate supervisor, a combination of estate steward and someone also able to assist the tenant farmers modernise their farming techniques and increase their profitability.

Hugh was very keen to have a go when Mary discussed her idea with him, especially when she told him that his duties would cover both the Longmire and Oakdale Estates. That meant that he could spend some of the year at home helping his father and brother.

'When would you be able to come down to the Longmire Estate Hugh?'

'Unfortunately, all graduating students at the College are expected to remain on site for at least two weeks after Graduation Day, which is in just over a month on the twenty third of November. I'm afraid it would be close to Christmas before I could get to the Longmire Estate Mary.'

John and Paul were thrilled to hear of Hugh's possible employment, especially when they heard that he would be working at the Oakdale Estate too. John had thought a lot about his younger son's evening discussions, but had wondered just how much the Oakdale Estate could afford to put into practice. Now he had Mary's approval without having to ask her!

Just over a week after Mr Lyon's return to Lewes, a letter arrived from the judge, stating that the court's ruling would apply to Mr Morris's bank accounts and safety deposit box at the Pocklington bank. He gave permission for the Countess to have access to both the account and safety deposit box, before the bank arranged to have the money transferred to her Lewes account.

John and Hugh travelled to Pocklington with Mary, where she opened the safety deposit box with the key that the judge had included with his letter. Inside were two small ledgers, an amount of cash and a gold hunter watch. John gasped when he saw the watch. 'That watch belonged to my grandfather Mary. It went missing, with some cash at about the time of Mr Morris's last visit, but we hadn't considered that he may have stolen it.'

As at the Longmire Estate, one ledger had the amount that John had signed for, with the increase to the amount to go into the Countess's account included, and the second with the original amount, with a very good forgery of John' signature. Mr Morris's bank account had an entry for the amount of the additional profit.

With the contents of the deposit box in Mary's bag and the contents of Mr Morris's bank book transferred to the Estate account Mary, John, and Hugh went to Amanda's house to collect Elizabeth, who was ready to go home. Mary met Amanda's husband Peter, who was just heading off to work, looking resplendent in his police uniform. John told him of finding his watch and money in the deposit box, while Mary explained that Mr Morris was already in prison.

Now that the bank issue had been sorted, Mary felt that she should return to Longmire Hall. Hugh had to return to the Agricultural College at Cirencester in Gloucestershire in a few days, so he agreed to accompany her to London, then head off to the college. When they arrived in London the following afternoon, Mary was surprised at how sad she felt as she watched Hugh stride off to catch the train for Cirencester, knowing that she wouldn't see him again for over two months.

With a heavy heart she followed the porter to the cab stand, where he loaded her luggage and gave instructions for her to be taken to the hotel where she had previously stayed.

CHAPTER 16

London
October – November 1886

Two days later, as Mary walked through Hyde Park on her way back to the hotel after lunch with some of her factory managers, she noticed a small girl huddled on a bench near the gate. She was dressed in a thin cotton dress, shivering violently in the cold wind, and appeared to be sobbing. When Mary approached her, the girl started then tried to curl up into a smaller shape and hide behind the branches of an overhanging shrub.

Before Mary could speak, another small girl raced through the gate and sat on the bench, grabbing the other girl, hugging her tightly and murmuring soothing words to her. While doing this, she glared at Mary, as if daring her to interfere.

Mary smiled at the girls. 'Could I please sit on the end of the bench to rest my tired legs?' and was answered by a brief nod from the second girl. As she sat on the bench, Mary glanced at the girls, noting that they appeared to be quite young and looked very alike.

'My name is Mary, and I have been walking around a lot in the city.' As she spoke, the girls appeared to relax. 'What are your names and where do you live?'

'We are Jane and Sally Martin. We don't have a home anymore. Now we sleep anywhere we can find shelter.'

Shocked at this response, Mary was becoming worried about how much both girls were shivering. 'I'm staying in a nearby hotel. Would you like to come with me to the hotel to warm up, and have something to eat before it gets dark?'

After some thought Jane agreed. As they walked beside Mary, the two girls clung to each other, and it became apparent that Sally, the first girl she had seen, was blind. Gently encouraging the girls to accompany her up the steps into the foyer of the hotel, Mary stopped beside the doorman. 'Please ask the housekeeper to meet me in my suite as quickly as possible.' Then she led the girls up the stairs to her suite on the first floor.

The housekeeper arrived as Mary was settling both girls in front of the fire in her sitting room. She quickly explained how she had found the girls. 'Could I please have a maid sent up to assist me bathe and feed the girls, and to be a witness that I'm not accosting or kidnapping them. Also, could you please ask the hotel doctor to call?'

A young woman named Meg arrived soon after the housekeeper left, carrying a tray with two glasses of warm milk and some bread and jam. While Meg ran the bath, Mary encouraged the girls to eat the bread and drink the milk. After some initial hesitation, they both devoured the food very quickly, Jane assisting Sally with the glass of milk and handing her the food.

Neither girl was at all keen to get into the bath, but once they were soaking together in the warm water after their hair had been washed, it was hard to entice them to get out. Eventually, each girl was wrapped in a warm, fluffy towel, sitting in front of the fire.

While the girls were in the bathroom with Meg, the hotel inspector spoke to Mary. 'I have been asking around to see if anyone knows the two young girls Your Ladyship. No one could tell me where they live, though a few shopkeepers said that they had found them sleeping near their back doors over the past few weeks.'

Mary was intrigued to see Sally constantly stroking her towel and rubbing it on her cheek. Jane noticed her watching her sister. 'That fluffy towel feels like a teddy bear that Sally used to love stroking and cuddling. She lost the bear when we had to leave our house after our grandmother died.'

Although she would have dearly loved to find out more about the girls, Mary could see that they were getting very sleepy, so she and Meg dressed them in a couple of Mary's work shirts, and put them to bed in the maid's room next to Mary's bedroom. 'Meg and I will stay in the suite next to your room all night while you sleep.'

The next morning, after breakfast of porridge, toast and milk, the doctor arrived and checked the girls. 'Both girls are surprisingly healthy, for the life they have recently been living, Your Ladyship.' He gave Mary the address of a nearby lawyer, and wrote a note of introduction for her before he left.

Both girls appeared to be more relaxed with Mary and Meg after breakfast, and were prepared to tell their story. Jane was very protective of Sally, assisting her with most activities, and she was also the main speaker.

'Sally and I are eight year old twins. We lived in Hoxton with our mother, after our father was killed at work. Then Mother was knocked down and killed by a runaway horse and cart a year later. Sally was with her, and was knocked unconscious, but seemed not to be hurt. But when she woke up in hospital she couldn't see.

We went to live with our grandmother, who lived near the river, until she died suddenly a few weeks ago. I don't know if we have any other relatives. Our next-door neighbour looked after us for a few days when the landlord rented our grandmother's house to another family the day after she died, but her husband said that we had to go to the workhouse. When I heard him say that we ran away and lived on the streets, until you found us in the park. I'm scared that Sally and I will be parted, because I heard that Sally being blind means that she will be sent to a different place to me.'

Mary knew, from her involvement with the local workhouses, that most workhouses didn't like having disabled people thrust upon them, and where possible segregated them from the other inmates. As an eight year old blind girl, separated from her twin, Sally's life would be a nightmare if she was put in the workhouse.

Before she left for her appointment with the lawyer, Mary sat with the girls. 'Would you like to visit my home in the country, while we try to find a suitable place where both of you can stay together?'

After a quiet discussion with her sister Jane replied. 'Yes, we would like to stay with you Mary, especially if Meg can come too, because Sally feels very comfortable with her.'

Mary took Jane aside for a moment. 'Jane, would you mind Meg taking over some of the responsibility for dealing with Sally's needs?'

'I love my sister Mary, and try hard to look after her, but I would be thrilled if Meg helps.'

Mary spoke to the housekeeper and Meg about the possibility of Meg travelling to Longmire Hall with the girls.

'Meg may have unpaid leave from the hotel to assist you Your Ladyship.'

Meg was excited at the idea of leaving London and spending some time in the country.

Mary left the girls in the suite with Meg after breakfast, while she went to see Mr Brown the lawyer, promising to take them shopping for some warmer clothes and boots when she returned. Mr Brown was a middle aged gentleman, who reminded Mary of a sleepy owl as he sat behind his desk wearing steel rimmed glasses, blinking often as he regularly turned his head to look out of the window, then back at Mary.

After reading the doctor's letter, he turned to Mary. 'I can see no reason why you can't look after the girls Your Ladyship, if that's what you desire.'

He seemed to be more interested in having a Countess in his office than about the girls' future. Mary had to ask him a couple of times if he would undertake a search for possible relatives. Eventually, by the time she left the office, Mary had his agreement to carry out an investigation on her behalf.

Following a quick lunch on her return to the hotel, Mary asked reception to book her four first class tickets on the following morning's early train to Lewes, then the four of them set off shopping. When Mary began walking towards the shops, Meg stopped her. 'Begging your pardon m'lady, if you want to buy serviceable clothes for the girl's I think we should go to the market, not to the nearby shops that just sell fancy, frilly dresses.'

At a stall run by a distant relative of Meg's, they found several pinafore dresses of suitable sizes made from warm material, so Mary gave the girls the choice of picking three dresses each. She was touched at how Jane held each dress up for Sally to hold, and explained the colour and style, before choosing her own. A warm woollen coat, and several articles of underwear and nightwear was purchased for each girl before they left the market to buy some boots. Mary was determined to have the girls fitted with good quality boots, so they set off down the street looking for the boot shop.

On the way, they passed a shop with some dolls displayed in the window, and on a whim, Mary led the way into the shop. Looking around, she saw many different types of dolls, plus all sorts of toys, and in an area near the counter, teddy bears of all sizes. As Meg walked ahead, with Sally holding her hand, Mary stood with Jane. 'Do you see any teddy bears similar to the one that Sally was so attached to Jane?' The little girl pointed to a furry yellow bear, so Mary picked it up. 'Would you like to give this bear to Sally?' The canny young lass shook her head. 'It would be better if Meg gave it to her.'

When Meg handed the bear to Sally, the look of surprise on her face was quickly lost, as the bear was clutched to her chest and her face was buried into its fur. Muffled words were heard as the young girl talked lovingly to the soft toy.

Hearing a faint sigh from Jane, Mary turned and saw a wistful look on her face. 'Did you have to leave a favourite toy behind too Jane?' Jane nodded, and pointed to a rag doll sitting to the side of all the fancily dressed porcelain dolls. Mary walked over to the shelf, and carefully picked up the doll and handed it to Jane, who burst into tears as she hugged it.

Mary was astounded. 'What's the matter Jane?'

'I'm crying because I'm so happy Mary!'

Finally they arrived at the boot shop, where Mary used her title, and ordered some sturdy boots, shoes, and slippers for the two girls, and was pleased to see the attendants take great care to pick footwear that was soft, comfortable, and well fitted. Both Mary and Meg had to cover their smiles at the look of bliss on both girls' faces as their feet were buttoned into their new boots. Apparently, they had always had second hand footwear that didn't always fit properly.

Dinner back at the hotel was a joyful affair, with both girls clutching their new toys. The girls were keen to go to bed early after the hectic afternoon's shopping, which left Mary and Meg free to pack their cases. Mary had bought each of the girls a small case, and had also bought Meg a warm woollen shawl, and some boots more suitable for country use. Meg left for a while, to pack her belongings and to say goodbye to her friends on the staff.

At first the girls were scared when the train pulled out of the station the next morning, but soon settled to enjoy the journey to Lewes. Jane and Meg spent a lot of the time describing the scenery to Sally, which allowed Mary time to sit back and think about her trip up north, and also of her return to Longmire Hall. Celia Lyons was waiting to meet them at Lewes station, having received a telegraph message of their expected arrival time. She took them home, and after a quick lunch the girls were very happy to have an afternoon sleep. That night the twins were introduced to Mr Lyons at dinner time, and Mary was thrilled to see both girls using manners that they had obviously been taught earlier in their short lives.

Mary decided to spend the next day in Lewes, before introducing the girls to all the people at Longmire Hall, so a message was sent to the Hall for Robert and James to bring the coach and cart the following day.

In the morning, while Meg and Celia took the twins for a walk to the local park, carrying a bag of bread crusts to feed the ducks, Mary visited Mr Lyons in his office, to discuss her extended trip to the Oakdale Estate, and also to explain her concern for the girls' future.

Early the next morning, Mary was woken by two very excited girls, who were ready to set off for Longmire Hall straight away, even though it was still dark. Mary managed to convince them that it was too dark for the horses to travel safely, so they climbed into bed with her for a cuddle before breakfast. When Meg came in later with a cup of tea for Mary, she found all three sound asleep.

With breakfast finally eaten, the girls went out to the front garden to await the arrival of Mary's coach. Although young, the girls had a vague idea of Mary's title, though, in their minds fact was heavily blended with fiction. By the time Robert and James arrived at the front gate, the girls had convinced each other that the coach would be golden, and the coachman wearing full regalia. Somewhat to their disappointment neither was the case, but they quickly regained their excitement when Robert sat them up on the seat beside him, while James went to the house to announce their arrival.

Finally, with the luggage on the cart, Mary and Meg in the coach, and the twins wrapped in a thick travelling rug sitting beside Robert, they set off for Longmire Hall. The girls had wanted to travel all the way on the driver's seat, but a compromise had been struck by Robert. 'You can travel through the town up here with me, but you must travel in the coach when we leave the town.'

So, the remainder of the trip was spent in the coach with Meg and Jane chatting to Sally, again explaining what they were travelling past, while Mary sat back and watched Meg dealing with the girls, amazed at the way she spoke and dealt with Sally as though she was sighted. Mary had noticed that when Meg walked with Sally, she encouraged the little girl to put her hand on her arm, rather than Meg holding her arm as they walked. Of course Meg guided Sally when necessary, but never made a fuss about it. If Sally wanted to hold hands, that was allowed, but she wasn't pulled along as so often happened when blind people were being assisted. Meg had already begun to encourage Sally to use a spoon to feed herself, and was teaching her to use a cup by herself.

The staff, Alfie and Jack were all waiting on the front steps when the coach came down the drive to Longmire Hall, and they cheered as it pulled up in front of them. Although Mary had only been in England for six months, and had been away from the Longmire Estate for three weeks, this felt like a great homecoming. The staff were thrilled to see their young Countess home safely, and were intrigued to see the twins in the coach.

When Mary stepped down from the coach she was knocked to the ground by Scruffy when he launched himself from the top step and landed in her arms. As she unsuccessfully tried to stop the excited hound licking her face Polly wrapped her arms around Scruffy and hauled him off Mary. Laughing, she stood up and dusted herself off, before greeting the quivering dog rolling at her feet, then the staff and boys waiting on the steps.

Once the greetings were over Mary looked at her waiting staff. Everyone please go to the sitting room, where I will introduce our visitors.'

While James restrained Scruffy, who would have loved to greet each girl with a lick, Meg and the girls followed Mary up the steps and into the hall. As Jane gazed in awe around the huge entrance, Meg quietly explained what she saw to Sally. Like the twins, Meg was aware of Mary's title, and had been slowly relaxing and trying hard to follow Mary's request to treat her in a less formal manner, especially when they were not in public. However, she was not prepared for the informal manner in which the staff greeted Mary, laughing when Scruffy knocked her over, and each giving her a welcoming hug as she walked up the steps.

When they were all together in the sitting room, Mary introduced each member of the staff and the boys to Meg and the girls, explaining that for the moment the girls were holidaying at the Hall, and Meg was to be their maid. Jack and Alfie each gave Mary a big hug, then stood back and watched the two young girls greet the staff. Mary could see that she would have to quickly allay their fears that their place in the household would not be usurped.

'Polly, please arrange for a bedroom on my floor with an attached maid's room, to be prepared for the girls and Meg'.

Like Mary, Meg had noticed the boy's wary greeting to the girls. 'I will take the girls up to help Polly prepare their room m'lady.'

Sitting together in front of the fire, Mary asked the boys what they had been doing in her absence. Quickly they forgot about the girls, and excitedly told Mary all about their days at school, which had started over a week ago. They also told her of the work that they had been doing at home. Jack had been helping Mrs Smith in the kitchen. 'I cooked the pie we are having for dessert tonight Mary.' Not to be out done, Alfie boasted 'And I helped Tom grow the vegetables, and I picked them all by myself!'

Congratulating them both on their endeavours, Mary explained who the visitors were. 'The girls will be holidaying with us until I can find a suitable permanent home for them. I want you boys to remember that Longmire Hall will always be your home, no matter who else comes to visit or stay, because you are now very much part of my family. Hearing this, both boys gave Mary a big hug.

'I hope that you will both make the girls feel welcome. Just remember that Sally is blind, so you will need to take extra care of her, and explain to her what you are doing.'

'Will the girls be coming to school with us while they are staying here Mary?'

Unsure of the girls' future, Mary hadn't thought about their immediate education. 'I will talk to Sarah before making that decision Alfie.'

Thrilled to be home again, Mary spent time chatting to all her staff, and she also visited all three farms, revelling at being on Gem's back again. Scruffy was in his element, loping along beside them wherever they went. Mary had asked the boys to show Jane, Sally and Meg around the grounds, gardens, and the stables while she was visiting the farms. Jane had a wonderful time chatting to the boys, while Sally was happy to have Meg's sole attention, as they followed slowly behind the other three.

The next day Mary walked to the village to meet Sarah and Lilly, who proudly showed her through the school. She was thrilled to hear how enthusiastically the villagers had supported the opening of the school, and how keen the ten girls and eight boys were to attend. The meal roster was working well, with plans to provide hot soup as the weather became colder. Sarah and Lilly had moved into the school house, and had offered the use of their kitchen to cook the soup, and possibly some stews later on.

Before returning to the Hall, Mary told Sarah about Jane and Sally, and asked what she thought about them attending school while staying at the Hall. Sarah could see no reason why Jane shouldn't attend, but was unsure how Sally would cope. Mary decided to discuss this with Meg, before she made a final decision about either girl's attendance.

When the children were in bed, Mary and Meg sat in front of the fire in the study to discuss the girl's education. Like Sarah, Meg felt that Jane would benefit from attending school, but thought that Sally would be better off staying with her, where she could teach her life skills, before she began to learn to read and maybe write.

Sally was already showing great aptitude in developing new skills as Meg showed her ways to cope with her blindness. She was starting to feed herself, was dressing herself in clothes put out for her, and was also much more confident walking around with her hand on Meg's arm, rather than clinging to her guide.

The next morning, Mary, her staff, Meg and the four children walked to church, the girls revealing that they had never been to church before. Both girls loved the singing, and sat quietly throughout the rest of the service. Sally coped quite well with the number of people coming up to Mary following the service to welcome her back, and she and Jane walked back to the Hall arm in arm, humming the tunes of the hymns that they had heard.

Before dinner that night, Mary and Meg took the girls into the study to have a talk about school. Jane was resigned to staying with Sally. 'I would love to go to school, but I don't think Sally will cope, so I will stay home too.'

Sally slapped Jane's arm. 'Don't be silly Jane. We will still be together after school, and I need to learn more from Meg.'

Mary found it hard to believe that the twins were only eight years old when she heard them talking in such a matter of fact way. Sally realised that her dependence on Jane was stopping her sister from doing things she liked to do, while Jane was fiercely protective of her sister, and had for the past two years unselfishly done everything for Sally.

So, the next morning Alfie and Jack took Jane to school with them, after Mary had asked them to help her settle in. Both boys were loving school, and were happy to take Jane with them. Mary had gone to the school earlier, to be there to introduce Jane to Sarah, then she left to wander through the village, chatting to the villagers she met, catching up on news from the weeks she had been away.

Back at the Hall, Sally was at the stables, where Robert was introducing her to the horses, speaking quietly to them as he carried Sally to the stable door. Rusty stretched out his head to be patted, and made Sally laugh when he blew hot air on her cheek. She loved the feel of his soft lips when he gently took the sugar that Robert had placed on her palm.

'Would you like to sit on Rusty's back Sally, if Meg holds your hand?' When Sally nodded her head, Rusty was led out of the stable, and Sally was lifted onto his back. Her right hand was placed on his mane, and she was instructed to hang onto the hair when he moved forward. Meg walked beside Rusty, holding Sally's left hand as Robert slowly led Rusty around the courtyard, and he was pleased to see Sally's big smile while they moved around.

As they were about to leave the stables, Meg noticed the coach whips hanging on the tack room wall. The handles reminded her of a thin cane that her blind cousin had used to help him walk unassisted. She pointed to the whips. 'Robert, might there be an old whip handle that I could use to make a walking cane for Sally?'

Robert looked puzzled and looked at Meg. 'My blind cousin walks with a thin cane extended in front of him to detect objects before he trips over them, not using it as a walking stick.'

Robert nodded. 'I see what you mean Meg. I'll see what I can find.'

That evening, after the evening meal, Robert presented Sally with a whip handle that he had cut down to reach a little above her waist. It had a thin leather loop at the top of the handle to put around her wrist, and also a small knob on the other end to stop it from being a dangerous point. After Sally thanked Robert, Meg turned to her. 'I will teach you how to use this tomorrow Sally.' This gift from Robert helped Sally cope with Jane's obvious excitement about her first day at school, the first time the girls had spent a day apart experiencing different activities.

During the following weeks, the girls settled into life at the Hall, the boys happy to accept them into their adopted family. After school, Jane and the boys would race into the kitchen for a glass of milk and a slice of Mrs Smith's cake. Sally would meet them there, and she and Jane would discuss their day's activities.

If the weather was too cold or wet, Jane and the boys were taken to and from school in a covered cart driven by James, with Sally sitting beside him on the driver's seat. The young blind girl was quickly becoming a favourite with the staff, who were impressed with her uncomplaining efforts to cope with her disability. Often, they would stop to chat to her, explaining what they were doing, and sometimes allowing her help them polish a table or to help make some scones.

CHAPTER 17

Longmire Estate
Sussex, England
November 1886

A month following her arrival home, Mary received a letter from the London lawyer Mr Brown informing her that his investigation had turned up a distant relative of the girls, who was very interested in giving them a home. Little more was said, other than a request for further instructions on how Mary wanted this to proceed. Not happy with what the letter told her, or more to the point, what hadn't been revealed about this distant relative, Mary went into Lewes to speak to Mr Lyons.

After reading the letter, he agreed with Mary. 'There is a lot more information required before those girls will be moved from your care Mary. I know a private detective living in Kensington, who deals with cases such as this.'

Immediately he wrote a note to his friend, while Ben made a copy of Mr Brown's letter to be included with the note, then Ben went out to post the letter.

Early in November Mr Lyons arrived at Longmire Hall, accompanied by his friend Richard Jones, the private detective he had written to.

'Your Ladyship, I used the information that Mr Brown gave me to track down Hester Martin, who claimed to be a relative of the girls. Before we met face to face, I sourced information from local people who knew Hester, but found few who had a good word to say about her. The local constabulary informed me that Hester was suspected of being involved in several thefts in the area, and also of entertaining gentlemen in her apartment, to supplement her income.

I followed Hester from her home in a dingy alley in Whitechapel, to a nearby public house where I watched her steadily drink gin for a couple of hours, bragging to anyone who would listen that soon she wouldn't have to work, and would have tons of money. Making sure that Hester didn't see me, I left before she staggered out into the street.

The next afternoon, I knocked on Hester's door, and was met by a very heavy-eyed Hester, clutching a grubby dressing gown around her. When I informed her that I was looking into her relationship with the girls, she pulled me into a dingy hall and slammed the front door shut. The stench in the hall nearly made me gag, and the kitchen was no better. The room was squalid, with dirty dishes stacked in the sink, and dishes with food stuck on them covered the grubby table. Empty gin bottles were stacked near the door, and cockroaches scuttled across the floor.

Hester used her arm to sweep dishes to one end of the table, then told me to sit down and tell her how soon she could have the girls to stay. I told her that I needed more information, which didn't please her, but eventually she sat down and answered my questions.

It turns out that Hester is the widow of the twin's paternal great uncle's step son, hence the same surname, but not a blood relation. She was looking forward to her 'young relations' doing all of the household duties for their board and keep. She didn't seem to care when I told her that the twins were only eight years old, but she became very angry when I informed her that Sally was blind and screamed at me. 'No way am I taking on a blind child. If I'm forced to take her, I'll leave her out on the street near the river to fend for herself'.'

He paused when he heard Mary gasp, then continued.

'I tried not to show how shocked I was at this statement, then Hester slyly confided that some of her clients preferred young girls, and would pay her a lot of money for the girl she took in. I hastily excused myself soon after this revelation, telling Hester that I had to send in my report before there could be further progress on her claim. On my way home,

I called in at the local police station, to tell them of Hester's admission that she had 'clients', some of them interested in young girls.

I later heard that the next day the police had placed a watch on Hester's apartment, and had entered the apartment ten minutes after a man had been ushered through the front door to find him in bed with Hester in the front parlour. Hester was furious when he admitted to the police that he had paid for her services, and worse still for Hester, a policeman recognised a stolen necklace that she was wearing. A thorough search of her upstairs rooms turned up quite a stash of jewellery, linking Hester to several recent burglaries, and she was arrested on the spot.'

Mary was horrified to hear this story, terrified that the twins might be forced to live with this woman. Mr Lyons assured her otherwise. 'Mary, there is little chance the girls will be sent to Hester on such a distant and tenuous family relationship, and even less chance now that she is in custody, and likely to be there for some time to come. To make sure, Richard and I are going straight to Lewes to discuss the case with Judge Stephens, to see if we can get an injunction on Hester's claim, and have you granted guardianship of the twins.'

While awaiting the outcome of this meeting, Mary didn't mention anything to the girls, but she did speak to Meg. 'If the girls could stay here permanently, would you be interested in a permanent position at Longmire Hall Meg?'

'I would love to m'lady.'

Like Mary, she could barely conceal her impatience while waiting for the outcome of the meeting to be revealed. Luckily, they only had to wait a couple of days before Mary was asked to attend a meeting with a local magistrate to sign the paperwork to become the girls' legal guardian for the period that no close blood relation deemed suitable to care for the young girls could be found. Immediately on her return to Longmire Hall Mary hugged the waiting girls. 'Jane and Sally, Longmire Hall is now your home for as long as you wish.'

Turning to Meg she smiled. 'Meg, you are now a permanent member of my Longmire Hall staff, to help look after Sally.' Like the two girls, Meg was thrilled with the news. 'Thank you m'lady. May I please have a few days off to go back to London to hand in my notice at the hotel and collect the remainder of my possessions held in storage there?'

'Take as long as you need Meg. I will pay for your return train ticket, plus give you money to cover your accommodation while you are in London.'

At first, Sally was upset at the thought of not having Meg with her, but soon found that there was always someone nearby, keeping an eye on her ready to be of assistance if she needed help.

While Meg was away, Robert met Mary at Gem's stall. 'Great news m'lady. I have finally found some well-bred ponies for sale near Lewes.' The next day she and Robert travelled to the other side of Lewes, to see if there were any ponies that they felt would be suitable for the boys. Mary had decided to also look for one for Jane.

On arrival at their destination, they were shown ten Shetland ponies in a yard beside some imposing stables, which housed a number of race horses. Mary and Robert stood near the yard with the foreman. 'May I please go into the yard alone with the ponies, Mr Hewitt?'

For a short time, Mary walked slowly amongst the small ponies, then stood near the fence, talking quietly to them and Robert would swear that they were conversing with her. The foreman obviously thought the same, as he stood there watching, shaking his head. When Mary left the yard, three ponies followed her to the gate. The foreman was stunned. 'Those are the exact same three that I would have chosen for children to learn to ride on Your Ladyship.' Mary just smiled. 'I will buy these three Shetlands. Could they please be delivered to Longmire Hall as soon as possible Mr Hewitt?'

Mary had previously decided that if the right ponies were available she would give them to the children as early Christmas presents. Both Robert and James were happy to teach them to ride, and how to look after their ponies. The plan was for the children to ride to school, once it was felt that they were competent enough. This left Mary with the issue of what to give Sally. She didn't feel that a pony would be advisable for her at this stage.

The next morning Mary took Sally to the stables and introduced her to Gem. Holding Sally's hand towards Gem, Mary spoke quietly to the horse who stretched her head out to allow Sally to touch her nose.

Mary encouraged Sally to rub Gem's forehead and between her ears, then Gem gave a soft nicker, and blew warm air down Sally's neck. When the startled girl heard Mary laugh, she relaxed, and allowed Gem to tickle her neck with her soft lips.

Following the introduction Mary saddled Gem, placed a pad across the saddle for a well rugged up Sally to sit on, then she swung up onto the saddle and walked the horse out of the courtyard. Mary allowed Gem to walk for a while, to get used to Sally's extra weight. 'We are going to visit my friend Tess at Home Farm Sally. Gem will begin to go faster now, but don't worry, because I will hold you tightly all the way.' As Gem began to trot Mary felt Sally tense, but when the filly broke into a slow canter she relaxed and rocked to the horse's gait until Gem slowed down as they neared Home Farm.

'This is great fun Mary; I want Gem to keep going. Why is she slowing down?'

Mary laughed. 'We have arrived at Home Farm Sally, and Gem is walking through the gate that Tess has kindly opened for us.'

When Mary swung Sally down into Tess's outstretched arms, and tied Gem to a post near the farm house, she watched Scruffy going through his usual routine with the farm dogs, and noticed a young dog with a yellow, curly coat creep out from under a cart and run to the back door while the other dogs were preoccupied with Scruffy. Tess was watching the dog too and sighed. 'I don't know what I'm going to do with that little dog. He turned up in the yard one morning last week, and spends most of his time hiding from the farm dogs. I haven't the heart to get rid of him, but he is constantly being set upon by the other dogs whenever they catch sight of him.'

While Tess was explaining about the dog, he crept in behind them as they entered the kitchen. Sally sat at the table, and was happy to drink a glass of milk and listen to Mary and Tess chatting, but after a while she sensed that she was being watched. When she asked 'Who is staring at me Mary?' they realised that the little dog was looking at Sally, with his head tilted to the side.

'It is a very sad, lonely little dog Sally, who is hoping that you will give him a pat. Why don't you put your hand down for him to sniff?' When Sally put her hand down, the dog crawled over to her and thrust his muzzle into her hand. As she bent over to pat him, he leant against her leg, and placed his head on her knee, staring up at her face. With a sigh, he shut his eyes and stayed with his head on Sally's lap until Tess stood up. 'Would you like to help collect the eggs with Mary and me Sally?'

Tess and Mary were astounded to see the dog stand beside Sally when she stood up, and then walk to the door with the young girl's hand resting on his back. With Tess leading the way, the dog followed, guiding Sally away from puddles and walking at a pace suitable for the small girl's short legs. Mary walked behind the girl and dog, explaining to Sally where they were walking, telling her that she was ready to assist if needed, but with every step, Sally appeared to gain more confidence in her new guide, and was walking quite naturally by the time the dog stopped beside Tess at the chook yard gate.

Both women stared at each other in amazement when the dog picked up the basket that Tess had put on the ground when she opened the gate. As Mary held Sally's hand to lead her into the chook yard the dog walked beside Sally, totally ignoring the chooks. Tess handed the warm eggs to the young girl, who gently placed them in the basket, still hanging from the dog's jaws.

Sally patted a couple of chooks that Mary held for her, but she was more interested in walking back to the kitchen with her new friend, once Tess had taken the basket from his mouth. Back in the kitchen Sally hugged him. 'You are such a wonderful dog!' The grin on his face went from ear to ear, and his tail thumped a tattoo on the floor. The next hour was spent in the kitchen, where Mary helped Tess make bread, and Sally and the dog curled up together on the mat in front of the stove.

Both women were still finding it hard to believe what they had just witnessed, and discussed it quietly as they kneaded the dough. Mary knew that many animals could sense someone in need, but had never witnessed it happen so quickly. Both women wondered if the dog could be trained to really help Sally, or whether what they had seen was just a once off occurrence. There was no doubt that the young girl and lonely dog had struck up an instant rapport, and Mary thought '*this could solve my problem of what to give Sally when the ponies arrive for the other children, as well as possibly helping her to become a little more independent.'*

'Tess, would you please allow Sally to have the dog as a pet at the Hall?'

'Yes of course Mary. That would certainly solve my problem of what to do with him. Would you like to take the dog home Sally?'

The young girl was ecstatic. Although Mary added 'Remember, that we will have to see how he gets on with Scruffy and the horses Sally,' both she and Tess knew that the little dog had found a new home. The issue of getting him to his new home was solved when Bob came in for lunch. 'I have to go to the Hall later Mary, so I can take Sally and the dog home in the cart after lunch.' Mary rode home alone with Scruffy, hoping that he would accept the new dog.

While having lunch with some of the staff, Mary warned them of the new arrival, and explained what had occurred at the farm. The twin maids set off after their meal to look for suitable bedding and bowls, while Mrs Smith told Mary 'I once heard of a man who had a dog trained to take him to the shops in his village in Wales. All by himself he was, and the dog took him wherever he needed to go.'

When the cart arrived Bob lifted Sally down and the little dog jumped down and stood beside her, looking around at the people waiting in the courtyard. 'Initially, the dog wouldn't let me lift Sally onto the cart Mary until she held my hand to let him sniff it and she told him that I was her friend.' With this in mind, Mary asked Sally to introduce each member of staff as they came over, and watched the dog look at each person, then wag his tail. The last introduction was to Scruffy, who Mary led over after speaking quietly in his ear. 'Sally, give Scruffy a hug, then hug your dog.' Surprisingly the dog sniffed Scruffy's nose, then walked straight back to stand beside Sally.

'Have you thought of a name for your dog yet Sally?'

Sally turned towards Polly. 'I have called him Mac. My name is Sally Martin, so he will be Mac Martin!'

When Mary turned to walk to the back door, Mac walked under Sally's hand and followed Mary, with the awestruck staff staring at Sally walking confidently beside him.

Mary was a little concerned that Mac was showing signs of overprotectiveness towards Sally, and wondered how he would act when Alfie, Jack, and particularly Jane, arrived home from school. She decided to walk to the village to meet the children at the school, to tell them about Mac and ask them not to make a fuss of him straight away before Sally introduce him to them.

Intrigued, the children rushed into the kitchen, to see Sally cuddling a small yellow dog. He looked at Jane with his head tilted, then at Sally who was smiling. Slowly he walked over to Jane, sniffed her hand, then to everyone's surprise, gently took her hand in his mouth and walked back with her to stand beside Sally. He let Jane stoke his head, then he walked back to the two boys, wagging his tail, and stood beside them to let them pat him as well.

Not a word had been said, yet the perceptive little dog seemed to understand that the children were Sally's friends, especially Jane, and were to be accepted as no threat to his new friend. He lay between the two girls, with his head on his paws as they excitedly swapped stories of their day's activities.

When they had finished their after school snack, Sally was keen to show off Mac's ability to help her walk by herself. Arm in arm with Jane, with her other hand on Mac's back, the four children walked out into the courtyard. There Sally let go of Jane's arm, and they all walked to the stables, then out into the parkland. Mary was pleased to see them keep pace with Sally and Mac, obviously pleased that she could be out with them.

When the girls were in bed, with Mac on his bed on the floor beside their bed, Mary read them a story. 'Sally, please don't try to walk downstairs with Mac, or leave the house by yourself until I feel it would be safe for you to do so.' She kissed the girls goodnight, then bent down to pat Mac, who sat up and gave her a big lick on the cheek. She ruffled his ears then whispered 'You are such a good dog Mac. I'm so pleased that you are here.'

In the morning while Jane and Sally were dressing, Mary took Mac and Scruffy outside, and was pleased to see them scamper around together until they followed her back inside. As soon as he finished his food, Mac went to sit beside Sally while she ate her breakfast.

As it was Saturday, the children spent the morning wandering around the estate, taking Jane to areas that she previously hadn't been to. Mary went with them to the lake, to keep an eye on all four youngsters, and was interested to watch Mac gently moving Sally away from the water's edge. Sally loved the various bird calls she could hear, and asked Mary to describe the different birds to her.

Soon after lunch a covered wagon trundled into the courtyard and stopped near the stables. The curious children watched as Robert, James and the driver unloaded three small ponies, and led them to the yard next to the stables. Mary took the children over to the yard and told them, 'These ponies are for you Alfie, Jack and Jane, to look after and learn to ride on.'

Mary had earlier told Sally about the ponies. 'You have Mac Sally, and the other children will have their ponies to ride to school.' Sworn to secrecy, Sally was just as excited as the others when the ponies arrived.

Quite amicably, the children decided that Jane would have the bay and Alfie the slightly taller pony with the white socks. Jack was thrilled to have the one with a white mark on its black face – he immediately called him Star. Needless to say, the three children spent the rest of the afternoon out in the yard, where three very patient ponies were subjected to much brushing and patting.

While the ponies were being brushed, Sally and Mac slipped away with Mary to walk around the lake. Scruffy was happy to keep them company, as the other children's attention was solely on their ponies.

On Sunday Sally proudly walked with the others to Church, and following a brief discussion between Mary and the Vicar, Mac was allowed to follow Mary to the front pew to lie at Sally's feet for the duration of the service. The villagers were asked not to pat Mac while he led Sally through the Church yard, but all were smiling as the dog and little girl walked past them.

The Hall staff were thrilled to see Sally looking so happy, and were careful to keep an eye on her and her dog as they found their way around the house and the yard.

The boys and Jane had their first riding lessons in the afternoon with Robert, James and Mary leading them around the yard, initially just walking, and then bumping along at the trot. At the end of the lesson they brushed and fed their ponies, then raced inside to excitedly tell everyone they met about their new found skills.

The next morning, after the ponies had been fed, James drove the children to school in the cart, with Sally and Mac sitting beside him. Villagers they met called out 'good morning Sally', and when James explained who had called out, Sally politely used their name when she replied.

When Meg returned two days later and James drove the cart around the corner of the Hall, she was amazed to see Sally walking alone with a dog in the courtyard. She noted that as soon as the cart came into view, the dog moved Sally to a safe place near the stables, Sally moving confidently wherever the dog led her.

Sally couldn't contain her delight at Meg's return, and Mac quickly picked up on her excitement. He sat quietly watching their reunion for a while, then gave a gentle woof as though reminding Sally to introduce him. This done, he looked at Meg with her arm around Sally's shoulder, wagged his tail then walked in front of them into the house. At first Sally was upset, thinking that he had run away, until Meg explained. 'Mac is letting me walk into the house with you Sally. There will be times when you will need people to help you, and don't forget that Mac will need some time off.' Happy with this, Sally hugged Meg and walked inside with her.

After watching the dog and child together during the following day, Meg and Mary sat together after dinner to discuss how best to progress the dog's training. He seemed to instinctively know how to guide her, but how could they teach him where to go when Sally couldn't see to tell him?

CHAPTER 18

Longmire Estate
Sussex, England
Early December 1886

One early December morning, just after James had left to take the children to school, a lone horseman astride a magnificent black horse rode down the drive. Opening the front door, Mary was delighted to see that it was Hugh Watson. As Hugh dismounted, Mary ran down the steps to greet him, Scruffy close behind her. He ran straight up to Hugh, and licked the hand held out to him, then walked beside him when Hugh and Mary walked around to the stable yard where Robert took Hugh's horse into the stables.

Delighted to see Hugh again, Mary led him into the Hall. 'It's so good to see you again Mary. I left Lewes as early as I could to get here, so I didn't have breakfast, and now I'm starving!'

Before Mary took Hugh to the breakfast room she turned to Polly, who had just entered the hall. 'Polly, please ask Mrs Smith to prepare a hot breakfast for Mr Watson, and bring us a pot of coffee as soon as it is ready.'

Hugh and Mary went into the breakfast room and stood near the fire while waiting for the coffee. 'How have you managed to arrive so much earlier than planned Hugh?'

'Following graduation we all had a final interview with the Master of the college to discuss possible employment. When I informed him that I was to be employed as the estate supervisor for your two estates when I left the college, he immediately released me from further duties and wished me luck with my new job. Lucky for me, one of the college staff arranged for me to stay the night with his family who have a horse stud just the other side of Lewes.

While I was there, I saw that beautiful black mare and decided to buy her, rather than to hire a horse in Lewes. Unfortunately, not long after leaving Lewes yesterday afternoon, my mare cast a shoe, so I had to return to town to have a new shoe fitted. By the time she was ready to leave it was too late to attempt to ride alone in the dark on an unknown road, so I stabled her for the night and stayed in a hotel, leaving for Longmire Hall this morning at dawn.'

While Hugh ate his breakfast, Mary went out to find Polly. 'Have a room prepared for Mr Watson please Polly. He will sleep at the Hall while his cottage is made ready for him'. Returning to the breakfast room, she poured herself another cup of coffee, and told Hugh how she had found Sally and Jane in London soon after his departure.

When Hugh was ready Mary showed him to his room and left him to freshen up after his ride, telling him that she would wait for him downstairs. In his room, Hugh was feeling rather uneasy, as, having seen the stately residence that Mary called home and the servants calling her My Lady, the realisation that she really was a Countess hit home. While Mary was at Oakdale, it just hadn't seemed real and had been easy to ignore when they were just two young people together. He had been so looking forward to seeing Mary again, as he had become very fond of the fun loving, friendly, hardworking young lady, and had missed her terribly since they parted company in London.

When Hugh met Mary downstairs she sensed that he was feeling unsure of himself, and tried to dispel his concerns. 'Hugh, I'm still the same person you knew at Oakdale, despite the grand setting here.' She introduced him to the indoor staff as the new estate supervisor, then took him out to the stables, where he met Robert again and James, who had just returned with Sally and Mac.

When Sally was lifted to the ground, Hugh was amused to see the dog jump down and stand beside her, watching him warily until Mary introduced him to Hugh. Then he relaxed, and waited while Mary introduced Sally and Hugh. When Meg appeared at the back door and called to Sally, Hugh stared in amazement as the young girl placed her hand on Mac's back, and walked confidently beside him straight to Meg, and in through the back door. Like everyone else, Hugh found it hard to believe that Sally and Mac had only been together for a short time, and that Mac had been a lost terrified dog before they met.

Mary returned to the kitchen to speak to Mrs Smith, before going up to her room to change into her riding habit. 'Mr Watson and I will be visiting the three farms later this morning Mrs Smith, to introduce him to the farmers he will be working with, so we will require a small cut lunch please.'

Meg turned to Mary. 'I will be spending time with Sally, teaching her how to use her cane while walking with Mac.'

Before they left, Mary showed Hugh through the cottage that Mr Morris had occupied. His possessions had been removed soon after his incarceration, so it would only need a quick dust and polish, and the larder restocked before Hugh moved in. 'Hugh, this cottage is available to you rent free as part of your remuneration as the estate supervisor. You may choose to have meals with the other staff in the Hall, or cook your own from provisions supplied from the kitchen.'

'I would like to move into my own home as soon as possible Mary, though I will enjoy the communal meals in the Hall when I'm on the estate.'

Mary and Hugh visited Home Farm first, where Mary introduced him to Bob, Tess and Will. The men were just about to move cows to the upper pasture, so Hugh went with them, while Mary helped Tess separate the cream, ready to make butter. On his return to the house, Hugh happily took the skim milk out to tip into the trough in the pigsty. At Old Joe's farm, as Farm Two was often still called, Matthew and John were keen to chat to Hugh and Mary, explaining the changes that they had made since Old Joe's departure. John in particular wanted to talk to Hugh about the Royal Agricultural College where Hugh had been studying.

On the way to Glendale Mary took Hugh up to the Lookout, a high hill overlooking much of the Longmire Estate, where they stopped to eat the lunch packed by Mrs Smith. They then rode up to Glendale to meet Thomas and Paul. Initially, a little hesitant to talk, the men soon relaxed as Hugh chatted about their sheep, and their work up in the hills, all the while fondling their two dogs, who normally didn't like strangers. They didn't linger too long, as, despite the weak sunshine, there was a cold breeze, and Mary was learning that the afternoons were getting quite short at this stage of the year in England.

Hugh had a lot to think about on their ride home, and was happy to go up to his room for a long hot bath before changing for dinner. He was excited at the prospect of becoming the estate supervisor, but also a little nervous about taking on the job. Apart from collecting rents and being responsible for the maintenance of estate infrastructure and machinery, he was also going to work initially with the estate farmers, to help them modernise their enterprises where possible, and improve their pastures and stock breeding.

As pasture/crop management and animal breeding were his strongest areas of interest, Hugh felt that he could help the farmers make their businesses more profitable. When established, he possibly would be asked to help neighbouring farmers, many who had expressed interest in what he had to offer when Mary had told them of her new estate supervisor's role.

After dinner that evening, served in the dining room for Mary, Hugh, the four children and Meg, Mary and Hugh retired to the study, where she showed him the estate account ledgers, as well as the rent books. Mary told him about Mr Morris and his demise, plus what she had done since then. Hugh was impressed that she had undertaken the job herself until a suitable replacement was found, not only because she was a Peer of the Realm, but also because she was a woman.

Breakfast the next morning was a new experience for Hugh, with all the staff, plus the four children and Mary, chatting away, with no hint of the subservience he understood most of the aristocracy commanded from their servants. Their one obvious recognition to Mary's title was to call her m'lady.

As the day was fine, after a quick look at the estate office, Mary, Hugh, Sally, Mac and Scruffy walked to the village, while Meg stayed home to prepare lessons for Sally. Scruffy as usual dashed all over the place, but Hugh was impressed to see that no matter what Scruffy was doing, Mac totally ignored him and concentrated on guiding Sally away from puddles and rough areas of the road. In order to save Sally from becoming too tired, Hugh offered to give her a piggyback ride. When Mac was satisfied that she didn't need him, he raced off to join Scruffy snuffling around in the hedge row along the side of the road.

Earlier in the morning, Hugh had checked Mac's teeth. 'I think he is about twelve months old, a little older than Scruffy.' To watch the two dogs scampering along the road, it was easy to see that they were still basically pups, one with a grey, shaggy coat and long legs, and the other lower to the ground with a yellow, curly coat.

On arrival at the village, Mary took Hugh into the shops, the pub and other business premises, plus the vicarage, to meet some of the villagers. She also introduced him to the many villagers who stopped to chat to her as they walked along the street. Hugh had never been in a village where a member of the gentry was genuinely recognised as a friend.

While walking back to the Hall, watching Hugh piggybacking Sally again, Mary decided that it would be a good idea to buy one of the new governess carts that she had seen advertised in a rural paper. Meg could use it when taking Sally around the estate, and she could also take the other children to and from school, freeing up James and the cart. 'Hugh, I think your first job should be the purchase of a governess cart and suitable pony as soon as possible.' As he had carried Sally nearly all the way back to the Hall, Hugh thought that was a jolly good idea.

Three days after his arrival at Longmire Hall, Hugh attended his first rent day. Mr Lyons and Mary sat in the estate office with him as each tenant entered to pay their rent. Those tenants who Hugh hadn't met were encouraged to tell him where they lived, and who they worked for, as well as their family status.

Despite the cold weather, most people were quite cheerful, lingering to chat, and to sample Mrs Smith's lamb shank and vegetable soup, and hot bread rolls, both supplied in copious amounts throughout the day. Both boys and Jane had been given the day off school, Alfie to help chop up the vegetables that Jack regularly brought into the kitchen. Jane helped Sissy and Julie wash the pots, while to the amazement of people who hadn't met them before, Sally and Mac both carried out baskets full of the hot bread rolls, and took the empty baskets back to the kitchen to be refilled.

Mary had discussed with Meg the possibility of her moving to the second cottage with Jane and Sally (and Mac of course). Meg thought that this would be a great idea, to give the girls a sense of having somewhere more akin to a family home. Mary wondered if the boys might like to join Meg and the girls, but when asked, both boys were adamant that they were happy in their own room in the Hall, and didn't want to move. Both Alfie and Jack adored Mary, and to them, the Hall was home.

The large bedroom next to Mary's was theirs to retreat to whenever they wished, which gave them both a great sense of security. They had their own bathroom, and plenty of room for the toys and games that they had accumulated. Provided they kept the room tidy Jane cleaned it and set the fire, but the boys made their own beds and carried up the coal for their fire. Scruffy slept in their room too, and they were sure that he would prefer to stay put as well.

As Mary's official duties increased, she was having to travel to Lewes more often. She now felt that she was beginning to impose on the Lyons hospitality too much, so asked Mr Lyons to look for a suitable house for her to buy.

A week later, he showed her through a thatched cottage with a lovely rose garden at the front, and a large back garden area with a vegetable garden, small orchard, and double stables, with attached groom's quarters, and access to the rear lane. The cottage had a large kitchen and scullery, plus dining and living rooms on the ground floor, and three bedrooms, one with a maid's room, a bathroom with running water, and an indoor water closet upstairs.

Mary loved the cottage, and decided that it would be best to have someone living in it; otherwise it would be empty for more days than it was used. Celia introduced Mary to a young lady was desperately looking for accommodation for herself and her two small children after she had been turned out of her house when her fisherman husband had drowned.

Mary arranged for Gwen and her children to move into the cottage as soon as the paperwork was signed. They had use of two of the bedrooms, while the third bedroom, with the maid's room, was to be kept in readiness for Mary to use, whenever she needed to stay overnight in Lewes.

Hugh quickly settled into his new role, riding out to the estate farms early in the mornings, often staying all day helping with whatever jobs needed doing. Some nights he arrived back quite late, and was very thankful for the meal that Mrs Smith would leave in his kitchen. The farmers were pleased to see Hugh, and were ready to listen when he discussed ways that might be more profitable, as well as make their job a bit easier.

The week before Christmas he visited the Grey brothers at Glendale, to find Thomas house bound with a badly swollen knee, the result of slipping in the icy yard the previous night. The brothers were very concerned that Paul would be unable to carry out all the work still needing to be done before it snowed on the higher land.

'Would you please ride down to the Hall Paul, and tell Her Ladyship that I will stay at Glendale to help you for a few days, and ask her to pack me some additional warm clothes.'

Mary returned with Paul at lunchtime, with both horses carrying packed saddlebags. Once in the cottage Mary checked Thomas's knee. 'You should stay inside and keep your leg up as much as possible Thomas, to give it a chance to heal more quickly.' Hugh fashioned a crutch from a small branch, then sent Mary on her way home, so that she would be riding in daylight.

The days were getting shorter, and once again Mary was having trouble dealing with the opposite seasons, especially as Christmas was rapidly approaching, and there had been a couple of snow falls already. A far cry from the scorching heat, with the constant threat of bushfires of her previous Christmases in Australia. Having never seen snow before, Mary was as excited as the children when out making snowmen and throwing snowballs. She however quickly realised that, despite its beauty, it made life so much harder for the farmers and outside staff.

Plans were made to have a Christmas party at the Hall for the villagers in the week prior to Christmas, plus a 'family' Christmas dinner for all the residents of the Hall, plus invited guests. While looking forward to the Christmas festivities, Mary was painfully aware that it would be the first anniversary of her mother's death just after Christmas. Also, she was missing her family members Aunt Clara and Graham, who were so far away. She had written numerous letters to them since her arrival in England, but so far had not received any letters from either her aunt or her brother.

Awoken by thunder early one dark, stormy morning a few days before Christmas, Mary lay thinking of the dramatic changes that had occurred since that fateful day, almost twelve months ago, when her mother had died. Then she was an unpaid worker on the small family dairy farm in Australia, and had since travelled to the other side of the world, and was now a Peer of the Realm, an extremely wealthy young lady living in a huge stately mansion, with staff and four young children dependant on her.

Thinking of all the amazing things that had happened since her arrival in England eight months ago, Mary wondered *'what more can the coming New Year possibly have in store for me?'*

The Compassionate Countess

CHAPTER 1

London
April 1888

Hugh Watson, the Longmire and Oakdale estate supervisor, was seated in the boardroom with eight of the Countess's business managers, when Lady Mary Evans entered the room with her solicitor and friend Mr Gordon Lyons. The men all stood and waited for the twenty year old Countess to be seated at the head of the table, with Mr Lyons beside her. 'Good morning, gentlemen. Thank you all for attending this morning's meeting. I hope that you will be interested in the details that Mr Lyons is about to discuss with you. I will leave you to listen to and debate our proposal. Mr Watson, will you please accompany me outside?'

As the door shut behind them, Mary heard Mr Lyons begin to speak, then she turned to Hugh and gave him a quick peck on the cheek. 'Oh, Hugh, I have missed you so much during the past three weeks.' Poor Hugh, desperately wishing to sweep her into a loving embrace, blushed then took her hand and gave it a quick kiss.

'I missed you too Mary.' He offered her his arm, and they walked out of the building and entered the tea shop next door. Understanding Hugh's embarrassment, Mary smiled over the lip of her tea cup. 'Please tell me about your trip up north, Hugh.'

Once Hugh began to tell her about the people he'd met, the businesses that he had visited, and the brief visit that he had made to his family at the Oakdale Estate in Yorkshire, Mary was pleased to see him relax, and become his usual good-humoured self. An hour later, after Mary had updated Hugh on the information that Mr Lyons was imparting to the managers, they returned to the boardroom to find the men chatting away so keenly that at first they didn't realise that she had entered the room. When they resumed their seats, Mary remained standing. 'So gentlemen, do I take it that you feel as enthusiastic as I am about my proposal?'

Mr Jenkins, manager of the china clay mine in Cornwall, stood up, a frown on his face. 'Your Ladyship, are you truly proposing to offer each of us a five percent share in the new shipping company that you recently purchased?'

'I am Mr Jenkins. Are you interested in the proposal, gentlemen?' All eight men agreed that they were. 'Very well then, we will meet here again in three weeks' time after you have spoken to your families and your bank managers. This is a risky business that you are looking to enter into, although steamships now tend to be safer and more reliable than sailing ships.'

During the previous two years since her arrival in England, as Mary had become more interested and involved in the many businesses that she owned, she had quickly developed an acute awareness of how dependent her numerous mining and manufacturing businesses were on various shipping companies to move raw materials and finished goods around Great Britain and overseas. The costs were high, and at times it was difficult to ensure that the goods were dealt with efficiently and honestly. Earlier in the year Mary had made enquiries about the possibility of owning some ships, and whether owning her own shipping company would enhance or be detrimental to her businesses.

A month ago, Gordon Lyons had been informed of a small family shipping company in Southampton about to be sold following the death of the owner. With no close male relative to take over the company, his widow wished to sell up as quickly as possible and move back to America. The company owned 6 relatively new steamships: two 3,000-ton ships, with facilities for 300 passengers and some trade, at present sailing the Australia route in 60 days; two similar-sized ships with limited passenger facilities trading with America; and two trading vessels plying India and the East Indies.

After rigorous investigation and serious negotiations, a price had been settled upon, and Mary had become the owner of the Rushmore Shipping Company. She agreed to continue to employ the manager, Charles Browning, who had practically run the company for a number of years, as the owner rarely visited the office.

Mary had also decided to offer her senior managers the opportunity to be shareholders in the shipping company, and the eight men who attended the meeting were the ones who had shown the greatest interest in the proposal for the purchase of a shipping company. Hugh had been away when the final papers were signed, but was aware of the proposed purchase, so it was no surprise to him that Mary now owned the shipping company.

When Hugh first met Mary nearly eighteen months ago, he had held similar views to most men of his time; that men were both physically and intellectually superior to women, who were best suited to be just wives, who oversaw domestic duties, brought up children, as well as being available for whatever pleasures her husband desired. He had rapidly changed his views as he came to know Mary, soon realising that it wouldn't be wise to comment on what he had been brought up to think a woman's role should be!

She was a quick learner, who knew as much about the running of the estate as he did. Her accounting skills were well developed, and she had no qualms arguing the point with either men or women. Whilst her title gave her the liberty to do this, she did so in such a manner that most people didn't take offence. But more than that, Hugh had found Mary to be a great companion on their regular rides around the estate, and during the evenings when they sat together in the study, doing the books or discussing not only the estate, but all manner of subjects.

After a quick lunch, Mary and Hugh caught the train to Lewes, leaving Mr Lyons to finalise the share arrangements with the managers. They were met at Lewes Station by Robert, the head groom, with the Countess's coach. To their surprise, he was accompanied by Alfie, Jack,

Jane, and Sally, Mary's four wards, who excitedly hugged both Mary and Hugh, chatting constantly while the luggage was loaded, until Robert told all four children to get up on the driver's seat. Although it was a bit cramped, he sat with the boys to one side and the girls on the other. Sally, who was blind, sat beside him, with her hand on his hand so that she could feel him controlling the horses with the reins.

CHAPTER 2

Lewes,
Sussex, England
May 1888

Two weeks later, Mary was in Lewes attending an afternoon tea at the residence of Lady Edith Pridmore, the wife of Sir Harold Pridmore, a London banker seeking election to Parliament. While Mary and the other five ladies in the sitting room were sipping their tea and discussing the upcoming Charity Ball, there was the sound of a scuffle in the garden outside the French windows, followed by a high-pitched voice shouting, 'No, no, leave me alone' then a scream and a thud.

Sitting nearest to the windows, Mary was the first out into the garden to find a young man with his trousers down around his knees, struggling with a girl lying on the path. Mary grabbed the adolescent by his coat collar, hauled him off the girl, and swung him face first into a large rose bush, where he struggled and screamed as the thorns ripped into his face, and the lower part of his anatomy exposed to the elements!

While Lady Pridmore ran to her sixteen-year-old son Phillip, and tried to disentangle him from the rose bush before too much damage was inflicted on his person, Mary helped the girl to her feet. She was dazed, and had a bruised cheek, with one eye rapidly closing. Her blouse was ripped open, so Mary placed her own jacket around the shivering girl's shoulders.

With her snivelling son now curled up on the lawn, hastily covered by his mother's stole, Lady Pridmore turned to the girl. 'What have you done to my son, you stupid girl?'

'Master Phillip grabbed me and took my purse Lady Pridmore.'

Lady Pridmore slapped the girl across the face. 'You have no right to accuse my son of such a gross untruth Amy. Go to your room, pack your bags, and leave immediately!' Mary was appalled at such callous treatment of an employee, so ignoring a ferocious glare from Lady Pridmore, she looked at Amy. 'Tell me what happened, Amy.'

Amy sobbed. 'Master Phillip grabbed me when I was on my way to the shops m'lady, and demanded that I give him my purse. Cook gave me two shillings to buy some material for an apron, plus I was taking my own three pounds to put in the bank. Once Master Phillip had my purse, he attacked me.' Mary turned to Phillip, who was now standing and hastily adjusting his trousers. 'Do you have Amy's purse, Phillip?'

The boy glared at her. 'Mind your f★★★ing business, you interfering bitch!' Before he knew what was happening, Mary grabbed his right wrist, swung him around and pulled his arm so high up his back, he screamed. 'Enough of that foul language lad, or I will break your arm! Lady Pridmore, please take the purse from your son's coat pocket and count the contents.'

Initially, the shocked woman hesitated, but with the other four women intently watching the drama unfold, she extracted a soft leather purse from the boy's pocket before Mary let go of his wrist, and counted out exactly three pounds and two shillings. Humiliated, Lady Pridmore tried to cover up for her son's behaviour. 'This maid has been flirting with Phillip and leading him astray.' Taking her lead, Phillip embellished the story. 'That's right. That little slut is always flirting with me when I'm home from school.'

Amy exclaimed 'We have never met before you grabbed me!'

Phillip smirked. 'You won't be able to prove that I've done anything wrong, you stupid girl. Any charges you might make won't stick. My father has ways to make sure that you will change your story.'

Listening to the last sentence of his rant, Mary decided that she had heard enough, and for once opted to use her titled status. She glared at Phillip. 'Do you know who I am, Phillip?' She wasn't at all surprised by his foul-mouthed response. His horrified mother, well aware of Mary's reason for asking the question, tried to apologise on her son's behalf, while attempting to push him towards the open French windows.

'Please let your son go, Lady Pridmore!'

'Phillip Pridmore, you will be charged with theft and attempted rape. As a local magistrate, and witness to your actions, I will ensure that justice is served, and I will also make sure that your father does not interfere with the legal process.'

Mary had trouble keeping a straight face when the full impact of her statement dawned on Phillip. A footman, who had appeared in the garden, was sent to the stables to summon James, Mary's groom, who hurried to the police station nearby, with instructions to request police attendance as quickly as possible.

'Lady Pridmore, please take Phillip into the sitting room and make sure that he stays there until the police arrive.'

Mary then followed Amy up to her small room in the attic, and watched the maid sob as she packed her meagre belongings into a pillowcase. 'Where will I go m'lady? I'm scared that the master will make me disappear like two maids did after they accused his other son of forcing himself on them until they became pregnant. No one has seen or heard of them since they were told to leave.'

Mary decided to take Amy to Longmire Hall until things settled down. They descended the stairs to the entrance hall where James was waiting. 'Amy, go to the stables and stay with James. I will be along soon.'

Just then, two constables who knew Mary, arrived and bowed as they greeted her, then listened intently while she described what had just occurred. Neither constable seemed surprised when Mary spoke. 'Phillip believes that his father will arrange for any record of his indiscretion to be erased.' However, they showed more interest when Mary added 'I'm going to do all I can to ensure that Phillip pays for his misdemeanours.'

When the policemen entered the sitting room, Lady Pridmore initially tried to tell them that it was all a misunderstanding, but stopped when she saw Mary standing at the doorway. The four other ladies gave their statements then hurried off, no doubt keen to spread news of the scandal. Phillip was arrested, and as he was marched out of the house and up the street, each arm gripped by a burly policeman, his mother sat slumped in an armchair, sobbing. 'My husband will be furious. A scandal like this will ruin his chances of being elected to Parliament.'

Mary rang for Lady Pridmore's maid, then went to the stables, where James was waiting with Amy, ready to take the coach straight back to Longmire Hall. By the time the coach had travelled the six miles to Longmire Hall, Mary's residence on the vast Longmire Estate, Amy had lost some of her embarrassment from sitting in a coach beside a Countess, and Mary had found out that Amy was fifteen, had been in service for a year since leaving the orphanage where she had grown up, and that she was thrilled to be out in the countryside for the first time in her life.

'I can read and write m'lady, and was really sorry that I had to stop my schooling when I went out to work as a scullery maid in the house of Mr Merrick, a businessman in Lewes, then I was sent to work with his elderly mother's cook. I really enjoyed working for old Mrs Merrick, and was really sad when she died a month ago. Mr Merrick arranged for me to be employed by Lady Pridmore, and I have been working there for the past three weeks. Today is the first time I've ever met Master Phillip, who arrived home from boarding school at lunchtime.'

Amy was surprised when James drove the coach round to the back of the impressive stately manor house, instead of stopping at the front steps to allow the Countess to alight, as she had seen Lady Pridmore demand of her groom each time she arrived home. Her jaw dropped even further, when the servants stopped their work to chat with Mary as they crossed the courtyard and entered the house through the back door. Mary left Amy in the kitchen with Mrs Smith, the cook. 'Please give Amy a cup of sweetened tea and something to eat Mrs Smith. I need to speak to Polly.'

Mary met Polly, the senior indoor staff member in the entrance hall, and explained what had occurred in Lewes. 'Polly, please organise a room for Amy, and put her to bed as soon as possible.' That night, after the children went to bed, Mary and her staff discussed Amy's dilemma. Polly sighed. 'The poor little lass was exhausted. She snuggled down in bed, and was asleep before I shut the door.'

Although upset at Amy's treatment, most of the staff remembered life as a servant before Mary's arrival at Longmire Hall, and they weren't nearly as shocked as she had been. All agreed to keep an eye on Amy while she stayed at Longmire Hall until the Pridmore boy's trial, to make sure that nobody tried to make her change her story.

Before Mary went to bed, she looked in on Alfie and Jack, who still shared the big bedroom next to hers, then went up to check on Amy, taking a mug of cocoa and a couple of slices of bread and jam with her. In the light of the fire glowing in the fireplace, Mary noticed that Amy was awake. 'May I come in Amy?' Accustomed to having little to no rights as a servant, Amy just nodded, then pulled the bedclothes up to her chin when Mary sat on the chair beside the bed.

'I've brought you some bread and cocoa, Amy. Mrs Smith thought that you might be hungry when you woke up.'

'Thank you, m'lady.' Amy quickly devoured the bread and gulped down the cocoa.

'When did you last have a meal, Amy?'

'Dinner time last night, m'lady. I had a glass of water and a crust of bread. Cook gave me a cup of tea before I started work this morning.'

'What did you usually eat at mealtimes?'

'Most meals were a slice of bread and some jam, with a cup of tea. Some nights, we shared the scraps from the master's dinner table, but there wasn't much left over for the maids.'

The next morning, Amy was awake early and followed the twins Sissy and Julie down to the kitchen. Not sure what to do, she helped them clean and set the fireplace in the breakfast room where, the twins informed her, the staff ate their meals. Amy couldn't believe how much the girls chatted and laughed while they worked. She had always had to work silently, and only speak when asked a question by a more senior member of staff.

When Mrs Smith entered the kitchen, Amy bobbed a curtsey as she had been made do by the Pridmore's housekeeper. Mrs Smith chuckled. 'You don't have to do that here lass. Just make us a nice hot cup of tea.' As they sat at the table drinking their tea, Mrs Smith chatted with Amy. 'You will find working here a lot different to other places, Amy. Lady Mary expects us all to work hard, but wants us to enjoy our work. We help each other and can talk while we work. You will call her My Lady, but don't be surprised when she and the boys join us for meals. Most of the time, Lady Mary disregards most formalities. However, when there are guests, everyone snaps into formal mode. Polly will explain your duties later.'

Polly entered the kitchen just as Mrs Smith finished speaking. 'I trust you slept well, Amy?'

'Oh yes, thank you, Polly.'

Amy sat dumfounded during breakfast, unaccustomed to the amount of food put in front of her, and to the constant chatter throughout the meal, as both indoor and outdoor staff sat at the table discussing local news and work to be done. But most astounding of all, was having Lady Mary and the two boys sitting at the same table, laughing, and joining in the conversation as they ate.

Following breakfast, Mary spoke to the boys. 'Alfie and Jack, please introduce Amy to Meg, Jane, and Sally, and show her around the buildings and gardens near the house. Please stay in sight of either the gardeners or the grooms, just in case Phillip's father sends someone to harm Amy.'

During the night, Mary had thought a lot about the previous day's incident, and decided to go back to Lewes to discuss the issue with Judge Stephens, the judge who had initially informed Mary of her duty, as a Peer of the Realm, to become a magistrate. Seeing her shock and knowing of her lack of upbringing as an aristocrat, he had offered to be her mentor and to instruct her in English law, and the role of a local magistrate. Judge Stephens had become a good friend to Mary, and had arranged for her to sit with other magistrates as they dispensed justice in the region.

When informed of the arrest of Phillip Pridmore, and the possible interference from his father, Judge Stephens agreed that it could lead to an interesting situation. On one hand, news of Phillip's arrest could harm his father's Parliamentary future; a court case definitely would! Many of the aristocracy felt themselves above the law, and spent a lot of money covering up misdemeanours of family members. However, Phillip's indiscretions had been so blatant, with little to no thought of the consequences, but worse still it was witnessed by a magistrate, upon whom he had unleashed some profane language.

Unfortunately for the lad, he had been caught doing what he had observed others doing, under the notion that any misdemeanour would be covered up by his father. Aware that the penalty for theft could be harsh, especially for a naïve sixteen-year-old boy, Mary was hoping that Judge Stephens might know of a legal alternative, without yielding to possible interference from Sir Harold Pridmore.

Mary and Judge Stephens lunched together, discussing possible penalties. 'I recall sending a young man to America to work for his brother, who had emigrated there a few years previously, mainly to save him from the life of crime his associates were leading him into. Would you mind if I discuss this with Sir Harold, Mary? I know his younger brother Mark well. He bought some land south of Perth in Australia, and has written asking me to try to find him some suitable workers.

What would you say to Phillip being offered, say two years, working for his uncle in Australia, instead of a conviction leading to several years in jail, with a possible whipping included? Working for Mark would be no cinch. His land is over fifty miles south of Perth, and he lives in a hut near a creek while he clears land, trying to make it sustainable for the horses and cattle that he had shipped from England when he purchased his land.'

While Mary considered this, the Judge continued. 'Phillip would not be sent as a convicted felon. He would, however, be known as a remittance man, and his parents would have to pay him an allowance for the two years he spent with his uncle. It would be made clear to Phillip and his family that should he choose this option, he must stay with his uncle for the full two years, or he would end up in jail on his return to England.'

'That could be a good alternative Judge Stephens. Thank you for offering to act as an intermediary in this case.'

'In the meantime, Mary I would advise you, in your capacity as a local magistrate, to have Phillip released from the police cells, on payment of a large bond, and on the condition that he doesn't leave his parents' house until the trial date is set.'

Two days later, Judge Stephens arrived at Longmire Hall to inform Mary of his discussions with Phillip's father and consequent events. 'Sir Harold tried to bluster his way through our first meeting, but when I informed him that his previous actions might be looked into more closely, he became more agreeable to my suggestions. I also made it clear that should Amy be harmed or intimidated in any way, Phillip's misdemeanours would be made public.

I have already found a couple of men willing to work for Mark, both younger sons having to seek a living away from their family farms, wishing to try their luck in Australia. These men are willing to make sure that Phillip arrives at Mark's farm with them, happy with the promise of additional payment on their arrival. My clerk had sourced three berths on the Arabella, a steam ship sailing for Australia in a week's time, subject to Sir Harold's and your agreement Lady Mary.'

Mary gasped. 'The Arabella is one of my ships Judge Stephens!'

The judge laughed. 'All the better. Your captain can keep an eye on the lad until they land in Freemantle.'

CHAPTER 3

When Judge Stephens rode back to Lewes after lunch, Mary summoned Amy to her study, and informed her of the proceedings to date. Not sure what this would mean for her future, Amy stood silently in front of the large desk.

'Would you like to work here at Longmire Hall, Amy?'

'Oh yes please, m'lady. But I don't have any references. Mrs Merrick's cook, Mrs Harvey, was teaching me to cook. Often, we would try new recipes when I read the recipe to her. Mrs Merrick had given Mrs Harvey the recipe book, but she couldn't read too well.'

Mary leant down to Scruffy, her shaggy grey dog. 'Should we employ Amy Scruff?' He immediately jumped up and gave Amy's hand a lick and sat at her feet. Mary laughed. 'That's reference enough for me. Go and ask Mrs Smith if you can help her prepare dinner Amy.'

When Amy left the study, Mary remained seated at the desk, tapping a pencil thoughtfully as she stared out of the window. Before attending Lady Pridmore's afternoon tea, Mary had spent the morning with Gordon Lyons, discussing the finalisation of the purchase of a farm on the boundary of the Longmire Estate. Mary and Hugh had plans for most of the new land to be added to Home Farm and to Farm Two, to allow for more crops to be sown. She also had a proposal for a few acres next to Longmire village, but had wanted to discuss this with Mr Lyons before informing anyone else.

Hoping to see Hugh soon, Mary went for a ride around the new farm. Within half an hour, she had ridden Gem around the farm boundaries, Scruffy loping along beside them. The fields were overgrown, as the elderly farmer had sold his cattle months before he died, and some of the wheat crop hadn't been harvested, but the house and farm buildings appeared to be in reasonable order.

While crossing the stream running through the property, Mary was impressed by the strong flow of water, despite the dry weather that they were having. Following the bank upstream, she discovered that the water flowed from a spring near the base of a small hill. On her way back to the Hall, Mary rode through some of the flattened wheat crop, remembering the elderly farmer's complaint that he hadn't harvested most of his wheat because he could no longer afford to take the grain to the nearest mill a few of miles on the other side of Lewes. Mary knew how annoying and costly it was to get grain crushed, but if local farmers wanted their grain to be milled for cattle feed or flour, there was no alternative. As she rode home, Mary wondered if there might be some way of minimising the cost. When an idea came to her, she couldn't wait to get back to her study to start putting her thoughts to paper.

Later that evening, Jane tapped on the study door. 'Excuse me, m'lady, dinner is ready to be served. Mary looked at the clock in surprise. 'I'm sorry Jane, I had no idea that it was dinner time. Please tell everyone to start without me. I'll go to the kitchen when I've finished here.' As Jane closed the study door she noted that the desk was littered with sheets of paper, covered with writing and numbers.

Impatient to discuss her thoughts with Gordon, Mary decided to go to Lewes early the next morning, in the hope that he might have time to see her briefly before his first appointments. After visiting the stables to arrange for a groom to be ready to leave at dawn, Mary went to the kitchen where Mrs Smith had a plate laden with food warming in the oven.

As she ate, Mary could hear the twins Sissy and Julie chatting and laughing while they washed the dishes in the scullery. Mrs Smith watched Mary listening to the chatter. 'Does the twins' noise bother you, m'lady?'

'Not at all, Mrs Smith. In fact, I was just thinking how happy they sound, despite facing that mountain of crockery and pans from dinner. Does it worry you?'

Mrs Smith placed a dish of trifle on the table in front of Mary and smiled. 'No, it doesn't, m'lady. At first I thought it would, but they are so happy when they work and chat together, they finish their work far more quickly and thoroughly than when they work alone. In fact, all the staff comment on how much they enjoy their work now. They are more interested in what they do, and are often asking each other why things are done a certain way, or could changes be made to make a job easier or better.'

Mary was thrilled to hear this, knowing that she felt more comfortable in her home with a happy staff. As she walked towards the door, she turned. 'Mrs Smith, I will be leaving early in the morning, so I will make tea and toast for James and myself. There is no need for either you or the girls to get up earlier than usual.'

'We'll see!' murmured the cook as the kitchen door closed.

Mary wasn't surprised when the twins and Amy greeted James and herself in the kitchen the next morning, with bowls of porridge, hot buttered toast, and cups of tea ready for them.

After spending half an hour listening to Mary's proposal, and reading her notes and calculations, Gordon sat back in amazement. This young lady across the desk from him never ceased to astound him. Her business acumen for someone so young (and not just a lady) was astonishing, especially when she had previously informed him that she'd had little formal education when she grew up in Australia. 'I used to ride my horse three miles to school each day, until just before my fifteenth birthday. When my father was killed fighting a bushfire I had to leave school to help my step brother Graham run the dairy farm.'

What Mary had put in front of Mr Lyons was a very plausible proposal for erecting a watermill on the stream of the new property, to be used primarily for milling estate grain, but also for local farmers to use, at a reduced rate as well as a large saving on cartage costs. Promising to look into the scheme more thoroughly when he had finished his appointments, Gordon suggested that Mary and James stop in at his house for a cup of tea with his wife, Celia, before travelling back to the Hall. Before his next appointment, Gordon asked Ben, one of his associates, to start looking into the location of watermills in Southern England, both working and closed down.

Following a brief stop at the Lyons residence for a quick cup of tea and chat with Celia, James drove Mary to the boundary of Lewes, where he turned the horse at an impressive gateway, and went through the arch formed by the gatehouse. Set well back from the road and hidden by a grove of mature elm and oak trees, the four-storied manor house was surrounded by manicured lawns and flower gardens, with stables and fields at the rear. The much smaller Dower House was nearby.

Mary had purchased this twenty-acre property six months ago, when it had become apparent that she required a more substantial residence in Lewes, more suited to her title than the small cottage that she had initially purchased for overnight stays in town.

Much as Mary would have preferred to stay and work on the Longmire Estate, as she had for the first twelve months after her arrival in England, it had soon become obvious that more was expected of her as the new Countess of Longmire and Oakdale. While she refused to live an idle life, being waited on by servants and spending her days socialising with ladies who wanted to be seen in her company, Mary accepted that there were times when she had to, as she put it, 'Go formal.'

Social functions in the Lewes area, and in London, were becoming unavoidable if Mary was to be accepted in society for more than just her title. Afternoon teas, luncheons, and dinners were essential for Mary to network with both men and women, who could someday assist her in her endeavour to improve the lot of those in the lower classes.

Having been brought up to work hard on a small Australian dairy farm, struggling to make enough to feed the family, Mary had a desire to use her new-found circumstances for improving the lot of those struggling to survive. She was realistic enough to know that she couldn't help everyone, but with more money than she could ever imagine, plus such a high-ranking title, Mary was in a position where she could help introduce some changes.

Mary was on the Board of Governors of the Lewes Workhouse, and had already initiated changes to the feeding and treatment of inmates and especially the children within its grim walls. At first sceptical of the proposed changes, her fellow governors now admitted that the inmates, on the whole, were healthier, happier, and the children better educated; plus, there hadn't been the riots many had predicted if the children weren't more strictly managed.

The Board members had been much more rigorous in the selection of the new master, matron, cook, and teachers, offering quarterly bonuses if all the Board members were satisfied with the treatment of the inmates and schooling of the children and any of the adults who wished to attend classes.

Also, at Mary's instigation, stricter guidelines had been drawn up for entrance into the workhouse, so children couldn't just be dumped because their parents didn't want them. Bullies, or children who regularly flouted the rules, were brought before the Board, and given the choice of behaving and staying at the Lewes Workhouse, or being sent to a London workhouse, notorious for its harsh treatment of inmates. Needless to say, few children put this offer to the test!

A number of more enlightened gentlemen, mainly businessmen, who could see the benefit of Mary's plan to have healthy, educated, and more socially accepted young teenagers entering the workforce, offered for election onto the Board and took their role seriously. Previously, the role of a Lewes Workhouse Board member had been looked upon as a well-paid job, with little to do but enjoy long lunches and drink too much port, but not any longer.

Mary was also becoming more involved in her role as a local magistrate. Under Judge Stephen's tutelage, Mary quite enjoyed learning about the law, and lately was being encouraged to attend as many court cases as she could. Understanding that she couldn't adjudicate cases on her own until she was twenty-one, Mary sat on a panel of three magistrates when required in court.

Recently, she had been on the bench with two other magistrates to hear a case of assault, where a man had thrown his three-year-old son against a brick wall when he hadn't picked up his father's cigarettes quickly enough, resulting in the boy suffering broken limbs and head injuries.

Warned by Judge Stephens that some of her fellow magistrates might be of the belief that the man had every right to chastise his family members however he wished, Mary wasn't surprised when one magistrate, who was in a hurry to go to his club for a drink, suggested that there was no case to answer. However, the other man disagreed, so the case proceeded. The defendant was well-known for injuring his wife and three young children in his drunken rages on his return home from the local alehouse. His family were starving, and had to beg for food on the streets, while he ate most of the food that his wife managed to scavenge, and drank nearly all of the money he earned.

At the end of the trial, the man was sentenced to a number of year's hard labour in prison, much to Mary's secret delight. Should the boy die, the charge would be changed to murder, and the man could hang. The wife and children were sent to the workhouse, but not before Mary had spoken to the woman, and assured her that she and her children would be looked after. She was to be allowed regular contact with her children, and Mary would make sure that she could spend time with her young son while he was in hospital.

CHAPTER 4

Everton Manor
Sussex, England
May 1888

The new manor house at Lewes had fifteen bedrooms, numerous reception rooms, a ballroom, nursery, and staff quarters, plus a huge cellar, still stocked with a considerable quantity of wine that Gordon Lyons was longing to catalogue and hopefully taste! Longmire Hall would still be Mary's home, but Everton Manor, as Mary had named the property in honour of her grandmother Lady Emma Everton, would be her place of residence when she needed to be in Lewes.

The property had originally been an extensive estate close to Lewes, owned by a titled family that had, over generations of mismanagement, lost hundreds of acres through gambling debts and death duties. As Lewes expanded, the previous owner had sold all but twenty acres and the manor house to developers, who in a short time had covered the land with houses. His elderly widow had sold the land and manor house to Mary, hoping to save that acreage from the same fate.

At the time of the property sale, there was just a cook and an elderly maid remaining from the large retinue of servants previously employed. Consequently, much of the interior of the house, the stables, and the gardens were very dilapidated, requiring what seemed like an army of tradesmen and gardeners, working for nearly six months, to bring them back to a semblance of their former glory.

The Dower House was a well-appointed three-bedroom residence, with its own garden. This residence was included in the refurbishment being carried out on the property buildings. While Mary quickly inspected some of the lower floor rooms and kitchen of the main house, James checked the stables and men's quarters. As part as the renovation work, gas lighting was connected throughout the house, the kitchen was modified considerably, and some rooms were refashioned into indoor bathrooms and toilets.

An acre of land behind the stables had been ploughed and planted with vegetables, with the idea of not only supplying the house, but also selling vegetables to grocers in Lewes.

Another reason Mary had for buying the property, was the potential for it to become a second home for her wards. Alfie, Jack, and Jane were thoroughly enjoying their school days at the village school, but Mary realised that if they were to progress with their education, they would need to be enrolled in a larger school at the end of the summer break. Aware of the children's fear of the workhouse and institutional life, Mary knew that sending them to boarding school would be a nightmare. No way would she consider such a move.

However, if the children lived at Everton Manor during the week to attend school in Lewes, they could return to Longmire Hall at weekends, and for school holidays. Not keen on the idea at first, Alfie, Jack, and Jane became more interested when they were shown over the new property, and were told that they could keep their ponies in the stables. Due to Sally's blindness, she would not be attending school in Lewes, but she would join the others at Everton Manor. Mary and Meg, Sally's tutor, were arranging for Sally to attend classes at the School for the Blind in London later in the year.

After consultation with Celia Lyons and Polly, regarding staff for the manor, Mary was informed that she would need to employ a butler, footman, housekeeper, cook, three maids, plus two gardeners and two grooms. When Mary questioned why she needed a butler and footman when they didn't have either at Longmire Hall, she was told that being closer to Lewes the perception of the people that she would be associating with was paramount to maintain her standing in society.

Celia Lyons offered to advertise for the new staff, then she and Polly interviewed all of the suitable applicants. Although the new butler and housekeeper would be in charge of setting and maintaining staff conduct and performance, Mrs Lyons made it clear that whoever was employed in those roles understood the Countess's somewhat radical approach to servant employment.

Whilst each member of her staff would have set formal roles, they would be expected to share jobs, and would be allowed to speak to each other while they worked, providing they completed each task satisfactorily without wasting time. Certainly, a novel approach to most of the applicants.

Finally, a married couple, both in their late thirties, were employed as butler and housekeeper. Arthur Atkins had been valet to a London businessman, and his wife Helen had been lady's maid to the gentleman's wife. Arthur and Helen had married, with their employer's permission, but four months ago, the family had moved to New York. Much as the newly married couple would have liked to accept their employers' offer to accompany them to America, Arthur felt duty-bound to stay in England to be near his parents and handicapped younger brother Toby, who lived in London

Unfortunately, few London houses employed married servants. The couple were about to apply for positions further from the City, when they saw Mrs Lyons's advertisement. If they were fortunate enough to be employed by the Countess, Arthur was hoping to be able to rent accommodation in or near Lewes for his family.

Margaret Peters, the new cook, was a middle-aged woman who had been the cook at the London residence of the recently deceased widow of a prominent London financier. The family had sold the house and dismissed all the staff when the house had been cleared and cleaned.

Arthur, Helen, and Margaret all had glowing references, attesting to their work ethic, honesty, and reliability. They were introduced to Mary, and she invited all three to stay at Longmire Hall for the week prior to their move to Everton Manor, to give them the chance to get to know each other and the staff at Longmire Hall, and also to see how Mary's staff worked together.

Their train fares were paid for them to return to London to collect their possessions, and it was arranged for Robert to collect them from Lewes Station at eleven o'clock two days later. Imagine their surprise when the trio arrived back at Lewes Station to find the Countess's coach, with two gleaming black horses, waiting for them. It was pouring with rain, and they had imagined a long, wet, uncomfortable journey on a farm cart of some description.

Robert quickly introduced himself, and ushered the trio into the coach before they became too wet, then organised for their luggage to be placed on a waiting cart and covered with a tarpaulin, prior to setting off for Longmire Hall. Warm and dry in his oilskins, Robert expertly drove the coach out of town, briefly stopping at the gates of Everton Manor to point out to the new staff where they would soon be living.

When the coach pulled up near the Longmire Hall stables, Polly greeted the visitors, and led them through the back door, where they could hear two girls singing, then laughing when one hit a wrong note. As they walked towards the kitchen Polly laughed. 'Please excuse the twins. Unfortunately, Mrs Smith our cook has a bad headache and has been sent up to bed, leaving Julie and Sissy to get lunch ready. I'm not sure what we will get, but they think they can cope.'

Following Polly into the kitchen, the new trio were introduced to Sissy and Julie who, while making bread rolls on the kitchen table, were covered in flour. Following their introduction to the twins, Margaret looked at the smiling girls, 'Could I possibly help you to prepare lunch?' Seeing the delight on their faces, she laughed. 'Do you have an apron that I could wear?'

When Polly led Arthur and Helen out of the kitchen to show them around the Hall, Margaret walked over to the table, 'What do you have planned for lunch Sissy?' 'There's soup on the stove and cold cuts, plus hopefully, bread rolls. Mrs Smith was going to prepare a salad, but we don't know what she was going to use or how to make the salad dressing.'

'How many will be having lunch Julie?'

'Thirteen.'

'No, fourteen, don't forget Mrs Smith. We are awfully glad you offered to help us Mrs Peters, aren't we Julie?'

Margaret put on the large apron that Sissy handed her. 'Julie, could you please go out to the garden and ask the gardener for enough ingredients to make a tasty salad for lunch. Sissy, please put those rolls into the oven and clean the table while I check the soup and prepare the cold cuts.'

By the time lunch was ready, Mary had arrived back from her visit to Home Farm, where she had discussed her plans for the new farm with Tess and Bob Telford, and their elder son Will. Once she had changed into drier clothes, everyone assembled in the breakfast room, where Mary introduced each staff member in turn, explaining their main duties.

The twins then proudly brought in two large soup tureens, and served everyone, before they too sat at the table. Following grace said by Mary, the soup was eaten, then everyone served themselves from a variety of cold cuts and salad on the large sideboard. Margaret thanked Tom, the gardener, on his selection for the salad, and the twins were also complimented on their bread rolls.

After lunch and a quick word with Margaret, Mary and Polly took a cup of tea up to Mrs Smith. Finding her too unwell to get up, Mary reassured her that Margaret and the twins were happy to work together in the kitchen, following Mrs Smith's menu while she was indisposed.

To allow Margaret, Sissy, and Julie time to begin preparing dinner, Arthur and Helen offered to do the washing up. Helen laughed as her husband tried hard to handle slippery plates in the hot sudsy water. 'Can you imagine us doing the dishes when we worked for Sir Isaac, Arthur? I know that he and his wife were more liberally minded than other employers we met, but could you imagine them sitting at the same table as the servants?' Arthur eyed off what looked like a mountain of dishes still to be washed. 'No, I can't. I could get used to the informality, but I don't think I'll be as keen to offer to do the dishes again.'

Later in their bedroom, where they had gone to change their clothing, wet partially from their dishwashing adventure, and also from their boisterous introduction to a still wet Scruffy, Helen said 'You know Arthur, I think that this idea of Lady Mary's to allow a more relaxed atmosphere with the servants works. Everyone we've met here seems to be so friendly and helpful, yet I have been assured that they carry out their formal roles in a serious manner when required.'

'Yes. Although Polly warned us that the Countess ate most of her meals with the servants, it still came as a bit of a shock having her sit with us, with everyone chatting away to her almost as equals. Although it is clear that everyone adores and respects her, and no liberties appear to be taken.'

'It's interesting, this concept of calling the servants staff, almost like in a hospital or school. It certainly seems to work here. Do you think we could do something similar at Everton Manor Arthur?'

Arthur tucked his dry shirt into his waistband. 'When we first met the Countess, she said that she would like us to run the manor along similar lines. That's why we are here this week to see how it works. Because we will be closer to Lewes, we will have to be more formal, but everyone seems to be a lot happier and work hard, being allowed to talk to each other and help one another when needs be.'

Helen laughed as they left their room. 'Lady Mary told me that she wouldn't always be dining with the staff at Everton Manor, but said that she would like to drop into the kitchen for a cup of tea whenever she wanted one. 'Why stop a maid working to fetch me a cup of tea to drink in splendid isolation, probably in a freezing room?' she asked me.'

Meg and the four children met Arthur, Helen, and Margaret after school on the first day of their visit, and the boys joined the staff and Mary for dinner.

The next few days were extremely busy, with interviews for the new maids. Arthur, Helen, Polly, Margaret, and Mrs Smith, who was fully recovered after a couple of days in bed, interviewed a number of applicants for the parlourmaid and general maid positions. Following discussion with Arthur, Mary had delayed the appointment of a footman until the new staff had settled into their new positions at Everton Manor.

Lottie, the elder daughter of the Longmire Village blacksmith, was selected for the parlourmaid position. She was twenty years old, and had a glowing reference from her previous employer, for whom she had worked since going into service at the age of fourteen. Robert had already found two experienced grooms, and two of the gardeners who had been working hard to restore the lawns and gardens at Everton Manor were employed as permanent gardeners.

Joy and Martha, two younger girls about to leave the workhouse to seek employment, were appointed for general duties, while Karen, an older girl who had been working in the workhouse kitchen, was hired as assistant cook. It was impressed on all of the new staff that their work would be varied, and not fixed as upstairs and downstairs positions. Arthur also stressed to all that they were to work as a team, bullying would not be tolerated, and that staff could talk to each other while working, provided that all work was completed satisfactorily, in a timely manner. Obviously, when guests were in the manor, a more formal approach to their work would be required.

James made daily trips to Everton Manor with one or more of the new senior staff, to allow them to become familiar with their new workplace and home. A seamstress in Lewes had the measurements of all the new staff, and was making new work and formal uniforms for everyone. The gardeners didn't have a uniform as such, but were to be issued with new work clothes, boots, and waterproofs. Mary was happy to leave this preparation to her senior staff, who were getting on well together, as it left her free to spend time going through proposals and reports for many of her businesses.

CHAPTER 5

Sussex & London
June 1888

Mary's business interests were taking up more of her time these days, as her business managers, like Gordon, were beginning to realise that Mary's interest was genuine, and her ability to quickly understand and make sensible contributions to their meetings was becoming invaluable. Much to her surprise, a number of her managers had individually contacted Mary, to discuss issues with their businesses that they previously would never have considered discussing with a woman. 'Must be her colonial upbringing,' was often muttered.

One afternoon, Mary was notified that a canal boat carrying china from their factory at Stoke-on-Trent in Staffordshire, had been late in arriving at Liverpool, due to one of the locks on the Trent and Mersey Canal being damaged by a barge crashing into the gates. Consequently, the shipment of fine china had not arrived in time to be loaded onto the scheduled ship, before it sailed for America. Aware that the shipment contained a specially monogramed dinner setting, to be used at the wedding of the eldest son of a wealthy Washington family in less than a month's time, Mary understood the necessity to find another ship as quickly as possible.

She immediately sent an urgent telegram to Charles Browning, manager of her new shipping line in Southampton, instructing him to find suitable transport for the consignment to reach New York well before the wedding date. Mary was extremely relieved when the postboy arrived at Longmire Hall the following afternoon, with a telegraph from Charles. 'Julianne docked early in Liverpool. Sails to New York tonight once fuelled and china loaded. Charles.' The postboy was also pleased when he rode back to Lewes, having been given two slices of Mrs Smith's fruit cake, and a large glass of milk. He also had an apple in his pocket for later.

While all this was going on, Mary's staff from both residences worked tirelessly to prepare Everton Manor for the new staff to take up residence. The butler's and housekeeper's rooms near the kitchen had been renovated to make them more suitable for a married couple, while Margaret had a bedroom and sitting room nearby. The maids' rooms were south facing on the third floor, with a bathroom and toilet along the corridor. The previous small rooms had been enlarged, and the girls were given the choice of a room each, or to share if they wished.

The men's quarters were across the courtyard, next to the stables. Each man had a room to himself, and there was a communal sitting room, plus bathroom and indoor toilet. These quarters were remarkable to men who had often lived in less than adequate quarters. Meals would be eaten in the staff dining hall next to the kitchen.

When the new staff took up residence at Everton Manor, Mary called the three senior staff into the sitting room and ordered tea to be served. 'As you are aware, I was not brought up in a house adhering to the formal running of a servant workforce, and Longmire Hall works well with the system that the staff and I have evolved. Now that you have moved to Everton Manor, it is your new home, and you three will be in charge of the smooth running of the household. The only stipulation I expect of you is that the staff under your control are treated fairly and not unjustly punished.'

A few days later, Arthur tapped on the study door.
'Come in.'

Arthur entered and stood in front of the desk. 'Excuse me Lady Mary, may I please speak to you on a personal matter?'

'Why certainly Arthur, take a seat. What is your problem?'

'As you are aware, m'lady, my parents and brother live in London. What I have not explained is that my father works in a Bermondsey tannery, living with my mother and fifteen-year-old brother in a single room, in a multi-storied tenement house close to the fetid low-tide mudflats of the River Thames.

Their living conditions are deplorable, but my parents barely earn enough to pay the rent, and can only provide skimpy meals consisting mainly of bread and potatoes. My brother Toby has a club foot, and is unable to walk without a crutch. Nobody will employ him, so now he rarely leaves the room, and his health is suffering from the unhealthy conditions.'

Mary stared in horror at Arthur. 'Oh, that's dreadful Arthur, how can I help?'

'I'm worried that Toby will die soon if he stays in Bermondsey, m'lady. Would Your Ladyship please give me permission to bring him to Everton Manor for a short holiday? He could sleep on a mattress in our rooms, and would be no bother to anyone.'

Seeing the anguish on her butler's face, Mary leant forward. 'Of course Arthur. Take a couple of days off to go to London and get Toby. I'm sure that Helen and Margaret will cope in your absence. Go and pack a bag, while I write you a letter of introduction to Hugh Watson, the estate supervisor, who is in London at the moment.'

When Arthur returned, Mary handed him a sealed letter with Hugh's address on the front, plus money for his train fare. 'Hugh will handle all of your costs in London. Away with you Arthur. Good luck.'

Arriving in London late in the afternoon, Arthur went straight to the address written on the envelope, and found himself at a hotel in Mayfair. When he informed the receptionist that he was looking for Mr Hugh Watson, a boy was sent up to Hugh's room to inform him that Lady Mary's butler was asking for him. Intrigued, Hugh hurried downstairs and introduced himself to Arthur, who handed him Mary's letter. 'Let's go into the lounge while I read this Arthur.'

Mary had explained Arthur's worry about his brother, and gave Hugh carte blanche to arrange overnight accommodation for Arthur and his brother, transport, and anything else that he required to get Toby safely to Everton Manor.

The following morning Hugh and Arthur set off for the Atkins' address in Bermondsey. Hugh was shocked by the squalor and the offensive smell of the tanneries when they stopped in front of a shabby, multistorey tenement. However, neither he nor Arthur were prepared for the sight they beheld when they reached Arthur's parents room.

The door had been smashed open and the room stripped totally bare. Arthur's parents and brother were huddled together in a corner of the room, covered by a dirty, threadbare blanket. Mr Atkins had a bloody bandage wrapped around his head, and appeared to be semi-conscious. Rushing over to them, Arthur held his sobbing mother, while Hugh turned to speak to a woman who had appeared from the room next door.

'Mr Atkins lost his job at the tannery a few weeks ago, after he cut his arm. When he couldn't pay this week's rent, the landlord's thugs came last night to evict them. Poor Mr Atkins argued with them, so he was beaten, then more men came up and took away all of their furniture and possessions.'

The woman paused to take a breath. 'Because Mr Atkins was still unconscious when the men were ready to leave, Mrs Atkins begged to be allowed to stay in the room until morning. The men will be returning before midday to make sure that they are gone. I lent them a blanket and bound up Mr Atkins's head wound. I'm sorry I couldn't do more, but my family will be sent packing as well if those thugs hear that I helped.' Thanking her, Hugh slipped a few shillings into her palm and handed her back the grubby blanket.

He turned to the shaken butler. 'Arthur, we need to get your family downstairs as quickly as we can, and get out of the area before those fellows return.' Hugh half-carried Mr Atkins down to the waiting cab, while Arthur and his sobbing mother helped Toby down the stairs. 'They even took Toby's crutch.'

Just as the cab moved off down the street, four men walking along the middle of the road stepped out of the way of the horse, and Mrs Atkins shrank down into her seat. 'Those are the men who beat my husband.' Hugh frowned. 'I'm afraid we can't do anything about them, Mrs Atkins. Let's get back to the hotel as quickly as we can, and get a doctor to see to your husband.'

At the hotel, Hugh briskly arranged for a suite to be made available in the Countess's name, and took the family up to the rooms. A maid delivered sandwiches and a large pot of tea to the suite, then she waited to help the stunned family take turns to soak in the large ornate bath, with hot water on tap and helped them into the luxuriant beds. While his family slept, Arthur sat in disbelief at what had happened to his family. Hugh handed him a glass of whisky and a telegram. 'I telegraphed Lady Mary to let her know what has happened and this is her reply.'

'Arthur, so sorry at news. Purchase whatever clothing is required. Bring everyone to Everton Manor. Rooms will be ready. Lady Mary Evans.'

'Why is she doing this? What will she expect in return?' he queried.

'Nothing Arthur. When you've worked for the Countess for a while, you'll find that she is a very kind-hearted, generous person. She can't abide seeing people, or animals, being mistreated and will do all that she can to help. Her Ladyship is not at all like most of the titled and landed gentry you come across.'

A doctor arrived an hour later to treat Mr Atkin's injuries. The cut on his arm was cleaned, disinfected, and bandaged, as was the gash on his forehead. No further injuries, other than severe bruising, were found, and bed rest was prescribed.

Following Mary's directive, Arthur, Hugh, and Mrs Atkins went to a local market to purchase a set of clothing and footwear for all of the family, plus nightwear and underclothing. Hugh would have gone to a clothing store, but Mrs Atkins convinced him that she would be happier shopping at a market.

Toby was happy to be left at the hotel with his father, who was sleeping off the sedative that the doctor had given him. The young lad spent time soaking in a hot bath, until the water cooled down too much, then he sat at the window, watching in wonderment the street scene outside as he nibbled from the platter of food that Hugh had ordered before he left.

As they were leaving the market, Hugh saw some crutches for sale, so he bought them for Toby. He had noticed that the boy's right leg with the club foot was shorter than the other. He could hobble short distances unaided, but crutches would give him greater balance, and save wear on the side of his foot.

The next morning Mr Atkins appeared to be more alert and aware of his surroundings, though it took his wife some time to convince him to swallow his pride and accept the Countess's generosity. Following a large breakfast, and equally generous lunch Hugh, Arthur, and his family caught the train to Lewes, arriving mid-afternoon, to be met by Robert with the Countess's coach. On their arrival at Everton Manor Mary and Helen were waiting at the front door. Arthur's parents had no idea of Mary's age or history, and were astounded when their son introduced them to their young hostess, the Countess.

Their shock was quickly dispelled by Mary's quiet, but genuine words of welcome, followed by the arrival of Scruffy, who had wriggled out of the maid's grasp when he heard Mary speak. The Lurcher ran straight to Toby, who had just descended from the coach, and to everyone's amazement, he sat in front of the boy with a big grin on his face. Mary was as surprised as everyone else, remembering her dog's usual boisterous welcomes. 'He is asking you to pat him, Toby.'

Hesitantly Toby put his hand out and patted the shaggy grey head, then to his parents' surprise, he sat on the coach steps and hugged the dog to him, burying his face in his shaggy fur. Embarrassed, his mother turned to Mary. 'I do apologise, Your Ladyship. Toby has always been so terrified of dogs, I've never seen him touch one before.'

Mary laughed. 'Don't worry Mrs Atkins, Scruffy has accepted your son into his family, and will take great care of him, like he does me. He appears to realise that he needs to be gentler with Toby, though he has been known to knock me over in his enthusiastic greetings when I've been away.'

While Arthur and Helen settled their family in adjoining rooms in the visitor's wing, Mary and Hugh went into the study, where after a moment's hesitation, they were in each other's arms, hugging and kissing. Mary paused for breath. 'Oh, Hugh, I miss you so much whenever you are away.' Hugh kissed her hair. 'I feel the same way Mary my love.' At that moment, a knock on the door caused them to pull away from each other. Helen, entering on Mary's directive, noticed her mistress's flushed complexion, but kept a straight face. 'Afternoon tea will be served in the drawing room when you are ready, m'lady.'

'Thank you, Helen. We will be there directly.'

Smiling to herself as she went through the green baize door to the kitchen, Helen thought, *'I wouldn't be surprised if we are preparing for a wedding sometime soon!'*

Mary and Hugh reluctantly left the study. 'I was shocked to see Toby when he stepped out of the coach Hugh. Not his foot, I was prepared for that, but I thought Arthur said that his brother was fifteen. He looks more like a ten-year-old.'

'If you had seen the conditions that they were living in Mary, it's a wonder that he is still alive, let alone growing. They had next to nothing to eat, and he was terrified of leaving the room. I gather boys on the streets tormented him about his foot, and made life a nightmare for him.'

During the next few weeks, the Atkins family settled into life at Everton Manor. Dr Wilson was called to examine Mr Atkin's wounds and advised bed rest for a few more days, to allow complete recovery from the concussion that he had suffered. After consultation with Mrs Atkins, Dr Wilson also examined Toby. He felt the boy's susceptibility to ill health would be remedied by good food, and plenty of fresh air and sunlight. About Toby's club foot he said little, other than that he would look into possible supports to help improve Toby's balance

Unable to sit around doing nothing, Mrs Atkins assisted her daughter-in-law Helen as much as she could, until Mary discovered that she had been a seamstress before her marriage. Happy to take over the mending and needlework required at both estates, Katherine Atkins, was kept pretty busy.

When allowed out of bed, Joseph Atkins spent time sitting in the garden when it was fine, then, as his arm healed and his headaches ceased, he began to assist the gardeners prepare beds in the vegetable garden, and also to assist the grooms repair and adjust harness from both estates.

As Toby grew more confident that he was safe with the people around him, he too ventured outside, accompanied by Scruffy when he was at Everton Manor with the Countess. To Toby's astonishment, nobody made fun of his disability, or treated him as a freak as he had been in London. When he went to the stables, he was introduced to the horses, and watched the grooms brush them and clean out the stalls. After a few days, Toby asked if he could help brush one of the horses, and was surprised that he could manage quite well by keeping his free hand on the horse as he brushed.

Gaining confidence, he began to help around the stables more each day. Nobody jeered at him if he made a mistake, or if there was a job that he couldn't carry out alone he found there was always someone to give advice or help if he needed it.

Hugh knew that Arthur was hoping to rent accommodation in Lewes for his family and, after some thought, decided to discuss the matter with Mary when they rode out of the courtyard one morning. 'Mary, what are your plans for the Dower House at Everton Manor?'

Mary glanced at her estate supervisor, who she was becoming so fond of. 'I haven't really given that much thought, Hugh. Why, do you have something in mind?'

'I was wondering if you would consider renting it to the Atkins family. I know that Arthur is trying to find somewhere for them to live in Lewes. The Dower House would allow Katherine to continue to help with the sewing, and also maybe do some needlework for ladies in Lewes. Joseph is an accomplished leather worker, and I'm sure that he could get a job at the Lewes Saddlery business that's not far from the Manor.'

Mary considered his comment for a moment. 'Yes, you're right, Hugh. That house should be lived in; it will just deteriorate again if left empty, and I know that Toby would be thrilled to live on the estate rather than in the town.'

'It's amazing to see the change in that boy since his arrival, isn't it?'

'He's put on weight and looks so much healthier, and more importantly, he is so much more confident in himself. It's hard to believe now that he thought of himself as a useless cripple when they first arrived.'

'It certainly is. Do you want to tell them, or shall I before I go into Lewes in the morning? I need to speak to Mr Lyons about a few things before the next rent day.'

'Would you please, Hugh? I have a meeting planned with some of the older villagers tomorrow, to discuss our allotment proposal.'

As they rode, Mary thought how much rent days had changed from the first one that she had attended not long after her arrival in England, where unbeknown to her, Hugh's predecessor had been embezzling money from her tenants, who were surly and distrusting of their new young Countess with the strange accent.

Now, each quarter rent days had become more like picnic days, with family members encouraged to come to Longmire Hall to eat the large quantities of food laid out on trestle tables. Mary was aware that Hugh had arranged for a lamb to be roasted on a spit on rent day next week, and that Mrs Smith and her team were busy preparing all manner of dishes to be served. The school students were to have the day off, to allow them to attend with their parents.

Mary cared deeply for these people, and was sorry that her duties were beginning to impinge on her time to work with them on the estate. Two people who Mary was determined to keep in close contact with were Bob and Tess Telford, the tenant farmers on Home Farm. Early on, Tess had recognised how confused and homesick the young colonial girl was, grieving her late mother, and totally bewildered by what now confronted her.

Quite soon, Mary became the daughter that Tess had never had, and Tess was like a surrogate mother to Mary. Often, the young Countess would ride over to Home Farm early in the morning to help with the milking, and have breakfast with Bob, Tess, and their son, Will, who helped his father on the farm.

Chapter 6

The aide ushered Mary into the ornate room. 'Lady Mary Evans, Ma'am.'

Mary walked across the room, and paused in front of the elderly lady sitting near the fire and curtseyed. 'Good morning, Your Majesty. I trust you are well.'

'As well as can be expected at my age Mary. Sit down and join me with a cup of tea, my child.'

Mary sat in the chair indicated, and both women sat silently as the butler poured the tea and handed each a cup, and a plate with a piece of shortbread on it. 'I brought the shortbread back from Balmoral. It is very tasty, don't you think?'

'Yes, Ma'am.' Mary tried hard not to spit out crumbs as she spoke.

'Now, Mary, I have been informed of some of your recent business deals, and am amazed at your business expertise. It must come from your father's side of the family, as I never knew your grandmother to show the slightest interest in anything that interfered with her social life. She was one of my best friends you know, but could be blind to anything around her that she didn't want to see.'

The Queen paused to sip her tea. 'Your recent social outings have been causing some interest, I gather. Your dealings with the young Pridmore boy was most unladylike, but very effective I have been told. I must say, sending the lad to his uncle in Australia was a sensible idea.

159

He just might have a chance of growing into a decent young man, away from his father. Don't mention this to others, but I can't abide that man. Don't look so surprised, Mary. You are the only grandchild of my dear friend Emma, and I like to be kept abreast of your somewhat unorthodox dealings with situations in your new life in England.'

For the next fifteen minutes or so, the conversation went on with Mary being coaxed to speak of her work with the underprivileged, and also the dramatic change in the estate village since the improvements Mary had instigated.

'Now, Mary, tell me about this young man in your life.'

Shocked, Mary sat speechless, staring at the Queen.

'Do you love him? More to the point, does he love you?'

'Yes, Ma'am, we love each other very much, but nothing more can come of our friendship I'm afraid.'

'Let me guess. He hasn't a drop of aristocratic blood in his body, is the son of your farm manager, is one of your employees and has no title. If you marry, you would keep your title and inheritance, but he would just be Mr Watson, your husband, and a kept man. Am I right?'

Mary was surprise at the Queen's summation. 'Yes, Ma'am. He thinks that he will be looked down on and laughed at by the more affluent of our acquaintances, if we were to marry. Besides, he wants to have his own income, and keep working at the job he loves.'

'Nonsense, my girl. You have done things your own way so far, without causing too many calamitous situations. You deal with everyone from me to the poor in the workhouse with similar flair.'

'Oh no, Ma'am,' I would never speak or treat you like—'

'You know what I mean, Mary. I commend you on your passion for improving the life of those struggling to survive, through little fault of their own. Now, back to your Hugh Watson. If he truly loves you he will swallow his pride, to some extent at least. Encourage him to keep working. I gather that he has some very interesting ideas for improving the agricultural practices on your farms. Support him in setting up his own agricultural consulting business, to work with other farmers as well as for your estate tenants. That would keep him busy and meeting landowners and workers of all classes. I know this from experience! We might even employ him at some of the royal farms! As far as a title, I will bestow on him a knighthood for agricultural innovation when you announce your engagement.'

Mary was dumbfounded. 'Ma'am, I don't know what to say.'

'Away with you, lass. I enjoy our little chats. You need to have one with your young man. I hope to hear the outcome soon! Send me a message when he proposes to you.'

As soon as Mary stood up and bade her monarch goodbye, the aide opened the door and ushered her out of the room, and led her to the palace entrance, where a coach was waiting to take her back to the hotel. 'Her Majesty likes to hear news about you, Lady Mary, and enjoys her meetings with you.'

Mary had been to Buckingham Palace a few times now, mostly for private meetings with the Queen, who showed genuine interest in her young Countess's progress. She had also attended the previous year's Opening of State Parliament, dressed in her grandmother's full parliamentary regalia that Polly had reverently removed from storage and and taken to Ede and Ravenscroft, robe makers in London, to be cleaned and adjusted to fit the new Countess.

Excused attendance during her first year in England, Mary had been informed that she would be expected to attend each year from then on. Aware that Mary had no idea of the procedure for ceremonial occasions, the Palace had assigned a lady-in-waiting, Anne Maschmann, to instruct her in the months leading up to the event. Anne was with Mary on the day of the Opening of State Parliament, dressing her and staying with her until the procession into the House of Lords, where Queen Victoria read the speech outlining the Government's plans for the parliamentary year. An incredible and awe-inspiring experience for someone so young and fresh from the Colonies.

Those who did not approve of Mary's elevation to the peerage were astounded to note her poise throughout the day. Luckily, they didn't see her collapse from emotional exhaustion when she returned to her suite in the hotel! And to think she would have to do it all again each spring. Also, she had been told that sometime in the future, she would be expected to attend the future King's coronation, which would be a much more drawn-out and impressive ceremony.

While Mary was at Buckingham Palace, Hugh, Toby, and his mother had attended an appointment with a surgical specialist in Harley Street, whom Dr Wilson had recommended. After lengthy observation and manipulation of Toby's club foot, Mr Smyth advised that following more manipulation, Toby's foot and leg should be placed in a cast, to be replaced weekly for a period of one month. A special boot, with a raised sole, should then be made to support his foot, and help compensate for his shortened leg.

The trio were sent away to discuss this proposed treatment, with instructions to make their decision as quickly as possible. Thanks to Dr Wilson's earlier discussions about possible treatments, this proposed treatment didn't come as a total shock, and appeared to be the least invasive choice. However, Katherine was more concerned about staying in London for a month. Where could they stay, and how would they be able to pay for accommodation, the treatment, and food? Hugh saw that she was getting upset as they drove back to the hotel. 'Try not to worry yourself, Katherine. We will sort things out. But first, let's order some tea and cake while we await Lady Mary's return from the Palace.'

Mary arrived not long after the trio, but hurried straight to her bedroom to change out of her fashionable finery, as she called the attire that she had donned for her Palace visit. Feeling much more comfortable in a long maroon skirt and simple white blouse, Mary sat down and gratefully accepted the cup of tea that Katherine handed her.

'Now, what did your specialist have to say?'

When Katherine told her of the proposed treatment, Mary turned to Toby. 'How do you feel about that, Toby?'

Not used to having his feelings considered, Toby looked towards his mother who nodded, then took a deep breath and shyly turned back to face Mary. 'I would very much like to see if my foot could be corrected, m'lady, but I know that my mother is awfully worried about how we could afford it.'

'You leave those details to me, Toby my lad. If you are prepared to put up with the treatment that I'm sure won't be pain free, Mr Watson and I will organise the rest.' Mary then turned to Katherine and told her a little of her visit to the Palace, though not of the actual conversation with the Queen.

That evening, when Katherine and Toby had retired to their rooms, Mary and Hugh sat together on the couch near the fire. 'Where do you think would be the most convenient place in London for Katherine and Toby to stay, Hugh? Here at the hotel or in my rooms at the residence in Eaton Place?'

'I think here would be better, Mary. The hotel lift will make it much easier for Toby to get about. Do you know that Toby has never been to school and can't read or write? He is going to get pretty bored sitting in the room with little to do.' Mary snuggled up against Hugh's shoulder. 'Do you think he would consider having lessons while he's having this treatment?'

After a lingering kiss, she told Hugh of the Queen's comments about their potential future together. 'We would have her blessing if we marry, Sir Hugh! Seriously though darling, what do you think about setting up your own business?'

'It's what I dreamt of doing all the way through College, my love. The work I've been doing as estate supervisor has been wonderful grounding for such a venture. If you can put up with a working husband, I'm sure that I can put up with a Countess for a wife!' Hugh ducked the playful cuff aimed at his ear.

Mary, snuggled back against him. 'Oh, Hugh, I love you so very, very much.'

'I love you too, Mary. I fell in love with you when we first met at the hotel in Pocklington. It has just taken me awhile to come to terms with the implications of being married to a Countess. I must say, the Queen's suggestions have given me a lot to think about.' Before Mary realised what he was about to do, Hugh sank to one knee before her and held her hands. 'Would you please do me the honour of becoming my wife, Mary?'

Mary threw her arms around him and kissed him passionately. 'Oh yes, of course I will, Hugh. I thought you would never ask me!' Eventually breaking their embrace, Hugh stood up and walked towards the door. 'I must go to my room now, Mary. I will dream of you all night, my love.'

Mary sat near the fire for a short time, scarcely able to believe that Hugh had finally asked her to marry him. Suddenly feeling exhausted after such an eventful day, she went to bed and, for a short while felt sad that she couldn't tell her parents her wonderful news, then she fell into a deep dreamless sleep.

Before breakfast the next morning, Mary and Hugh decided not to share their news until they had discussed the ramifications of their situation a bit more in private. Katherine was aware of a change in the young couple at the breakfast table, but kept her thoughts to herself, and listened in astonishment to the suggestions being put to her and her young son.

Mary was adamant that if Toby was willing to endure the treatment, she would pay all medical and hotel costs. She turned to Toby. 'Toby, I know that you weren't able to attend school when you were younger. If I employed a tutor, would you be interested in learning to read and write while you stay in London? It would certainly be a way to fill in your time while you are dealing with your treatment.'

Toby nodded his head vigorously. 'Oh yes please, m'lady. I would love to be able to read and write. Oh, Mama, please say that I can.'

Katherine looked at her son's beseeching face. 'Yes, Toby, you can. Lady Mary, I will forever be in your debt for what you are doing for our family.' Mary stood up and hugged Katherine. 'You are part of the estate family now, Katherine, and we all look after each other.'

Hugh ruffled Toby's hair as he walked past the lad. 'So, shall I tell Mr Smyth to book you in to start treatment, Toby? Lady Mary and I have some business to attend to in the city today, so we can drop by his rooms on our way. Why don't you take your mother to the gardens and show her how well you can use those crutches?'

Riding in the cab going into the city, Hugh said, 'While I was in London last month, I met one of my college friends who lost his lower leg following an industrial accident last year. He was staying at the residence while being fitted for an artificial limb and was pretty down in the dumps, wondering what he could do with his life now. I wonder if he would consider tutoring Toby.'

'Why don't you ask him, Hugh? Is he still staying in London?'

'I'll go and see later this afternoon. Now, let's go to look at engagement rings.'

Mary looked at Hugh, chewing her lower lip. 'My love, would it upset you too much if I wore my grandmother's ring? It was meant to be given to my mother when she became engaged, but as you know, Grandmother had no idea where my mother was when my parents met and married.'

Hugh planted a kiss on his fiancé's nose. 'Of course I don't mind, Mary. I know how much it would mean to you to wear the ring that by rights should have been your mother's. I will, however, buy your wedding ring.'

Following a leisurely lunch at the Claridge Hotel, the couple went to the house that had originally been Mary's family's London residence which, since Mary's arrival in England, had been transformed into an upmarket boarding house for young men working in London. There they met Hugh's friend Adam Sinclair, who, although tired from a session with a physiotherapist where he was learning to use his new prosthesis, welcomed his visitors and offered them refreshments.

Hugh explained Toby's situation to Adam. 'Do you think you might be interested in tutoring Toby?'

'I would be delighted to Hugh. I need something to take my mind off this.' Adam tapped his leg. 'Toby and I could limp around London together!'

Mary was pleased. 'Thank you Adam. I will make arrangements for transport to be available whenever you require it. Also, when you feel up to it, you and Hugh can go shopping for books and other items that you think you will need.'

For the rest of the afternoon, the young couple wandered around Hyde Park, beginning to make plans, firstly for their engagement announcement and wedding, then the possible business that Hugh could start up. Mary was pleased to see how enthusiastic he was about the idea, and encouraged him to look at future possibilities once he became an agricultural consultant in his own right.

'The estate farms could become your first clients, Hugh, if you feel that they could pay your rates!'

Chapter 7

Windsor Castle
Train journey from York
August 1888

Toby's first treatment was booked for the following week, so Mary, Hugh, Katherine and Toby caught the train to Lewes, then a cab out to Everton Manor. All the staff were happy to welcome everyone back, and were keen to hear about Toby's proposed treatment and Mary's visit to the Palace.

Early next morning, Robert arrived in the coach to take Mary and Hugh home to Longmire Hall. As the coach passed through the Longmire Estate gateway Mary smiled. 'Everton Manor is lovely, and very nice to stay in after a long day in London and the train trip to Lewes, but Longmire Hall is my home and always will be.'

Hugh cuddled her to him. 'Soon, it will be our home.'

On her arrival back at the Hall, Mary searched through her grandmother's jewellery, and found her engagement ring wrapped up in tissue. It was a beautiful sapphire, surrounded by ten diamonds and with it was a magnificent gold necklace with a similar setting. To her delight the ring fitted perfectly when Hugh placed it gently on her ring finger. However she decided to wear the ring on a chain around her neck until their engagement was officially announced.

The day before Toby's appointment to begin his treatment, the foursome travelled back to London. A message regarding Mary's and Hugh's engagement had been sent to the Palace, and they were invited to Windsor Castle for a meeting with the Queen two days after their arrival in London. They caught the train to Windsor and Eton Riverside Station, then a cab to the Castle.

When they were ushered into the Queen's presence, Hugh bowed and Mary curtsied, then they sat in the chairs next to the monarch. For the next half hour, the three had a most informal meeting, with Queen Victoria talking mostly to Hugh, asking him about his family, his agricultural studies, and the work that he had been doing since being employed as Mary's estate supervisor.

When she heard that Hugh and his family had holidayed in Scotland near Balmoral Castle, the Queen became quite animated, and Mary was left to listen to the lively chatter between her betrothed and her monarch.

Finally, Queen Victoria turned to Mary. 'Do you have a ring yet, Mary?'

Mary took the ring from around her neck and handed it to the Queen. 'Yes, Ma'am. This was my grandmother's ring.'

'How appropriate my dear. I remember admiring it on Emma's hand. There was also a beautiful matching necklace. When do you plan to announce your engagement?'

Hugh looked at Queen Victoria. 'We haven't made any announcement yet, Ma'am. We were waiting to inform you first.'

'Thank you both for such a thoughtful gesture.'

Calling an aide to her side, the queen gave a quiet order, and a few moments later, the aide came back carrying a small sword. 'Hugh, as you know I told Mary that I would bestow a knighthood on you upon your engagement. The next formal investiture is not until after Christmas, but please kneel before me and we will have a private ceremony.'

Hugh knelt before his Queen, and she gently tapped him on each side of his neck with the sword. 'Arise, Sir Hugh Watson.' When Hugh stood up, a maroon ribbon was pinned to his chest. 'When you attend the formal inauguration next year, you will receive your medal. However, from today, you may formally be known as Sir Hugh Watson and so it will be gazetted.'

Bidding farewell to the monarch, the couple left the palace, Mary wearing her engagement ring on her left hand, and Hugh with his ribbon still pinned to his chest. When they arrived back in London, Hugh sent a telegram to his parents, informing them of his engagement to Lady Mary, and also of his knighthood. Notices were sent to the major newspapers, announcing the engagement of Lady Mary Emma Evans, Countess of Longmire and Oakdale to Sir Hugh Watson, agricultural consultant from Yorkshire. The date for the wedding later in the year was yet to be set.

Katherine and Toby were thrilled to hear the news firsthand, and to be taken out for a celebratory dinner. Toby's initial treatment was quite painful, and being taken out for dinner helped take his mind off his discomfort. Adam had visited earlier, and had left an alphabet for Toby to copy, which had kept him busy until Mary and Hugh returned with their news.

On their return to Everton Manor, and then Longmire Hall, the couple were congratulated on their engagement, and Hugh on his knighthood, by the two staffs; each time, bottles of champagne were opened to toast the couple. 'About time too,' Mrs Smith was heard to mutter, as she left the room to return to her kitchen to start baking an engagement cake.

Leaving the staff to enjoy their champagne, Mary and Hugh saddled their horses and rode over to Home Farm, to personally inform Tess and Bob Telford of their engagement. Hugging Mary, Tess laughed and cried at the same time. 'Mary, my love, I'm so happy for you both.' Bob grinned, and shyly gave her a brief peck on the cheek. He felt more comfortable pumping Hugh's hand and thumping him on the back. 'So, we'll have to tug our forelock and call you Sir Hugh from now on, will we lad?'

Hugh laughed. 'No, Bob, we will still be Mary and Hugh to you and Tess. How is John getting on at College?'

Bob's and Tess's youngest son, John, was currently studying at the Royal Agricultural College in Gloucestershire, the college that Hugh had graduated from before being employed by Mary. Bob chuckled. 'He is loving every minute of his time there Hugh, and says that he is learning all there is to know about agriculture! Little does he know what he has yet to learn!'

Tess led Mary into the kitchen and gave her another big hug. 'Oh Mary, I have prayed for this day for a while now. I'm so glad that Hugh has overcome his obvious misgivings about marrying a Countess. Have you thought when you would like to have your wedding?'

'I'm not sure yet Tess. I don't want a long engagement and neither of us wants a big wedding. Just Hugh's family, and as I don't have any family here, just close friends and my staff, of course. If possible, I would like the wedding to be before Christmas.'

'Do you think that your Aunt Clara and Graham might be able to travel to England for your wedding? With the new telegraph system, you wouldn't have to send a message with a ship and wait months for a reply.'

'I'll certainly look into it, Tess. Thanks for reminding me. Now, let's get a pot of tea ready to take back to the men.' As they drank their tea, Mary thought of Tess's comment about sending a telegraph message to Aunt Clara and Graham, and how much she would love to see them again.

Mary felt she owed her aunt a great debt of gratitude for the dedication that she had shown to the family, following her brother's tragic death fighting a bushfire. Riding slowly back to the Hall, horses almost touching, Mary told Hugh about Tess's suggestion of sending a telegraph message to Australia.

Hugh nodded. 'I agree that it would be a good idea.' He looked at Mary. 'Bob suggested that I move away from the Hall, and live at Everton Manor until we are wed, to save malevolent whispers from our noble connections.'

'Tess hinted that as well. She is worried that there will be enough snide remarks being thrown around about us getting married, without giving them more assumptions to work on Hugh. I would happily thumb my nose at them, but I don't want your chance of fitting in to society, plus your business, to suffer from incorrect, malicious gossip.'

As soon as they arrived back at the Hall, James was sent into Lewes to send a telegram to Aunt Clara, inviting her and Graham, if he could spare the time, to the wedding later in the year, adding that Mary would pay for their tickets.

The next day, the village church was so full, many people had to stand outside throughout the service. Everyone wanted to congratulate Mary and Hugh on their engagement, and also to acknowledge Hugh's new title. Mary was flattered at such goodwill being offered to them both, knowing the hardship many of their well-wishers still experienced.

Hugh received a telegram from his father, offering their congratulations, but also telling Hugh that his mother was quite unwell and wished to see them both. Mary didn't hesitate. 'Let's go to Yorkshire tomorrow Hugh. Our staff seem to be able to cope quite well in our absence these days.'

Early the next morning, Robert drove the young couple to Lewes, where they caught a train to London, then to York, where they stayed the night before travelling to Pocklington, the nearest station to Mary's northern Oakdale Estate, managed by Hugh's father John Watson. Hugh's brother Paul was waiting for them at the station, and greeted them with a deep bow. 'Welcome, Lady Mary and Sir Hugh.' He swiftly stepped backwards to avoid his brother's playful swipe at his head. After warmly embracing Mary, and thumping his brother's back, they set off for the Oakdale Estate.

Half an hour later, they alighted from the carriage, and were met by John Watson. 'Congratulations to the two of you. We were all thrilled to hear of your engagement. And what's this, my boy, you being knighted? You could have blown me down with a feather when I read your telegram!' 'I will tell you all about it later, Father. Firstly though, what is wrong with Mother?'

'Your mother caught a chill a couple of weeks ago, and developed a bad case of bronchitis. The doctor was worried it might turn into pneumonia, but thank goodness, that hasn't occurred. Your sister has been staying here to nurse Elizabeth.'

'Who is looking after the three children?'

'Peter has taken time off work Mary, which means that the children can stay at home in Pocklington. Anyway, do come in. I know that Elizabeth is so looking forward to seeing you both.'

Mary and Hugh were pleased to see that his mother was feeling well enough to sit before the fire in the cosy sitting room. After a very emotional welcome to her son and future daughter-in-law, Elizabeth sat back and looked at them. She knew that Hugh had fallen in love with Mary, but never in her wildest dreams had she envisioned that it would eventuate in marriage. They had met a number of times since Mary's first visit to the estate two years ago, and Elizabeth had grown very fond of her, becoming less self-conscious in her presence, but she was still a Countess after all, and was also Hugh's and their employer. She knew that John held the same reservations as herself for their son's future.

However, when Elizabeth saw Mary and Hugh together, she could see that they were blissfully happy, and that they were relieved to be able to make public their future aspirations. Elizabeth just couldn't believe that her son had had an audience with the Queen, or as he put it 'a cosy chat', and that he now had a knighthood and was engaged to be married to a Peer of the Realm. Who would ever have thought it of her little boy!

Following a restful few day with the family, Mary and Hugh set off on their return journey to Sussex, pleased to see Elizabeth recovering her health and energy, assuring her that they would set a wedding date and venue as soon as they could.

Night was falling as the York train neared London, and the weather had become very wet and windy. Mary was dozing, with her head on Hugh's shoulder, when she was woken by a loud bang, and the carriage began to sway violently. She felt Hugh grab her to him, then everything went black.

Slowly regaining consciousness, Mary felt something hard beneath her back, and water running on her face. As she tried to wipe her face, she heard a far-off voice. 'Lie still my dear.' Opening her eyes slightly, she saw a bearded man with a high black hat leaning over her. She opened her mouth to scream. 'Don't be afraid, I won't hurt you. You've had a nasty bang on your head and must lie still.'

Mary closed her eyes, then opened them again, wincing at the stabbing pain in her chest as she tried to sit up. 'Where's Hugh?' she whispered before sinking back to the ground with a groan.

The man wiped her brow. 'If you mean the young man who carried you from the carriage, and wrapped you in his coat, he is valiantly trying to save more passengers before the carriages catch fire.'

Mary didn't hear the end of the sentence, as she had again slipped into unconsciousness. The next thing she recalled was waking up in a large bed in a sunny room, with Hugh sitting beside her, holding her hand. He had a white bandage around his forehead, and his left arm was in a sling.

Hugh kissed her hand. 'At last you are awake, my darling.'

'What happened? Why can't I open my eyes properly Hugh?' Mary could only whisper, and it hurt to breathe.

'The steam engine hit a fallen tree and plunged down an embankment, taking our carriage and another with it. You received a nasty blow to the side of your head, and your eyes are nearly swollen shut. The doctor thinks that you have also some cracked, or maybe broken ribs.'

'No wonder it hurts to breathe,' muttered Mary as she fell asleep.

At that moment, the bearded gentleman that Mary had seen at the site of the accident entered the room. 'So, she is back with us, thank goodness.'

Mary was later to learn that the man was Dr Markham, the local doctor. 'Don't worry Hugh, she is asleep, not unconscious as before. Sleep will do her more good than harm. Come down for a bite to eat, and then rest. After your herculean efforts following the accident, you must be exhausted. There are a number of people who owe you their lives. If you hadn't managed to get them out of that carriage before it caught fire, they wouldn't have survived.'

When all those who could be saved were out of the train and the two wrecked carriages, Mary and Hugh had been taken to Dr Markham's home in nearby Stevenage, a small town about thirty miles north of London, while other badly injured passengers were taken to the local cottage hospital, where they were treated by Dr Markham and another physician. As the accident had occurred on the York side of Stevenage, the railway line to London was still open, so a special train carrying medical personnel had quickly been sent to the town, to treat then transport as many of the injured as possible to larger London hospitals.

Mid-afternoon, Mary wakened with an awful headache, and a great need to go to the toilet. A nurse sitting by her bed while Hugh slept helped Mary to the commode near her bed, then gave her a bitter drink that she said would help dull the headache. Gratefully lying back on the bed, Mary groggily tried to remember what had happened. She recalled being on the train with Hugh but little more, until waking to see Hugh with a bandaged head and injured arm.

'Where is Hugh?'

A different nurse was sitting beside the bed. 'Mr Watson is asleep in the room next door m'lady. He is fine, and will be in to see you when he awakes.'

'You mean Sir Hugh Watson,' murmured Mary as she again drifted off to sleep.

Midway through the second morning, not long after Hugh had entered Mary's bedroom, the door was pushed open by a well-dressed, white-haired lady, who glared at Hugh. 'How dare you enter this lady's bedroom Sir. Please leave at once!'

As she started to raise her walking stick, Dr Markham rushed into the room. 'Stop that, Mother. This is Sir Hugh Watson, Lady Mary's fiancé, and he has my permission to be by her side while she recovers from her injuries.'

Startled, the old lady turned to face her son. 'Lady Mary, Sir Hugh? Do you mean to tell me that is Lady Mary Evans in bed?'

'Yes, Mother.'

The lady turned to Hugh. 'I am so sorry, Sir Hugh. Nobody informed me that you and the Countess were visiting us. Is Lady Mary unwell?'

Dr Markham gently answered for Hugh. 'Lady Mary and Sir Hugh were injured in the train accident the other night Mother, and are staying with us until Lady Mary is well enough to travel to Sussex.'

He took his mother's arm. 'Please come with me, Mother. I will introduce you to our guests when Lady Mary is feeling better.'

When they left the room, Hugh and Mary, who had been woken by the loud voices, looked at each other and started to laugh, although Mary found this so painful she had to stop.

During the next few days, Mary's headache diminished, and she became more aware of her surroundings and those attending her. Hugh rarely left her side, and spent hours sitting beside her bed, holding her hand, and talking softly to her, whether she was awake or asleep.

When he felt that Mary was ready, Hugh told her more about the accident. 'Apparently, the strong wind blew a tree down across the rail line not far from the Stevenage station. Coming around the corner, the train driver wasn't able to stop in time, and the train left the track on impact with the tree, tumbling down an embankment, pulling the first two carriages with it. Luckily, the more crowded carriages remained on the track.

At first, no one realised that coals from the wrecked train had landed in the first carriage, until it caught on fire. It then became a race against the spread of the fire, to remove as many of the injured passengers as was possible, before the two wrecked carriages were totally engulfed in flames.

When our carriage stopped rolling, I landed on something soft between the seats that saved me from serious injury. I'm sorry my love, that something soft was you! Luckily, I only broke a few of your ribs! I managed to find a way out of the carriage, and carried you to safety. Then some other men and I tried to pull out as many people as we could, before the flames became too intense. I'm just sorry that we couldn't get everyone out.'

'But Hugh, you were injured too. You have a gashed forehead and an injured arm.'

'I wasn't really aware of that at the time, Mary. The blood dripping in my eyes was annoying, but a handkerchief tied around my head helped stop that. We were all just so desperate to get the injured passengers to safety. Luckily, Dr Markham and his colleague, accompanied by the townspeople, arrived on the scene so quickly with lanterns and pitch torches.'

Once Mary felt well enough to be dressed in a loose-fitting dress of Mrs Markham's, Hugh carried her downstairs, where she was settled in a comfortable armchair near the fire in the sitting room. There she was formally introduced to the elder Mrs Markham. Realising that the elderly lady was overjoyed at being in the company of a Countess, Mary overcame her embarrassment and spent some time chatting with her, before her daughter-in-law took Mrs Markham back to her room.

CHAPTER 8

Longmire Estate
Sussex, England
September 1888

Ten days following the accident, Mary was finally allowed to travel home, with strict instructions to take it easy and to contact Dr Wilson if the headaches returned, or her ribs remained painful. Hugh insisted that they stayed overnight in London, and again at Everton Manor, before the coach journey to Longmire Hall. A message had been sent to order the coach, and also to instruct the staff to have Scruffy restrained, so he didn't bowl his mistress over on her arrival home.

Despite her bravado, Mary was exhausted by the time the swaying coach entered the gates to the Longmire Estate late in the morning. There they were met by the four children, excitedly waiting astride their ponies, with James the groom, who had Sally's pony on a lead rope. Mary leant out of the coach window. 'Hello, my darlings. I'm so pleased that you've come to escort us back to the Hall.'

With that, the coach progressed down the long drive toward the stately manor house, with the horse and ponies trotting, then cantering in front of the coach. As Mary watched Sally on her pony, confidently cantering beside James's horse, she thought back to when the children had been given their ponies. Initially, Sally hadn't been given a pony of her own, but she had shown such a natural talent for riding, Robert had purchased a quiet, gentle-natured pony for her to ride.

From the moment they met, there was an instant bond between the young blind girl and Cass, the small bay pony, who seemed to recognise Sally's disability. Quite often, Sally would be seen sitting in the field behind the stables, with Mac, her golden dog, and Cass, sitting and standing close beside her as she chatted to them about all manner of things.

The Longmire staff were all waiting on the steps where, for once, Robert stopped the coach at the front door for Mary to alight. Tiredly, she stepped out of the coach and leant heavily on Hugh's arm as they climbed the steps.

'Hello, everyone, it's lovely to be home at last.' As she swayed, Hugh swept her into his arms and carried her through into the hall. 'Oops, I have just carried you over the threshold, and we aren't yet married.' When Mary didn't reply, he glanced down and saw that she was asleep. He winked at Polly, who was walking beside him as they reached the stairs. 'That was a practice run, in case she puts on weight before the wedding!'

'I heard that!' murmured Mary, eyes still shut.

'Lady Mary's bed is turned down for her, Sir.' Polly was struggling to stop laughing.

Once Mary was placed on the bed, Hugh left Polly and Amy to put her to bed, aware that here at home, he had to adhere strictly to convention. Going down to the kitchen, Hugh drank the mug of tea handed to him by Mrs Smith, then gave the staff a brief version of the accident, and their stay in Stevenage. 'I'm still very worried about Lady Mary. She was more severely injured than she cares to admit.'

Just then Polly entered the kitchen. 'I know it won't be an easy task Polly, but could you please keep an eye on Lady Mary, and don't let her try to do too much too soon. I'm afraid I have to attend a briefing in London about the accident, so I will have to be away for a few days.'

'If she won't listen to me, Sir, I will ask Tess Telford to come to the Hall to look after her Ladyship.'

Later in the afternoon, when Amy looked in on Mary, she found her awake and gently fondling Scruffy's ears, as he sat beside her bed with his muzzle on her chest.

'Oh my goodness, m'lady. How in the world did he get in here?'

Amy bent to grab Scruffy's collar. 'No, leave him here please Amy.' He isn't doing any harm and he is great company. Could you please bring me a cup of tea and some of Mrs Smith's cake?'

'Certainly, m'lady.'

Amy hurried back to the kitchen to announce that her Ladyship was awake, and that Scruffy was keeping her company. Polly laughed. 'If he keeps her in bed, he can stay there as long as he likes. Now Amy, take the tray up to her Ladyship and ask her what she would like for dinner.'

Polly had no need to summon Tess from Home Farm, as the lady herself arrived at the back door not long after Amy returned to the kitchen. Word had spread around the estate that Lady Mary was home but unwell, and Tess wanted to see for herself just how unwell her darling Mary was.

Polly was very relieved to see Tess, as she wasn't looking forward to ordering her young mistress around, having just been told by Amy that Lady Mary was determined to get dressed and join them all for dinner. She knew that Tess would have no qualms about being more forthright with her.

Mary was delighted to see Tess when she entered the bedroom. Ignoring Scruffy's quiet growl, Tess leant over and gave the pale, bruised face a gentle kiss. 'Mary, my darling. What in the world have you been up to while you were away? Just as well the wedding won't be for a few months yet.'

Tess was totally unprepared for the tears that welled up in Mary's eyes and started to run down her cheeks. Lying on the bed beside the sobbing girl, Tess gently hugged Mary to her, and let her cry on her shoulder. Polly, who had entered the bedroom with Tess, quietly led Scruffy out of the room and shut the door. Taking Scruffy outside, Polly leant against the water pump and thought that Tess was probably the best medicine for Mary at the moment, but kept her thoughts to herself when she went inside.

Tess held Mary for some time, soothing her with soft words as she let her cry for as long as she needed. This was the first time she had known Mary to lose her composure since her arrival in England, over two years ago. For an eighteen year old girl to lose her mother, sail to the other side of the world, and take on the responsibilities that Mary had in such a short time, with such apparent self-control, there had to be a build-up of emotions and anxieties. Now it appeared, the emotional dam had burst, and Tess was so thankful that she was with Mary when it happened.

Later when Polly peeped around the door, Mary had finally cried herself to sleep, still lying in Tess's arms. Quietly, Polly whispered, 'Are you able to stay with her for a little longer, Tess?'

'Of course I will, but could you please put a rug over me Polly? It's getting a little chilly in here.'

Mary awoke to find the room dimly lit by a turned-down lantern, with Tess still holding her, just like her mother had whenever she'd hurt herself when she was a little girl. Tess noticed Mary's eyes open. 'How are you feeling now, lass?'

'Oh, Tess, I'm so pleased that you are here. I'm sorry I cried all over you, but I just couldn't help it.'

'Mary, my love, you can cry on my shoulder any time you need to. It's the best thing to do, rather than bottling things up, and trying to sort everything out by yourself. It looks like you needed a good crack on that thick skull of yours to get you to see that. Now, what's this I hear that you are planning on going downstairs for dinner?'

'I can't expect the staff to nurse me now that I'm home Tess.'

Mary was startled at Tess's blunt reply. 'You most certainly can, and most certainly will, my girl. You don't appear to realise that you were seriously injured in that accident. It will take more than a few days for you to recover from that blow to your head, and your ribs will take even longer. Your staff are only too happy to look after you, for as long as needs be, after all you have done for them. They just want you to make a full recovery. You could get a nurse in, but I know that I would much rather have your staff look after me, than a bossy nurse. And don't forget, looking after your needs is what you actually employ them to do! Hugh has had to go to a meeting in London for a few days, but he has asked Dr Wilson to see you tomorrow, and he told Polly to make sure that you follow his instructions.'

Tess looked severely at Mary. 'Will you promise me that you will rest up for as long as is needed Mary, and not make life too difficult for your staff?'

Mary was apologetic. 'I'm sorry Tess, I will try to rest. To be honest, I've been a bit scared by my slow progress. In the past, I've normally recovered more quickly from injuries and illness.'

'I'll bet you were never involved in an accident like that one last week or been as badly injured. Concussion and shock can take a long time to recover from if you don't rest, and your broken ribs need to mend properly before you start getting too active, or you will suffer for much longer.'

Mary grinned. 'Yes Mum! No, seriously Tess, I will follow Dr Wilson's instructions and let the staff boss me around.'

'Right, shall we see what's for dinner? I will eat with you, then I had better go home to feed my poor men.'

Following a meal of a very tasty lamb broth, poached fish, and a light dessert, Tess was driven back to Home Farm by Robert, and Mary settled down for the night, feeling much better for the visit of her dear friend. Scruffy had once again taken his place on the mat beside Mary's bed, and stared threateningly at anyone who looked like they might try to remove him.

Mary felt much better after an unbroken night's sleep. After a visit to the toilet, she settled back in bed and meekly accepted a breakfast tray brought up by Amy. The children spent about half an hour chatting with her, regaling her with stories of their school days and their plans for the upcoming summer holidays. Aware that Mary would find their chatter tiring, Polly soon shepherded them down to the kitchen, allowing Mary time to rest before Dr Wilson's visit.

Not long before Dr Wilson's arrival, Mary was thrilled to hear that a telegram Aunt Clara had sent just before she set sail from Melbourne had arrived while they were in Yorkshire. Hopefully, she would arrive in England by early November.

Removing the dressing from the side of Mary's face, Dr Wilson examined the stitched wound just above her left temple, tested the reaction of her pupils, and then checked her ribs. 'Take as deep a breath as you can until it starts to hurt, Lady Mary.'

He noticed Mary give a slight gasp as she began to inhale. 'That's enough m'lady. Your ribs are going to take some time to heal properly. You must limit your activity to careful walking up and down the stairs, and walking around the house for the next week. No lifting or carrying anything heavier than a cup of tea. Horse riding is definitely out for a number of weeks, and it would be preferable if you refrain from any form of travel for the next fortnight. Your concussion appears to be diminishing, but you will still tire easily for a while. I will return in a few days to remove your stitches, and by then, I would expect your impressive bruising to have diminished considerably. If the headaches return, contact me immediately.'

Knowing that Dr Wilson would leave the same instructions with Polly, Mary returned to bed and slept until lunch. Following her meal, she sat at her bedroom window, and started to think seriously about the children's schooling. At the end of term Alfie, Jack, and Jane would be leaving the village school, and starting the next term at Lewes Grammar School while Sally would be going to London for the first six weeks of the term to attend the School for the Blind.

'*They are growing up so fast,*' thought Mary. Anyone meeting her foursome would not recognise the scraggy, malnourished children who she had become legal guardian to two years ago.

Assisted by Amy, who had been appointed her personal maid, Mary dressed in a skirt and blouse and walked slowly down the stairs to the kitchen before dinner. There she sat in a chair next to the range and had a cup of tea with Mrs Smith. Although delighted to be eating her meal at the table with her friends, Mary was surprised how quickly she tired, and was pleased when ever-watchful Polly told Amy to take her back to her room. Amy was thrilled to be able to offer Mary her arm as they went upstairs, and Mary swallowed her pride and accepted the girl's willing help.

Tess visited each day to spend time with Mary, sometimes in her room or sitting out in the garden. Mary was very grateful to have Tess's regular visits and sensible advice, and was happy for Tess to step into her mother's shoes to discuss married life.

Knowing how busy Tess usually was at home, Mary began to wonder how she could spend so much time at the Hall with her so asked 'Tess, how are you keeping up with your work on the farm, when you are here with me each day?'

'Bob has a young lad helping him for a few days,' was the reply.

By the time Hugh arrived back at Longmire Hall, Dr Wilson had removed Mary's stitches, and told her that he was pleased that she was heeding his advice. 'I have little choice, Dr Wilson. My staff watch my every move, and only allow me to do as little as possible. Polly even has one of the girls working near my bedroom during the day, so that if I make the slightest noise, she checks that I'm okay.'

Dr Wilson scowled. 'You probably don't realise it, Lady Mary, but being waited on hand and foot is the normal expectation of the majority of your peers. Many won't lift a finger when they have servants in the house. The big difference here though, is that your servants—sorry, staff—really want to help you, and look on it as an honour that you are allowing them to look after you while you are incapacitated.'

Mary was dozing in the rose garden when Hugh arrived. A low 'woof' from the ever-present Scruffy alerted Mary to Hugh's presence. Immediately, she was enfolded in his arms and was so enthralled by his kisses that she didn't at first feel her ribs hurting. Hugh loosened his embrace and nuzzled her neck. 'Oh, Mary, Mary, I don't want to let go of you. Being away from you these past days have been absolute hell. If only we could be married tomorrow.'

Sitting on a chair next to Mary's, Hugh looked at his fiancée's face and noted that the bruising and swelling had all but disappeared. 'Thank goodness Dr Markham followed the new practice of working with clean instruments, and keeping wounds as clean as possible', he thought as he noted that the wound on her temple had healed well, as had the gash on his forehead.

Hugh stayed on at Longmire Hall, defying convention, but he did sleep in his cottage, to the relief of the staff. Mrs Smith discussed Hugh's presence with Polly. 'We can keep an eye on them during the day, but I'm too old to give up my sleep during the night, and I need my girls to get their sleep too. We are going to be extra busy getting ready for the wedding. I just hope they are sensible.'

During one of their leisurely walks around the lake, Mary and Hugh were discussing the staff. 'Hugh, when we are married, we will need a new estate supervisor to liaise with the tenants, and carry out your original duties, minus the farmer consultancy that you have developed so well. Do you, by any chance, have any thoughts of a possible replacement? It would be a good idea to have someone appointed to attend the next rent day in the New Year.'

'You're right as usual, Mary. I have given it some thought, and wondered if Adam Sinclair might fit the bill.'

'But what about Toby's tutoring, Hugh? He has been doing so well with Adam.'

'Yes I know, my darling. But at the moment, Toby is staying at Home Farm, and Adam is at Everton Manor looking for work in Lewes.'

'Good grief. Did they have a falling out while we were away?'

'No. I gather Bob Telford met Toby a few times when delivering milk to Everton Manor. As the boy seemed at a loose end, Bob asked if he would like to help in the Home Farm dairy for a few days while Tess was spending so much time with you. Toby leapt at the idea, and is currently staying in their house, learning to milk, separate the cream, and make butter.'

'I vaguely remember Tess saying something about a boy helping Bob while she was visiting me, but I never thought that it would be Toby. How is he managing in the dairy?'

'Bob says he is a natural with the cows, and has taken to milking like a duck to water. His foot is no drawback when he is milking or working in the separating room. Others are happy to carry the pails and dishes of milk for him, and of course, he doesn't go into the fields.' Hugh looked at Mary. 'Bob and Tess are going to ask Toby's parents if he can live with them, and have a permanent job working in the dairy with Tess.'

'What a great idea. Tess will certainly appreciate some assistance. You know Hugh, I can just see Toby sweet-talking the cows while he milks. Look at how the horses respond to him when he visits the stables.'

Hugh kissed the top of Mary's head. 'Yes, he certainly loves animals, and they seem to respond well to him.'

'Mm. If Adam is the new estate supervisor living in your cottage, he and Toby could continue with lessons if they wanted to. Have you asked Adam about the job, Hugh?'

'No, I wanted to talk to you first, to see what you thought of my idea. After all, you will be employing him.' Hugh, clutched his shoulder when Mary playfully punched him.

'I suppose I will have to start looking for a new farm consultant as well! Ouch!' Hugh swung her around and gave her a lingering kiss on the lips. While Mary clung to him, savouring his lips on hers, Hugh gasped. 'I think we should get back to the Hall my love, before we forget that we are not yet married.' Wishing that she could flout every convention in the book, Mary begrudgingly stepped back, and they walked hand in hand back to the stables. There they spoke to the horses, until they felt ready to go into the Hall.

That evening after dinner, Mary and Hugh sat in front of the study fire. 'We really should start making serious plans for our wedding Hugh.'

'I think I can guess what sort of wedding you would prefer Mary. Out in the garden, under the big old oak tree. However, convention will not allow that, nor I should think will the weather later in the year.'

'If only! What I would like Hugh, would be a small wedding with your family, my close friends, and staff. Oh, and your friends too of course. If we could be married in the village church, that would be perfect, and the villagers could come to the reception in the ballroom.'

'I wonder if we would be allowed to have such a small wedding. It would suit me, but do titled people have to have more lavish affairs?' queried Hugh.

'On our wedding day Hugh, you will be marrying me, Mary Emma Evans, not my title!'

'Thanks Mary. And you will be marrying Hugh Edward Watson.'

'So, you are HEW either way!'

'Hmm. Now what about a date? How does Saturday, the first of December sound? If we have the wedding in the village church, many of the villagers will be home.'

'That sounds a wonderful idea. It should give Aunt Clara plenty of time to arrive and settle. Her ship is due to arrive in Southampton next month. I'm so looking forward to seeing her Hugh. Also, I was thinking of asking Katherine Atkins to make my dress. She is a beautiful seamstress, and that would give her plenty of time.'

At ten o'clock, Amy brought in a tray with two mugs of cocoa. 'Thank you Amy. We will wash the cups; you can go off to bed now.'

Amy was grateful to be able to head off up to her bedroom. 'Thank you, m'lady. I have warmed your bed and turned it back for you.'

During the last week of the holidays, the four children and Meg moved to Everton Manor to prepare for their new school term. Alfie and Jane were quite excited, looking forward to their new venture, but Jack, being a bit younger, wasn't quite so sure. Mary decided to spend a couple of weeks at Everton Manor, to help settle the pre-school nerves, and to be there when school actually started. Her Everton Manor staff were thrilled to have her stay for a while, and were keen to show her how well they had settled to their duties.

Katherine Atkins spent some time sewing name tags on uniforms, but was primarily busy working on Mary's wedding dress. At first, rather hesitant to commit to such a task, she had finally accepted the challenge and was thrilled when Mary took her shopping for material and accoutrements in London. When they arrived back at the Dower House, she discovered a new Singer sewing machine set up in the spare bedroom.

'That will be part of your commission for my gown, Katherine.'

Mary had asked Tess to be her Matron of Honour, and she, Katherine, and Mary had spent some time discussing the style of wedding dress that Mary would wear. Knowing her aversion to the bustle, they settled on a long-sleeved white satin dress, with a V-neck bodice. From the waistline, the front of the dress fell straight to the hem, while the back of the dress was more flowing and a two-metre train flowed from the waist.

Hugh's brother Paul, was to be his best man, while Sally and Jane were thrilled to be Mary's flower girls. Jack and Alfie would be young groomsmen, having refused to be dressed as page boys. In the absence of her father, Gordon had delightedly agreed when he was asked to give Mary away.

Much to Mary's disappointment, her plans for a small, simple wedding were dashed, when Gordon pointed out to her that the wedding of someone of her standing was a significant event in the county, and for her family. 'You must realise my dear that in your position there are some conventions that you must adhere to. Generations of your family weddings have taken place at St Anne's Church in Lewes. Whether you like it or not, you have a family tradition to uphold, and your marriage to Hugh will become part of that tradition.' Mary gracefully accepted his sage advice. Consequently, the wedding was to take place in St Anne's Church in Lewes at one o'clock on Saturday, first of December, with the Bishop of Lewes officiating.

Mary had officially been excused from attending the Opening of Parliament, which fell while she was recovering from her injuries. She was relieved in a way not to have to attend, although in a perverse way, she wished she had been able to attend. Although nearly frightened out of her wits last year, she had quite enjoyed being involved in the spectacular proceedings. The pageantry and strict adherence to tradition fascinated her, and she felt that had she been able to attend, knowing what to expect, she would have enjoyed herself much more this year.

Chapter 9

Longmire Estate
Sussex, England
October 1888

Finally, more than a month after the accident, Mary was allowed to ride Gem, who had been ridden daily by James while Mary was recovering from her injuries. When Gem saw Mary walking towards her, she whickered excitedly and snuffled noisily into Mary's outstretched hand. Aware that swinging up onto the saddle could put pressure on her ribs, Mary meekly submitted to using a mounting block brought into the courtyard by Robert.

It felt so good to sit on Gem again, Mary nearly forgot her promise to keep Gem at a walk for this first ride. Robert accompanied her up to the gatehouse and back, watching carefully for any signs of discomfort. The next day, Gem was saddled again, and this time, Robert watched as Mary went for a short trot. Noticing his mistress grimace a little, he suggested that she move Gem to a slow canter. For Mary, this was pure bliss. Gem had such a smooth canter Mary felt no discomfort at all. Just a wonderful sense of freedom, riding her darling horse again, with the wind on her face and in her hair.

After about a hundred yards, she slowed Gem down and waited for Robert, a huge smile on her face. 'That was wonderful Robert. It didn't hurt a bit.'

'That's good m'lady, but you mustn't overdo it. Wait till we see how you feel in the morning!'

The next morning, Mary felt fine, so she rode over to Home Farm to have a chat with Tess. She was met at the farmyard gate by Toby, who had walked from the dairy aided by just a walking stick. Mary was surprised when Gem greeted him with a little nicker and stretched out her head to allow him to scratch her between the ears. He held Gem's bridle and fondled her head as Mary dismounted, much to the amazement of Tess, who was waiting at the back door. Everyone who knew Gem was aware that although Mary could do anything with her, no one who hadn't been introduced to her by Mary could normally go near her. After a hug from Tess, and a shy greeting from Toby, Mary tethered Gem to a post in the shade, then the three walked to the house.

'You are looking well Toby. You've grown and your walking has improved so much I nearly didn't recognise you. What have you been doing to him Tess?'

'Nothing more than three good meals a day, fresh country air, and Toby's obstinate determination to succeed.' Tess ruffled Toby's hair as he put the kettle on the stove.

'I hear that you have become a dairyman Toby. How are you enjoying your new job?'

'It is wonderful, m'lady. I help Uncle Bob and Will milk the cows, and work with Auntie Tess, separating the cream and making butter. I feed the chooks and collect their eggs. Will lets me help him feed the pigs now.' Toby was so enthusiastic about his work he lost his usual shyness with Mary.

Mary laughed. 'You will soon be out of a job Tess.'

'Toby is my right-hand man now. All the animals love him, even the geese. They let him walk near them, without a hiss or a ruffled feather.'

'I love all the animals, but the cows are my favourites.' Toby walked to the kitchen door. 'I will tell Uncle Bob and Will that the kettle is on, and that Lady Mary has come to visit.'

When the door closed, Mary raised her eyebrows. 'Uncle Bob and Auntie Tess?'

Tess laughed. 'He asked what he should call us, and Bob replied, 'Why don't you think of us as your new aunt and uncle?'

'That boy has changed so much since I first saw him Tess. Not just his ability to walk so much more steadily, but his whole demeanour is different. To think he spent most of his life until a few months ago, sitting in a single tenement room, too scared to venture outside.'

Tess looked over her cup at Mary. 'You know Mary, he reminds me a bit of you, when it comes to handling animals. I swear they listen to him, and at times they appear to answer him back. The gander certainly does!'

'Mm. I must say I was surprised at Gem's instant acceptance of him at the gate.'

'Will enjoys his company too. I think he misses his brothers more than he lets on. The two of them often sit at the table after dinner working their way through the study sheets that Adam left for Toby. He is certainly a quick learner, that lad. Toby goes wherever he can with Will. I even caught him carrying a small pail of swill, when he and Will fed the pigs yesterday. I don't know how he kept his balance, but he didn't fall over.'

'Has Toby been in touch with Adam about his schoolwork Tess?'

'Bob started taking Toby on the milk delivery rounds this week, and he met up with Adam when they delivered the Everton Manor milk. Adam told him he would keep in touch while he was still in Lewes.'

'Hugh is going to speak to Adam about the estate supervisor's position. He thinks that Adam would do well in the job, despite his injury. He can't ride around the estates, but he can drive a horse and buggy.'

'What a great idea Mary. I assume that Adam will take over Hugh's cottage after your wedding, which will mean that he and Toby can keep in contact. I would like the lad to learn to read and write properly, then, who knows what he will end up doing.'

Just then, the kitchen door opened, and Bob and Toby entered, both carrying some apples from the orchard.

Toby looked shyly at Mary. 'May I please give Gem an apple, m'lady?'

Mary smiled. 'Of course you can Toby. Just tell her to chew it properly.'

As Toby headed back to the door, he turned. 'What is it like to ride a horse, Lady Mary?'

Mary looked at him in surprise, then remembered his life in London. 'Oh, it's the most wonderful feeling Toby. Would you like to learn to ride?'

The smile on Toby's face faded. 'I would love to m'lady, but my boot won't fit in the stirrup.'

'You don't need stirrups to learn to ride Toby. I always rode bareback until I was about your age. I refused to ride side-saddle, and only started using my father's saddle after he died. I will ask Robert if he knows of a suitable pony for you to ride.'

'Oh, thank you m'lady.' Toby turned as quickly as he could, and escaped outside to tell Gem that he was going to learn to ride a horse like her.

CHAPTER 10

Southampton, England
November 1888

When Mary received notification that Aunt Clara's ship was due to dock at Southampton during the first week of November, she and Hugh travelled by train from London to Southampton. They were accompanied by Amy, partially to follow social conventions, but also for her to assist Mary dress in her more formal attire when in Southampton. For once Mary was travelling in her titled capacity, mainly to introduce her fiancé, Sir Hugh Watson, to her peers. They had been invited to attend a formal dinner to be held by the Mayor of Southampton when he heard of their planned visit to his city.

Mary also wanted to visit the headquarters of her new shipping company and meet the manager, Charles Browning who had been busy securing many lucrative import and export shipments for their new company. Mary was pleased to hear that the shipping company was developing a reputation for reliability and trustworthiness.

Once Mary's initial nervousness of again travelling on a train abated, she quite enjoyed herself. She had never been to the south-west of the country, and was interested in the changing landscape. Also, Amy's obvious delight in all aspects of the journey was quite entertaining to Mary and Hugh. The young maid had a new wardrobe of serviceable dresses, and a new pair of soft leather boots. These, along with a warm winter coat that Mary had insisted she have, were Amy's pride and joy. Never before had she owned new clothes or footwear that weren't uniform.

On their arrival at Southampton Station, a waiting coach transported the trio to the Star Hotel, where Mary and Hugh were welcomed as extremely honoured guests. Bookings had been made in Mary's name for a two-bedroomed suite for Mary and Aunt Clara, plus a single room for Hugh. A small maid's room for Amy was included in the suite. A little taken aback by the level of deferential treatment that they were receiving, Mary noted with a smile that Amy, standing nearby, was basking in being attached to them.

Leaving Amy to unpack their luggage, Mary and Hugh went down to the dining room for lunch, after telling Amy that they would have a meal sent up for her. However, when they were ordering their meal, and Mary asked for a meal to be taken up to her suite for her maid, the maître d'hôtel, who was standing nearby stepped forward. 'Begging your pardon, Your Ladyship, maids eat in the servants' hall near the kitchen.'

Taken aback, Mary replied a little more sharply than she intended. 'My maid will eat the meal I ordered for her in our suite, or would you rather she joined Sir Hugh and myself here at our table?'

The embarrassed man bowed slightly. 'I apologise, Your Ladyship. Whatever you order will be delivered to your suite while you are dining.'

Seeing the smile on Hugh's face when the maître d'hôtel hurried to place their order, Mary apologised. 'Sorry Hugh, I forget that away from home, my staff are just servants to other people and treated as such.'

Hugh laughed. 'If you stand up for me like you do for your staff when you feel they are being maligned, I shall have no worries.'

'I shouldn't have snapped at him like that. I will apologise when he returns.'

'No, don't do that my love.' Hugh held her hand. 'Unfortunately, that is the manner of response that he and the other staff are used to hearing. He will ensure that everything is to your liking from now on, just you wait and see.'

When they returned to the suite, they found Amy sitting at a small table near the window, dreamily eating the same meal that they had ordered in the dining room, served on good hotel china. When Amy realised that Mary and Hugh had entered the room, she stood up. 'A waiter brought this meal up on a trolley and said that you had ordered it for me, m'lady. I hope it was right for me to eat it before it went cold, but I was awfully hungry, and it smelt so nice.'

Mary patted the girl's shoulder. 'Of course you were Amy. When meals are ordered for you in the future, just eat and enjoy them. This afternoon, Sir Hugh and I will be going to the shipping office, so you are free to do as you wish until four o'clock, but I wouldn't go too far from the hotel if you go outside. Here is the spare key.'

'I think I would rather stay here and sleep off that huge lunch, m'lady.'

A coach was waiting at the hotel steps for Mary and Hugh when they left the hotel. The concierge handed Mary up into the coach and closed the door after Hugh had seated himself beside her. Hugh gave the driver the shipping office address, then he and Mary sat back and held hands as they drove through the crowded streets.

'I'm sure Tess had ulterior motives when she insisted that Amy accompany us to Southampton Hugh.' Mary laughed as she removed his hand from her knee.

Hugh put his hand in his coat pocket. 'I'm sure she did, and much as I wish it was otherwise, she was right. I wish we could just disappear and marry tomorrow, in the first church we came to.'

'It's only a month to wait, and you are going to be away for quite a lot of that time. Luckily, I will have Aunt Clara to help me stop pining for you!'

When they alighted at the shipping office, they were met by a tall middle-aged man with the reddest hair Mary had ever seen. Holding her hand, he bowed, then he shook hands with Hugh. 'Welcome to Southampton, Your Ladyship and Sir Hugh. Please come inside.'

Charles led them up to a large well-appointed office on the second floor of the building, with a large window offering an extensive view of the port. There, Mary, Hugh, and Charles Browning spent the next hour going through the books and schedules of all their ships. Mary also asked Charles to give her a résumé of the six captains.

When Mary left the room to freshen up in the bathroom, Charles turned to Hugh. 'My goodness, Sir Hugh, I have never before met a lady with such business insight as Lady Mary. Am I right in thinking that she has not yet reached her majority?'

'Yes, Lady Mary will be twenty-one in a couple of months' time. Her grasp of all her business interests still astounds me. I have dealings with many men with much less business sense.'

On Mary's return to the office, Charles accompanied them back to the front door. 'Would you like me to meet you at the docks tomorrow, when you go to meet your aunt Lady Mary? I might be able to expedite your meeting.'

'That would be wonderful, thank you Charles. I wasn't looking forward to fighting my way through the crowd, looking for Aunt Clara.'

'I will send one of my clerks to your hotel in the morning to let you know when the ship is berthing, and he will direct the coachman where to meet me on the docks. It has been a pleasure meeting you both. Goodbye until tomorrow.' Charles stepped back from their coach after shutting the door.

The next morning, not long after they had all eaten breakfast in Mary's suite, a bellboy announced that a gentleman at reception was asking to see the Countess and Sir Hugh.

Hugh handed the boy a coin. 'Please inform the gentleman that we will meet him at reception in ten minutes, and also please advise the coachman that we will be requiring his services at that time.'

Hugh looked at Mary, who was donning a beautifully styled three-quarter length emerald-green velvet coat over her white silk blouse, and thought how beautiful she looked. Amy pinned a small brimmed green hat, with a feather wrapped around the crown, on to Mary's head, then the three of them went down the lift to meet Charles's clerk Tom Larkin who rode in the coach with them, and directed the coachman to a quieter roped-off area near to where a large steamship had just docked. There they were met by Charles.

'Your aunt will be escorted off the ship to meet you here, Your Ladyship, once the customs formalities have been completed. Her luggage is being collected as we speak. I apologise that I can't stay, but an urgent order arrived this morning that I must deal with as quickly as possible. Tom will stay with you until you are ready to leave.'

Mary smiled at her shipping manager. 'Thank you Charles. I look forward to our next meeting.'

Unbeknown to the group waiting on the dock, a woman up on the top deck of the ship was watching them, thinking how smart the young lady looked in her emerald-green coat and skirt. For a fleeting moment she thought there was something familiar about the lady, but then turned away as she heard her name being called by the purser walking towards her.

'Mrs Wilkinson, would you please accompany me to your cabin to collect your carryon luggage? I will be escorting you off the ship to meet your niece. Your trunk is being brought up from the hold.'

Entering the cabin that had been her home for the past two months, Clara breathed a sigh of relief, as she had been getting quite anxious about leaving the ship, worrying how she would pick Mary out in that huge crowd milling around on the dock.

While in Australia, Clara had been concerned when she hadn't heard from her niece since her sudden departure for England over two years ago, and was upset that she had no idea how to contact her. Then suddenly, two months ago, she had received the telegram from Mary, inviting her to her wedding, and offering to pay for her ticket to England. The cabin had been extremely comfortable, and Clara had often wondered how Mary could afford to pay for a first-class cabin for her. The man she was marrying must have a lot of money.

Following the purser down the gangplank, Clara looked in vain for Mary, and was surprised when she was ushered through the crowd to the clearer area that she had been looking at from the deck. She gasped with astonishment when the elegant young lady wearing the green suit ran towards her, crying out, 'Aunt Clara!' and hugged her tightly. Mary was delighted to see her Aunt Clara again, but was shocked to see how much she had changed in the past two years. Her hair was greying and she looked many years older.

Following a very emotional coach journey back to the hotel, with her aunt sobbing most of the time into Hugh's handkerchief, Hugh suggested that he and Amy might go for a walk around the old town walls to leave Mary and her aunt time alone together. Once Mary had settled Clara into a comfortable armchair near the window and ordered some tea, she too sat down, and watched her aunt slowly calm down and take in the luxurious room.

Clara's mouth dropped open when the waiter addressed Mary as 'Your Ladyship' and poured the tea for them. When the waiter left, Clara stared at her niece. 'Mary, you and Hugh aren't married yet. How can you use his title before the wedding, and surely you are not sharing this suite?'

Mary gave her a bewildered look. 'Haven't you received any of my letters Aunt Clara? I must have sent over a dozen to you, but have been puzzled that you never replied.' Mary leant over to grasp Clara's hand. 'Has something happened at home Aunt Clara? Is Graham all right?'

Taking a deep breath, Clara turned to face her niece. 'I haven't seen any letters from you Mary, other than the one you sent from Melbourne before you sailed. I'm afraid that Graham is not all right, and yes, a number of things have happened since you left.

Following Patricia's death and your departure, Graham lost interest in the farm. He was often late milking the cows, and did very little work during the day. Then he started to go into town, and would often come home drunk.'

'But Graham never drank!'

'Well, he does now! A few weeks after you left, he arrived home with that blonde hussy of a barmaid from the hotel, and informed me that they were married! Annette did absolutely nothing in the house. She wouldn't cook or do any housework, and expected me to do everything. 'You did it before, so you can keep doing it now,' was her reply when I asked for some assistance. When I spoke to Graham, and told him that I wasn't going to be an unpaid slave while Annette sat in the house doing nothing, he lost his temper and threw me out. Can you believe that Mary, after all the years I looked after him?'

Mary was shocked, and sat back in her chair. 'Good grief Aunt Clara, what in the world did you do?'

'I packed my bags, saddled Trixie, and rode to a friend's farm in the next valley. I was so furious, I didn't let him know where I had gone.'

'But what have you been doing since you left the farm Aunt Clara?'

Clara dabbed her eyes with her handkerchief. 'When I recovered from the shock of Graham's outburst, I travelled to Melbourne, where I was lucky enough to be employed as a live-in housekeeper for a lovely retired doctor. Following his death last July, I decided to return to the farm to speak to Graham, only to find that he had sold the farm not long after I left, and that neither he nor Annette have been seen since. No one knows where they are now.'

Mary opened her mouth to speak, but Clara hastily added. 'He did own the farm, Mary. I'm sorry, but I don't know what happened to your letters. It was just pure luck that I was in town the day your telegram arrived, and the post boy saw me.'

Mary was finding it hard to believe what she was hearing. 'Oh, Aunt Clara that is awful. How could Graham turn into such a monster?'

'I don't think he could cope with the responsibility of owning the farm Mary. Then that hussy turned his head. I know that she hated being on the farm, and I would say she convinced him to sell.'

'Well, all I can say is thank goodness you were able to come to England. I will look after you from now on.' Mary gave her aunt another hug and a kiss on top of her head.

A few minutes later, Clara looked at Mary. 'So what in the world have you been up to since you left Australia, my girl? Again I ask, how can you be staying in a suite like this, when you aren't yet married to Hugh?'

'Well, do you remember how Mother was referred to as Lady Patricia in the letter she received before she died?' When Clara slowly nodded, Mary continued. 'Her mother, my grandmother, was a Countess. She died a week before her daughter, so when Mother died, I inherited the title and all that goes with it!'

To give her aunt time to take in this information, Mary showed Clara her engagement ring. 'This was Grandmother's engagement ring, and was meant to be given to Mother.'

'It is beautiful Mary, and suits your hand so well.' Clara, held the ring up to the light. 'So, tell me about this young man you are marrying.'

'Actually, he is the son of the manager of one of my estates.' Mary hid a smile at Clara's expression.

'One of your estates? How many do you have?!'

'Two. Hugh has been working for me for nearly two years, and we have fallen blissfully in love. To make Hugh's transition into aristocratic circles easier, Queen Victoria knighted him when we announced our engagement.'

Clara sat back in her chair and stared at Mary. 'You have met Queen Victoria?'

Mary chuckled. 'A number of times actually. She and my Grandmother were great friends, and Her Majesty appears to have taken me under her wing.'

'Well, I never. I think I need another cup of tea!'

Just then, the door opened and Hugh and Amy entered the suite.

'What perfect timing Hugh. We were just going to ring for more tea.'

'How about lunch instead, if you two have caught up on important matters? Amy and I are both famished.'

'Goodness, is it lunchtime already? Aunt Clara, may I formally introduce you to my fiancé, Sir Hugh Watson.'

Hugh took Clara's right hand and kissed it. 'It is a pleasure to meet you Mrs Wilkinson, or might I call you Aunt Clara?'

Clara blushed. 'How do you do, Sir Hugh? But could you both please just call me Clara?'

'And to you Clara, we shall always be Mary and Hugh. Now, how about some lunch? Oh, I nearly forgot.' Hugh turned to Amy to bring her to stand in front of Clara. 'Clara, may I introduce you to Amy, who works for Mary, and has come along to keep an eye on us both. Amy, this lady is Mrs Wilkinson.'

Amy bobbed a curtsey. 'Good afternoon, Mrs Wilkinson.'

Collecting their warm coats, all four went to a nearby restaurant and had lunch. Amy was surprised how quickly she grew to like Mary's aunt who, like Amy, was a little overawed to be dining in such a splendid restaurant. Clara was fascinated to watch the interaction between Amy,

Mary, and Hugh. While Amy appeared to be at ease to talk freely, Clara noted that she always called Mary, m'lady and Hugh, Sir, and was always alert to assist them if the need arose.

When they were alone in the suite for a short time in the afternoon, while Mary and Hugh met with one of Mary's business managers, Amy told Clara about Longmire Hall and Everton Manor. 'Working for Lady Mary is fun, Mrs Wilkinson. She lets us talk while we work together, and as you have seen today, she treats me as a person, not just an employee of no account. All her staff love her.'

'Staff? Don't you mean servants?'

'No, Mrs Wilkinson. Lady Mary says that we are her staff, like the people employed in all her businesses.'

'*What in the world has this niece of mine become involved in?*' wondered a bewildered Clara.

CHAPTER 11

Lewes,
Sussex, England
November 1888

Clara was amazed to see the respect shown to her young niece throughout their journey to London and on to Lewes. She was proud to see that the Mary she knew hadn't changed, despite the honours and wealth bestowed upon her. Yes, she did dress more formally when required, and Clara had seen Mary put a couple of people in their place, when she felt it was required, but she was still the loving, friendly, down-to-earth girl Clara had always loved and treasured. Clara noticed that Mary spoke respectfully to everyone, whether they were her aristocratic peers, the manager of the hotel, or the paper boy outside on the street.

What really surprised Clara though, was the genuine respect the men they met had for Mary. Word was spreading that, despite her youth and gender, this young colonial Countess was not only an astute businesswoman, but also a benevolent aristocrat, who could be relied on to give sound advice and assistance if needs be. She seemed to instinctively recognise people who weren't genuine in their dealings with her, and was quick to deal with them with an authority that allowed no room for argument. She appeared to not tolerate people abusing their power, in any form.

Mary had intended to take Clara to Longmire Hall after a week at Everton Manor, but not long after their arrival at the Manor Mary was called to sit on a Magistrate's Panel for a larceny trial. A lady was to be tried for stealing a large amount of jewellery from houses in Lewes. The police had found the jewellery in a local pawnshop, and the lady was arrested.

When brought before the magistrates, and questioned about the theft, the lady denied the charge. 'It weren't me. I aint done nothing wrong.'

One of the magistrates glared at her. 'Mrs Green, the pawn ticket for the jewellery was found in your kitchen behind the tea caddy.'

Thinking that the young lady on the bench would take her side, Mrs Green looked towards Mary, and tried to sound aggrieved. 'It musta been that good-for-nothing daughter what stole the stuff.'

Mary smiled at the lady. 'How many children do you have Mrs Green?'

'Three pathetic brats!' The woman suddenly remembered where she was. 'Sorry, I'm a bit unwell at the moment. I have three children, Your Honour.'

Mary turned to the other two magistrates. 'Do either of you know where the children are?' Both men shook their heads. 'Do you mind if we adjourn the case until we have spoken to them? If we are to convict this lady, we need to know what will happen to her children.' Both men had thought that Mary would take the woman's side, like in the last case, and were astounded when she appeared to be showing no sympathy towards the woman, and talking about a possible custodial sentence. As it was already mid-afternoon, the men agreed to adjourn the case until the next day, and asked the police to bring the children to the courthouse the next morning, for a closed meeting with the magistrates.

All three were shocked, when the next morning three unkempt children were brought into the room. They were dirty and gaunt, their clothing basically in tatters. The older girl held an emaciated baby in a grubby shawl, while the younger girl clung to her sister's garment that was a threadbare man's shirt, with a piece of string tied around her waist.

Mary was appalled. 'Please sit down, children.' She turned to the policeman who was standing near the door. 'Constable, please have some bread and milk brought to these chambers immediately. And also please have some milk warmed for the baby.'

Mary looked at the older girl. 'Please don't be afraid lass. You are not in any trouble. My friends and I want to know how we can help you.' The girl looked at her for a moment, then nodded. 'First of all, what are your names?'

'My name is Ruth, this is Chloe, and this here is Christopher.' She glanced at the bundle in her arms.

'How old are you Ruth?'

'I'm seven, Chloe is five, and Christopher is only five months old.'

'Your mother said that you left the pawn ticket behind the tea caddy Ruth. Is that correct?'

'She aint our real mam! That old hag would blame the Lord, if she thought it would get her off the charge!'

'Now steady on young girl.' The elder man stopped when Mary laid a hand on his arm, and shook her head slightly.

'Who pawned the jewellery Ruth?'

Before Ruth could answer, Chloe interrupted. 'Mam did, and she bought a lot of food, but us didn't get any of it to eat. We just got dry old crusts.'

Ruth ruefully nodded. 'Chloe's right. What mam didn't spend on food for herself, she drank at the ale house. She hates us because we aint hers. Our dad married her after our real ma died when Christopher was born. He's a sailor, and when he went back to sea after the wedding, she drank and ate everything that she earned. We don't know where he is.'

'Where have you been getting food from?' Mary thought that maybe the children had resorted to stealing themselves.

'Our neighbours give us some food sometimes, but usually, Chloe and I get food from the bins at the back of the posh eating places. That aint stealing, is it?'

Just then, the baby gave a weak cry, and the three magistrates looked on in pity as the young girl gave him her finger to suck, and rocked him to try to soothe him. Mary was worried about the baby. 'How have you managed to feed Christopher Ruth?'

The girl began to sob. 'A neighbour has been feeding him with her baby that was born just before Christopher. She told me yesterday that she won't be able to feed him anymore cause her milk's drying up. I don't know what to feed him now.'

Just then the policeman returned with a jug of milk and some ham sandwiches, and was followed into the room by a lady carrying a bowl of warm milk, with some small pieces of bread soaking in it. 'Begging you pardon, Your Honours. I took the liberty of bringing some of the sandwiches prepared for your morning tea. Mrs Hughes here is a midwife. I thought she might be able to help with the baby.'

'Well done Constable. I'm sure that my colleagues and I can forgo a few sandwiches.' Mary turned to the midwife and spoke quietly. 'Mrs Hughes, I'm really worried about the baby. He looks quite ill.' She turned to Ruth, 'May I hold your brother please Ruth? I promise we won't take him away from you, and we will feed him while you eat.'

Reluctantly, the young girl handed over the baby, but it was obvious, by the way that she and her sister devoured the milk and sandwiches that they were starving, although Ruth barely took her eyes off her brother while she ate. Mary anxiously watched as Mrs Hughes patiently held a piece of milk-soaked bread against Christopher's lips, and breathed a sigh of relief when he greedily began to suck hard, and nibbled the bread with toothless gums.

Handing the baby to Mrs Hughes, Mary took her colleagues aside. 'For the children's sake, I think that they should be removed from their mother and made wards of the state. At least until we can find their father. Would you agree to me arranging for their care? That baby wouldn't last a week in the workhouse.'

Thankful to be relieved of having to deal with the children, the men agreed to hand them over to Mary, then suggested that they call the court back to order. Without further ado, following the evidence of a neighbour, who supported the children's story, Mrs Green was found guilty of stealing the jewellery, and was sentenced to five years in Reading Jail.

While the two men went off to lunch, Mary returned to the room where the children were waiting. Mary noticed that Christopher was wrapped in a clean shawl and was sleeping in Ruth's arms.

Mrs Hughes walked over to Mary. 'Before you leave the court, m'lady, I will bring a baby's bottle and some formula to feed him.'

Thanking the midwife for her assistance, Mary passed her some money. 'For your time and kindness.'

The clerk of the court was summonsed. 'My aunt Mrs Wilkinson is waiting for me in the visitors' gallery. Would you please bring her here?' The clerk gave a brief nod of his head. 'Certainly, Lady Mary.'

Chloe stared at Mary. 'Is you one of them lardy-da ladies Miss?'

Mary laughed. 'Well yes, I do have a title, but I'm not at all lardy-da.'

When Clara was ushered into the room, Mary introduced her to the girls. 'This is my aunt, Mrs Wilkinson, and she is not at all lardy-da, as you so eloquently put it Chloe.' Mary tried not to laugh at the shocked look on Clara's face. 'Aunt Clara, this is Ruth, Chloe, and young Christopher, who we will be looking after for a while.'

When Clara smiled at the girls, Chloe looked at the older woman for a moment, then stepped forward. 'Would you give me a hug Aunt Clara?' Totally disregarding the dirty clothes and grimy body, Clara wrapped the young child in her arms and held her tightly, muffling Chloe's 'Did you hang our mam, titled lady?'

Clara, gently stroked the little girl's filthy head. 'Chloe, her name is Lady Mary, and no, your mother won't be hanged. But she has been sent to jail.'

'Let's get this little family back to Everton Manor Clara, and we will send for Dr Wilson to check them.' Mary put her court notes into a leather satchel, and prepared to leave the court.

Enthralled at being driven in a real coach, the two girls were quiet, until they saw Everton Manor. Ruth looked at Mary in wonder. 'Do you live in a palace, Lady Mary?'

Chloe interrupted. 'Is you a queen, Lady Maresy?' Mary was amused at Chloe's pronunciation of her name. 'No girls, I'm not a queen, and while this is certainly a large house, it is not a palace. When we go inside we will give you something else to eat, then you will both have a long hot bath.'

'Are you going to drown us like our mam threatened to?' the ever-questioning Chloe asked. Ruth just stared reproachfully at Mary.

Trying hard to sound stern while struggling not to laugh Mary replied 'Listen to me carefully, Ruth and Chloe. No one is going to hurt you. Aunt Clara and I are going to look after you. You must have a bath to get clean, but I assure you that neither of you will be allowed to drown!'

While the two girls happily devoured part of a rabbit pie that Mrs Peters had just removed from the oven, Mary took Clara into the study. 'I'm sorry to land you with this mess Clara, but will you please help me with the children?'

'Of course I will, my darling girl. Please don't apologise, I need something to do. Like you, I can't just sit around doing nothing. I adore children, and always wished that your uncle and I had been blessed with some. Why don't you have Helen organise making up a couple of beds in the nursery, and maybe the governess's room for me? Oh, and we will need a cot for Christopher.'

Mary smiled, thinking how wonderful it was to have Aunt Clara in her life again.

By the time the girls had overcome their fear of the large bath half full of warm water, and had been scrubbed and had their hair washed by Joy and Martha, the tiled floor of the nursery bathroom was awash with water and soap suds. Martha laughed at the horrified look on Ruth's face, as she stood wrapped in a big fluffy towel, surveying the wet floor. 'Don't worry lass. Joy and I will have this cleaned up before you are dressed in your fancy new clothes.'

Clara was waiting in the girls' bedroom, where two dresses, underclothes, and shoes and socks were laid out on the large double bed. She handed a dress to each girl. 'I hope these dresses fit you. We had to guess your sizes. We will get more clothes for you both tomorrow.'

'Where is Christopher, Aunt Clara?' Ruth was less suspicious now, confident that they wouldn't be separated.

Clara answered, while helping Chloe dress. 'He is still down in the kitchen where it's warm Ruth. Helen has given him a warm bath, and he has been given some semolina mixed with stewed apple. Dr Wilson was examining him while you had your bath, and now he is waiting to see you both.'

Chloe clutched Clara's hand as she rang the bell to summons Dr Wilson. 'Will you stay with us, Aunt Clara? 'Mam used to tell us that doctors stuck needles in children, then took them away!'

Chloe's explanation horrified Clara. 'Dr Wilson is a very nice, kind man. He will try hard not to hurt you, but if he needs to give you an injection, I will hold you tight.'

Dr Wilson chatted with the girls while he examined them, putting them at ease. His announcement that they would not need an injection was met with great relief, as was his statement that they were to eat three proper meals a day.

While the girls played with some dolls that Clara had found in a nursery cupboard, Dr Wilson spoke to her. 'Those girls are as healthy as can be expected, considering the conditions they have been living under. Regular nourishing meals and plenty of exercise and fresh air should be all the treatment they require. If you have any worries, call me.'

'What about Christopher Dr Wilson?'

'You are right to be concerned about the baby Mrs Wilkinson. He is severely malnourished, and I am not sure what his future holds. By rights, he should be in hospital, but understanding his sisters' fear of separation, I would like to send a qualified nurse to assist you with the children.'

'I will willingly accept whatever help you think is necessary, to help that tiny lad recover Dr Wilson. I'm sure that Lady Mary will agree.'

That night, Clara tucked the two girls up in the large double bed, and read them a story from a book that she remembered reading to Mary when she was a little girl. Mary came in to wish the girls and her aunt goodnight, then went down to her other four children to explain why Aunt Clara was upstairs in the nursery with the two younger girls and a baby. They all expressed a desire to meet these newcomers before school the next morning.

When the girls were asleep, with the lamp turned down low, Clara went to her bedroom next door, leaving the connecting door ajar. She sat on the bed and looked at Christopher, sleeping in the bassinet that Martha had found in the attic, and scrubbed to ensure that it was as clean as possible. All the staff were concerned about the health of the children, the little baby in particular. Margaret Peters and Karen were busy looking up recipes of nourishing baby foods, while Joy and Martha were keen to accompany Mrs Atkins to the market in the morning, to buy more clothes for the girls and baby.

Mary in the meantime, was in her study, reading through the copious notes that Gordon's staff had gathered on watermills. The more she read, the more determined she became to build a mill on the new land. How she wished that Hugh was at Everton Manor. Not just to be with her, but also to discuss her ideas. Unfortunately he was in Kent, having received an invitation to attend a local county fair, to meet with some influential farmers who had heard about his new business. He had been gone since the first day of the recent trial.

Early the next morning, Clara was woken by the two girls climbing into bed with her. Far from being angry with them, she was thrilled that they felt relaxed enough to take such liberties. A quick glance into the bassinet assured her that Christopher was asleep and breathing normally, so Clara cuddled each girl to her and fell asleep. When Mary arrived later with a cup of tea for her aunt, the three in the bed were still asleep and Christopher was just stirring. Gently waking Clara, Mary handed her the cup, then lifted Christopher from his bassinet and held him to her chest. Watching her niece cuddling the tiny mite, Clara prayed that Mary and Hugh would be blessed with healthy children following their wedding.

Everyone was thrilled to see that Christopher had survived the night, and appeared to be a little more alert to the people around him. He hungrily ate the food that Margaret had prepared for him, and would have eaten more if Mary hadn't reminded them that he was to have small amounts often. Halfway through his bottle, he fell asleep, which Karen interpreted for them all as 'I've had enough!'

Ruth and Chloe were introduced to Alfie, Jack, Jane, and Sally when they met at the breakfast table. Both girls were fascinated to see Mac, Sally's dog, lying beside her. The only dogs that they had previously seen were dogs roaming the streets searching for food. Ruth shuddered when she thought of the times she had been forced to grab scraps of food before the scavenging dogs did. She kept watching Mac, waiting for him to steal food from Sally's plate, but he took no notice and only stood up when Sally asked to be excused from the table. Both girls watched in amazement as Sally walked out of the kitchen with her hand on his collar, not hesitating for a moment.

Alfie chuckled, watching Ruth and Chloe. 'Pretty cool, eh? He didn't have to be taught to look after Sally. He just knows what to do and she trusts him completely.'

Mid-morning, while Mary was showing the girls the stables, a young lady arrived at the back door carrying a Gladstone bag. Assuming that this was the nurse for Christopher, Mary left the girls with the groom and walked over to introduce herself. Before she could utter a word, the lady interrupted. 'Excuse me miss, I'm Elin Davies, the nurse. Could you please inform her Ladyship that I have arrived?'

Mary stopped, entranced by the lilting Welsh accent, and then stepped forward. 'Welcome, Elin. I'm Lady Mary.' Aware of the girl's embarrassment, Mary added swiftly, 'Do come in, Elin,' and led the way to the kitchen where she introduced her to the staff there.

'Where did you study nursing, Elin?'

'I trained at the Nightingale Training School, which is part of St Thomas's Hospital in London, m'lady and I currently work at St Thomas's in the maternity ward.' Elin handed an envelope to Mary. 'Here are my papers Lady Mary.'

The first sheet that Mary removed was Elin's nursing certificate, showing that she had graduated four years ago; the second was confirmation that Elin Davies had topped her class in nursing.

'How is it that you have come to us here at Everton Manor Elin?'

'Matron's sister is married to Dr Wilson. When Mrs Wilson spoke to Matron and explained the situation, she asked me if I would like to be assigned to care for the baby that you are so generously looking after.'

This time it was Mary's turn to blush with embarrassment, much to her staff's amusement. Noting that Elin had finished her cup of tea, Mary stood up. 'I'll show you up to the nursery, Elin, and will introduce you to my aunt, who is looking after the children.'

Clara was thrilled to meet Elin, and immediately took her to see Christopher, who was intently watching the small spoonful of mashed pumpkin that Karen was moving slowly towards his open mouth. As they watched, he swallowed quickly and opened his mouth for more. 'Like a little bird, isn't he?' Karen laughed, and filled another spoonful.

Moving silently out of the room so as not to distract him from his meal, Clara looked at Elin. 'The little lad appears to be becoming more alert each time he wakens Elin. Surely that is a good sign, isn't it?' Elin put her bag in the bedroom next to the nursery. 'He is terribly malnourished, Mrs Wilkinson, but I hope that between us, we can help him gain weight, and look forward to a much happier future for him. Matron gave me permission to bring whatever I thought I might need from the maternity supplies, so I have a quantity of formula and bottles, plus napkins.'

Chapter 12

Longmire Estate,
Sussex, England
November 1888

With Clara and Elin looking after the children, and her foursome happy for them to be at Everton Manor, Mary headed back to Longmire Hall. When she visited Tess, to tell her about their journey to Southampton, Graham's treatment of Clara, and the trial resulting in her rescuing three more children, Tess sat back in her chair and stared at Mary.

'Nothing you do now surprises me, Mary my dear. I'm terribly sorry to hear that your aunt was so shabbily treated by you brother, and am so glad that she has come to England for your wedding. I'm very much looking forward to meeting your Aunt Clara. Did you say that she has taken over looking after those poor children?'

'Yes Tess, she needed something to do, and she is bossing me about just like she used to at home.'

'And you are loving every minute of it, aren't you!'

Tess poured boiling water into the teapot. 'If Clara doesn't have a home in Australia now, would you consider asking her to live here in England?' Seeing the startled look on Mary's face, Tess quickly added 'She wouldn't need to live with you and Hugh. There are plenty of places nearby where she could live.'

'What a wonderful idea Tess. I've been so happy to have Clara here, I really hadn't given her future a thought.'

Tess placed a cup of tea on the table in front of Mary. 'You've had a bit on your mind over the past couple of months lass. Don't blame yourself for forgetting or not thinking of a few things. It's a wonder you can think of anything, after that blow to your head. Do you realise just how lucky you were Mary?'

'Yes Tess, I do. I also know that I wouldn't be here if Hugh hadn't been with me.' She laughed. 'Though I still haven't forgiven him for landing on me and breaking my ribs!'

Seeing the pensive look on Tess's face, Mary grasped her hand. 'Tess, you know that you and Bob mean the world to me. I wouldn't have accomplished half the things I have without your love, encouragement, and sage advice. I know that Clara is a relative, however you both mean just as much to me, and will continue to do so whether Clara stays in England or goes back to Australia.'

Tess hugged her tightly. 'Thank you Mary. You are like a daughter to me now, and I hope that your mother would approve of the love and guidance I have tried to give you. Now, let's get this bread in the oven before I become too tearful.'

Mary rode away from Home Farm, thinking about Tess's comment regarding Clara's future, and decided to ask Clara herself what she would like to do. As she rode, her thoughts changed to how much she preferred to be out riding Gem with Scruffy beside her, rather than having to carry out her increasing social duties. However, she knew that she was finding these duties less onerous, as she became more confident in her ability to deal with the variety of tasks that she was being expected to undertake.

Mary was really enjoying her introduction to the business world, and was as surprised as everyone else how quickly she was able to grasp the concepts important to be successful. She realised that her privileged position had made it much easier for her to enter such a male-dominated domain, but it was her business insight that some businessmen were now seeking.

Once she and Gem neared the stream on the new farm, Mary's thoughts switched to her plans for a watermill. Recalling the information that she'd read about the various mills in Gordon's report, she started to ride slowly along the stream, looking for what she thought could be possible sites for a mill. Taking a pencil and pad from her saddlebag, she made notes while Gem munched grass each time they stopped for Mary to write. Scruffy would have preferred to keep running, but each time the horse stopped, he returned to lie beside her.

One particular area of the stream bank, where the water ran swiftly between four-feet-high banks on either side around a gentle curve, attracted Mary's attention. The ground was flat near the stream banks, with a slight rise further back on one side, and the area was within easy access to the track leading to the village. Moving away from the stream, Mary headed towards the farm boundary with Longmire Village.

Mary and Hugh had discussed setting aside an area near the village to start a small market garden to grow vegetables for the village, and later possibly to supply surrounding villages. At the moment, the villagers had to rely on vegetables from Lewes Market being delivered to the village grocer. Some had small vegetable gardens, but had to rely on the grocer for the bulk of their vegetables.

Bob's son Matt had ploughed about an acre that was to lie fallow during the winter. Hugh had made a list of some of the villagers without jobs, to make a roster of working days, and wages to be paid by the estate. A committee was currently having meetings to decide on varieties of vegetables and sowing plans for the venture. Already, the one-acre vegetable plot at Everton Manor was producing some vegetables, and the plan was to increase that area after winter, to send vegetables to the Lewes and London markets.

Mary's progress through the village was slow, as she was constantly stopping to speak to villagers on the street. Finally, when past the last house, Mary encouraged Gem into a canter along the road to the Hall. Back in the kitchen for a quick cup of tea, Mrs Smith handed Mary a telegram. 'Back for lunch tomorrow. Love Hugh.' Mary was delighted, and ran up the staircase in a most unladylike manner to her bedroom, to change out of her riding habit.

In the meantime, at the Dower House, Katherine was meticulously sowing satin onto the buttons for the front of the bodice of Mary's wedding dress. Three small buttons were to hold the v neckline modestly closed, but still open enough for the magnificent sapphire and diamond necklace to be seen in all its glory. *Something old, something new, something borrowed, and something blue,* thought Katherine as she finished the last button.

The wedding dress was almost finished, and was awaiting Mary's final fitting. Looking at the long white dress hanging in her sewing room, Katherine thought how her family's fortunes had changed since the day that Arthur and Sir Hugh had walked into their room in London.

During Mary's convalescence from the train accident, Katherine's husband Joseph had approached the owner of the Lewes Saddlery business to apply for a job. Seeing some of his work, especially the embossing samples, Joseph was offered a job to start immediately, at a pay rate that took his breath away. A bicycle was also made available for him to travel to and from work each day. He was sure that his connection with the Countess, all be it slight, had some bearing on his instant employment.

Joseph was in his element, working at the Lewes Saddlery business, and was getting a name for his leather embossing skills. Katherine had never seen him happier, and he genuinely looked forward to going to work each morning, although Katherine was a little concerned about his journey to and from work once winter really set in. For the first time in their married life, they had a bank account, and were saving quite a lot of money from his generous wage.

Toby and Adam had become good friends while in London. Adam had found a quick, eager student in Toby, who seemed to absorb information like a sponge. With Hugh's encouragement, Adam had moved to Everton Manor, where he continued with Toby's lessons, even when he moved to live at Home Farm

Katherine almost didn't recognise the cheerful, confident lad that Toby had become since living with Bob and Tess. He had grown and put on weight, and had lost the pallid complexion and lethargy that had so worried her. Although not completely cured by the month's treatment in London, Toby's foot had been turned to the point that he could put the sole of his foot on the ground. The special boot with a built-up sole had been fitted, and Toby had learnt to walk with less reliance on a crutch. Thanks to the treatment that Lady Mary had organised and paid for, Toby now walked with only the aid of a stick, and was so keen to attempt new jobs, one almost forgot that he still had a club foot.

Robert and James, from the Longmire stables, had found a suitable pony for him and were teaching him to ride bareback. 'A born rider, this lad. We could put him in a circus' Robert had declared when he and Toby had ridden the six miles to Everton Manor, to collect some harness that her husband had mended.

Katherine herself was loving working on Lady Mary's wedding dress. At first not sure that her sewing ability would be sufficient for such a task, she was thrilled to find that her natural talent and the training she had received before her marriage, gave her the confidence to attempt whatever Lady Mary requested. And the sewing machine was a marvel to work with. She was beginning to wonder if she might be able to sew dresses for the ladies of Lewes at some stage.

CHAPTER 13

Despite everything that clamoured for her attention, Mary was determined to make time for her four children. She was pleased how well Alfie, Jack, and Jane had settled in at their new school, and they were coping well with their schoolwork. Sally was learning a lot in her short spells at the School for the Blind in London, though she was always pleased to be back at Everton Manor to be with Jane after school.

Although Jane missed her twin terribly when Sally was at school in London, she found that her new school offered her so much more than the village school, and loved going to all her classes. She had been quickly accepted into a small group of girls who had similar interests, so had little time to feel lonely.

Alfie, being a little older, and keen on playing any type of sport, had settled into the new larger school more quickly than his younger brother. While Jack coped well with his schoolwork, he didn't enjoy the rough and tumble that his brother revelled in. Consequently, he found the new school a lonely place, and was keen to return to Everton Manor immediately after the school day ended.

Jack had found an ally in Margaret Peters when, soon after the children moved to Everton Manor prior to the start of the new school term, the young boy had wandered into her kitchen and watched her making pastry. Shyly he had asked 'Mrs Peters, could I please help you? Mrs Smith sometimes lets me help her make pastry.' Very quickly Margaret recognised the enthusiasm the young boy had for cooking, and he became a regular occupant in the kitchen, prepared to help with any job needing to be done, and also cooking recipes that Margaret gave him. Everyone was very proud of the budding young chef when his first pie was served for dinner, no one more so than his brother Alfie.

Alfie knew that Jack spent most of his time sitting alone in the quadrangle reading a book when not in class, but was at a loss as to what he could do to help. Alfie had made it clear that his brother was not to be bullied, when he dealt servery with two of the school bullies who had taunted Jack on the way home after school, but he couldn't spend all his time with his brother.

The headmaster had called on Mary to notify her of the incident, and to explain the school's policy on fighting. Secretly, Mary was very proud of Alfie. 'I will speak to Alfie Headmaster, and will inform him that, whilst I understand and applaud his defence of Jack, I do not want him to lower his standards to become a school bully, like the two boys that he dealt with!' Not quite the reply the headmaster expected to hear from the young lady sitting opposite him, but he wasn't going to argue with her. Most women, and many men, shrank from his steely stare and booming voice, agreeing to his every demand, but this young lady wasn't fazed in the slightest.

Early in November, Jack made friends with a boy in his class who, like him spent his free time sitting alone in the quad. Ryan Murphy, a small Irish lad, who lived in the poorer area of Lewes, was one of the school's sponsored students, and was not at all popular with the other boys. Noticing that Ryan rarely ate lunch, Jack offered him a piece of pie that Margaret had packed for his lunch, and was astounded when, after an initial refusal, Ryan devoured the pie so quickly that Jack was sure he hadn't chewed it at all. That night, Jack told Margaret about Ryan, so from then on she packed an extra lunch in Jack's bag.

The two boys ate their lunch together and slowly, Ryan began to talk to Jack, embarrassed to tell him how poor they were, when he knew that Jack lived with the Countess. 'I haven't always lived with Lady Mary Ryan. Alfie and I were in the workhouse when we were younger.' When Ryan scoffed and appeared not to believe him, Jack pulled up his shirt to reveal the scars still visible on his back. 'The master at the workhouse whipped me two years ago Ryan, before Lady Mary saved us.' From then on, the two boys became firm friends, and eventually Ryan told Jack about his family. 'I'm the oldest of four children, my father works at the livery stable in town, and my mother takes in washing and ironing, to try to make enough to feed us.'

While Mary's business and social commitments took up a lot of her time, she tried to spend time each week wherever the children were staying. All four spent time with Mary, chatting about school and what they and their friends had been up to. Consequently, it wasn't long before Mary heard about Ryan.

She was aware that Jack loved spending time in the kitchen and had a great ally in Margaret, who had urged Jack to seek Mary's permission to keep taking extra food to school for Ryan each day. Mary encouraged the children to bring their friends to Everton Manor if they wished, but could understand Ryan's hesitancy to visit the Manor.

One day, when she and Hugh were in Lewes, they passed the livery stable where occasionally Hugh hired a horse to ride to Longmire Hall. On impulse, Mary grabbed Hugh's arm. 'Hugh, do you remember an Irishman working at the livery stable?'

'There is a chap called Mick, who I think is Irish. I haven't actually dealt with him, as he was always busy mucking out stalls when I visited.' Glancing across the road at the stables, he noticed a thin man in ragged clothes near the door. 'That's the chap near the door, Mary. Do you think he might be Ryan's father?'

'Hmm, I think he might be. He looks like a puff of wind would blow him over, doesn't he?'

Later that day, Mary contacted the school to ask the bursar for Ryan Murphy's address. Knowing that the Countess was one of the patrons of the sponsored student program, he had no hesitation in disclosing the information.

The next morning, Mary was driven to the laneway running behind the Murphy's home, and asked the groom to wait at the end of the alley. Walking along the cobbled surface, Mary was pleased that she was wearing sensible walking shoes. She could hear some children squabbling as she approached the back gate, and as she entered the backyard, she saw two children tugging on a soft toy, watched by a baby sitting in a high chair. A lady was struggling to peg some heavy wet sheets onto a long line, stretching the length of the yard.

Mary started to introduce herself to the startled woman. 'Good morning Mrs Murphy. I'm M—' but was interrupted by a scream from the baby, who had been thrown into the air when the little girl let go of the toy, sending the boy reeling backwards against the high chair. Mary and Mrs Murphy reached the baby at the same time, and saw her lying limply on the path with blood on her face

'Mrs Murphy, get a clean towel as quickly as you can!'

While she was gone, Mary gently ran her hands over the small body, as Dr Wilson had shown her when Alfie had fallen off his pony. She noted a large lump quickly developing over one eye, and the right arm was at an abnormal angle. Otherwise, she could feel no other obvious injuries.

Mrs Murphy ran out with two tea towels and looked at Mary in distress. 'Try to wipe the blood from her face Mrs Murphy, so that we can see where it is coming from. I'm pretty sure her arm is broken, but only a doctor can say for sure how badly she is hurt.'

Mrs Murphy stared at her in shock. 'We can't afford to call a doctor, miss.'

'We must get her to a doctor as soon as possible Mrs Murphy. My groom is waiting at the end of the laneway with a carriage. Send your lad out to tell him to come here straightaway.'

This was said with such authority that Mrs Murphy immediately sent the boy out to the road to get Mike. The tall groom, who entered the yard a few moments later, looked at the baby, then at Mary. 'Is there a problem, Lady Mary?'

Mary gently handed the baby to her mother, who was staring at Mary in astonishment. 'We need to get this baby and her mother to Dr Wilson's surgery as quickly as possible Mike. Do you know where it is?'

'Yes, m'lady, we can be there in a short time.'

'Mrs Murphy, please trust me and go with my groom. Tell the receptionist that Lady Mary sent you, and I will explain more when you return. I will look after the other children while you are gone.'

As the speechless lady followed the groom through the gate, Mary called to the two young children. 'Could you two please help me with your mother's washing? You hand me the pegs, and I will hang it on the line.' The boy who had crashed into the high chair frowned at Mary. 'Ma don't let us touch the posh peoples' stuff,'

'Oh, I think on this occasion she won't mind you helping me. When we have finished, do you think we should buy some cream cakes for when she comes back?' Mary saw the eyes of both children light up, then the boy scowled again. 'We don't have no money to buy them sort of things.' Struggling to lift a large sheet onto the line, Mary took some pegs handed to her by the little girl. 'That's all right. I will buy them. By the way, what are your names?'

'I'm Fergus. That's Niamh and the baby is Roisin. Is she going to be all right Miss? I didn't mean to knock her out of the high chair, it were an accident.'

'I know it was Fergus. We will pray that Roisin will be better soon. My name is Mary. Now, let's get this washing hung out, and then we can go to the cake shop.'

Just as Mary was picking up the empty washing basket after the last sheet had been hung up, an elderly lady looked over the neighbouring fence. 'Who are you? What are you doing with Bridget's washing?'

'It's all right Mrs Baker. This here is Mary, and she is going to buy us some cakes. Ma has taken Roisin to the doctor cause she fell out of the high chair and bumped her head.'

'Oh my goodness! Is she seriously injured Mary?'

'I hope not Mrs Baker. I think she may have a broken arm, and she was knocked out. But I'm hoping that Dr Wilson will be able to help her.'

Not wanting Fergus to have all the say, Niamh butted in. 'Mary sent Ma and Roisin to the doctor with a man dressed in a uniform, and said to tell him that Lady Mary had sent them.'

The lady screwed up her eyes a little, to peer short-sightedly at Mary. 'Are you the Countess Lady Mary that's to be married next month?'

'Yes I am Mrs Baker, but at the moment I would rather not broadcast the fact, and want to keep things as normal as possible for these children, while their mother is away.'

'Yes, of course Your Ladyship. I understand.'

About an hour later Mike arrived back with the man that Hugh and Mary had seen at the stables the day before. 'Dr Wilson wants to keep the baby and her mother at his surgery overnight, m'lady. This is Mick Murphy, the children's father who has come home to look after them. Mick, this is Lady Mary Evans.'

When Mary and Mike were about to leave, Fergus shyly looked at Mary. 'Thank you for the cakes Mary. They was wonderful.'

As Mike drove back to Everton Manor, he turned to Mary. 'Lady Mary, when Mick Murphy heard the news about his daughter's accident, and his children being at home alone, he asked for time off to be with them. His boss refused, and said that he would be sacked if he left early.'

Mary was horrified, and couldn't believe that an employer could be so heartless.

'Unfortunately, some people don't like the Irish, m'lady. He was probably waiting for the first opportunity to put him off.'

Early the next morning, Mary and Mike went back into town, with a big basket of nourishing food, and a small can of fresh milk. Buying some freshly baked bread from the baker, they arrived at the Murphy's house in time for the three hungry children and their father to have a tasty, and ample breakfast before Ryan left for school. When they had finished, Mick and his other two children were bundled into the carriage to go to Dr Wilson's surgery.

Mick Murphy was still trying to come to grips with having a titled lady being so involved with his family, and was also worried how he could explain to his wife that he no longer had a job.

When they arrived at the surgery, Dr Wilson was about to leave for an out-of-town appointment, but he stayed long enough to speak to Mary. 'Little Roisin regained consciousness not long after she and her mother arrived here yesterday Lady Mary, and she slept normally throughout the night. I have set her arm and feel that if she can be kept quiet for a few days, she should make a full recovery.'

'Thank you, Dr Wilson, I will be paying for Roisin's treatment.'

Back at the Murphy's house, Mary remembered how she had felt after the train crash, and how important it had been for her to have peace and quiet for a complete recovery, and wondered how that could occur in such a cramped home with two other small children, plus Ryan when he was home from school.

Mrs Murphy put Roisin in her cot upstairs, while Mary sat in the kitchen with Mr Murphy. 'How long have you and your family been in England, Mr Murphy?'

'Tis Mick and Bridget to you, m'lady. I was a carpenter in Ireland and was offered a job building houses on an estate in London three years ago. Unfortunately, the owner of the company died, and we were all put off. Since then I have been doing any job I can get, to try to keep my family fed and room over our heads. We have been here in Lewes twelve months since.'

'Mick, please don't take this the wrong way, but would you allow me to offer you and your family somewhere to stay, at least until young Roisin is better? I know that you are no longer working, and Bridget is worried about the rent due to be paid at the end of the week.' Before Mick could speak, Mary continued 'Are you aware that your Ryan is friends with my ward Jack? They would have a great time together at Everton Manor. My aunt is at the moment looking after two young girls, and she would love a couple more small children to pamper, while your wife tends to Roisin.'

Mary could see the anguish on Mick's face as he tried to make a decision. 'Do you like gardening, Mick?'

Startled, he looked at her to see if she was joking, then smiled. 'I love growing vegetables, m'lady. We had a small glasshouse in Ireland, and I used to grow seedlings and replant them in my parents' garden.'

'Would you be interested in working in the market garden we are developing at Everton Manor, Mick? We are looking for more gardeners at the moment.'

'Oh my Lord, yes, I would, m'lady!'

'Very well Mick, consider yourself employed. Your first task is to clear your possessions from this house, so that it can be cleaned before rent day. Bridget and the children will go back to the Manor with me this morning, and I will send a cart to collect you and your belongings this afternoon.'

Mick, who had never before been spoken to like that by a woman could just stammer 'Yes, m'lady.'

Leaving food for Mick's lunch, Mary and the rest of his family set off towards Everton Manor, stopping briefly at the school to leave a message for Ryan to go home with Jack and Alfie after school. On their arrival at the Manor, Mary introduced Bridget to Clara and Elin. Soon, Bridget and Roisin were taken to the area of the nursery that had been set aside for Elin and Christopher, while Clara took Fergus and Niamh to meet Ruth and Chloe, who were playing in the garden.

Clara was thrilled with the idea of having a couple more children to look after, while Bridget spent time with her baby. Helen quickly organised two adjoining rooms for the Murphy family, after Bridget told her that Fergus and Niamh were still young enough to share a bed. A spare bed had been put in Alfie's and Jack's room for Ryan.

After lunch, Hugh and Mary were in the study when Mary told him about the Murphy family. He was not in the least surprised when she told him that the Murphy family were coming to stay, and that she had offered Mick a job in the vegetable garden.

'I wonder if the Gatehouse would offer the Murphys suitable accommodation Mary. I've never really taken the time to have more than a cursory glance in there. Have you been inside?'

'It's been empty for a long time I think Hugh. When I bought the property I looked through the front door, but have never been inside.'

'Let's go and have a look through it now. It would be ideal for a family of six. Mick would be virtually living on the job, plus it would be a bonus to have people living in the Gatehouse again.'

Hugh pulled Mary to her feet, and after giving her a quick kiss on the cheek, he took the Gatehouse key from the desk drawer, then led her out of the front door to walk up the drive to the front gate. When they entered the empty building, Mary was surprised at the spaciousness of the rooms, but even more so, that despite the layers of dust everywhere, the rooms seemed to be in quite good condition.

The kitchen, dining room, and sitting room were on the ground floor on one side of the arch, with stairs leading up to a large bedroom and a passageway across the gateway, to two upstairs bedrooms and three more rooms downstairs.

Mary was impressed. 'Well, there's certainly plenty of room. Apart from a jolly good clean, do you think there is much to repair, Hugh?'

'No, I don't think so. It would pay to have gas lighting put in, and that stove needs to be replaced. Other than that, I can't see any major repairs. You said that Mick was a carpenter, didn't you Mary?'

'Yes he is, and I'm sure that he would be willing to look through the place with you. I'll get Helen to organise some cleaners from town, to give the place a good scrubbing.'

As they were about to leave, Mike drove the cart carrying the Murphy's possessions through the gateway, and pulled the horses up when he saw Mary and Hugh. 'Hugh, this is Mick Murphy. Mick, this is my fiancé, Sir Hugh Watson.'

As the two men shook hands, Mary continued, 'Mick, Sir Hugh and I were wondering if you and your family would care to live in the Gatehouse, once it is cleaned up.'

Mick looked in disbelief at the imposing arch, with buildings either side of the gates. 'You surely don't mean all of it do you, m'lady?'

'Yes, we do Mick. Why don't you and Sir Hugh have a look through, while I ride to the Manor with Mike? Do you mind Hugh?'

Hugh grinned. 'No, of course not m'lady!'

Mary next saw Hugh when he, Mick, Alfie, Jack, and Ryan walked back down the drive together. Ryan couldn't believe that he was going to be staying in the big house, and then living on the estate.

While Alfie quickly changed into his working clothes, and raced out to help the gardeners, Jack took Ryan down to the kitchen to introduce him to his friend, Mrs Peters. Sitting at the table with a hot cup of tea in his hands, Ryan shyly looked at the cook. 'Thank you very much for all the lunches that you made for me, Mrs Peters. They really gave me the energy to keep up with my schoolwork.'

'That's been a pleasure Ryan.' Looking at the gaunt face, Margaret thought *'At least from now on, he will get three square meals a day.'*

By mid-November, the Gatehouse had been thoroughly cleaned, and the Murphy family had taken up residence. Each morning, Fergus and Niamh would ride to the Manor house with Bob or Will, when they were returning from their town milk run. There, they would play happily with Ruth and Chloe, share lunch with them, then return to the Gatehouse in time for tea with their parents.

Dr Wilson had been pleased with little Roisin's recovery, and had told a relieved Bridget that he expected to remove the cast from the baby's arm in a couple more weeks.

Bridget was also happy to see the change in her husband since their arrival at Everton Manor. No longer too malnourished to be able to do much physical labour, he was now up at daybreak and working like a navvy in the acre plot until dusk.

The plentiful food the family were now eating was certainly helping to increase his stamina, but it was the return of his zest for life that thrilled her. He was playing with the children again, and after the evening meal was making furniture from timber left over from the Manor renovations. He was also back to his vigorous self in bed, which worried Bridget somewhat, as she really didn't want another baby just yet!

Chapter 14

Longmire Estate
Sussex, England
Late November 1888

In late November, the weather turned very cold, wet, and windy. Forced to stay inside one day due to the inclement weather, Mary decided to look through her grandmother's jewellery box that was kept in the wardrobe of her bedroom.

When Mary had first arrived at Longmire Hall, her grandmother's clothes had been packed into trunks, and taken up to the attics, clearing the large room for Mary's use. Her copious amount of jewellery had been kept in Mary's room, but Mary hadn't bothered to look in the jewellery box or in the trunks in the attic.

It had been Polly who had packed the Countess's jewellery, and had remembered the engagement ring and necklace wrapped in tissue paper. When she had spoken to Mary about them, Mary had asked her to bring them to her study, so she had not seen the other jewellery. At a loose end, not even welcome in the kitchen because Mrs Smith and the girls were busy preparing for a special pre-wedding luncheon for the villagers, now that the wedding would be in Lewes, Mary decided to look through her grandmother's jewellery.

Tipping the contents of the box onto her bed, she began to sort the jewellery into piles of rings, necklaces, bracelets, brooches, and headpieces. A sparkling tiara caught Mary's eye, and when she held it up to the light, she realised that it was inlayed with numerous diamonds.

Suddenly, it dawned on Mary that the jewellery in front of her was of high quality, and undoubtedly of great value. Much of it was inlaid with precious stones, and there appeared to be a lot of gold and silver. The Countess's coronet was there too, packed in its own special satin-lined box.

Thoughtfully putting everything back into the box, Mary decided to go up to the attic to look at her grandmother's clothes. Opening a large trunk, Mary removed some paper and found a beautiful brown three-quarter mink coat. On a whim, Mary took it out of the trunk and tried it on. To her surprise, it fitted her perfectly. Delving further into the trunk, Mary found some framed family photos under a lighter mink stole. One photo in particular caught her eye, and she discovered that it was of her mother and her grandmother, standing arm in arm in the rose garden.

Tears clouded Mary's vision for a while as she stared at her mother's smiling face. One of her greatest regrets was that she didn't have a photo of Patricia, and here was one that Mary assumed was taken not long before she disappeared. Clutching the photo to her chest, Mary ran down the stairs to the kitchen. 'Mrs Smith, I know that you are busy, but could I please speak to you for a moment.'

Staring at the photo that Mary held out to her, Mrs Smith sighed then looked at Mary. 'That photo was taken on your mother's eighteenth birthday, m'lady, and both of them were so happy. Then the next day, she disappeared.' The cook gave a sob and wiped her eyes with her apron.

'They were very alike, weren't they?'

'Like two peas in a pod they were. And you look so much like your mother did then. Now you know why I, like others who knew and loved her, were so shocked when we first met you, m'lady.'

'My mother and I used to joke that we could wear each other's clothes. I found a mink coat in a chest in the attic, and it fitted me perfectly. Was that my grandmother's coat or my mother's, Mrs Smith?'

'It was your grandmother's birthday present to you mother, m'lady. Unfortunately, she never had the pleasure of wearing it. The Countess kept it in her wardrobe in her bedroom, but it has never been worn.'

'Thank you, Mrs Smith. I think I shall wear it instead.' Mary left the kitchen and made her way up to her bedroom, where she placed the framed photo on her bedside table.

The weather improved in the latter part of November, and the weekend before the wedding, a special church service was held in the village church where the vicar blessed the impending union of their Countess and Sir Hugh Watson. Not a wedding ceremony as such, but an important occasion for Mary's tenants to feel part of their forthcoming nuptials. All were invited to a banquet that evening in the Longmire Hall ballroom, where they were treated as special guests by Mary, Hugh, and their staff.

Mary and Hugh left for Everton Manor the next morning, accompanied again by Amy, who had now become Mary's maid, and who was to assist with dressing her in her wedding dress. Mary had become quite fond of the young girl, finding her to have a quick mind and a wicked sense of humour. She was aware that while Amy was capable of being an entertaining conversationalist, and often chatted quite freely with her, she always called her m'lady and never overstepped her station.

It had been agreed that Mary and Hugh should leave Longmire Hall early, in case the weather changed again, and made travel to Lewes difficult. Hugh was to stay with the Lyons prior to the wedding, while Mary was staying at Everton Manor. The staff were excited getting ready for the big day, and also to be looking after the guests who would be staying at the Manor. Hugh's parents and Paul were to arrive midweek, and two elderly ladies, who had known the old Countess well and had been Patricia's godmothers, were invited following a private message from the Palace.

Both ladies were in their eighties, and had been courtiers to the Queen until recently. Now retired and living together in a cottage on the Sandringham Estate, Lady Stella and Lady Bella had everyone in stitches with their anecdotes of the royal court. The two ladies were thrilled to meet Mary, and were only too ready to regale her with stories of her mother as a young girl. Neither had a good word for David; as Stella said tersely 'Emma should have drowned that brat at birth!'

Much to Mary's surprise, Stella and Bella asked her if they could visit Longmire Hall for 'old times' sake. Apparently, they had been frequent guests of her grandmother, and knew the place well. Before arrangements could be made for a coach to take them, the two octogenarians had hitched a lift with Bob and Toby on the milk cart! Wrapped up in large horse rugs, they had a very pleasant ride, keeping Bob and Toby entertained with their recollections.

Mrs Smith couldn't believe it when her kitchen was invaded by the two elderly ladies, who remembered her cooking all too well. However, once she overcame her self-consciousness at entertaining ladies who had only known her as a below stairs servant, they had a wonderful time reminiscing.

The ladies Stella and Bella stayed at Longmire until the afternoon before the wedding, when all the staff travelled to Everton Manor. The coach and all the estate carriages were used to transport the Longmire staff, so all horses were harnessed up. James enlisted Toby's help to lead Gem from the back of the carriage that he was driving, so that she wouldn't be left alone in the stables.

Because the entire staff was attending the wedding, and probably staying away for two nights, the blacksmith, and a couple of other villagers were staying in the men's quarters to guard the Hall and surrounds.

Tess travelled with the staff as well, leaving Bob and Will to milk that night. Bob would stay for the wedding after his early morning milk run, and return to Home Farm following the ceremony.

It was a very jovial party that descended on Everton Manor mid-afternoon, where after some afternoon tea, rooms were allocated and beds made up.

Dinner that evening was served to Mary and her guests by a mixture of her staff from Longmire Hall and Everton Manor, who enjoyed showing off their formal waitressing skills. Then the staff ate in the staff dining hall in two sittings, served by each other.

Hugh returned to the Lyons', after spending the day with Mary and his family. They had been to see Longmire Hall, and had spent some time in Lewes, shopping and looking through some of Lewes Castle.

Clara and Elin had their meals as usual in the nursery with Ruth and Chloe, not just to supervise their food intake, but also to try to teach the girls some table manners. Once the girls realised that their meals would be regular and filling, they were happy to chew their food more, rather than grabbing and gulping as they'd had to do at home. They were also both quite willing to follow the two grownups use of cutlery and table manners.

Clara was in her element, looking after the two young girls, and was becoming very fond of them both. Each day, their trust in her grew, as did their love for her. Christopher was gaining weight and was far more alert, much to Clara's and Elin's relief. He was thriving on the formula Elin had brought and was also very interested in eating the variety of soft food sent up from the kitchen. Margaret's experience in preparing nourishing baby food for her previous employer's baby, and Elin's medical knowledge, resulted in his meals being both nourishing and appetising.

CHAPTER 15

Everton Manor
Lewes
Sussex, England
December 1888

The day of the wedding dawned fine but cold. Amy tapped on Mary's door, bringing her a cup of tea. 'Lady Mary, when you are married, will I still bring up cups of tea for you and Sir Hugh, first thing in the morning?'

Mary looked at Amy in surprise. 'Yes please Amy, though it would be best to wait until one of us calls for you to enter!' Blushing, Amy beat a hasty retreat to the door, while Mary smothered her laughter in her pillow.

Realisation that tonight would be her wedding night suddenly hit Mary, and she thought, '*Tomorrow morning I'll be waking up with Hugh in bed beside me!*' She began to remember remarks that she had heard from some ladies about their revulsion of being with their husbands, but then Tess's sensible advice wiped those thoughts from her mind. 'When you love each other as much as you two obviously do my darling, just relax, trust each other, and enjoy yourselves.'

Mary puzzled everyone when she entered the kitchen dressed in her riding habit, grabbed a piece of toast, and headed for the door. Mrs Smith, who was helping Margaret prepare breakfast, stared at her young mistress. 'You can't go riding on your wedding morning, m'lady!'

'Why not, Mrs Smith? It's a beautiful morning, and Gem is waiting in the stables.'

'You just can't, m'lady. It's not the done thing, not on your wedding day.'

'I'll be back before you know it!'

Mary disappeared out the door, Scruffy at her heels. When she reached the stables, Gem was waiting in her stall, already saddled, and James was there too with his horse.

Surprised, Mary stopped at the stall, and James smiled at her. 'Good morning, Lady Mary. We assumed that you would like to take Gem out for an early morning ride. However, as we are so close to the township, Robert has instructed me to accompany you. You never know who might be up and about at this time of the day.'

Mary was touched by their consideration. 'Thank you James, company this morning would be greatly appreciated.'

As they rode away from the stables, Mary noticed that all the men from both properties were either grooming the horses, or polishing the vehicles and harness. All turned and called out 'Good morning Lady Mary,' as they passed.

Mary laughed. 'Good morning, gentlemen. If you groom those horses much longer, they'll have no hair left!'

Mrs Smith, Tess, and Clara watched as Mary and James cantered away from the Manor towards the back of the property. Tess was nonplussed. 'Why is she doing such a reckless thing on her wedding day?'

Clara answered her. 'When Mary was growing up, she always went for a ride before any event where she had to perform before a crowd. It was her way of calming her nerves, I guess,'

Mrs Smith replied 'Well, there will certainly be a crowd in the church today, so she has cause to be nervous! I can't say that I've noticed her to be nervous, but she does go out on Gem a lot, and seems to do a lot of thinking when she is out. Polly says that quite often she will go straight to her study when she returns, and spend time writing notes.'

An hour later, the ladies were relieved to hear Mary and James return to the stable, and not much later, Mary and Scruffy entered the kitchen, both ready for a hearty breakfast.

Following a long hot bath, Mary was kept entertained for an hour by her two elderly ex-courtiers, who regaled her with more stories of her mother's early life, then she was taken up to her room by Tess and Amy to dress for her wedding.

All the staff and visitors were transported to the church an hour before the wedding. While Elin remained in the nursery with Ruth, Chloe, and Christopher, two police constables patrolled the Manor grounds while everyone was in Lewes.

While Clara and Meg made sure that the children were correctly dressed, Tess and Amy dressed Mary. Tess was amazed how calm Mary was and thought, 'Clara's statement about her early morning ride must be true.'

When Mary walked down the stairs, resplendent in her flowing white satin gown, with her grandmother's sparkling diamond tiara holding her veil on her styled hair, and the sapphire necklace around her neck, Gordon, waiting in the hallway, could just stare in amazement at the radiant young lady walking down the stairs towards him.

Gordon bowed as Mary reached the bottom of the staircase. 'Mary, my dear, you look absolutely exquisite. Your parents would be so proud of you. I am truly honoured to be walking you down the aisle this afternoon in their stead.'

Taking her arm, he led Mary into the sitting room to wait while Clara, Tess, and Meg, plus the four children, set off in three carriages for the church, with Tess holding Mary's train wrapped in a sheet on her knees. Fifteen minutes before the hour, Gordon and Mary stepped out of the front door to where Robert, dressed in his formal coachman's uniform, was waiting with her coach.

The vehicle gleamed and the crest had been repainted, while the two black horses looked magnificent with their shining coats and gleaming harnesses and brasses. Each horse had a large white plume attached to the top of their bridle.

James, also dressed in his finest uniform, handed Mary up into the coach, then shut the door once Gordons had seated himself carefully away from Mary's dress. As the coach progressed into Lewes they were met by two policemen on horseback, who escorted the coach through the town. People stopped and waved, and the men removed their hats and bowed as the coach slowly passed by.

Mary was stunned by the display of respect being shown towards her. 'I had no idea it would be like this.'

'Mary my dear, you sadly underestimate the esteem in which you are held in this community. It is not just your tenants who have benefited since you became the Countess in this county.'

Before Mary could reply, the coach stopped in front of the church. James waited for Gordon to alight, before assisting Mary to step down from the coach. As she thanked him, Robert leant down from the driver's seat and said softly, 'God bless, Lady Mary.' Flashing him a brilliant smile Mary turned, gathered her dress, and walked into the nave to be greeted by Tess, Jane, and Sally. Mac was with Sally, having travelled to Lewes earlier with the Longmire Hall staff, while Alfie and Jack were already in the church waiting near the altar with Hugh and Paul.

Quickly Tess hooked the long train onto the waistband of Mary's dress, spread it out, and then stepped around to face Mary. 'We are all so very proud of you, my love,' whispered Tess, kissing Mary lightly on the cheek, then she carefully brought the veil down over Mary's face, and walked to stand beside the two beaming flower girls.

When the organ began to play the wedding march, Gordon tucked Mary's left arm into the crook of his right arm. 'Ready my dear?'

When Mary nodded and replied, 'Yes,' Tess said, 'Off you go girls, just like we practiced.' Jane, Sally and Mac walked slowly down the aisle, followed by Mary and Gordon, then Tess who walked behind the train. Heads turned as the girls walked past, Jane holding Sally's right hand, while Sally's left hand held the short handle attached to the soft leather harness that Mac was wearing. He walked beside her, looking straight ahead, taking no notice of the large crowd on either side of him.

As Mary and Gordon walked behind the girls Mary noticed some of the Longmire villagers were sitting in the back rows. Recognising them with a slight nod, Mary looked over the girls' heads, to see Hugh waiting at the end of the nave aisle with Paul and the two boys. Both men looked resplendent in their black tailcoats, over dove-grey waistcoats and pinstripe trousers. Alfie and Jack, self-conscious at wearing long trousers for the first time, wore dark grey trousers and black jackets.

As they progressed towards the front of the church, Mary was pleased to see that the staff from both houses were seated behind the front rows on either side of the aisle. Hugh's parents sat on the front right-hand pew with the Everton Manor staff behind them, while Aunt Clara sat on the left with Celia Lyons and Bob Telford, leaving room for Gordon, Tess, and the two flower girls to sit during the service. The Longmire staff sat behind Clara, with Stella and Bella in their midst. The two boys had been adamant that they would stay with Paul throughout the ceremony.

When Mary stopped beside Hugh, and Gordon carefully lifted her veil away from her face, Hugh grinned and whispered, 'Thank goodness it is you under there my love!' making Mary giggle.

For Mary, the ceremony passed in a blur, though she remembered making her vows, and exchanging rings with Hugh. Then the Bishop announced 'I now pronounce you husband and wife.' Hugh leant down and kissed her gently on the mouth, before they were led into a side room to sign the register in front of the Bishop, Paul, and Tess.

Hugh was thrilled when he saw that Mary had signed Lady Mary Emma Evans Watson under her title. Mary looked up and gave him a wide smile. 'I'm your wife as well as a Countess now Hugh.'

As Hugh and Mary walked arm in arm out of the church, the bells were pealing, making conversation a little difficult. When the bells finally stopped, Robert brought the coach to the church yard for Mary and Hugh to travel through the cheering crowds near the church, and along the route out of town back to Everton Manor.

A procession of private and hired vehicles followed the coach.

CHAPTER 16

Mary awoke early the next morning to see Hugh lying next to her, smiling as he watched her open her eyes. He gently moved a strand of hair from Mary's face. 'Good morning, Mrs Watson. Happy?'

'Deliriously so!' Remembering their first night together, Mary thought how Tess's wise advice had been so true!

Following their reception, Mary and Hugh had been driven to Lewes station, from where they travelled to Brighton. Hugh had booked the honeymoon suite at the Old Ship Hotel, right on the Brighton seafront, in the name of Mr and Mrs Watson. Before the wedding, the couple had decided to try to spend their honeymoon as anonymously as possible. 'This might be the only time you can be plain Mrs Watson, Mary.'

The young couple spent a blissful week in Brighton, at times wandering around the town or strolling along the beach, so happy to be able to be a couple in public, without the restrictions of the past. But a good deal of their time was spent in their suite, truly getting to know one another.

Reluctant though they were to end such an idyllic start to their married life, both Mary and Hugh understood the need to get back to their real life, with Christmas only three weeks away, and Hugh had meetings scheduled with a number of farmers wishing to employ his services. Eating breakfast in their suite on the final morning of their honeymoon, Mary looked at her husband. 'Hugh, my darling, you have made me the happiest woman in the world. I had no idea making love could be so exhilarating and gratifying.'

'You are magnificent, my love. I think we were made for each other, I truly do.' Hugh clasped her hand and led her back into the bedroom.

Back in Lewes later in the morning, Hugh grimaced as they were greeted by their formal titles, and whispered, 'Goodbye Mrs Watson,' to which Mary softly replied, 'Whenever we're alone in our bedroom Mr Watson, I'll definitely be your wife, not the Countess!'

Everyone was delighted to greet the new couple when the cab drew up at the front door at Everton Manor. Aunt Clara was pleased to see her niece looking so happy and relaxed as she walked arm in arm with Hugh through the front door. Clara joined Mary and Hugh for lunch, and filled them in with news since the wedding. She was thrilled to tell them that all three children appeared to be happy in their new surroundings, and were putting on weight and looking much healthier.

Mary could see that Clara was becoming very fond of the children, but could also sense that her aunt was concerned about something. Hugh had discerned the same thing, so while they had a moment to themselves in the garden he broached the subject. 'Mary, do you think Clara is anxious about something?'

'Yes, I do Hugh. I know that she is concerned about the children's future, but I think there's something else. I wonder if she's worried about her future as well.'

'Has Clara said anything to you about returning to Australia?'

'No, we haven't spoken about Australia since she told us what happened with Graham. And I must confess, I haven't discussed her future with her. I've just let her settle in, and I guess have just taken it for granted that she will stay here with us.'

'Does she have a personal income of any sort, or money saved for her future?'

Mary felt quite ashamed. 'To be honest Hugh, I've never enquired about Clara's financial situation. She came to live on the farm after her husband died, but I don't know how she was left financially, nor do I know if she was paid for the work that she did in the house. I doubt it, as money was very short.'

'So, she could be getting rather worried about not only where she will live, but also what she will live on.'

That evening, after dinner, Hugh went to the study to read mail that had been delivered while they were in Brighton. Mary sat with Clara in the sitting room and decided to come straight to the point. 'Clara, you seem to be worried about something. Is it anything that Hugh and I can help you with?'

Clara looked startled for a moment, then looked at her niece. 'You continue to be a very perceptive person Mary. Yes, I'm worried about where I'm to live, and what I can do to earn enough to live on. I'm very grateful for your help in travelling to England for your wedding and for your hospitality, but I can't just be a permanent guest living off your generosity.'

Going to her aunt, Mary gave her a big hug. 'Oh Clara, I would love you to stay with us, but I do understand what you mean. Firstly, do you want to stay in England, or would you rather go back to Australia?'

Clara looked sadly at her niece. 'Even if I had the money to pay to sail back to Australia, there's nothing there for me now. I would dearly love to live near you, but I would need to seek employment so that I can have an independent income.'

'I understand Clara. However, you are certainly not overstaying your welcome. The work you're doing with those three children has been marvellous. Worth way above and beyond any bed and board you might think you owe.'

'I have become very fond of them Mary, and I think they are fond of me. I really hope the trust the two girls are developing in Elin and myself is not dashed when their father returns to port.'

'I've asked my shipping manager to find out where Mr Green's ship is at the moment Clara. Please try not to worry about them. I will do all I can to keep them out of harm's way, and will also help you in any way I can.'

'Thank you so much Mary, I shall sleep more soundly tonight. Goodnight, my dear.' She kissed Mary on the cheek, then walked out of the room. Mary soon followed her aunt out of the room, and went to the study where Hugh was just putting his pen in its holder. He flashed her a cheeky grin. 'What great timing, my love. Are you ready for bed?'

'I thought you would never ask!'

As they walked arm in arm towards the staircase, they passed Helen. 'Goodnight, m'lady, Sir. Sleep well.'

'Goodnight Helen.'

'I'd say those two had a very enjoyable honeymoon Arthur,' said Helen quietly to her husband who had just entered the hall.

'They're a wonderful couple, and also make a great team. I don't think the estates will fall into decline while those two are at the helm.'

The next morning, the kitchen staff were surprised to see Mary and Hugh up and dressed, having an early morning cup of tea before going for a pre-breakfast ride. Although Gem and Hugh's mare Ebony were back at Longmire, there were a couple of riding horses in the stable. Before they returned, a message from Gordon was delivered, asking if it might be possible to meet Mary and Hugh at his office before their return to Longmire Hall.

When they arrived at the solicitor's office, they were told that following Mary's request to find Ruth, Chloe, and Christopher's father, Gordon had received news from Charles Browning that Mr Green's ship had been lost with no survivors during a hurricane in the Caribbean Sea about a month previously. Having travelled to Reading to inform the Prison Governor of the tragedy, Mr Lyons was in the Governor's office, when the Governor informed Mrs Green of her husband's death. 'She broke down sobbing at the news, so both the Governor and I were totally unprepared for her outburst when the Governor told her that she would have sole responsibility for the three children.'

She screamed 'Not bloody likely! You aint shoving responsibility for them three pathetic brats onto me. They aint mine and never were. The marriage was a sham.' Mrs Green stopped when she realised what she had just uttered. When she refused to say more, Mrs Green was threatened with time in solitary confinement until she explained what she meant about a sham marriage.

'Me and Fred Green had sometimes talked about marriage, so when his ship was due to sail the next day, and he was on a farewell drinking binge, I arranged for a friend to pretend to be a travelling priest, who had the authority to carry out home weddings. Too drunk to realise what he was doing, Fred signed a phoney marriage certificate and, more importantly, a letter saying that his new wife was to receive his wages while he was at sea. The next morning, my friend and I took the hungover fool to his ship, where he was dragged on board by some sailors, and dumped on the deck as the ship was made ready to sail.'

Mary was horrified. 'So that means those poor children are now orphans!'

'I'm afraid so, my dear. Margaret Giles, the prisoner's real name, has given the Governor access to the sham marriage certificate, and also a letter stating that she claims no legal responsibility to the children, now or in the future.'

'The poor little mites. They've been progressing so well with Aunt Clara and Elin. Dr Wilson has been amazed at Christopher's progress, but he wouldn't survive long in an institute. Could they possibly stay at Everton Manor for a while longer, do you think Gordon?'

'There's no need to move the children just yet Mary. I'm sure this will take some time to be sorted out. There's something else before you go Mary. While you were away, your tenant in Rose Cottage informed me that her brother has asked her to move to his home in Brentwood, a town north of London. Would you like me to start looking for a new tenant?'

'I think we should wait till she moves out, then see if any work needs doing, rather than putting someone else in straight away. I must see Gwen before she leaves. Do we have time today Hugh?'

'I should think so my love, providing you keep the visit short.' Hugh winked at Gordon.

When they arrived at the cottage, they found Gwen in the middle of packing clothes into boxes. While Hugh went to check the stables, Mary helped Gwen pack while they chatted. 'I can't thank you enough for allowing me to rent this cottage after my Tom was drowned, Lady Mary. The children and I have loved being here for the past two years. However, my brother who is a doctor in Brentwood, has asked me to be his housekeeper. The children and I will live in a cottage at the back of the house, which will give the children more freedom than they would have living in rooms in the house.'

'I understand completely Gwen. You and the children have been excellent tenants. Now that I have Everton Manor so close to Lewes, I shan't be using the cottage as before, so your timing is perfect if I decide to sell it.'

CHAPTER 17

Longmire Estate,
Sussex, England
December 1888

Finally, late in the afternoon, Mary and Hugh arrived back at Longmire Hall. All the staff were waiting at the front steps to welcome them home. After the couple had greeted each individual, plus Scruffy who was ecstatic at having Mary home again, Mary and Hugh walked towards the front door.

Suddenly Hugh bent down, swept Mary into his arms, and to everyone's delight, carried her over the threshold. When he put Mary down in the hall, he turned to Polly and winked. 'She hasn't put on too much weight!'

Dinner was a jovial affair, with everyone sharing their news with the young couple, who shared some news about their stay in Brighton before the conversation turned to preparations for Christmas.

The next morning, there was a gentle tap on the bedroom door. 'Would you like a cup of tea, m'lady, Sir?'

Mary smothered a chuckle. 'Yes please Amy. Come in.'

Amy entered carrying a tray with a pot of tea and two cups and saucers, averting her eyes until she realised that Hugh was standing at the window, wearing his thick woollen dressing gown.

Mary and Hugh had decided while in Brighton that they would ignore the upper-class custom of husband and wife having separate bedrooms. Polly had been informed of the arrangement before their return to Longmire Hall, so Hugh's clothing had been temporarily placed in the maid's room next to Mary's room. Plans for a new changing room and clothes storage were being developed for the bedroom beyond Mary's bathroom.

'Amy, would it embarrass you terribly if Sir Hugh and I were both in bed when you come into our room in the morning?

Amy thought for a moment, then smiled. 'No, I don't think so, m'lady. I'll just make sure that I wait until you tell me to enter. Will you be down for breakfast?'

Hugh and Mary both laughed. 'Away with you, Amy. I think we should make it downstairs in time for breakfast!'

Later that week Mary rode over to Home Farm, where Tess was delighted to hear a lot more about the honeymoon than everyone else had been told. She was thrilled when Mary coyly confided that she and Hugh both thoroughly enjoyed being in bed together, and thanked her for her earlier advice on what to expect.

'Your wedding dress is the talk of the town Mary. When it became known that Katherine made it, she has been inundated with requests for new dresses. It looks like her dream of opening a dressmaking premises in town might be realised.'

'Tess, do you think Katherine and Joseph might be interested in moving to Rose Cottage in Lewes? Gwen is leaving to housekeep for her brother, so it will be empty before Christmas.'

'You know Mary, they just might be. Katherine told me that she is worried about Joseph cycling to work each day, now that winter is setting in. If I remember correctly, the leather business he works for is just a block away from the cottage.' Tess paused for a moment. 'Just what are you scheming now Mary?'

'Well, I've been wondering, if the Dower House was free I could offer it to Clara to make her home. She's worried about her future living arrangements and income. She's also become extremely fond of the three children, and the two girls are fond of her and are learning to trust her. Now that it has been revealed that they are orphans, I thought I might ask Clara if she would like to look after them on a more permanent basis.'

'There are lot of pieces that need to fall into place, Mary. Think carefully before you act, as a lot of people's feelings and futures are involved.'

As it turned out, when Mary arrived at Everton Manor a couple of days later, Katherine approached her, to tell her of the many requests for dresses that she had received from ladies in Lewes. Sitting in the morning room with Mary, Katherine was quite nervous. 'Our family is so indebted to Your Ladyship for your kindness and generosity in allowing us to rent the Dower House, and for encouraging the three of us to make the most of the opportunities offered to us. But Lady Mary, would you mind if we looked for a place to rent in Lewes, where I could set up my own dressmaking business?'

Mary looked at Katherine, and could see how excited she was. 'Of course I don't mind Katherine. My wedding dress was a wonderful example of your dressmaking skills, and I think that you could have a lucrative business, once you get established. Katherine, I have a cottage in Lewes that you and Joseph might be interested in looking at. It's quite close to the town centre, and is also not far from Joseph's workplace.'

'Oh Lady Mary, I would love to see it. Joseph is really busy with Christmas nearly upon us, and won't have time to look for rental properties until the New Year.'

'Why don't we go and have a look now Katherine? The previous tenant left a few days ago, so it's empty at the moment.'

Katherine stopped at the gate of Rose Cottage, and stared in delight at the lovely thatched building. 'Oh what a pretty cottage. It must look a picture when all those roses are in bloom.' When they entered Rose Cottage, Mary showed Katherine the large kitchen and scullery, then the dining and sitting rooms on the ground floor and the three bedrooms upstairs. Katherine couldn't believe that there was also a bathroom with running water and an indoor water closet upstairs. She had become accustomed to such luxury at the Dower House, but hadn't expected the same in a rented home. Rose Cottage had gas lighting in all rooms, and the kitchen had a gas stove, as well as the coal-fired range.

There was a large back garden area with a vegetable garden, small orchard, and a double stable, with attached groom's quarters, and access to the rear lane.

'To start with, you could set up the back bedroom as your sewing room Katherine, and use the sitting room as your showroom and fitting area.'

Poor Katherine was speechless, so to give her time to gather her thoughts, Mary put the kettle on and made a pot of tea, using tea and milk that Margaret had put in a basket for them, along with a couple of slices of cake.

'Actually Katherine, what would you think of going into partnership with Sir Hugh and me? If we set the business up and built rooms to the side of the cottage, you could lease the whole property, and run the business as you wish. Mary placed the key in Katherine's hand. 'Here's the key, so you and Joseph can look through the cottage together, and discuss my proposal.'

After lunch, Mary told Clara the news about the children's father and their so-called mother's rejection of them. 'I think it would be best to speak to Ruth first Mary. There's quite an old head on those young shoulders.'

Not sure how much a seven-year-old would understand about the situation, Mary agreed to let Clara do the talking when she and Ruth met Mary in her study. Clara sat beside Ruth near the fire and held her hand. 'I'm afraid I have some sad news about your father Ruth.'

'He's dead aint he, sorry, isn't he, Aunt Clara?'

'Yes my dear, I'm afraid he is. His ship sank in a storm.' Clara hugged the sobbing young girl tightly.

Suddenly, Ruth pushed her away. 'Oh my Gawd, that now means that the old witch he married is all we have to look after us, and she hates us to death.'

Listening to the distress in the little girl's voice, Mary sat beside her, 'No Ruth, you will have nothing more to worry about from that lady. She wasn't really married to your father.'

'So, we don't have neither a Ma nor a Pa now! Does that mean we will have to live in the workhouse now?'

Clara looked in anguish at Mary, who took a deep breath. 'I sincerely hope not Ruth. For the moment, you will all remain here with Aunt Clara, while I try to arrange a more permanent home for all three of you.'

Ruth turned to Clara. 'Aunt Clara, please don't tell Chloe yet about our father. I don't want her to worry too.'

'My darling, try not to worry too much. I'm sure that Lady Mary will work something good out of this.'

When Clara returned from taking Ruth back to the nursery, Mary was staring into the fire, deep in thought. As Clara sat in the chair opposite her, she looked at her aunt. 'Clara, I know that you have grown very fond of those three children and enjoy looking after them. Would you, by any chance, be interested in making that a more permanent arrangement?'

Clara sat dumfounded, staring at her niece. 'What on earth do you mean Mary?'

'As you know, I'm Alfie, Jack, Jane, and Sally's legal guardian. They are all orphans, the boys from the workhouse and the girls from the streets of London. Would you consider putting your name forward to be the legal guardian for those three upstairs? With my recommendation and support, I think it could be arranged.'

'I would love to Mary, but how could I, with no home or income?'

'Just give me a little time to sort things out Clara, and you give a bit of thought to the implications of such an undertaking before you definitely say yes.'

Looking at her niece, Clara saw before her a self-assured, accomplished young woman, so different from the grieving girl she had waved goodbye to nearly three years ago in Australia. Instead of being overwhelmed by the authority, privileges, and wealth that had been bestowed upon her, Mary appeared to have thrived and developed confidence in herself, and a passion to use her position to help those less fortunate than herself. Clara had no doubt that when Mary set her mind to it, arrangements to suit the children and herself would fall into place. And to think that she was not yet twenty-one.

With Christmas rapidly approaching everyone was extremely busy preparing for the festive season. It had been decided that Mary, Hugh, and their four children would have Christmas dinner at Longmire Hall, then travel to Everton Manor to dine there with the staff on Christmas evening.

The children were looking forward to having two weeks' holidays at Longmire Hall. While they enjoyed staying at Everton Manor during the week, Longmire Hall was still home. Mary and Hugh had both attended the school Christmas concert to watch the children participate in the carol singing, and the nativity play. Mary thought that Jack and Ryan were wonderful lambs!

Mary had also been invited to present the prizes at the end of year awards night. Although the headmaster was wary of crossing swords with Mary again, he was well aware of the prestige to the school of having the Countess as the principal guest. Alfie, Jack, Jane, and Ryan were thrilled to see Mary up on stage, dressed in all her finery, in front of the whole school. Usually, when she attended school functions, she dressed in a much less imposing manner. For the children, it was confirmation to their peers that their Mary really was a Countess and a Peer of the Realm.

Mary, Hugh, and the four children travelled to Longmire Hall the following day. Meg was taking some time off to visit her family for Christmas, confident that Sally was much more capable of coping without her constant company. A large fir tree had been placed in the front hall that morning, ready for the children to decorate. By the end of the day, with a little help from Mary and Hugh, and a degree of hindrance from Scruffy, the tree was a mass of tinsel and decorations.

The days leading up to Christmas were as hectic as ever. The kitchen was a hive of activity, and Jack was in his element there, while Alfie helped as much as he could in the vegetable garden. Both girls helped the twins with their duties, Sally cheerfully following directions from Sissy and Julie.

Mary and Hugh spent a day visiting Glendale, the third and largest Longmire Estate farm, situated in the higher country, where tenants Thomas and Paul Grey ran large flocks of Suffolk and Border Leicester sheep. Hugh, in his position of estate supervisor, had been a regular visitor to the high farm, but Mary hadn't seen the brothers for a few months.

At first, totally overawed by visits from the Countess, the brothers were now much more at ease, though still very respectful in Mary's company. Shyly, Thomas said, 'Congratulations, Lady Mary and Sir

Hugh. Paul and I were very pleased to hear the news of your wedding.' Paul then handed them each a beautiful sheepskin coat, which to Mary's delight, fitted them perfectly.

Mary in turn, gave the men a large hamper of food after Hugh had removed it from the pack horse that he'd led from Longmire Hall. Each man was also given a new pair of leather boots.

As usual, the two shaggy sheepdogs gave Mary an enthusiastic welcome, and happily followed her as their owners proudly showed Mary and Hugh around their barn full of pens of sheep.

Mary was surprised when Thomas invited them into the small thatched cottage for a warm drink. Usually, the men were hesitant to invite Mary into their home, but when she entered the living room, it was warmed by a large fire and was very neat and tidy. To her amazement, an older woman entered the room, carrying a tray with four steaming mugs. Placing the tray on a side table, the lady turned to Mary and gave a slight curtsey. 'It is an honour to meet you, Lady Mary. My brothers have told me a lot about you.' She turned to Hugh. 'Congratulations to you too, Sir Hugh.' Thomas stepped forward. 'Lady Mary, this is our sister Mabel, who has come to visit us for Christmas.'

'It's lovely to meet you Mabel. Be careful that these two don't get too used to you looking after them, or they mightn't let you leave!'

Startled, Mabel looked at her elder brother, who grinned. 'It has crossed our minds, m'lady. It would be wonderful for us all to be together again, but it would be too cramped. Paul is sleeping in the barn at the moment so Mabel has a bed.'

When they were about to leave, Mary took Thomas aside. 'Thomas, were you serious about wishing that Mabel could live here with you and Paul?'

'Yes, m'lady, Mabel would be in her element up here with us and the sheep. She and her husband Hector, were tenant farmers near Horsham until his death five years ago. Mabel went to live with our mother and looked after her until she died earlier this year, and now she's living alone in the big house. She is very lonely and would love come up here to live with Paul and me'

Mary turned to Hugh. 'Do you think it would be possible to build an extra room onto the cottage after Christmas Hugh?'

'I'm sure it would be Mary. There are men in the village desperate for work at this time of the year, and we could ask Mick Murphy to oversee the job. He's already shown himself to be a skilled carpenter.'

'What a great idea. Well Thomas, do you think Paul would survive sleeping in the barn for a little longer?' Mary grinned at the stunned look on the weathered face. 'I'm sure he will, m'lady. We will take turns. Thank you so much.' Thomas gave Mary a slight bow.

Leaving Thomas to excitedly inform his siblings of Mary's offer, Mary and Hugh rode out of the yard wearing their new coats, leading the pack horse with their other coats rolled up and strapped to the pack saddle. Turning to Mary Hugh smiled. 'You can't help yourself, can you my love?'

'What in the world do you mean Hugh?'

Hugh leant over to kiss his wife. 'Helping to solve other people's problems.'

'Well, I don't like to see people suffer Hugh. I get far more pleasure helping people who I feel will benefit from my support, than from spending money on frivolous things and swanning around expecting everyone to kowtow to me. As far as I'm concerned, the reason I ended up with this title, and the fortune that goes with it, is to help others not as fortunate as I am. I don't think I could live with myself, if I just sat back and expected everyone to do things for me.'

'That's one of the many things I love about you, my darling, your selflessness.' Her proud husband leant over to kiss her again. 'You certainly are a very caring Countess.'

The next few days Mary and Hugh spent visiting Home Farm and the boys working on Farm Two, plus all of the villagers. They also made plenty of time to spend with the children, riding around the estate, helping to make Christmas decorations, wrapping presents, and preparing stockings to hang on the mantelpiece.

Katherine and Joseph accepted Mary's offer of Rose Cottage, and moved there, with the help of the grooms and gardeners. Arthur and Helen had been given Christmas Day off to spend with his parents and Toby in their new home.

Mary and Hugh rode to Everton Manor, and took Clara through the Dower House, on the pretext that they were checking the empty building. As they were leaving the house, Mary turned to Clara. 'Would you like to move in here Clara, and make the Dower House your home from now on?' Speechless, Clara stared at her niece, then at Hugh. 'I would love to Mary. If I gain custody of the children, it will be an ideal home for them.' She hugged Mary tightly. 'I knew that you would come up with a suitable solution my dear. Thank you so much.'

On Christmas Eve the whole family, plus the entire Longmire staff, attended the midnight service in the village church. After wishing everyone a Merry Christmas, they all walked back to the Hall, had a hot cup of cocoa, and retired to bed.

Christmas morning, the children were up bright and early, ready to open their stockings. Hugh and Mary quickly made their way down to the kitchen to put the kettle on, and had tea ready for Sissy, Julie, and Amy who were usually first down to the kitchen.

While the girls gratefully drank their tea, Mary and Hugh took trays of tea and toast to Mrs Smith and Polly. Both were delighted to have a little longer in bed, although Mrs Smith said that she had a lot to do before lunch. Back down in the kitchen, Jack, Sissy, and Julie were busy cooking breakfast for everyone.

Due to the need to be at Everton Manor for the evening meal, Christmas dinner at Longmire Hall was served in the dining room before midday. Much to everyone's delight, Hugh and Mary played their part as Master and Mistress of the household, sitting at either end of the long table. Hugh skilfully carved the poultry, while Bob Telford was invited to carve the other roasts. The women took turns to serve different dishes, while the men served the wine. Tess Telford sat midway down the table, and watched with satisfaction as the happy couple smiled at each other from either end of the table.

All too quickly, it was time to leave; Mary, Hugh, the two girls, and Mac were inside the coach, with the two boys huddled under a thick horse blanket on the driver's seat with Robert. Mary yawned as the coach pulled away from the Hall. 'I feel awful leaving the staff with all those dishes, although, at the moment I don't think I could lift a dish, let alone wash it. That was a wonderful dinner. How are we going to do justice to a similar meal in a few hours?'

Mary and the girls were all fast asleep before the coach went through the estate gateway, and slept until Hugh dug Mary in the ribs as they passed under the gateway arch at Everton Manor.

Clara was thrilled to see them all, but particularly Mary as, like her niece, it was the first Christmas she had spent with a relation since Mary had left Australia. She had spent most of the day looking after the girls and Christopher, plus the four younger Murphy children until Mick collected everyone, Christopher included, to take them to the Gatehouse, where he and Katherine would look after them until after breakfast the next morning.

Elin had returned home to Wales for Christmas, and would return in the early New Year. While Christopher's condition was greatly improved, Dr Wilson felt that it would be wise for Elin to stay on for a while longer. Elin and Will Telford were thrilled to hear this, as they were becoming very fond of each other, following their frequent meetings when he now did all the morning milk runs.

As at Longmire Hall, the Everton Manor staff shared the serving roles, and the kitchen staff provided an excellent meal. At the end of the evening, all the staff moved to the kitchen to share the washing up, plus another bottle of wine. After the children were put to bed, Ryan again in the boy's room, Mary and Hugh decided to retire to their bedroom, where they agreed that the evening meal had been a great success.

CHAPTER 18

Longmire Estate
Sussex, England
December 1888

When the children woke up the next morning, they discovered that it had snowed throughout the night, and everything outside was covered by a thick layer of snow. After breakfast, they all went out and frolicked in the snow, then proceeded to make a large snowman. Hugh had given them an old hat to put on its head, and Arthur had found an old scarf. With a carrot nose and two plums for eyes, it looked quite smart.

At lunchtime it began to snow again, heavy enough to keep them indoors until mid-afternoon. Keen to be outside again, they all wrapped up in coats, hats, scarves, mittens, and boots before trooping out into a white wonderland. Their snowman had a thick new coating of snow, so Jane took Sally over to pat the soft snow onto the snowman. When they stood back to admire their handiwork, Jack playfully tossed a snowball at Alfie, who returned one with glee. Soon, snowballs were flying all over the place.

Scooping up a handful of snow, Alfie yelled, 'Watch me knock his hat off,' and hurled a snowball at the snowman, just as Sally stepped out from behind the large icy creation. Unfortunately, Alfie's off-target missile hit Sally on the side of her head, spinning her around and causing her to fall face down in the snow. Mary, who had been watching the snow fight from the safety of the back porch, raced over to help the stunned girl. 'Are you all right Sally?' The young girl clung to Mary. 'I think so Mary, though my head hurts. Can I go inside and sit down?'

Picking up the shaken girl Mary carried her inside, and was about to take her up to the bedroom that she shared with Jane, when Helen and Arthur returned to the Hall. 'Helen, please get a warming pan for Sally's bed, and have the fire lit in the girls' bedroom immediately.' While Mary stripped the wet clothes off the now shivering girl, and rubbed her hard with a soft towel, Lottie warmed the bed with a copper warming pan containing hot coals from the stove. She then lit the fire, and tended it until the coals were glowing.

Sally gratefully crawled between the warmed sheets and dozed off, clutching her bear. Mary looked at her anxiously, then sent Lottie to find Hugh, who arrived a few minutes later with Mac hot on his heels. The little dog who had been in the kitchen during the snowball fight, leapt onto the bed and lay beside Sally, glaring at Mary and Hugh, as though defying them to make him move.

'Do you think we should call Dr Wilson Hugh?'

'Let's see how she is at teatime Mary. We'll get him if we need to, but it's not a pleasant night to be out and about.'

'I'll get my coat and sit here with Sally until she wakes up. Hugh, I'm worried about the head injury that blinded her a few years ago.'

Mary returned immediately to the bedroom wearing her lambskin coat and carrying a blanket, then sat in the chair pulled up to the bed, where she stayed for the next hour, holding Sally's hand, talking gently to the girl and her dog. Hugh brought up two mugs of tea and sat with her for a while. When they had finished their drink he stood up. 'I think I should go down to the other children Mary. They're terribly worried, especially Alfie who threw the snowball.'

'Thank you darling. That's a very good idea.'

Not long after Hugh left the room, Mary was staring at the fire, praying that her little Sal would be fine, when she heard Sally whisper 'I didn't know you had brown hair Mary.' Startled, Mary turned around to stare at Sally, who was looking at her with her eyes half closed. 'What did you just say Sally?'

'I can see you Mary! I can really see you!'

Mary held up one finger. 'How many fingers am I holding up Sal?' and nearly wept when Sally replied 'One, but it's a bit blurry.'

Mary hugged Sally. 'Oh Sal, that's incredible.'

Slowly turning her head, Sally stared at Mac. 'Oh what a pretty dog you are Mac. Look at your curls,' to which Mary burst into tears. Sally patted her hand. 'Please don't cry Mary, I'm not blind anymore.'

'My darling, these are tears of joy!'

'Mary, can we wait 'till the morning to tell everyone, just in case it doesn't last all night?' 'Of course we can, though let's pray that you'll be able to see even better in the morning. Can I please tell Hugh?'

'Yes, of course tell Hugh.'

'Would you like something to eat Sal, or would you rather settle down and get a good sleep?' Sally yawned. 'Sleep, I think. Night Mary, night Mac.' Sally kissed Mary and her dog, then she fell asleep as soon as she put her head back on the pillow. When Lottie later tiptoed in to check the fire, Mary said quietly, 'I think I'll spend the night here with Sally Lottie. Could you please ask Joy and Martha if they could make up a bed for Jane in one of their rooms?'

'Yes, of course m'lady. Would you like a tray brought up?'

'Yes please, Lottie.' Mary, warmed her hands in front of the fire until Hugh brought up a tray with two meals and ate his meal with her while she told him the wonderful news. After a while, he left to say goodnight to the other children, intending to return to sit with Mary.

Before he could return to the bedroom Hugh was called to the stables where one of the horses had cast itself in a stall. As most of the stable staff had the day off, Hugh spent the next couple of hours helping the remaining groom. By the time he had washed up and returned to the house it was late in the evening, and only Helen and Arthur were still up.

'Is the horse all right Sir?'

'I think so, thanks Arthur. He doesn't appear to be too injured, and is now standing in the stall eating from the hay net. I'll take a cup of tea up to Lady Mary, after we have finished ours down here.' When Hugh opened the door to the girls' bedroom, the lamp had been dimmed, and he found both his wife and Sally sound asleep in bed, with Mac lying between them. Quietly closing the door he went to bed alone.

Early the next morning, Mary was woken by Sally shaking her. 'Mary, Mary, I can still see!' 'Oh, my darling, that is wonderful.' Mary cuddled both the girl and Mac, who was licking the excited girl's face. 'Can you really see properly, or just blurred shapes?'

'I can see like I used to before the accident. Oh Mary, I can really see again.' The excited young girl flung her arms around Mary's neck. Mary sat up and swung her feet to the floor, grimacing when her foot missed her slipper, and touched the cold floor. 'Let's put on your warm dressing gown, and go down to get you something to eat and drink.'

Stopping at their bedroom to tell Hugh that Sally could still see, and where they were going, Mary held Sally's hand as they walked down the stairs to the kitchen, Mac following close behind. All the time, Sally was staring around her in delight, actually seeing the house and its splendid fixtures for the first time. Hugh caught up with them before they reached the kitchen, and swept Sally up into his arms. 'I'm so pleased that you can see again, Sally. Won't everyone be delighted when they hear your wonderful news?'

Sally looked at Hugh, then turned to Mary. 'Mary, Hugh is very handsome, isn't he? I would marry him if you hadn't!' Laughing, Hugh put Sally down, and gave Mary a quick kiss. 'I'll go up and get Jane. She'll be overjoyed when she hears your great news Sally.'

'Hugh, can you please just tell her that I'm awake and in the kitchen? I want to see her face when she hears the news.'

Sally was sitting near the range when Jane tumbled into the kitchen and ran to her sister. She hugged her twin. 'Are you feeling ok, Sal? I was so worried about you.' Sally looked at her sister. 'That's a lovely blue dressing gown you're wearing Jane.'

Jane stared at her sister in disbelief. 'Sally, can you truly see, or did someone tell you that my dressing gown is blue?'

'You also have blue slippers, and you'll knock that cup off the table if you are not careful!'

Screaming with delight, Jane grabbed her sister to her, and started to dance her around the kitchen until Mary intervened. 'Sit down Jane and Sally. We need to take things quietly, until Dr Wilson has checked Sally. That snowball gave you a pretty hard whack, my love.'

It wasn't long before the kitchen was full of people who had heard Jane's scream. All were delighted with the wonderful news, and it was a very joyous group who sat down for breakfast half an hour later. Alfie was delighted that Sally could see again, then began to boast that he was the one who had made it happen, until Hugh beckoned for him to follow him out of the kitchen.

'Alfie, it's wonderful that Sally has her sight back, but you are very lucky indeed that she wasn't seriously injured when that snowball hit her head.' Alfie hung his head. 'I'm sorry Hugh. I truly am relieved that Sally wasn't badly hurt and that she can see again.'

'Good lad Alfie. Just be pleased for her and look after her like a big brother should.' He put his arm around Alfie's shoulders and they walked back into the kitchen.

Dr Wilson arrived mid-morning, and after hearing what had occurred the day before, gave Sally a thorough examination.

'Is your sight still blurry Sally?'

'No Dr Wilson. It was a bit last night, but I can see quite clearly now. I can see those big black birds in the trees in the park.' Dr Wilson looked to where she was pointing, and saw some ravens perched on the bare branches of a big oak tree beyond the garden.

'Well done young lady. Do you have a headache?'

'No Dr Wilson. My head is a bit sore where the snowball hit me, but that's all. Will I stay not blind now?'

'Well now my dear, I sincerely hope so. Just take things easy for a few days. No racing around, especially outside where it's slippery, in case you fall and bang your head again.' The doctor snapped his bag shut. 'Now, off you go with your sister.'

When the girls left the room, Mary looked at the doctor. 'I've heard of people regaining their sight following a traumatic incident Lady Mary, but this is the first time I've witnessed it firsthand. I'd like to think that Sally's return of sight will be permanent. Try to keep her from running around, in case she was concussed, but other than that, I'm afraid we'll just have to wait and see.'

'Thank you Dr Wilson, we will do what we can. Would you like a hot drink before you venture outside again?'

'Much as I would love to Lady Mary, I have a few more patients to see, before I can head home.'

When Mary caught up with the girls again, they were up in their bedroom, looking at their dresses, and she heard Sally say, 'You were very good at explaining everything to me Jane. As soon as you took that dress from the wardrobe, I knew that it was the yellow one with the small pockets, because you would tell me the colour of everything I wore. Thank you.'

Quietly, Mary went downstairs again, leaving the twins to get used to Sally's new state by themselves.

Following lunch the family was driven back to Longmire Hall. Listening to Jane's quiet chatter to help Sally recognise sights that she had only heard of, Mary was reminded of the first trip they'd made when Jane and Meg had described the same scenes for her blind twin. Sally couldn't believe what she was seeing when Longmire Hall came into sight. She had known that it was large, but had never realised that it was such a magnificent building.

The staff at Longmire Hall had been informed of Sally's returned sight, and were all waiting to congratulate her. They were surprised when she greeted each of them by name before Mary or Jane introduced them. Seeing the looks of surprise, Sally laughed. 'I know your voices.'

The young girl gasped and turned to Mary, when she heard Polly say, 'Meg will certainly be surprised when she arrives back tomorrow Sally,'

'Oh Mary, now that I can see, what will happen to Meg?' Mary looked puzzled. 'What do you mean Sally?'

'Well, Meg's job was to look after me when I couldn't see. Now that I can see, will Meg still be able to look after Jane and me?'

'Sally, it's going to take you some time to adjust to being able to see again, and I'm sure that Meg will want to help you. I will speak to her when she arrives back tomorrow.'

Happy with the thought that Mary would sort things out, the two girls wandered all over the house, chatting all the way, with Mac always close to Sally. Polly and Mary went into the study to discuss the household budget for the next few weeks. 'It's unbelievable m'lady. Imagine waking up and suddenly being able to see again.'

Hugh went to the estate office to meet with Adam Sinclair, who had moved into Hugh's old cottage and was now the estate supervisor. The two men were going to spend some time going through the books, and then Hugh planned to take Adam up to Glendale to meet the Grey brothers.

The next morning, aware of Adam's inability to ride due to his leg injury, Hugh took him to the stables to meet Robert, who had shown himself to be quite an innovator when it came to adapting saddlery to suit both horses and riders. Before Christmas Robert had designed a specially shaped stirrup to allow for the turn in Toby's foot, and had asked the Longmire blacksmith to construct it for him. With some minor adjustments, Toby was now happily learning to ride in a saddle.

Robert asked Adam about his riding experience prior to his accident and examined the foot of the prosthesis. 'Mr Sinclair, I realise that you have no feeling in your lower leg, and are worried that your foot might get caught in the stirrup if you fell; but would you be willing to try riding a quiet horse, if I make you a stirrup that would release your foot if you fell?' Adam looked doubtful, but was aware that his new job would be easier if he could ride. 'Yes Robert, I'll give it a go.'

Robert nodded, then said to Hugh. 'Sir, if you are planning to go up to Glendale today, Mr Sinclair could drive the cart pulled by Rusty, then ride him bareback up the last steep pitch. Mick Murphy was up there yesterday, and said that the track was just passable.'

'Thank you Robert. That's a great idea. We should leave immediately Adam. Get your warmest coat.' While Adam collected his coat, Hugh thought of the quick chat he'd had with Mick Murphy before Christmas. Mick was sure that it wouldn't take long to build a suitable room for Mabel, and was planning to show Hugh plans and a list of materials required before the New Year.

When Hugh and Adam returned from Glendale just before dusk, Robert handed Adam what, at first sight, seemed to be a large flat-bottomed hook. Looking more closely, he realised that it was a stirrup, with a cutaway side. Robert noticed Adam's puzzled look. 'It's a stirrup to help you stay balanced in the saddle, Mr Sinclair. I wouldn't recommend hunting or galloping around, but I should think that, after some practice, you could ride a horse that you were comfortable with. If you were to fall, your foot won't be held by the stirrup iron.'

Taking the iron from Adam, Hugh turned it around in his hand, and whistled as he recognised the simplicity of the design. He slapped the coachman on the back. 'You could go into business designing remedial equipment, Robert.'

'If this works Hugh, I could have my favourite horse brought here. It's been one of my greatest regrets to not be able to ride her since the accident.'

'Where is she at the moment Adam?'

'She's at the family farm at Basingstoke. My younger brother rides her sometimes, but he prefers to ride his hunter.'

'If you feel confident riding with Robert's modified stirrup, what say we go to Basingstoke early next month to get your mare? I could do some business while we're there.'

Following dinner, Hugh and Mary retreated to the study, which was very snug with a well-set fire burning in the hearth. Sitting on Hugh's lap, Mary told him about Meg's reaction to Sally's regained sight.

'When Meg hopped out of the carriage, Sally met her at the door, and while they were hugging, Sally whispered in her ear, 'Meg, I can see again.' Meg froze for a few moments, then held Sally at arm's length and stared at her before saying, 'Oh Sally, that's the most wonderful news I could hear. When did this happen?' Sally gave a graphic account of the snowball incident, and what had occurred later. Then of all things, she looked at Meg and said, 'Please don't be angry with me Meg. I can't help seeing again.' We were all speechless, then I grabbed Meg and whispered, 'Don't worry, Meg, I'll explain later,' then we all went into the kitchen.'

'Poor Meg.' Hugh, curled a lock of Mary's hair around his finger.

'As soon as I could, I brought Meg in here and explained what had happened, and Sally's concern for Meg's future now that she can see. Meg told me that just because Sally can see, she will have a lot of catching up to do. While she can read some braille, she has never seen writing in a book. She won't be able to attend school with Jane; she is so far behind.

I agreed, then I asked her would she stay on to look after the girls in the cottage as before, and to also become Sally's tutor to try to help her with her education in all aspects. Meg was so pleased. The girls have become like family to her, and she will be continuing as before, minus the trips to London.'

'That's great news my love. Adam and I went to Glendale today, and Mick Murphy has already marked out the area for the new room. He told Thomas that he will draw up some plans to show us, then plans to start building next week if possible.'

'Mick's in his element working as a carpenter again, isn't he? How stupid people can be, to ignore someone's obvious talent and passion, just because they're Irish.' Mary spoke more passionately than Hugh had heard her speak before.

'I think I'd best whisk you away to bed, my little Australian firebrand, before you get too fired up!' He pulled Mary to her feet then gave her lips a hard, lingering kiss. Pulling away to take a breath, Mary gasped 'I think you'd better my love, or one of the staff might interrupt us on the mat in front of the fire!' Laughing, they raced hand in hand up the stairs to their bedroom.

Mrs Smith, hearing the racing footsteps, turned to Polly. 'Isn't it wonderful to hear that young couple so happy to be together, Polly? When I first started here, the place was full of laughter, especially when Lady Patricia was a little girl. But once Mr David started to throw his weight around when he came home from school, everyone was very wary. When the Master died and Lady Patricia disappeared, the Countess lost interest in everything and just shut herself away in the Hall.'

Polly grimaced. 'My earliest memories from when I started here, are how hard we tried to stay out of sight of Mr David. He'd punish us if he so much as set eyes on us when we were working. I really detested him, and the only thing I felt when he died was relief! I can't believe how quickly our lives changed for the better once Lady Mary arrived and took charge. Now it's wonderful to see her so happy as well.'

CHAPTER 19

Longmire Estate,
Sussex, England
End of December 1888

Hugh had to leave before breakfast the next morning to attend a farm meeting near Lewes, so Mary decided to ride Gem over to Home Farm. Tess saw Mary, Gem, and Scruffy enter the farmyard and called 'We're in the cream room Mary.' Tess knew that this particular day was a difficult one for Mary. It was three years to the day, since her mother's death, and while she had overcome her initial grief, Tess knew that Mary still missed Patricia.

When Mary entered the cream room, she saw Toby manfully turning the cream separator handle, and Tess churning butter. Determined to keep Mary busy, Tess stood up and stretched. 'Good morning, my dear. What wonderful timing. You've arrived just in time to give my poor old back a rest, and you look like you need something to do.' Giving Mary a kiss on the cheek before she sat down to take up the churning, Tess picked up two butter pats and started to form a lump of butter into a small block, which she then stamped with the Longmire crest. By the time Bob returned from taking the cows to a fresh field, the two women and Toby had just finished cleaning up, and were about to go back to the kitchen for breakfast.

'Run along and collect the eggs please Toby.'

Mary was amazed to watch Toby hurry across to the henhouse, with neither a crutch nor a stick, while Scruffy joyfully scampered beside him. Toby had a rolling stride, but nothing like the limp when they'd first met six months ago. Bob watched Mary looking at Toby's retreating back. 'That lad is a born farmer Mary, and is willing to try anything. He's a wonder at improvising to compensate for his gammy foot, and there aren't many jobs that he can't carry out now.'

'I'm so pleased he's become such a help to you both.' Mary walked arm in arm with Tess across the yard. Bob growled 'Just as well he's here. Will seems to take a lot longer doing the milk run these days, now that Elin is back at Everton Manor.'

Mary laughed. 'They seem to be quite keen on each other, don't they?'

'I've never seen Will smitten like this before. I think it was love at first sight, as far as he was concerned.' Tess, threw some bacon in the hot pan.

'What about Elin? Do you think she would be willing to give up her nursing to live on the farm?'

Tess shrugged. 'I don't think they're quite at that stage yet, but she lived on a farm in Wales, and loves coming here to help with whatever jobs need doing when she has time off,. We might have to rethink our accommodation, sometime in the future.'

'When Will does marry, whenever that may be, what do you and Bob plan to do Tess?' Mary hoped that Tess wasn't planning to move away from the estate.

'Bob and I always planned to move out into the old cottage near the barn, though we'd have to do a bit of work on it. Maybe we could get Mick to give me a hand some time.'

Mary didn't say anything, but it gave her a lot to think of as the four of them ate breakfast. In fact, when she was about to leave and Tess said, 'Will should have dropped Clara off at the Hall by now,' Mary realised with a shock, that for a short time she had forgotten about the anniversary of her mother's death.

Twelve months ago Mary had arranged for a marble tablet to be placed in the family mausoleum in the Longmire Village church graveyard, in memory of her mother. Clara had asked if she could accompany Mary to the graveyard to lay some flowers, and arrangements had been made for her to ride to Longmire Hall with Will.

Mary met Will on her way back to the Hall. 'Good morning, Lady Mary. Your aunt is waiting at the Hall for you.'

'Thanks Will.'

When Mary entered the kitchen, Clara was chatting to Mrs Smith. 'Good morning Mary. I've just seen Jane and Sally running around outside. Isn't it wonderful, not just for Sally, but for Jane as well, that Sally has her sight back?'

'You're so right Clara. Although Meg and Mac relieved Jane of much of the responsibility she felt for her sister, Jane really missed being able to share everything with her twin.' Clara turned as she put on her coat and boots. 'Is Meg still staying now that Sally has her sight back, Mary?'

'Oh, most definitely, she will Clara. This is her home now.' Mary put on her sheepskin coat again. 'She and the girls will stay in the cottage, and her role now will be to assist Sally readjust to being sighted again. She needs to learn to read and write for starters, and also to recognise sights that she has only been told about or sensed. Her early sighted memories are of city life. She had never been to the country before she lost her sight.'

Walking arm in arm with her aunt towards the village, Mary felt a great sense of contentment. She missed her mother, especially at this time of the year, but the sense of loss was diminishing. She and Hugh were real soul mates, and treated each other as equals in both their business and personal lives. Having Clara living at Everton Manor was a comfort too, and of course, there was always Tess at Home Farm, who was a perfect surrogate mother.

'How are the children settling into the Dower House, Clara?' Mary slowed as they neared the church yard.

'Ruth and Chloe can't quite believe what is happening to them at the moment Mary. Living in their own house with a garden is still such an incredible experience for them both they keep seeking my reassurance that it is really happening. Hopefully, my application for guardianship will be formalised soon, so that I can show them the signed paperwork.'

'I heard that your application to be the children's guardian has been accepted Clara. The Christmas break has slowed the delivery of the paperwork, but you should have it early in the New Year.' Clara looked lovingly at her young niece. 'Thank you for all that you have done for me, my dear. You have no idea how happy you have made me since my arrival in England.'

'It has been my pleasure Clara, and is little compared to your care and support to our family following Father's death.'

Mary led Clara to the mausoleum standing under a large yew tree near the church. Taking a key from her pocket, she unlocked the door and led Clara into the cool interior. Leaving the door propped open, to allow light into the small room, the two women went to stand in front of the black marble tablet with gold lettering, standing against the side wall.

In loving memory
of

Lady Patricia Victoria Evans (nee Everton)
Countess of Longmire and Oakdale
Born 12-6-1845 Died 29-12-1885
Beloved wife of Thomas Evans
Buried in Australia

Loving mother of Lady Mary Emma Evans

Reverently laying an arrangement of winter flowers that Tom had picked from the garden that morning beside the marble tablet, Mary and Clara both stood silently remembering Patricia, mother and sister-in-law, who had died far too early. After a short time, Clara left Mary alone in the mausoleum, and wandered amongst the gravestones until Mary was ready to leave.

The villagers, well aware of the reason for Mary's visit to the graveyard that day, had not greeted her when she arrived in the village, but as she and Clara departed, they constantly paused to chat to women and men who stopped to greet them, or called out from their front doors. Once again, Clara marvelled at the esteem in which these people held Mary.

As they left the village, Mary could see in the distance that work had started on the watermill. A closed-down mill in West Sussex had been dismantled, and transported to near the site that Mary had selected, and was now in the process of being reassembled by tradesmen experienced in constructing mills. The miller, who had worked the mill before the owner closed it, had been employed, and was currently staying at the local public house. Hopefully, his accommodation near the mill would soon be built, and the mill should be ready to crush the next season's grain.

Mary and Clara were met near the Hall by the four children riding their ponies. Sally had been ecstatic when she first saw Cass, and realised what the colour *bay* meant. Now she rode everywhere with the other three children, showing more natural riding ability than any of them. The four children were making the most of their holiday time, as school started again at the beginning of the New Year. All four, plus Meg, would go back to Everton Manor the weekend before the new school term commenced.

The schoolroom near the nursery at Everton Manor had been cleaned and set up for Meg to take classes for Sally and Ruth, who had declared that she would love to learn to read and write if Meg would teach her. Chloe however wasn't so sure, telling Clara that she would rather not have classes, as people with learning had to stay inside and read silly books! She was having far too much fun playing in their garden, talking to the horses in the stables and climbing trees when the weather was fine, to stay inside and learn stuff!

Forever asking questions, Chloe wanted to know why things were as they were, and Clara was sure that she would soon want to know why she wasn't having lessons with the others, and demand that she be allowed to learn to read and write as well!

Clara had always dreamed of having children, but the early death of her husband had prevented that. Now she was in her element, looking after three children, whom she loved dearly and would soon be able to call her own. But she wryly thought that Chloe was pushing her developing parenting skills to the limit. Luckily, Elin seemed to have

Chloe's measure, and with her help, Clara was slowly getting the upper hand with little miss Chloe.

The New Year dawned windy and wet, so Mary, Meg, and the children were driven to Everton Manor a day earlier than planned. Many of the farmers were preparing for snow when the wind dropped, and Mick Murphy was pleased to be sitting beside Robert, having completed the new room at Glendale before more snow fell. He had thoroughly enjoyed building again, plus the two men from the village helping him had been both friendly and competent. Mick planned to ask Mary if they could be employed again for other building jobs that she had mentioned might be started when the weather improved.

Dropping Mick off at the Gatehouse, Robert drove the coach to the Manor, and parked as close to the back door as possible, to allow Mary and the children to move inside without getting too wet. While Mary went to the kitchen for a cup of tea, the children scampered up the stairs to their rooms, Mac trotting up behind them. He was still Sally's constant companion, but he seemed to understand that she no longer required him to be within touch, as before.

Hugh was riding to Everton Manor later in the day, after he'd visited a couple of local farmers who had employed him to assist them with their animal breeding programs, so Mary walked over to the Dower House to spend some time with Clara and the children. Opening the back door, Mary could hear voices in the kitchen so, after removing her coat, she walked into the kitchen where Clara was making bread, 'assisted' by Ruth and Chloe, both of whom were liberally coated with flour. In fact, Mary suspected that there was more flour on Chloe than on the small dirty lump of dough she was meant to be kneading.

Seeing Mary at the door, Chloe shrieked 'It's our Maresy,' and launched herself towards Mary so quickly that the dough went flying, and Mary had little chance to stop the flour-covered body clinging to her legs, thereby transferring a fair amount of the white flour to Mary's dark blue skirt. Mary quickly lifted Chloe up, gave her a quick kiss on her snowy cheek, then held her at arms' length. 'My goodness Chloe, I thought you were a snowman!' When she put the young girl down, Chloe picked up the dough off the floor. 'We's helping Clara make bread, Maresy.'

Mary tried hard not to laugh at the look on her aunt's face. 'Good morning, Clara and Ruth. Would you like me to put the kettle on?' 'Good morning my dear, that would be lovely.' Clara placed the dough that she had been kneading onto an oven tray, ready to put it into the oven. 'As you can see, the girls have been helping me this morning. Ruth, put your loaf next to mine, and we will put them in the oven.'

'What about mine, Clara?' Chloe dumped her grubby lump of dough onto the table.

'I don't think we should cook that dough, since it's been on the floor Chloe, especially now that it also has your footprint on it! You can share my loaf, and next time, your dough will go into the oven first.'

Clara turned to Mary. 'I'll just take these two up to the bathroom to dust them off, then we'll have that cup of tea.' Five minutes later, Clara returned to the kitchen, minus the girls, and thankfully sat in the chair near the range. Mary raised her eyebrows. 'They are up with Iris and Christopher.'

Handing Clara a cup of tea, Mary sat in the other chair. 'How is Iris settling in Clara?'

'Oh, I think she will be fine. The girls like her, and she's good with Christopher. I just have to get used to having someone working for me, rather than the other way around!'

When Clara and the children moved to the Dower House, Mary had convinced Clara that she would need some help with the house and the children. Christopher's health was improving daily, and Elin's assistance in her nursing capacity was no longer necessary. Clara soon realised how much easier it was to cope with two people than just by herself, so she didn't take much convincing when Mary discussed the possibility of employing some additional help.

Elin's secondment was coming to an end, though at the moment, decisions were being made as to whether she would return to her nursing career in London, or marry Will and become a farmer's wife. Mary was expecting the latter to be the case, as she was well aware of the strong attraction that the young couple had for each other.

Just after Christmas, the matron at the Lewes Workhouse had spoken to Mary about a seventeen-year-old female resident suffering from Mongolism. While she had the distinct facial appearance of the affliction, and was mildly intellectually disabled, she was a friendly, helpful lass, who spent most of her time assisting staff with the younger children. Iris was capable of following instructions, and was totally trustworthy looking after the little ones. Unfortunately, the matron was finding it very difficult to place Iris in a household outside the workhouse, mainly because of her physical appearance.

Mary had taken Clara to meet Iris, and was thrilled when she agreed to give the lass a trial period at the Dower House. Clara was relieved to find that Iris was more than capable of dealing with the wilful Chloe. At their first meeting, Chloe asked Iris, 'Why do you look different?' to which Iris replied without batting an eyelid, 'I just do. Why do you ask silly questions?' Chloe looked a little stumped at that reply, then said quietly, 'I just do.' She paused, then said, 'Will you be Ruth's and my friend, Ilis?' When Iris nodded, the two younger girls took her on a tour of their home.

Ruth and Chloe both thought Iris was wonderful, and Clara was soon quite happy to leave Christopher in her care. Iris was very gentle with him, and seemed to sense his needs almost before he did!

CHAPTER 20

Longmire Estate,
Sussex, England
January – May 1889

Life finally began to settle down after the children went back to school, and Sally worked with Meg, who was teaching her to read and write. Meg also spent a lot of time taking Sally into Lewes, and around the countryside, explaining everything they saw.

Mary and Hugh began to work out a schedule that allowed them to spend as much time as possible together, as well as with the children. Both of them had to accept that there were times their work necessitated days and nights away, but they tried hard to coordinate them, so that they were away at the same time.

On Mary's twenty-first birthday, Hugh took her to London where, following a beautiful dinner with a string quartet playing throughout their meal, and a night at the opera, they retired to their suite in Claridge's Hotel. Later the next morning they travelled back to Longmire Hall, and life continued as before, although now Mary would be expected to adjudicate more regularly at the Lewes Magistrates Court.

It didn't take long for the local magistrates and the court attorneys, to realise that Judge Stephen's young prodigy was not going to be the pushover that they had first assumed. During the next few months, the majority of her fellow magistrates began to look forward to having Mary on the panel. If Mary thought witnesses, plaintiffs, or defendants were only giving evidence as coached by the attorneys, she would often ask questions of her own, and demand an immediate answer. Quite often, when questioned by Mary, the witness would look helplessly at their furious attorney, whom she forbade to interrupt. Her questions at first appeared to be quite harmless enquiries, from a lady concerned for the person's welfare, but her fellow magistrates and the local attorneys soon learnt that Mary was able to get to the truth, more often than not, with her seemingly innocuous questions.

Two older magistrates, with well-known prejudiced views about women, who refused to sit on a panel with Mary, soon found that they were no longer selected to sit on cases, whether Mary was attending or not.

Elin returned to nursing in London in the New Year, but at midsummer she and Will announced their engagement, and their intention to marry before Christmas. Knowing that Tess and Bob planned to allow the newly married couple to move into the farmhouse, a week after the engagement announcement Mary rode to Home Farm to have a chat with them.

'Remember Bob, last year you said that you might do up the old cottage if Will and Elin were to marry? I'm planning to employ Mick Murphy and the two men who helped him with the building at Glendale full time, and would like their first job to be the renovation of your cottage, to your specifications.' Tess and Bob stared at her, dumbstruck for a moment, then Bob shook his head. 'You don't have to do that lass.'

Mary stood up and hugged them both to her. 'Oh yes I do! Apart from the fact that the cottage is an estate property, it is the least I can do for the two wonderful people who are like parents to me.' Eventually, over a cup of tea and a piece of fruit cake, Bob and Tess admitted that Mary's offer would relieve them from worrying about their future, and they agreed to discuss with Mick changes that they would like made while the cottage was being renovated.

'When Mick and his crew finish your cottage, I want him to build a couple more cottages in the village, plus design and build a row of self-contained accommodation, for the single farm workers and employees who will be working at the mill, and in the planned village market garden.'

When Bob left to have a look at the old cottage, Tess sat beside Mary. 'My love, you spend far too much of your time thinking of, and worrying about, everyone else but yourself. It's time you let others do the work you pay them to do. Remember that saying, 'Don't keep a dog and bark yourself!'' When Mary opened her mouth to respond, Tess placed her finger against Mary's lips. 'Mary, I know that you and Hugh both want children, so the sooner you slow down a bit to give yourself the chance to start your family, the better.'

Mary smiled and looked shyly at Tess. 'I think there might already be an heir to the title on the way Tess!'

The Countess
Connections

CHAPTER 1

Melbourne Australia
April 1895

Solicitor Charles Mee looked up in alarm as a dishevelled man with long hair and a shaggy beard barged into his office and staggered towards his desk. As the man grabbed hold of the back of one of the two visitor's chairs in front of the desk, he gasped 'Help m..' then slumped to the floor.

Charles stood up and looked at the frightened receptionist who was staring through the doorway. 'Ring the police Carol!'

Placing his fingers on the side of the man's neck, Charles could feel a faint pulse and noted from the slight movement of the unconscious man's chest that he was still breathing. Looking more closely at the man's chest, he saw a large stain on the left side of his coat. Gingerly opening the grubby coat, and lifting the equally filthy shirt, he saw what looked like a bullet wound still oozing blood on the left side of the man's chest,. He pressed his folded handkerchief over the wound, and called urgently to his receptionist. 'Carol, please throw me the towel from the washstand, then telephone the ambulance station behind the Windsor Hotel. This man is seriously injured!'

When two policemen arrived, Charles had staunched some of the bleeding, and the man was slowly showing signs of recovering consciousness, but was very confused and incoherent. The older policeman looked at the man lying on the floor, then turned to Charles. 'My name is Sergeant Taylor, Mr Mee. Do you know this man?' The sergeant flipped open his notebook as they heard the bell signalling the arrival in King Street of the new horse drawn ambulance

'No sergeant, I have no idea who he is, nor why he has come to my office.' Charles sat back in his chair, as his legs threatened to give way. 'Do you think there may be some identification in that oilskin covered package that you took from his coat pocket?'

The sergeant remained silent when two puffing ambulance men carrying a canvas stretcher entered the office. The man's wound was bandaged, and he was carried down to the ambulance waiting in the street.

'I'm not sure. Inspector Brown will open it and read the contents before deciding what action to take. We will go to the Melbourne Hospital now to wait for the man to hopefully recover enough to talk to us.' Sergeant Taylor headed for the door, beckoning to the constable to follow him. 'We will be in touch when he does Mr Mee. He appears to have wanted to speak to you for some reason. Goodbye for now.'

Carol entered the office in response to the buzzer sounding on her desk. 'Thank you for your help Carol. This has been a shock to both of us. I suggest that you go home now, and take tomorrow off as we have no pressing appointments for the day. I'll shut the office early, and head home soon.'

When Carol left, Charles removed a bottle of whisky from the bottom draw of his desk and poured himself a stiff drink. He wished that his Associate, Peter Jones was there to share a drink with him, and to talk through what had just happened. But, as Peter was away for the week, he was left to sip his whisky alone, and ponder why a man suffering such a wound had come up three flights of stairs to his office, when surely it would have been easier to go into a ground floor office or shop to seek help.

The next morning, when Charles arrived at his office building, the young constable that he'd met the previous day stepped out of the doorway. 'Mr Mee, your presence is required at the Melbourne Hospital.' Puzzled, he accompanied the policeman to walk to the hospital, where he was met by Sergeant Taylor, who was clearly annoyed. 'Sorry to disrupt your morning Mr Mee, but that tramp who collapsed in your rooms yesterday has recovered consciousness, and is demanding to speak only to you.'

'Why me? I've no idea who he is, or why he chose my office to collapse in.'

'Let's go and see, shall we?' Sergeant Taylor led the way through a number of corridors to a small room, where a burly policeman was sitting outside the door. On entering the room, Charles saw the stranger lying on the bed. His clothes had been removed, and an attempt had been made to clean his face. The man stared at Charles. 'Mr Mee, I'm Graham Evans, Mary Evan's brother.'

Graham spoke in a faltering voice. 'Please take the package in my coat pocket Mr Mee, and follow the terms of my enclosed will, should I not survive. I have money to pay for your services.' Following this effort to speak, Graham shut his eyes, breathing painfully. A nurse ushered the men out of the room, and called a passing doctor into the room.

Charles and the Sergeant waited outside the hospital room. 'Mary Evans was a client I met briefly about five years ago. Where is the package Sergeant Taylor? As I accept this man Graham Evans as a client, I will need to go through his papers as quickly as possible, considering his current state of health.'

'Here it is.' Sergeant Taylor took the package from his pocket. 'Inspector Brown wasn't in his office when I returned to the station last night, so I brought it with me when I was told that the patient was awake and asking for you.' He handed the package to Charles. 'Please let me know if there is anything untoward enclosed – after all, someone appears to be after Mr Evans for some reason. You take care they don't have a go at you too!' As the two men were about to leave the hospital, Sergeant Taylor handed Charles a card. 'If you have any trouble, you can telephone me on this number.'

Quickly walking back to his office Charles was acutely conscious of the package in his pocket, and was relieved when he entered his rooms and locked the door behind him. Carefully slitting the top of the package with his paper knife, Charles slid the contents out on to the surface of his desk. Thoroughly documenting all of the contents into a receipt book, he then carefully opened Graham Evans will. The one page document, signed by Graham and two witnesses, simply stated that, after expenses, all of his worldly goods, other than a bequest of £1,000 to his Aunt Clara Wilkinson, if she could be found, were to go to his step sister Mary Emma Evans. Solicitor Mr Charles Mee, Kings Street, Melbourne, was named as the executor.

Putting the will to one side, Charles picked up a small silver key with a tag attached, and saw that it was for a deposit box at the English, Scottish and Australian Bank in Collins Street. Thinking of the unkempt appearance of the man calling himself Graham Evans, Charles wondered why he would have such a key

Two other documents turned out to be land titles for adjoining rural properties in Gippsland, in the name of Graham Thomas Evans, and were dated six months ago. Seeing the addresses and names on the property titles, Charles wondered if Graham had bought land adjoining his farm.

As he had no appointments for the day he walked to the E, S & A Bank, and produced the key, plus Graham's will, to request access to the bank safety deposit box to view the contents. This request was granted, on the proviso that the escorting teller stayed in the room with him while he handled the contents. When the box was opened, it was found to contain numerous documents, plus Tom Evan's engraved gold hunter watch and two leather purses, one full of gold sovereigns, and the other with gold nuggets. There were also a number of bank books from different banks in Bendigo, Ballarat, and Echuca, all in Graham's name, with multiple thousands of pounds in each, plus an E, S & A Bank statement for £20,000.

Amazed at the large sum of money that Graham appeared to possess, Charles noticed an envelope with his name on it. Opening it, he found the following hand written letter:

Melbourne April 1895

Dear Mr Mee,

Please excuse me for nominating you as executor for my will without prior consultation, but you are the only person I know who may have contact with my step sister Mary Emma Evans, and possibly through her, contact details for my Aunt Clara Wilkinson.

I fear for my life, so when you read this it is likely that I am either dead or incapable of talking to you, so please bear with me while I explain my circumstances.

When Mary left our farm in January 1886, she wrote to tell Aunt Clara and myself that you had arranged for her to sail to England, soon after her arrival in Melbourne. Since then, we have had no further correspondence from her, so I have no knowledge of her whereabouts or her circumstances.

Unfortunately, following Mary's departure from the farm, I lost interest in farming, and I'm afraid I made a huge mistake when I allowed myself to be hoodwinked by a lady in town, who professed to love me and in whom I foolishly fell in love.

Despite Aunt Clara's misgivings and words of advice, Annette and I married, and she moved out to the farm. It soon became apparent that Annette wanted me to sell the farm and move to Melbourne, which like a besotted fool I did.

On arrival in Melbourne, Annette introduced me to a man she claimed was her brother. Inadvertently, I overheard some of their conversation in reception when he left, and I realised what a fool I had been. All she was after was my money.

When Annette was out shopping, I removed the money from the farm sale and deposited it in the E, S & A Bank. I weighted and locked the Gladstone bag that had contained the money, and put it back into the wardrobe in our room.

The following morning when I awoke, both Annette and the bag were gone. When I spoke to the receptionist, he told me that she had left at dawn with her brother, who was carrying my bag.

Two weeks later, I was informed by the police that Annette had been arrested, following a botched robbery that she and her 'brother' had attempted at a bank in Ballarat.

Simon escaped after a young teller was killed, leaving Annette when she fell while trying to flee. As her husband, I was questioned by the police, but quickly cleared of being involved. Annette was hanged a week following her trial, while the police are still searching for Simon Lester.

Charles remembered the trial some years ago, where the female defendant had tried to lay the blame on everyone she could think of. Little did he know that she was Mary Evans step sister in law!

Following the trial, I travelled to Bendigo, and wandered around some of the less accessible areas prospecting for gold. To my surprise and delight, I discovered a sizable and extremely profitable deposit of gold in the gravel bed of a small stream high in the hills. To allay suspicion, I only took small amounts to different towns to be weighed and sold. After two years, I had several thousand pounds in various banks.

On a trip up to Echuca, I signed on as a deck hand on the paddle steamer Lancashire Lass, and spent two years taking supplies up the Darling River to Wilcannia, and returning to Echuca with wool bales. Last year I returned home, to discover that the neighbour who had bought the farm had just died, so I bought both properties from his widow. She and her two adult sons are staying on to manage both farms.

Unfortunately, Simon Lester was in the area at that time, but disappeared when he realised that I had recognised him. Since then, I have been receiving threatening messages, demanding that I pay him what he believes should have been Annette's half share of my income since she died. The threats have become quite violent recently, to the point I have reported them to the police.

Hopefully I will be able to explain more to you in person Mr Mee. If I can't, please implement my will as I have stated.

Yours sincerely
Graham Evans

When the teller had packed everything except the letter back into the deposit box, he locked it, then handed the key to Charles. 'As the named executor in Mr Evan's will, you may keep the key sir.'

Conscious of the key and will in his pocket, Charles hurried back to his office and locked the door behind him when he entered his rooms. After making a strong cup of tea, he sat at his desk, and wondered what on earth he had unconsciously become a party to.

Taking the letter out of the envelope again, he reread it, and wondered why Graham had not heard from Mary, other than the letter she'd sent before she sailed. In the short period of time that he had known her, she had appeared to be very fond of Graham and their Aunt Clara. Also, Graham must have found a very rich gold deposit, to explain the substantial sum of money in his bank accounts.

The telephone rang while Charles was eating his lunch, and he was asked to meet Sergeant Taylor at the hospital as quickly as possible. At first, Charles wondered if it might be a trap, so he rang the number on the card Sergeant Taylor had given him. When his call was answered by a policeman at the nearby police station, who confirmed that Sergeant Taylor had been called to the hospital earlier, Charles set off to meet him.

A policeman waiting at the front of the hospital took Charles straight up to Graham's room, where a number of policemen were waiting outside the door. Looking into the room Charles saw that the bed was empty, and became aware of an awful smell in the room. Before he could speak, Sergeant Taylor arrived and led him to another room further down the corridor, where Graham was lying unconscious on the bed.

'Earlier this morning, a man wearing a doctor's white coat entered the room after saying good morning to the policeman on duty. Mistakenly believing him to be a doctor, the policeman had stayed outside when the man entered Mr Evan's room. Luckily, a nurse passing the door glanced through the window, and saw the man holding a pillow over Mr Evans' head. She rushed into the room, and struck the man over the head with the heavy enamel bedpan she was carrying. As the man fell unconscious to the floor, she removed the pillow from Mr Evans' face, and made sure that he was able to breathe. Unfortunately, she was taking the used bedpan to be emptied, so the contents went all over the attacker, Mr Evans and herself!'

'Good grief! No wonder the room smells so terrible!' Charles, tried hard not to laugh. 'Was Graham injured any further?'

'Mr Evans is unconscious at the moment, but the doctors don't think further harm has been done, thanks to the nurse's swift action. Her colleagues who had to clean Mr Evans weren't so thankful though, and nor will the cleaners be. The prisoner had to be doused under a pump at the horse trough before he was put in the police van!'

When they both stopped laughing Charles handed the letter to the policeman. 'I think you should read this Sergeant Taylor. It was in a bank safety deposit box in Mr Evans' name, along with a number of gold nuggets and coins, his bank books, and statements showing that he possesses a small fortune.'

Handing the letter back to Charles, Sergeant Taylor looked thoughtful. 'I wonder if the prisoner is Simon Lester, or more likely someone doing his bidding? What became of Mr Evans' sister Mary? Do you know if she ever landed in England Mr Mee?'

'Oh yes, she arrived in England in April 1886, to discover that she came from an aristocratic family, and had inherited the hereditary title of Countess. She is now an extremely wealthy young woman, but I can't understand why she didn't contact her brother or aunt before they left the farm. I will contact her solicitor in England, and ask him if he knows what has happened to her.'

During the fortnight following Charles Mee's surprise meeting with Graham Evans, Graham was dangerously ill for a number of days, but gradually showed signs of recovery, to the point that he was awake and quite lucid on the early May morning when a nurse ushered Charles into his hospital room. As Charles sat on the chair beside the bed, Graham smiled. 'Good morning Mr Mee, or may I call you Charles?' When Charles nodded, he continued, 'Today I'm finally starting to believe that I will recover from my injuries, and I have you to thank for that.'

'I'm certainly relieved to hear that you're on the road to recovery Graham, but I wasn't the only one involved in saving you.'

'Well, thank you anyway. Did you manage to get access to my safety deposit box without too much obstruction?'

'Yes, I went to the bank the day after you collapsed in my office, and had no trouble getting access to the box, once I showed them your will, and proof of my identity. After I read your letter, I sent a telegraph to your sister's solicitor in England, stating that you had been seriously injured, and that you were concerned that you had lost contact with Mary and your Aunt Clara.'

Graham looked annoyed. 'So, Mary arrived in England nine years ago, and is now living there? Why hasn't she written to let me know?'

'Graham, I have been in regular contact with Gordon Lyons, Mary's solicitor during the past two weeks, and he said that Mary only stopped writing after two years of hearing nothing from you. It was just by chance that your Aunt Clara was in town when Mary's wedding invitation to you both arrived in mid-1888, but by then you had left the area. Clara is now living on one of Mary's estates in southern England.'

Graham looked at Charles in shock. 'So, she married a chap with a bit of money and land did she? Good for her. But Charles, as I never received any letters from Mary after she sailed, I had no address to write to. I wonder...' Graham stopped mid-sentence, then continued, 'I wonder if Annette intercepted Mary's letters? Now I come to think of it, she used to collect the mail then handed it out at lunch time, which annoyed Aunt Clara no end. Annette and Aunt Clara didn't get on at all well, and I regret to say I sided with Annette, and at her urging I finally told Aunt Clara that she had to leave. I sold the farm not long after she left, and the rest you know from my letter, other than that Annette and I weren't actually legally married, as she and Simon Lester were husband & wife, not siblings. Oh, I feel such an idiot.'

'I see. Well, I think you can remedy that somewhat by sending your Aunt Clara a telegram, telling her that you are sorry, then when you feel stronger in the coming days you should write to Mary, a letter similar to the one you wrote to me. Clara has told her about Annette, and the sale of the farm, but like you, they are upset about losing contact with you. I must tell you Graham, I thought about sending a copy of your letter to Mr Lyons, but decided not to until I spoke to you. I have however kept them informed of your daily progress.'

By this time Graham was starting to tire, so Charles stood up to leave. 'I'll see you tomorrow Graham, and will bring some writing paper, pen and ink.'

'Thanks Charles. As you are aware, I have the money to repay you, so please keep account of all that I owe you.'

When Charles left the hospital, he wondered how long Graham would remain under police guard in hospital. The man who had attacked him was currently languishing in Melbourne Gaol, hoping to escape execution by telling the police that he'd been paid £10 by a man, said to be Simon Lester, to kill Graham, and to retrieve the safety deposit box key from the package that Graham was known to keep in his coat pocket.

The next day, when Charles visited the hospital, Graham was sitting up in bed, propped up by several pillows and looking much better. 'Great news Charles. They think that I should be able to leave hospital in a couple of days.'

'Where will you go Graham?' Charles was mindful of the dishevelled man who had crashed into his office. 'Do you have a house or rooms to go to?'

'No, not yet. I was going to ask if you would mind booking me a suite in a hotel.' Before Charles could comment, a nurse who had entered the room and heard Graham's comment, looked at him severely. 'A person recovering from the injury you suffered Mr Evans will not be released to stay alone in a hotel.'

'What if I employed a valet to stay with me?'

'That might be considered Mr Evans. You will need to ask the doctor.' The nurse checked the chart at the foot of the bed before leaving the room.

Graham looked at Charles and raised an eyebrow. 'Could your receptionist possibly book me a suite at the Windsor Hotel when they set a date for my release Charles? And also, could she ask if they have a man suitable to be a valet for a few weeks? I'll sign a letter to the bank manager giving you access to the contents of my safety deposit box and bank accounts as required.' Charles drafted a letter there and then, which Graham signed and was witnessed by a passing nurse. 'I'll arrange the hotel rooms Graham, but how do we protect you from Simon Lester?'

CHAPTER 2

Gordon Lyons, a Lewes solicitor, stared at the telegram from Charles Mee that had just been delivered to his office. Although the telegram was brief, Mr Lyons understood that Mary's brother Graham had been seriously injured, and was worried about Mary and their Aunt Clara, having had no contact with either since 1886.

Unbeknown to Graham, since he last saw his sister in January 1886, following his step mother Patricia's death, Mary had become Lady Mary Emma Evans (Watson) Countess of Longmire and Oakdale, and was now an incredibly wealthy young woman. She was married to Sir Hugh Watson, formerly the estate supervisor, and they had two children, the Honourable William Thomas aged 5 and Lady Patricia Elizabeth aged 3, Both children were happy, lively youngsters, adored by their parents, and all the staff at both of their homes at Longmire Hall and Everton Manor.

While Mary's four wards had attended school in Lewes, they'd stayed at Everton Manor, and Mary had tried to spend equal time between Longmire Hall and Everton Manor. Now, only Alfie remained at the Manor, while the other three lived in London. He and Ryan Murphy both lived at the manor, working in the estate market garden, and the garden office set up in one of the Manor's smaller ground floor rooms.

When William began attending the Longmire Village School earlier in the year, Mary and Hugh had settled back at Longmire Hall, again using Everton Manor as a stopover for their business trips to Lewes, London and beyond. Both houses were fully staffed, and kept in readiness for the family at all times.

Gordon Lyons had been responsible for Mary's arrival in England, and had taken the homesick eighteen year old Australian girl under his wing. During the following nine years he had become a close friend as well as her trusted solicitor. He and his wife Celia had helped Mary deal with the authority, privileges and wealth that have been bestowed upon her, as well as the social requirements that her title decreed.

As it was late afternoon, Gordon left his office early to discuss the telegram with Celia, and to work out how best to break the news about Graham to Mary. Celia read the telegram. 'Mary and the children are at Longmire Hall at the moment Gordon, though I think Hugh was planning to stay overnight at Everton Manor when he returned from London today.'

'Thank you my dear. I'll telephone the Manor, to see if he's arrived yet.'

'Everton Manor.' Gordon recognised the butler's voice in the phone's ear piece. 'Good evening Arthur, Gordon Lyons here. Is Sir Hugh home yet?'

'Good evening Mr Lyons. Sir Hugh has just returned from London, and is having a cup of tea in the kitchen. Do you wish to speak to him?'

'Yes please Arthur, on a matter of some urgency I think.' Gordon looking fondly at Celia, who had just placed a glass of whisky on his desk. Not long after, Hugh Watson came to the phone. 'Good evening Gordon, Arthur said that you need to speak to me on a matter of some urgency. Is there a problem at the Hall?'

'No Hugh, the issue is to do with Mary's brother in Australia. Would you be able to see me at home tonight? I'd like to talk to you, before we speak to Mary.'

'I'll borrow Alfie's bicycle, and should be at your place in five minutes Gordon.' Hugh was perplexed by Gordon's last statement. Was Graham dead? True to his word, Hugh arrived at the Lyon's house within minutes, and was ushered into the study by Celia, after she'd invited him to stay for supper.

'Thanks for coming so quickly Hugh.' Gordon handed him a glass of whisky and offered him a chair in front of the fire. When Hugh was seated Gordon gave him the telegram, and sank into the other fireside chair. 'I'm hoping for more details to follow in the morning, but wanted to talk to you first before speaking to Mary.'

Hugh sipped his whisky. 'I agree that we should discuss this before telling Mary. It still upsets her that she hasn't heard from Graham since she left Australia. Knowing my wife, she would want to sail to Australia tomorrow if we showed her that telegram. We need to get more information from Mr Mee before we speak to her.'

'That's why I wanted to discuss this with you first tonight Hugh.'

After ringing the Manor to let them know that he would be having supper with the Lyons, Hugh, Celia, and Gordon spent the evening discussing the possibilities implied in the telegram. Finally, they agreed that it would be best to await further information, which hopefully would help clarify the situation.

Early the next morning, Hugh rode his glossy black mare Ebony the six miles to Longmire Hall. Pausing briefly to greet the elderly gateman, Hugh rode slowly along the tree lined drive, until the imposing multi storied Longmire Hall came into sight. He stopped to take in its grandeur, still marvelling that this was his home. Cantering the last hundred yards towards the front steps, he was pleased to see Mary open the front door to greet him. Before he could dismount a small boy wearing only a nightshirt raced down the steps, calling 'Father, Father,' and stood with his arms outstretched to be lifted onto the mare. Laughing, Mary lifted him up, giving Hugh a quick kiss when he leant down to lift his son onto the saddle in front of him.

'Good morning my love. I swear that young Bill hears Ebony before you reach the front gates. I thought he was still asleep when I saw you from the landing window.'

Holding his young son in front of him, Hugh walked Ebony around to the back of the Hall, where James the head groom was waiting near the stables.

'Good morning James.'

James smiled. 'Good morning Sir Hugh. Would you like me to take Ebony and Master Bill for a walk around the courtyard, before I unsaddle and feed her?'

'Thank you James, I'm sure he would love that.' Hugh carefully dismounted, while Mary moved the excited boy back onto the saddle and placed his small hands on the pommel.

'Hang on tight Bill. Don't forget to thank James and Ebony before you come into the kitchen.' Mary hugged Hugh and walked arm in arm with him through the back door.

James happily walked Ebony around the courtyard twice, watching the laughing child sitting on the saddle, totally relaxed, though his short bare legs stuck out sideways. '*The boy is a natural rider,*' thought James as he lifted Bill down. The lad patted the soft nose of the large horse when she lowered her head to gently nibble the piece of apple that James had put on Bill's small outstretched hand. 'Thank you Ebony, thank you James.' Giving another gurgle of laughter, he turned and ran to the backdoor, where Sissy, one of the maids, was holding the door open for him.

'Good morning Master Bill,' she said as he ran past her calling, 'Morning Sissy.'

Mrs Smith the cook, ruffled Bill's unruly hair. 'There you are you little minx. Wash your hands before I give you a mug of the fresh milk that Toby delivered earlier this morning.' She smiled as he scurried into the scullery, thinking how lovely it was to have young children in the Hall again.

A stranger entering the kitchen, would have been shocked to see the Countess and her husband sitting at the kitchen table, drinking tea, and to hear the cook speak to their son and heir in such a manner. They would not know that soon after Mary's arrival at Longmire Hall nine years ago, she had relaxed the authoritarian manner in which servants at that time were forced to work, and had also started calling the servants her staff. Most of Mary's aristocratic peers where horrified at such a deviation to the strict master/servant traditions of the day, predicting a rapid decline in both effort and lack of respect for the servants' employer and visitors.

To their surprise, and in some cases annoyance, the opposite occurred. Mary's indoor and outdoor staff were devoted to her, happy in their less autocratic workplace, and while not servile, they respected Mary and her title. She was always referred to as m'lady or Lady Mary, and Hugh was Sir or Sir Hugh. The children were called Master Bill and Miss Pat; rarely were they called by their formal names.

All staff were ready to snap into 'formal mode' whenever there were visitors, though they worked with smiles on their faces, and often spoke to each other while they worked. Needless to say, staff on Mary's estates were the envy of those in many of the aristocratic households in Sussex.

Before her marriage, just over six years ago, Mary had taken to having her meals with her staff, reasoning that it saved money preparing just one meal; plus, she was lonely eating by herself. Once the staff lost their self-consciousness, they enjoyed her company, as well as the meals that they were being served. Now Mary and Hugh had most of their meals in the breakfast room, with the minimum of staff involvement. That didn't prevent them dropping into the kitchen for a cup of tea, and some of Mrs Smith's cake or scones during the day.

Although the children had a nanny and two nursery maids, who cared for them in a new nursery area on the same floor as their parent's rooms, as soon as Bill could sit in a high chair, he ate many of his meals with his parents. When Bill had finished his milk, Mary wiped his mouth with a napkin. 'Off you go upstairs to get dressed Bill, then you can come down to have breakfast with your father and me. Please tell Nanny Roberts that you will be eating breakfast with us this morning.'

Margaret Roberts looked up from her book when Bill charged into the nursery, minus the night shirt that he had pulled off at the top of the stairs. 'Master William where..,' started Nanny, only to be interrupted by the excited boy shouting, 'I is having beckfast with my mother and father.'

Nanny's correction 'I am' was lost on Bill, as he tried to put his jacket on his bare torso. 'Now hold on my lad. You will be going nowhere until you slow down, and dress yourself properly,' threatened

Nanny, in a voice that pulled Bill up short. 'Sorry Nanny Woberts,' he muttered, then carefully put on his singlet and shirt, then his under draws and long shorts. He allowed her to help him put on his long socks and shoes, then his jacket.

'There now.' said Nanny, holding Bill's arm to stop him running off, then in a voice that brooked no argument 'You will walk down the stairs, unless you wish to have breakfast with Patricia and me.' Margaret smiled as she heard the slow footsteps on the stairs change to a run as fast as his little legs could go to get to the breakfast room. Hearing a noise behind her, she turned to see Patricia standing up in her cot.

'Hello my little lady.' She said lifting the young girl from the cot. 'We'll be having a peaceful breakfast this morning, while your brother is downstairs disrupting your parents' reunion!'

Actually, contrary to speculation, Bill was on his best behaviour, sitting beside his father at the table like a big boy, raised by a thick cushion discretely placed on the chair by Fran, the parlour maid, before his father lifted him onto the chair. While Bill concentrated on eating a small bowl of porridge without spilling any, Mary looked across the table at Hugh. 'Did you have a successful trip to Hereford Hugh?' Before answering, Hugh lent over to help his son scoop up the last of the milk from his bowl. 'Oh my word I did Mary. I purchased two beautiful stud Hereford bulls, and four two year old cows with calves at foot.'

Knowing well Hugh's passion to develop the genetics and productivity in the local beef herds, Mary could understand his enthusiastic answer. She walked to the sideboard where Fran had just placed the cooked breakfast dishes, keeping hot under silver covers. 'That's wonderful darling. The local farmers will be happy to hear that news.'

While Mary served three plates of hot food, Fran removed the porridge bowls from the table. 'Well done Master Bill. I'm sure Mrs Smith will be thrilled when I tell her that you finished a bowl of porridge.'

'No, I'll tell her!' Bill slid from his chair, and ran out through the door in front of Fran.

Mary laughed. 'Well, that was a short breakfast with our son. Still, it gives us time to enjoy some time alone before our day's work begins.'

She placed a plate of hot food in front of Hugh, and gave him a lingering kiss on the lips, before collecting her plate from the sideboard and sitting down to eat. Laughter was heard from the kitchen, which Mary and Hugh presumed was due to some antic of their young son.

CHAPTER 3

Everton Manor,
Sussex England
May 1895

Since her arrival in England, Mary had refused to conform to the popular view that women were less intelligent than men, and should not be involved in business, so should stay at home, and socialise with their peers. Although her title necessitated many social commitments, Mary had arranged most of hers to fit with her desire to alleviate the suffering of those struggling to survive.

She had, overtime, set up a number of societies, whose main objectives were to improve the lot of the poor, comprising of women with similar ideals, and others who joined because they coveted the acclaim of being associated with one of the Countess's committees. Well aware who those ladies were, Mary made sure that although they were made welcome, they were closely monitored and kept busy with administrative tasks, with no actual contact with the clients, until it was felt that their disdain for the poor had diminished.

Whilst many of the noble class believed that the poor couldn't improve themselves, Mary would use the Murphy and Atkins families as examples of how, when given a little help, people desiring to better themselves could do just that.

When Mary first met the Murphy family, Mick Murphy, a skilled Irish carpenter, was struggling to find work of any kind due to his Irish ancestry, and the family of six was reliant on money that his wife could earn taking in washing, and the pittance he received from cleaning the stalls at the local livery stables. With Mary's sponsorship, Mick was now running a prosperous building enterprise in Lewes, and their seventeen year old son Ryan was working full time in the Everton Manor market garden with Alfie.

Mary had rescued the Atkins family from the slums of London, on the behest of their elder son Arthur, Mary's Everton Manor butler, after they had been evicted from their derelict dwelling. Now living in Lewes, Joseph Atkins was a skilled employee at a reputable local leather works, Katherine Atkins had a flourishing dressmaking business in town, and their younger son Toby, a strapping twenty two year old, was a valued employee on the Longmire Estate Home Farm, despite having a club foot.

Owing to their business and community commitments, Mary and Hugh had established a routine of residing at Longmire Hall for four days of the week, including the weekends, then travelling the six miles to Everton Manor late each Sunday afternoon. This allowed more time on Monday, Tuesday, and Wednesday for travel by train to London, for meetings, court hearings, or for Hugh to visit clients of his expanding farm consulting business on the other side of Lewes.

When back at Longmire Hall, Mary made time available to meet with her tenants, both in Longmire Village and on the three farms of the Estate as well as to spend as much time as possible with her children. Mary was also actively involved in the many businesses she owned, ranging from a small shipping company, to mining ventures and manufacturing businesses in Britain and overseas. With her involvement, the majority of her commercial interests had developed into very profitable enterprises. Rather than augmenting her fortune with all of the profits, she'd encouraged her managers to increase wages, and improve working conditions and hours, especially for children. Her rationale that the workers would be happier to work, and would put more effort into their work, was soon realised when production in most of her enterprises increased considerably, much to the disbelief of many of her competitors.

Thankfully, with the connection of the telephone to Longmire Hall and the Manor, she could speak to her managers on a regular basis, rather than having to travel to attend meetings in London, or further afield. It also allowed Gordon Lyons to keep Hugh up to date with Graham's progress in Australia. When he rang to inform Hugh that Graham was recovering from his injuries, they both thought it would be prudent to tell Mary and Clara, so Hugh decided to do so on their next visit to Everton Manor.

Hugh had to keep a firm hold on Bill, as the coach turned to pass under the impressive gateway arch formed by the gatehouse to Everton Manor, Mary's second residence on the outskirts of Lewes. His son had just sighted Roisin Murphy, the eight year old daughter of the gatekeeper, playing in the small garden and he wanted to join her. 'Sit down Bill. You can play with Roisin tomorrow, when she goes to Aunt Clara's after breakfast.'

Bill knew from previous attempts, that it would be no use to appeal to his mother, who was holding a sleeping Patricia on her knee, so he consoled himself by hugging Scruffy, Mary's large shaggy grey dog, who had sat up from the coach floor when he heard Hugh's stern voice. When the coach stopped in front of the Manor house, and the coach door was opened, Scruffy leapt out, closely followed by Bill. They both quickly disappeared around the house, heading towards the stables, then to the Dower House further on. As it was late afternoon, Mary and Hugh knew that their young son would soon return to claim a toasted bun from Helen the cook.

Patricia, now wide awake, tried to follow her brother, but was distracted by Mary, who pointed out through the other window. 'Look Pat, there's Ryan coming to see you.' When Ryan Murphy stopped beside the coach and greeted Mary and Hugh, he swung the giggling Patricia up onto his shoulders, and carried her through the open front door, past Arthur Atkins, who was waiting for his employers to leave the coach.

'Good afternoon Lady Mary and Sir Hugh. I trust you had a good journey. I'll bring some tea and cake into the sitting room immediately.'

'Thank you Arthur. A cup of tea would be lovely. Is all well with everyone?'

Before answering, Arthur glanced at Hugh, who briefly shook his head, a movement quickly noted by his wife. 'Everyone is well thankyou m'lady. Mrs Wilkinson will be over to see you shortly.'

When Arthur left to collect the tea tray from the kitchen, Mary and Hugh entered the sitting room, and stood near the glowing coal fire. 'What's going on Hugh?' Mary looked at her husband, who was busily poking the fire. 'Please leave the fire alone, and tell me what has happened.' Hugh stood up and put the poker on its stand. 'Mary, Gordon Lyons has received some news from Melbourne about Graham.' Seeing her shocked look, and the colour drain from her face, he put his arm around her shoulders, and added quickly, 'Graham is alright, but I would prefer to tell you everything when Clara arrives.'

Nodding, Mary sat in a lounge chair near the fire, wondering what on earth Graham had been up to since her departure from Australia. Soon after, Arthur entered with the tea tray and set it down on the small table beside Mary's chair. While he was pouring the tea, Clara Wilkinson, Mary's aunt who had moved to England in late 1888, and was now living in the Dower House, entered the room.

She gave both Mary and Hugh a quick kiss on the cheek. 'Welcome back. I left Bill in the kitchen regaling Helen and two maids with his adventures at Longmire Hall since they saw him last.'

'Hello Clara, it never ceases to amaze me how much a young lad can fit into four days.' Mary gave her aunt a hug. How is your young family?'

Clara sat in the chair that Hugh had moved nearer to the fire for her. 'Oh, they are fine. Ruth had a wonderful report from school – her teacher has asked if she can sit for a scholarship to the Grammar School. Chloe on the other hand, is the bane of her teacher's life. I know that I should take her to task, but she's never spiteful; just a young lass who likes to speak her mind.'

Mary laughed. 'That's wonderful news for Ruth. Iris is one of the few people I know who can better Chloe, and funnily enough Chloe accepts it.'

'Employing Iris was the best thing I ever did when I took on the guardianship of those three children seven years ago. Despite her slight disabilities, she's wonderful with the children, and a great help around the house too.'

Mary remembered the shy seventeen year old female workhouse resident, suffering from mild mongolism, who immediately had the measure of the wilful five year old Chloe from the day she started work at the Dower House. While she had the distinct facial appearance of her condition, Iris had developed into a responsible, hardworking young lady, who had learnt to read and write, and was treated more as one of the family than a maid.

'Chris can't wait to see Bill tomorrow. They certainly get on well those two.' Clara sipped her tea, thinking back to when, not long after her arrival in England, she had been in court when Mary had presided over a case where three starving orphans, seven year old Ruth, five year old Chloe and five month old Christopher were left homeless. Certain that the baby would not have survived for long in the workhouse, and knowing of her aunt's regret at not having children of her own, Mary had asked her if she would consider taking on the guardianship of the three children. Clara had agreed with alacrity, and with Mary's sponsorship, the children were soon living with Clara in the Dower House at Everton Manor.

Now that Clara was with them, and they had finished their tea and cake, Mary turned to Hugh. 'Darling, please enlighten us how and why Gordon has had recent contact with Graham.' Noting Clara's shock, she added 'I have just heard about this Clara. Hugh wanted to tell us both why Graham has finally made contact, after all these years of silence.'

Standing with his back to the fire, Hugh looked at the two ladies sitting in front of him, hoping that they would not be too upset by what he was about to tell them. He cleared his throat. 'Recently, Gordon received a telegram from Charles Mee, your solicitor in Melbourne Mary, saying that he had been in contact with Graham, who had been seriously injured, and was in the Melbourne Hospital.'

Mary clasped Clara's hand. 'Seriously injured! How, and how badly?'

'Let me finish my love. Since the initial telegram, Gordon and Charles have been in daily contact. Graham was attacked on the street when he was in Melbourne, and he managed to make his way up to

Charles's office. He was taken to the Melbourne Hospital, where he's recovering from his wound, and hopefully will soon be released.'

'Why didn't Gordon let me know straight away?'

'What could you have done Mary, apart from worrying yourself sick? You couldn't just jump on a ship to go to him; who knows what would have eventuated in the two and a half months it would have taken you to get to Melbourne.' Hugh put his arm around Mary's shoulders. 'Gordon and I decided to wait a few days, to hear how Graham progressed, to save you both the anguish of not knowing what was going on.'

Clara gave Hugh a loving smile. 'Thank you for your consideration Hugh, you are right. There wasn't anything we could do but worry. At least now we know that he is recovering from whatever happened to him.'

'Something that might help as well, is a possible answer to why you lost touch with your brother Mary. He often wondered why he had never received any letters from you, and now thinks that his wife Annette...' Hugh broke off at a snort of contempt from Clara. 'Graham asked Gordon to pass on his sincere apology to you Clara, for the way he treated you, and he hopes that you can forgive him. He thinks that his wife, who collected the daily mail, destroyed your letters Mary, so that neither Graham or nor Clara had an address to write to you. It was just pure luck Clara that you were in town on the day that Mary's telegram inviting you to our wedding arrived.

Mary and Clara looked at each other, knowing how upset they had both been by Graham's apparent snubbing of them. Mary dearly loved her step brother, and Clara had been close to Graham from the day of his birth. She had lived on the farm with Tom's second wife Patricia, Mary, and Graham, following her brother Tom's tragic death while fighting a bushfire. Her nephew's rejection of her at the urging of his wife still hurt, but she was prepared to forgive him, if he was truly contrite.

Mary was as ready to forgive her step brother too. 'Do you know what Graham has been doing since he sold the farm Hugh?'

'Sorry darling, I don't know.' Hugh sat on the arm of Mary's chair. 'He apparently wrote a letter to Charles Mee, leaving it in a bank safety deposit box. The key was found on Graham when he was taken to hospital. Charles will post a copy of the letter to you, but in the interim he is hoping that a newspaper editor might send it, via an abbreviated form of communication called telegraphic reporting, to keep the words to a minimum. We should receive that in a few days. I can tell you though, Graham and Annette parted company, soon after they arrived in Melbourne after selling the farm.'

'I don't know what to say. I hate not being there with him when he needs help.'

'I think you will find that Charles Mee has taken him under his wing Mary, and will keep us informed on Graham's recovery. Gordon Lyons has sent additional money to Charles's bank account, to cover his time, and any costs Graham may need covered.'

Clara stood up and straightened her skirt. 'Well, I'm just glad the poor boy is being looked after. I'll leave you now, as my lot need their tea. Goodnight my dears.'

When Mary came back to the sitting room, after seeing Clara on her way back to the Dower House, Hugh gave her a big hug. 'We will keep you informed of all news from Australia from now on Mary. Now, I think that it's time that we rounded up our missing son.'

CHAPTER 4

Melbourne, Australia
Late May 1895

When Charles visited Graham after work, he found the patient to be very despondent. 'What's the matter, old chap? Is your wound painful today?'

'Hello Charles, I've just been speaking to my doctor; well rather he spoke to me. He warned me that the bullet has caused significant muscle, and some nerve damage to my chest, which may cause some permanent weakness. It could be months before I can go back to work on the farm, or any other job, for that matter, requiring physical activity. What can I do Charles? I've always worked outdoors, and enjoy hard physical work. I'll go mad sitting around not being able to work. Being stuck in bed here is bad enough.'

Knowing that Graham's life, until now, had involved a lot of hard strenuous outdoor labour, Charles could understand his dejection. He handed Graham a bunch of telegrams from England. 'Mary and Clara send their love, and wish that they were closer to be able to be with you.' As Graham read the messages, a sudden thought flashed into Charles's mind. *'Would Graham possibly consider, or even be well enough, to travel to England?'* The Police now had confirmation that Simon Lester was behind the attacks on Graham, and that he was determined to get hold of the contents of the safety deposit box. Being out of the country for a few months could keep Graham out of danger of further attacks.

298

When Charles arrived home that evening he ate a quick supper, then spent time thinking more seriously about the possibility of Graham undertaking a lengthy sea journey. He decided to ask the doctor first, before speaking to Graham, then he rang the harbour master to enquire about ships expected to be sailing to England in the next fortnight.

Now that he had officially been employed by Mary to help Graham, the next morning Charles rearranged less pressing appointments, then went to the hospital to speak to Graham's surgeon about the possibility of his patient undertaking a long sea voyage. The surgeon thought for a bit. 'If it's a larger ship, with suitable accommodation and some medical personnel on board, it could be quite beneficial. Mr Mee would get plenty of fresh air, and would be forced to lead a more sedentary life than he has been used to in the past. It could maybe even hasten his recovery.'

Leaving the hospital, Charles went straight to the harbour master's office, to learn that one of Mary's steam ships, the Esmeralda, was expected to dock in Melbourne in three days' time, and would be sailing two days later. Although predominately a trade ship, the Esmeralda had facilities catering for about thirty passengers, who were not looking for the fastest journey to England. The well-appointed cabins were towards the bow of the ship, situated below the passenger dining room and lounge that opened onto the deck area set aside for the passengers. When Charles explained that the proposed booking was for Lady Mary's brother, the harbour master immediately spoke to someone in the booking office, who arranged for a cabin to be reserved for Graham. Charles then returned to the hospital, and received permission from the matron to visit Graham out of visiting hours.

'Graham, last night I wondered if you might consider sailing to England to see Mary and Clara.' When Graham opened his mouth to speak, Charles held up a hand. 'Now, hear me out before you disagree Graham. If you sail to England, you'll solve part of the problem of what to do while your muscles repair. Two and a half months sailing to England, plus two and a half months back, added to the time you spend with your family in England, would be six months at least. By the time you return, you should be able to do light work on the farm, while employing others to carry out the more physically demanding jobs,'

Graham was about to dismiss the idea out of hand, until Charles added 'There is also Simon Lester to consider. While he's still at large, you will be constantly looking over your shoulder. The only thing stopping him from attacking you at the moment, is the current police guard on your room, and that won't last forever.' 'It's a tempting idea Charles, but I can't afford to spend too much of my money, especially now that I might not be able to work like I have before.'

'Well, it just happens that one of Mary's ships is about to berth in Melbourne ...,' Graham interrupted 'What do you mean 'one of Mary's ships?' Is her husband into shipping?'

Charles gave Graham a brief account of Mary's position in the English upper-class, and explained that she personally owned a shipping company, the Esmeralda being one of her ships. Dumbfounded, Graham listened to Charles's proposal that he sail for England later in the week. Charles also explained that Mary had insisted that she would pay all of his expenses, so he would send Peter, who was about Graham's build, out to buy the clothing and other goods that Graham would require on board the ship. Charles stood up and prepared to leave the room. 'One thing Graham, we should keep your proposed journey quiet, so Simon Lester doesn't get wind of it. I'm sure the police would agree to that.'

Charles had a long meeting with Sergeant Taylor, explaining the proposed plans following Graham's release from hospital. 'The inspector will be pleased to be able to stop guarding his room, but what will Simon Lester do when he loses track of Graham? He seems desperate to get hold of the contents of that safety deposit box. Do you realise that you might be the next one he will target Mr Mee?' Following further discussion with Sergeant Taylor, Charles went back to the bank and opened a new safety deposit box in his own name, into which under the watchful eye of the manager, he transferred all of the contents of Graham's box. Before taking the two keys home, Charles explained that someone else might try to open the empty box, and that the police would be watching.

The day the Esmeralda docked in Melbourne, Sergeant Taylor met her captain in the harbour master's office. When Captain Ferguson was informed of Graham's situation, and the possibility that he might be followed when he left hospital, he happily entered into the plans for making Graham's boarding as inconspicuous as possible. 'My officers and I usually go to the Seaman's Club for dinner the night before we sail Sergeant. If Mr Evans met us at the Club, and left with us dressed in one of my officer's uniforms, we could return to the ship with him as part of our group. The officer left behind would then dress in a sailor's uniform, and return with the others later. In the meantime, if anyone was watching the ship, they would have no idea whose luggage was taken aboard by the porters. Just to be sure to label Mr Evans' luggage in my name.'

Graham was released from hospital the afternoon before the Esmeralda was due to sail, and was taken to the Seaman's Club in a police cab. He signed the register for a room booked in his name, and was helped upstairs to his room by a policeman, who came straight down and left within minutes in the cab. Unbeknown to any of the staff, other than the manager, Graham was immediately taken to the room next door to his booked room, where the constable, who had originally accompanied Sergeant Taylor to Charles's office, sat reading beside the fire. Dressed in plain clothes, he'd arrived at the club before lunch, and been given the duty of guarding Graham until he left with Captain Ferguson.

The constable had earlier placed the package that Graham had been carrying in his coat pocket in a drawer of the bedside table in the empty room. Apart from some old receipts and letters, the only other content of the package was the safety deposit box key. He'd hung some clothes in the wardrobe, and rumpled the bed to make it look as though someone had been lying on it. A note from Charles, inviting Graham to dinner that evening, was left lying on top of the bedside table.

That night, while Graham was being smuggled onto the Esmeralda, the constable heard someone enter the room next door. Listening with his ear against the wall, he heard the wardrobe being opened, then a hiss of satisfaction when a drawer was pulled open. *'Great, the bait has been taken!'* When he went downstairs a few minutes later, he asked the concierge to describe the man who had just preceded him into the foyer. Scribbling this description into his notebook, the constable immediately left the Seaman's Club and returned to the police station.

By the time the Esmeralda's officers arrived back at the dock, Graham was almost at the point of collapse and had to be helped up the gangplank. 'You'd better be sober by sailing time in the morning Jack, or I'll have your guts for garters!' Captain Ferguson played up the pretence that Graham was a drunk second mate, then left his officers to assist Graham down to his cabin.

When Graham awoke the next morning, the Esmeralda was heading towards the entrance to Bass Strait. At first disorientated as to his whereabouts, he was soon enlightened by the purser, who entered the cabin to see how he was feeling.

At lunchtime the next day, after the Esmeralda had entered Bass Strait, Charles received a phone call from Sergeant Taylor, informing him that a man matching Simon Lester's description had been apprehended at the bank, with the opened empty cash box in his hands. It had taken four policemen to apprehend him, but he was now under lock and key, swearing vengeance on Graham. Charles was relieved to hear that, because Simon Lester was such a violent prisoner, his trial for attempted robbery and the murder of the bank teller in Ballarat, plus the ordered attacks on Graham, would be given priority scheduling, possibly within a week. It was a forgone conclusion that he would be sentenced to hang, as his sister had been, years before.

Although Graham didn't suffer from sea sickness, he found trying to stand and brace himself against the movement of the ship incredibly painful and tiring, so he was advised to rest as much as possible, and to stay in his cabin, where he could stand and walk for short periods of time, before sitting or lying down again. The Esmeralda had left Freemantle, and was well on her way up the west coast of Australia, before Graham felt strong enough to venture out onto the deck, assisted by a young doctor who was travelling to England to work in his uncle's country practice in Scotland. They spent a lot of time slowly pacing around the ship's deck, occasionally stopping on the bridge to chat with Captain Ferguson.

Soon after the ship had sailed, Dr Iain Campbell had been approached by Captain Ferguson, who had offered him a reduction to his fare if he would keep an eye on Graham, who was the ship owner's brother. Not looking forward to nearly three months of enforced idleness, Iain had happily agreed to attend to any medical needs Graham might require, regardless of the offer of a reduced fare. By the time the ship approached Galle, a port in Ceylon, the two men had become good friends, having spent hours reminiscing about their childhoods in Victoria, both in their cabins and out on the deck. Graham's wound had finally healed, and thanks to the fresh air, good food and gradually increased exercise supervised by Iain, his muscles were almost back to full strength.

While the Esmeralda was loading a shipment of tea at Galle, Graham and Iain left the ship, to stretch their legs wandering about the port until it was time to reboard before the ship sailed to Aden, then through the Red Sea to the Suez Canal. Before the ship entered the narrow canal, Captain Ferguson invited Graham and Iain onto the bridge for the duration of the passage through to Port Said on the Mediterranean Sea. Both men were amazed as the large ship steamed through the canal that had been hand built, and opened twenty six years ago, cutting weeks of travel off the voyage between Australia and England.

Leaving Port Said, the Esmeralda sailed through the Mediterranean Sea, the passengers and crew enjoying the balmy weather and calm seas, knowing that this could change dramatically when the ship left the Mediterranean, and headed into the North Atlantic Ocean to travel northwards to England. Sure enough, once through the Straits of Gibraltar, the Esmeralda had to negotiate huge waves, driven by gale force winds. All the passengers were forced to stay in their cabins for a day, eating sandwiches and drinking lukewarm tea, delivered to them by the weary purser and crew members, who were assigned to cater to the passengers.

Luckily, the wild weather abated as they headed northward, and it was a fine day when the Esmeralda finally docked at Southampton in early August. Before the passengers were given permission to leave the ship, Captain Ferguson asked Iain to join him in his cabin, where he thanked him for his care of Graham, and handed him a refund for his ticket. 'Iain, I have just received a telegram that concerns you from our company manager. Your father contacted the office a couple of weeks ago, to tell you that your Uncle Robbie in Scotland died not long after we sailed from Melbourne. His son has sold his father's medical practice, so now there is no longer a practice for you to work in.'

Iain looked at the captain in shock, then shook his head. 'Although my cousin Ross and I never met, he bitterly resented his parents keeping contact with my family in Australia. I'm sure that Uncle Robbie would have told him of his plans for me to travel to Scotland to work with him, and I'll bet he sold the practise just to spite me.'

'I'm sorry my boy, I know how much you were looking forward to working with your uncle.' Captain Ferguson, patted Iain on the shoulder. 'Maybe you could spend a few days with Graham, while you sort out your future plans. I'm sure that Lady Mary would welcome you with open arms, knowing how well you looked after her brother on the voyage.'

Chapter 5

Mary stared in amazement at the telegram in her hand. 'Graham on board Esmeralda. Left Melbourne May 28, due Southampton mid–August. Charles Mee.' Polly looked at Mary as she stood clasping the telegram. 'Is everything alright m'lady?'

'Oh yes, Polly very much alright. It appears that my brother is on his way to England!'

'That is good news m'lady. When is he due to arrive?'

'Mid-August the telegram says Polly. He's on one of our ships, so I'll be able to keep track of their progress.'

'Is there anything I can get for you m'lady?'

'No thanks Polly, I was about to go out for a ride with Master Bill when the telegram arrived. I'd better go to the stables before he gets too impatient, and rides off without me!'

Gathering her hat and crop from the hall table, Mary hurried out to the stables, where Bill was riding around the courtyard on Star, his small black pony with a white star on his forehead that had been Jack's beloved pony, until he'd grown too tall to ride him. Mary looked with pride at her young son sitting upright in the small saddle, gently guiding the pony with the reins held low near the pony's neck. Bill saw his mother walk into the courtyard, and called impatiently, 'Hurry up Mother. Star can't wait!'

'I'll be with you in a minute Bill. Thanks James.' Mary patted the neck of her grey mare Gem when James handed her the reins. Quickly putting her left foot in the stirrup she swung up onto the saddle, gathering the reins as she placed her right foot in the stirrup. Unlike most noble women, Mary rode astride, refusing to ride side saddle. She was an accomplished rider, and had broken Gem in, soon after arriving at Longmire Hall, astounding the experienced horsemen in the district, by using a much gentler method that they had never seen before.

Once they left the stable yard, Mary let Gem trot along the track to Home Farm, with Star cantering beside her. Bill was in his element, determined to show his mother that he was riding properly, not just bouncing around on the saddle like he used to. To his delight, Mary allowed Gem to break into a slow canter, which meant that Star had to canter faster to keep up. Before they reached the Home Farm gate, Mary slowed Gem to a walk. 'Slow down now Bill to give Star a breather.'

She was pleased to see him gently bring his pony to a walk. 'You're riding very well now Bill.'

The young boy grinned and patted Star. 'I love riding Mother, Its fun isn't it?'

'Yes it is Bill, especially when your pony enjoys having you riding him.'

'James makes sure that I take care of Star, just like you and Father do with Gem and Ebony.'

As the two riders approached the Home Farm yard, a young man limped forward to open the heavy wooden gate. 'Good morning Lady Mary, good morning Master Bill.' Toby Atkins smiled as the two horses passed through. 'Good morning Toby.' Mary and her son replied in unison. Mary added 'Where is Tess at the moment Toby?'

'She was in the dairy making butter a few minutes ago m'lady. Would you like me to take Master Bill and the horses to the stable?' 'Thank you Toby.' Mary dismounted and handed him Gem's reins. She turned to Bill, who was looking at Toby with a big grin on his face, 'Off you go with Toby Bill. Make sure that you do as he tells you.' As she walked towards the dairy, Mary watched Bill and Toby chatting together as the horses walked towards the stables. Tess Telford met her at the dairy door, and gave her a big hug and a kiss on the cheek. 'Good morning my dear. Those two get on well together don't they?'

'Bill idolises Toby. I think after Hugh, he is the favourite man in his life.' Mary laughed as she walked arm in arm across the yard with Tess. Despite being the wife of one of Mary's tenant farmers, over the years Tess had been like a surrogate mother to Mary. Soon after Mary's arrival in England, Tess had comforted the lonely girl, who was missing her recently deceased mother, and having to cope with her unexpected entry into an aristocratic life.

'I've just had the most wonderful news Tess. Graham is on board a ship sailing for England, and should arrive in mid-August.'

'That's great news Mary. He must have recovered from his injuries.'

'I've the feeling that they may have put him on board the Esmeralda to get him out of harm's way Tess. As far as I know, they haven't caught the man who attacked him.' Mary couldn't help sounding worried.

'Well, he'll have plenty of time to rest on the journey Mary, so here's hoping that he will feel a lot better when he lands.' Tess poured boiling water over the tea leaves in the brown ceramic tea pot. 'Have you told Clara yet?' 'No, Bill and I rode straight over to see you, after I received the telegram from Charles Mee. I can't wait to see Graham again, and find out what's been going on since I left Australia.'

Tess placed two cups and saucers on the table. 'How do you think Clara will feel, meeting Graham again after his insensitive treatment, when he sent her from the farm?' Mary laughed as Tess handed her a cup of tea. 'Knowing my loving aunt, I think she'll give him a big welcoming hug and forgive him!'.

Just then the kitchen door opened and Bill hurried in, carefully carrying a brown egg in each hand. He held them up and beamed. 'Look what I found Auntie Tess. Can I take them home for Pat's and my beckfast?'

'Please,' Mary prompted.

'Please Auntie Tess.' Bill put the eggs gently on the table, making sure that they didn't roll off.

'Yes, you may Bill, but how will you hold Star's reins if you carry the eggs back to the Hall?' Tess tried hard not to laugh at the crestfallen look that replaced Bill's smile.

'Oh, I..,' Bill paused, then turned to Mary with a broad smile 'You can carry them Mother, because you can ride Gem without using reins!' Having solved that dilemma, Bill ran outside again to help Toby feed the pigs.

'It's like living with a whirlwind at times. Were your boys so energetic at his age Tess?'

'I'm afraid so my love. Just you wait till young Pat is old enough to keep up with him. Then it will be twice as hectic!'

CHAPTER 6

Southampton, England
Early August 1895

Walking down the gangplank after the Esmeralda had berthed at Southampton, both Graham and Iain noticed the elegantly dressed couple, with a small boy sitting on the man's shoulders, standing slightly to the side of the excited crowd being kept back from the foot of the gangplank. 'Would that be your sister over there Graham?'

Iain was looking towards the couple, as they waited halfway down the gangplank as an elderly man made his way slowly to the dock. Graham nodded his head uncertainly. 'Yes, I'm pretty sure that's Mary. I guess that's her husband and son with her.'

Finally, they stepped onto the dock. 'I'll wait here while you go over to greet them Graham.' When Graham tentatively moved towards Mary and Hugh, then stopped, she walked swiftly over to him and smiled. 'Hello Graham, aren't you going to give your sister a hug?'

Hugging her tightly to him, he murmured, 'How do I greet a Countess?' Pushing back in his arms and looking up at his face, Mary laughed. 'I'm still your sister, you goose. My name hasn't changed.'

'What, do I call you Sis, like I did when we were back at home?' Graham chuckled, a big grin on his face.

'Sure.' Mary linked arms with her brother, and they walked towards Hugh and Bill. 'But maybe Mary would be better when we have company.'

They stopped in front of Hugh. 'Graham, this is my husband Hugh and your nephew Bill. Bill this is your Uncle Graham from Australia.' Hugh stepped forward and shook Graham's hand. 'Welcome to England Graham. I hope you had a pleasant voyage.'

Bill stared at Graham for a moment, then smiled. 'Do you ride a horse or a kangaroo in 'Stralia, Uncle Graham?' When everyone laughed, he looked a bit annoyed. 'I have a pony called Star, and Mother says I'm a good rider.'

Graham looked at his vexed young nephew. 'I'm sure you are Bill. I ride a horse at home. In fact, I still have Trixie, your mother's horse on the farm, and I rode her when I was there earlier this year.' Seeing Mary's surprised glance, he added, 'The neighbour where Clara left her returned her to me when I bought the farm back.'

Graham then looked towards Iain. 'Mary, can I ask a big favour of you, and invite a friend to stay for a few days?'

'Why, of course you can Graham. Longmire Hall is certainly not short of spare guest bedrooms.' She followed Graham's gaze. 'Do you mean the chap who came down the gangplank with you, and is now standing over there by himself?'

'Yes, that's him.' Graham beckoned to Iain. 'Iain is the doctor who looked after me on board the Esmeralda.'

When Iain stood beside him, Graham introduced Mary. 'Iain, this is my sister Lady Mary..,' He paused and looked embarrassed. 'I don't actually know what your title is Mary!'

'When we're being formal, it's Lady Mary and Sir Hugh Watson Graham, but to family and friends, Mary and Hugh will be just fine.' Mary turned to Iain, who removed his hat and bowed his head. 'It's a pleasure to meet you Lady Mary and Sir Hugh. I'm Dr Iain Campbell.' As he and Hugh shook hands, Iain looked down at Bill, who was now standing on the dock, firmly held by his father's left hand. 'And who might this young gentleman be?'

'I'm Bill. I'm five and I'm a good rider,' was the immediate response from said young gentleman.

'Right Bill, how about you, Dr Campbell and I go and help the porter collect the luggage, and leave your mother and Uncle Graham to chat. Then we can go back to the hotel for some lunch.'

Graham laughed as he watched Bill, now holding hands with both men, walk towards the stack of luggage being deposited on the dock. 'He's a bonny lad Mary. Do you have any other children?'

'We also have a three year old daughter called Patricia. She is waiting for us at Longmire Hall. Graham smiled. 'Mother would have been delighted to have a granddaughter named after her.'

Before Mary could respond, Graham continued, 'I'm so sorry that we lost touch over the past few years Sis. By the time I came to my senses, and realised what a fool I'd been when I was with Annette, I had no idea where Aunt Clara was, and I had no address for you here in England. It was only when I was in Melbourne earlier this year that I saw Charles Mee's advertisement in the Argus newspaper and remembered that he was the solicitor you were going to see, before you sailed to England.'

'Oh Graham, it's so lucky that you saw that advertisement. I've missed you so much.' Mary hugged her brother again. 'But let's wait 'till we get back to the hotel before we go into details.'

'Sure Sis, but have you heard anything from Aunt Clara? I feel terrible about the way I treated her when you left. I can't believe I behaved like that.'

'Aunt Clara came to England for our wedding in December 1888 Graham. She's been living happily on my estate near Lewes, south of London for nearly seven years now and is looking forward to seeing you.'

Back at the hotel, Hugh quickly arranged for a room for Iain, then they all met in Mary and Hugh's suite on the next floor, where the two men were introduced to Mary's maid Amy, who was also deputising as Bill's nanny for the journey. Graham and Iain were intrigued to see the interaction between Mary and Amy. Both had visited houses in Australia where servants were employed, but had never seen such a relaxed interaction between mistress and servant. While Amy was courteous and helpful, she wasn't submissive, and she and Mary gave the appearance of being friends, though it was noted that Amy always called Mary m'lady.

While they waited for the meal ordered for Amy and Bill to be delivered, Hugh reminisced. 'Remember the first time we stayed here Mary, and you ordered room service for Amy?'

Mary smiled. 'The maître d' wasn't too pleased, was he?'

Hugh turned to Graham. 'Mary doesn't often assert her title, but she saw red when the maître d' told her that servants weren't allowed to eat in the rooms, but must go to the kitchen for their meals. She glared at the poor man and said softly, 'My maid will eat the meal I ordered for her in our suite, or would you rather she joins us at our table here in the dining room?' From that day, room service has always been splendid, hasn't it Amy?'

Amy chuckled. 'Yes Sir, there is always far too much for me, and the waiters treat me like a lady. Should I remind them that Master Bill is actually The Honourable William m'lady?'

'No, I think his head is big enough at the moment Amy, and I don't want him to abuse his title at the expense of others. Just make sure that he minds his manners.'

A young waiter delivered William's and Amy's lunch on a trolley covered with dishes of food that Bill eyed with delight. As the waiter was about to leave, Bill walked over to him, said 'Thank you sir,' and handed the surprised man a coin.

During a leisurely lunch in the hotel dining room, Mary, Hugh, Graham, and Iain chatted and shared some of their more immediate news, including Iain's unexpected change to his plans. Mary insisted that he accompany them back to Longmire Hall, to give him time to rethink his plans.

Graham couldn't believe that the sophisticated lady sitting opposite him was his younger step sister, who, though a very capable worker on the farm, had never shown any inclination for business matters or decision making, though she had been better than he was at keeping the farm books. Now here she was, seemingly unaware of the esteem in which she was being held by all in the dining room, reminiscing about their early years on the farm, and telling stories of life at Longmire Hall.

By the time they left the dining room, Iain felt totally at ease with both Mary and Hugh. While Hugh and Graham went out to get some money from a nearby bank, Mary and Iain headed back upstairs. 'Iain, I can't thank you enough for looking after Graham on the voyage over here, especially during the first few weeks, when I gather his wound hadn't completely healed. If there's anything I can do to help you, please don't hesitate to let me know.'

'Thank you Lady Mary.' Mary interrupted him. 'Mary, please Iain. You seem so like family already, Bill has asked if he can have you for an uncle!'

'Thank you Mary, I would be honoured to have Bill call me Uncle Iain, and maybe Patricia might too. As an only child, I have no nephews or nieces in Australia, and only my aunt and a cousin in Scotland. As to your other offer, I would be happy to discuss my plans with you and Graham, who has become a good friend to me.'

The train journey back to London, then Lewes, passed in a blur of news swapping between Mary and Graham. Leaving the siblings together in the carriage, Hugh took Iain and Bill to the lounge, where they kept the excited youngster entertained until he fell asleep. Hugh spent some time explaining to Iain Mary's position in society, and a little of her accomplishments since her arrival in England nine years ago. Iain's respect for Mary grew as Hugh spoke. He had no idea that the younger sister that Graham had spoken about, was such a strongminded, resourceful and above all, compassionate woman.

When the coach left Lewes in mid-afternoon, Mary pointed to Everton Manor as they passed the gatehouse. 'That's home when we need to be in Lewes or London, and it is also where Clara lives, Graham.'

'Do you really think she wants to see me Mary?'

Mary looked lovingly at her brother. 'She can't wait to see you, you goose. She's waiting at Longmire Hall to meet you, so cheer up.'

Following Mary's earlier instructions, Robert stopped the coach on the drive when Longmire Hall came into sight. Graham and Iain both stared in amazement at the imposing white four storied building, with six elegant marble steps leading up to an impressive portico and stout wooden front door. Windows seemed to cover the whole of the building's façade, with numerous dormer attic windows under a high pitched roof with countless chimneys. A lake sparkled at the bottom of an immaculate sloping lawn to the side of the building.

'Wow! Is that really your house Sis; sorry Mary? It's a bit different to the old farm house isn't it! How on earth did you cope when you arrived here?'

'It was a bit daunting at first, until I grew to know the staff and people on the estate. Gordon Lyons, the solicitor who wrote that letter to Mother, and his wife Celia, were wonderful supports from the start, and Tess Telford at Home Farm was a life line for me.'

When the coach neared the Hall, Graham could see a group of people standing at the base of the steps, one lady holding a young curly haired girl, and another holding the collar of a large shaggy grey dog. Tears welled in Graham's eyes when he recognised his beloved Aunt Clara standing in the group. He still couldn't understand how he had allowed himself to be persuaded to treat someone so dear to him in such an insensitive manner.

Bill's shrill, 'Look Mother, Scruffy's waiting for me,' had everyone laughing when the coach stopped near the waiting group, where the dog was straining to get to the coach. Scruffy had been a tiny pup when Mary had saved him from drowning in the lake, soon after her arrival at Longmire Hall, and he was devoted to her; though now he shared his devotion with her young children as well.

As Graham stepped down from the coach, Clara hurried forward and flung her arms around her nephew. 'Oh Graham, it is so good to see you again.' As he stooped to kiss the top of her head Graham murmured, 'Aunt Clara I'm so, so sorry for the way I treated you. I hope you can forgive me, as I'll never forgive myself for what I did.' Clara looked up at him with tears in her eyes. 'Of course I forgive you my darling boy. Let us put that terrible time in our lives behind us, and enjoy being together as a family again. Life is too short to hold grudges.'

Graham turned to Iain, who was standing back near the coach. 'Iain, come over and meet my aunt Mrs Clara Wilkinson. Aunt Clara, this is Dr Iain Campbell, who was a passenger on the ship with me.' Iain clasped Clara's extended hand. 'Good afternoon Mrs Wilkinson. Graham has often spoken of you.'

'Good afternoon to you too Dr Campbell. Thank you for delivering our boy safely to us. And please, both of you call me Clara. Aunt Clara and Mrs Wilkinson makes me feel much older than I think I should feel!'

By this time, Bill and Scruffy were rolling around at the base of the steps, so Hugh deftly plucked his young son up off the ground, and deposited him onto the driving seat beside Robert. 'Please take this grubby scamp round the back with you Robert. I'll collect him shortly.'

'With pleasure Sir Hugh.' Bill snuggled up beside Robert and held the end of the reins. 'Should I toss him in the horse trough while he's at the stables Sir?' asked Robert, with a grin. Seeing the horrified look on Bill's face Hugh tried hard not to laugh. 'Not this time Robert. We'll give Nanny Roberts the pleasure of bathing him.'

After greeting her waiting staff, Mary introduced her guests. 'I'd like you all to meet my brother Graham, and his fellow traveller from Australia, Dr Iain Campbell. I shan't introduce you all individually as I'm sure that they are too tired to remember your names. So, when you meet, just introduce yourself.'

Polly stepped forward. 'The gentlemen's rooms have been prepared m'lady. Fran will show them the way when they are ready.' 'Thank you Polly, I'm sure they would appreciate a chance to freshen up before dinner.' As everyone entered the huge, high ceilinged hallway with a black and white tiled floor, Mary pointed to the sitting room door. 'We shall meet in the sitting room in an hour.'

CHAPTER 7

Sussex, England
Early September 1895

Like many before him, Graham was fascinated watching the interaction between Mary and Hugh with the servants, or as Mary called them 'her staff'. Although Mary was always referred to as m'lady and Hugh as Sir, exchanges were friendly and casual. It was not unusual to see Mary sitting in the kitchen, chatting to Mrs Smith over a cup of tea, or rubbing down her horse in the stables after a ride. Yet, when visitors arrived, the staff could be very formal when required. Polly, the head of the household staff, seemed to know instinctively the level of formality visitors might require or expect, and she would immediately inform the staff.

Graham and Iain were quickly accepted as family members, and spent the first few days at Longmire Hall riding around the estate with either Hugh or Mary, meeting the tenants on the three farms, and in Longmire Village. Graham was particularly keen to meet Tess Telford, who had apparently taken Mary under her wing. It didn't take him long to see how much she cared for his sister, having her best interest at heart.

Seeing them together brought a lump to Graham's throat, remembering how lonely he had felt when Patricia died. She was the only mother he knew, and she had loved and cared for her stepson just as she had her precious daughter. Clara had tried to help him in his grief when Mary left, but he now knew, after long discussions with Iain, that he had sunk into a deep depression, easy prey for a con artist like

Annette, who had duped him with her female allure, plied him with alcohol and constantly undermined Clara's efforts to help him. How he regretted those days.

Now he was thrilled to have both Mary and Clara back in his life. He and Hugh had ridden to Everton Manor when Clara returned home to the Dower House, and he'd met her wards Ruby, Chloe and Christopher, as well as all the staff at Everton Manor.

While they were there, Hugh was informed that a local dairy farmer, George Edwards, had broken his leg when he'd fallen off a haystack. His two daughters were trying to keep the farm running, but Mrs Edwards hoped that Sir Hugh might know of a farm worker who could help while her husband was in hospital. Immediately, Hugh and Graham rode back towards Longmire Hall, until they reached the small farm about three miles from the Hall. The farm yard was neat and clean, but the men could hear a cow bellowing in the barn. Leaping from their horses, they ran into the barn, where they saw two young ladies struggling to calve a cow tied in a stall, with a calf's foot showing from under her tail. While Hugh introduced themselves, Graham removed his coat, rolled up his sleeves and took the rope from the grateful girls. 'Could you please get me a bucket of warm water and another rope?'

Graham felt inside the cow until he located the other front leg and pulled it out beside the other one, making sure that the calf's nose was lying on the legs. With a rope on each leg, Graham and Hugh pulled until the calf's nose, then head appeared. Pausing for a moment, Graham put his finger in the calf's mouth and felt the tongue move. He grinned at the girls, 'It's alive; we shouldn't be long now.' True to his word, it wasn't long before a wet brown and white heifer calf lay on the straw, taking her first breaths. The calf was carried to the front of the stall, where the now untied cow immediately started licking her calf from head to tail.

'Thank you so much Sir Hugh and Mr... I'm sorry, I don't know your name sir.' The elder girl looked embarrassed.

'Sorry Bethany, this is Mr Graham Evans, Lady Mary's brother, who's visiting from Australia. Graham, this is Bethany Edwards and her sister Heather. Bethany blushed. 'Thank you Mr Evans. I don't know how we would have coped if you and Sir Hugh hadn't arrived when you did. Father will be so pleased that you saved Bella and her calf.'

'Stop prattling Beth,' hissed Heather, digging Bethany in the ribs. 'I'll go and put the kettle on for a cup of tea.

Yes, of course. Please come to the house for a cup of tea after you've finished washing.

'Thank you Bethany. Mr Evans and I will join you soon, providing that we sit in the kitchen.'

While drinking their tea and eating a slice of fruit cake, the girls explained that while Bethany normally helped their father milk the twenty cows and feed the pigs, and Heather helped their mother make the butter and some cheese, they had never worked alone without their parents, and Heather had little experience with milking. Hence the need for an experienced farm hand. Graham looked at Hugh. 'I could help until you find someone suitable Hugh. Would some of your father's old work clothes fit me, do you think Bethany?'

Before Hugh left, Mrs Edwards arrived home, and accepted Graham's offer for help after he had explained that he had been brought up on the same dairy farm as Lady Mary. Graham went outside with Hugh, who had promised to send over some clothes for Graham, and to look for a suitable worker. 'Don't be in too much of a hurry to find someone just yet Hugh. I need something to do, so let's see how I go first.'

Graham was in his element being back on a farm, although it was a lot different to farming in Australia, with the cows housed in the barn instead of being out in the paddocks day and night, all year round. He hadn't realised how much he had missed working with the animals. He and Bethany quickly developed a routine for milking the herd, and he thought that she was nearly as capable at milking as Mary had been, which was praise indeed. They shared jobs such as feeding the cows, calves, and pigs, while Graham insisted on cleaning the pig sties and the cow barn himself.

At night, he was happy to sit down to dinner with Mrs Edwards and her girls, then after the dishes were washed, they discussed the day's events and planned for the next day. Despite initial qualms about Lady Mary's brother working on their farm, Mrs Edwards soon realised that Graham knew what he was doing, and enjoyed the work. Another half dozen cows calved during the week without any problems, and she was pleased to see how gently Graham handled the new born calves, making sure that they drank from their mothers, and then a few days later he taught them to drink warm milk from a bucket. She felt comfortable leaving Graham working with her daughters when she visited her husband in hospital, happy to tell him that his beloved cows were being well looked after by a capable farmer. Looking at Gordon's leg encased in plaster, she wondered how long Graham might be able to stay.

CHAPTER 8

A few days after Graham began working on the Edward's farm, Iain caught the train to Edinburgh, then a coach to the village of Roslin, where his uncle had had his practice. Iain's father Lachlan, had lived there too, until their widowed father had been killed in a coal mine accident in 1839. Following the accident, Lachlan had applied for an assisted passage for his family to Melbourne in Australia, leaving his brother Robbie and his family living in the village.

When he arrived in Roslin, Iain headed straight to his uncle's house and surgery, to find strangers living there, who had no idea where his aunt had moved to. Mystified, he knocked on neighbouring front doors, until an elderly lady four doors down from the surgery dragged him into her hallway, and slammed the door shut behind them.

'I believe you are looking for Edith Campbell. Who might you be?' She looked hard at Iain. 'You have the look of poor Dr Campbell, God bless his soul. Would you, by any chance, be Lachlan's lad who he was so looking forward to have working with him?'

'Yes, I'm Dr Iain Campbell. You must be Mrs Gordon, my Aunt Edith's good friend. She sent my father a photo of you, my uncle Robbie and herself at a fair in 1890.' Mrs Gordon gave a gasp, then wrapped her arms around a surprised Iain. 'Och, 'tis so good that you have come at this sad time young Iain.' Letting him go she added, 'Where are my manners, come away into the kitchen where it is warmer, and I will put the kettle on for a cup of tea.'

'Where is my Aunt Edith, Mrs Gordon? There are strangers living in my uncle's house now.'

'Aye, 'tis all your cousin Ross's doing, so it is. He's a mean man that one, and greedy too.' Mrs Gordon sat at the table, after passing Iain a cup of tea and a slice of cake. 'When poor Dr Campbell took sick with the pneumonia, Ross returned to the village with a friend who was a doctor, and installed him as a locum, for just while his father was sick, so he said.' Mrs Douglas sniffed. 'But when the good doctor died, Ross immediately sold the practice to his friend, despite poor Edith's objections, because she knew that you were coming to work with Dr Campbell. No one could believe that Ross would do such a thing, even before his father's funeral, it was. He managed to convince the solicitor that you wouldn't arrive for months, if at all, which would leave the village without a doctor.'

Taking a number of sips of tea, Mrs Douglas continued angrily. 'Ross gave his mother the two days before the funeral to clear out her personal possessions, with orders to leave all the furniture and surgery equipment in place. Poor Edith was still in shock from Dr Campbell's death, and her son's heartless demand distressed her to the point of collapse. After putting Edith to bed, Joan McDonald from next door and I cleaned out all of Edith's and Dr Campbell's clothing, and personal possessions, plus all the books and materials from Dr Campbell's study and desk. Ross doesn't know that I've stored it all in my spare room!

At the funeral, Ross played the dutiful son, supporting his shocked mother, telling her that he would buy her a cottage in the village, so that she could live near her friends. That pretence vanished once the will was read after the funeral.

Ross was furious when it was announced that the practice and house had been left to you Iain, plus the rest of Dr Campbell's estate, on the condition that Edith would be allowed to live on in the house and receive a small allowance. Dr Campbell also stated that, due to his only son Ross's self-imposed separation from his parents for over twenty years, he was to receive nothing from his father's estate.'

Iain looked up in amazement. 'I had no idea that Uncle Robbie would leave me his practice, Mrs Douglas. We'd never met.'

'Maybe not Iain, but he was kept well informed of your progress over the years, and was so proud when you became a qualified doctor. He looked on you more as his son than Ross, who went off the rails in his teenage years, and has become a despicable animal, in my eyes!'

Iain felt a growing sense of dread. 'So where is my Aunt Edith now Mrs Gordon?'

'After the will was read, Dr Campbell's solicitor declared that the money from the sale of the house and practice was to be kept in trust, until he could contact you. Ross was livid, and stormed out of the house, dragging Edith with him. It wasn't until just a week ago that we discovered that he had signed his mother into the Charity Workhouse in Edinburgh!'

'He what!' Iain exclaimed, so loudly Mrs Gordon jumped. 'Sorry Mrs Gordon, did you really say that Aunt Edie is in a workhouse?' When Mrs Gordon sadly nodded her head, he continued. 'What sort of a reprehensible brute would do that to his own mother, who was grieving for her husband?' Iain sat with his head in his hands for a moment. 'Thank you for telling me this terrible news Mrs Gordon. From the way you hurried me into the house earlier, are you worried that Ross might do you harm?'

'I'm terrified that he will punish me for talking to you. He threatened to kill us if we spoke to anyone asking about his parents. But you need to know what's happened to your aunt!'

Iain sipped his now tepid tea. 'How did you find out where Aunt Edith is Mrs Douglas?

'My eldest son works for the butcher who supplies the workhouse with meat, or gristle more like, he says. He recognised Edith in the kitchen when he delivered an order last week. He couldn't believe his eyes, and he said she looks terrible.'

'Do you know the address of Dr Campbell's solicitor's office Mrs Douglas?'

'I can give you his card that he left with Edith after the funeral. Ross doesn't know that I have the card, plus a copy of Dr Campbell's will that was with other papers in his desk when we cleared the house. Come with me.'

Iain followed Mrs Douglas to her back room, where boxes of clothes, books, and paperwork were stacked against the walls. She handed him a leather satchel that he discovered contained not just the will and solicitor's card, but also a pile of stocks and shares, plus titles to a number of properties in the village, all in the name of Dr Robert Campbell. Iain whistled in surprise while flicking through the pile of papers. 'Uncle Robbie sure was a canny Scot, salting away his money like that. His solicitor is in Edinburgh, so I had best get back there as soon as I can, to see how I can get my aunt out of that hideous place.'

He turned to the elderly lady. 'Mrs Douglas, would you consider accompanying me to Edinburgh, partially to keep you away from retribution from Ross, but also to help me with Aunt Edith, if we can secure her release?' Noting her hesitation, he quickly added, 'I will cover all your costs while you're away from the village, and will endeavour to keep your home safe. Do you know of any likely lads I could pay to keep an eye on your house while you're away?'

'My three nephews are brawny lads and live nearby. I'm sure they'd love to stay in my house for a while, especially if they were being paid.'

'Right, you go to speak to your nephews, while I organise transport back to the city.'

Early the next morning, after accepting Mrs Douglas's offer of an evening meal and a bed for the night, Iain and Mrs Douglas left the village in the hotelier's personal cab, driven by his son, while Mrs Douglas's three nephews, all in their late teens, were installed in the house, tucking into a substantial breakfast left by their aunt.

Mr Roberts, Dr Campbell's solicitor, was horrified to hear of Edith's incarceration in the workhouse, and Ross's attempt to illegally contravene his father's will. He frowned when he said 'Unfortunately, if there was any suggestion of insanity when Ross signed his mother in to the workhouse, it could be extremely difficult to have her released, without the written permission from Ross.

Looking at the telephone on the desk, Iain thought back to the discussion that he and Hugh had had while on the train to London, when Hugh told him about Mary's involvement in the business world, and of her ownership of businesses all over Britain. He was sure that Scotland had been mentioned. '*I wonder if Mary could help*' he thought.

'Excuse me Mr Roberts. My friend's sister is a magistrate, and I gather that she has rather a reputation for dealing with the legalities of releasing people unfairly committed to workhouses. Would it be possible for me to ring her in Sussex, to explain this situation to her?'

'Of course Iain. Anything we can do to rectify this travesty of justice must be tried.'

Consequently, half an hour later, Iain was explaining the sorry tale to Mary. She replied without hesitation. 'Iain, I own a biscuit factory in Edinburgh, and the manager's brother is the Police Chief Constable there. He should be able to help you.' She gave Iain the name and phone number of her manager, and asked him to keep in touch.

When Iain rang the biscuit factory manager, and told him that he was Lady Mary's guest, and the reason that she had suggested he be contacted, Fergus Walker agreed to send a cab to the solicitor's office immediately, and told Iain that he would try to set up a meeting with his brother for that afternoon. Before the cab arrived, Mr Roberts suggested that, as Mrs Douglas was beginning to show signs of exhaustion, he would take her to wait at the hotel, where rooms had been reserved in Lady Mary's name, while Iain went to meet Fergus Walker, and hopefully his brother.

Chief Constable Walker was waiting in his brother's office, his curiosity aroused when Fergus had mentioned, that in some way Lady Mary Evans Watson was involved. He had met Mary a couple of times when she had visited Edinburgh, and had been impressed by her no nonsense approach to dealing with social issues of the day. He was also aware of her work as a magistrate in Sussex. Once Iain explained his relationship to Mary, the chief constable listened silently to his account of the situation. He frowned when Ross Campbell's name was first mentioned, but made no comment until Iain finished speaking.

He looked intently at Iain. 'Do you know where Ross Campbell is at the moment, Dr Campbell?'

'No Chief Constable, I have never met him and have no idea where he might be.'

'I'm sorry to inform you Dr Campbell that your cousin is a member of a notoriously vicious gang in this city, and we would dearly like to arrest him and his fellow members, as soon as possible.'

'But what about my aunt? Can you please help to have her released to my care?'

'All in good time, my boy. Let's get your cousin under lock and key first. Then he won't be able to interfere with her release.'

Iain could see that there was no use arguing. 'Chief Constable Walker, if it was made known that some paperwork that Ross might be interested in is in Mrs Douglas's house in Roslin, I would lay odds on that Ross and possibly some of his mates would be visiting her house as soon as they could. If you had some men waiting in the house, you might be able to catch him red handed.'

The chief constable looked at Iain with respect. 'That's a great idea. Do you want a job on my force young man?'

Before dawn the next morning, Mrs Douglas's nephews were surprised when six plain clothed policemen arrived at the house, slipping in one at the time before the sun rose. The boys were happy to leave when it was light, following instructions to make it obvious to anyone watching or listening, that they'd had enough of guarding their aunt's place against burglars while she was away, and as they had run out of food, they were going home for breakfast. As Iain had predicted, not long after dark that night Ross and four of his gang members broke into the back of the house where they were quickly over powered by the waiting policemen. They were shackled for their journey back to Edinburgh, to await court appearances for a string of vicious attacks and audacious robberies. Ross in particular was going to have the book thrown at him.

When he was asked to sign for his mother's release from the workhouse, he tried to bargain with the police prosecutor, but when that failed, Ross laughed, and sneered, 'She can rot in there for all I care.' This callous retort earned him a quick jab in the face by one of his police guards, leaving him spitting out broken teeth, and nursing a broken, bleeding nose.

The day after Ross's capture, Iain, Mrs Douglas, and Chief Constable Walker called at the workhouse, and were immediately taken to the master's office. When asked to release Edith Campbell, he started to sermonise. 'Only her son can sign for her release,' but the furious look on the chief constable's face pulled him up short. 'Her son is in jail, and is unlikely to be released in the near future. You will release his mother immediately, or you may soon join him. I'm sure that if I went through your books, I could find ample proof to send you away for a good period of your future.'

Five minutes later, an emaciated, white haired lady dressed in a filthy, torn garment shuffled into the office, her oversized boots making walking difficult. Looking at the ground, she didn't see the visitors until Iain sobbed, 'Oh Aunt Edie, what have they done to you?' She looked up and stared at Iain, then said faintly, 'I prayed so hard that you would come young Iain,' then crumpled to the floor in a dead faint. Disregarding the men in the room, Mrs Douglas followed Iain's terse instructions to strip the dirty rags off his aunt, and they both gasped when they saw how distressingly thin she was. 'Edith was never a big woman, but this is appalling!' Iain and Mrs Douglas quickly wrapped the frail woman in Mrs Douglas's woollen shawl and Iain's coat.

The chief constable grabbed the frightened master by his shirt front, and lifted his feet off the floor. 'How much did Ross Campbell pay you to starve his mother to death?'

'I got to keep half of what it costs to feed a female inmate. He threatened to harm my wife if I didn't follow his instructions.' The chief constable was furious. 'Is that so? How many other inmates are being treated like this? I think your books will make for interesting reading after all!' He dropped the terrified man to the floor, and turned to a constable standing at the doorway. 'Arrest this man, constable, and lock the door when you leave. You will be returning later to confiscate all the workhouse account books.'

Iain was weeping as he gently carried his aunt out through the daunting gates of the workhouse, and laid her in the waiting carriage, that was to convey her straight to the Royal Infirmary. A fortnight later, Edith was transferred to London in a private sleeping carriage, organised and paid for by Mary. This carriage was then coupled to a train travelling to Lewes, where Mary's coach took Edith and her nephew to the Lewes Hospital, to be placed under the supervision of Dr Wilson.

CHAPTER 9

Sussex, England
Late September – early October 1895

Mary invited Iain to stay at Everton Manor, to allow him to be near the hospital where Edith was being treated. He spent a lot of time at the hospital, sitting with his aunt, and soon became known to Dr Wilson.

Well known as the Longmire Estate doctor, Dr Wilson had first met Mary soon after her arrival at Longmire Hall, when the housekeeper had died suddenly of a stroke. Over the following years, he had been called to both residences and also Longmire Village to treat family, staff and tenants' illnesses and injuries, and he had delivered Mary's two children. Now a close friend of Mary's, Colin Wilson was on the lookout for another doctor to join his widespread practice.

Sharing a pot of tea with Mary in the Everton Manor sitting room, he sort her advice on the possibility of employing Iain. 'Colin, I know that Iain has no intention of returning to Australia, and would like to practice medicine over here. But at the moment, his Aunt Edith is his main priority.'

'I'm pleased to say that Mrs Campbell is making rapid progress towards good health Mary. Once she became aware that Iain had come to England and wants to stay, her improvement has been amazing. The will to live is truly extraordinary.'

'Colin, why don't you just arrange a meeting with Iain, and tell him your needs, and ask if he might be interested?'

Colin laughed. 'Straight to the point as usual, eh Mary? I might just do that.'

The next morning, Colin met Iain on the ward when he was doing his rounds, and asked if they could meet in his office after lunch.

'Aunt Edie is alright isn't she?'

'She is doing fine, and should be allowed out of bed in a couple of days. I would just like to have a chat to you about your future Iain.'

Later that afternoon, Colin and Iain were seated in his office. 'Iain, would you be interested in joining my practice here in Lewes, with the possibility of a partnership, if we get on well together?' Taken by surprise, Iain didn't reply straight away, so Colin added, 'There is accommodation available in my house, and your Aunt could stay there too, when she leaves hospital.'

'That sounds a wonderful offer Colin. Do you mind if I give your proposal some thought, before I give you my answer?'

'Not at all my boy, talk to whoever you think could help you understand my practice.' Colin stood up, and offered Iain his hand. 'In fact, come to the surgery tomorrow morning to have a look around, before you make your decision.'

Iain spent the rest of the afternoon at the hospital, chatting to Edith, who encouraged her nephew to think seriously about Colin's offer. 'Would you be happy to live in England Aunt Edie, because I would dearly love you to stay with me, when I start work again? I know my intention was to work in Scotland, but now that Uncle Robbie isn't there, I really don't mind staying down here in the south.'

'My sentiments entirely Iain. I would love to live with you, and look after you, wherever you decide to settle. I know my friends are in Roslin, but with train travel these days, we can visit I'm sure.'

For the next few minutes Edith lay quietly staring out of the window, then she turned to Iain. 'It is such a beautiful sunny afternoon Iain. Do you think Sister might let you take me outside in a wheelchair?'

'Do you really feel that you are strong enough Aunt Edie?' When she nodded her head, he smiled. 'All right, I'll go and ask Sister.'

Five minutes later, he arrived next to Edith's bed with a wheelchair and a nurse, who helped him to settle his aunt in the chair, and to wrap her in a blanket. 'Off you go Mrs Campbell. Enjoy some fresh air and sunshine, but don't stay out too long.'

Iain was careful to find a sunny area in the rose garden, sheltered from the breeze that had sprung up just after they left the building. He was pleased to see the delight Edith showed sitting with the sun on her face. She had lost the skeletal appearance of their first meeting in the workhouse, and was now gaining weight at a steady rate, thanks to the nutritious diet that Colin Wilson had prescribed for her, and the compassionate care of the nursing staff. After ten minutes, Iain slowly wheeled Edith back to her ward, and waited until the nurse had tucked her up in bed. 'I think I'll go back to Everton Manor to speak to Lady Mary and Sir Hugh while they are there, Aunt Edie. I'll see you later tomorrow, as I intend to have a look at Dr Wilson's surgery and house before I come to the hospital.'

'Thank you for a lovely afternoon Iain, I really enjoyed being outside again, and I love having you here for company. However, now that I'm feeling stronger, you need to get out and about more yourself, and maybe pop in before you go home in the evening, to tell me of your ventures.'

The next morning, after spending the evening discussing Colin Wilson's surprising offer with Mary and Hugh, Iain was walking towards Colin's house, when he heard a loud crash, a horse squealing, and then people screaming. Running over the bridge, he came across an upturned farm cart, with a struggling horse still in the shafts. Two people lay still on the cobblestones, while a number of people were standing nearby, some silent, others screaming. Quickly looking at the two people lying on the road, Iain noted that the man was unconscious but breathing, and at first sight didn't appear to have bleeding wounds. The young boy, on the other hand, was bleeding profusely from a large gash on his leg, so Iain quickly made a pad from his handkerchief and cravat, and pressed it over the wound. He spoke to the distressed woman kneeling beside the boy. 'Are you this boy's mother?' When she nodded, he continued, 'Press hard on this pad, to help stop the bleeding.' While talking, he quickly ran his hands over the boy, to feel for other injuries. Finding none, he patted the boy gently on the head. 'You're a brave lad. I'm a doctor, and will be back to you soon.'

Going over to the unconscious man, Iain was pleased to hear people shouting for someone to get Dr Wilson. He also noted that the horse had been released from the cart, and was being calmed by a couple of men, who were restraining the trembling animal further down the street. The man lying on the road had a large bump above his right eye, and his left arm was twisted at an abnormal angle, but Iain was pleased to see that he was slowly regaining consciousness. While he was checking for further injuries, he thought he could hear someone moaning, so shouted for everyone to be quiet. Startled by the sudden yell, everyone fell silent and, like Iain, they heard a low moan coming from near the upturned cart. A lady standing near the cart screamed, 'That's my Tommy. He's trapped under the cart,'

Thankfully, Iain saw Colin Wilson push his way through the crowd. 'What do we have here, Dr Campbell?' Colin spoke loudly, to make sure that the crowd heard who he was talking to. Iain pointed to the lad. 'Gashed leg. This man was unconscious when I arrived. Looks like a broken arm, but we've just heard that someone is trapped under the cart.' Colin cast his eye over the patients on the ground. 'Let's have a look under the cart, to see what we are dealing with Iain.'

Iain turned to the distraught lady standing near the cart, while Colin lay down on the road to look under the upturned cart. 'How old is your Tommy madam?'

She sobbed into her apron. 'He's only four.'

Colin stood up, and spoke quietly to Iain. 'Have a look Iain. It looks like he's pinned by his arm.' Sure enough, when Iain peered under the cart he saw a small boy lying face down on the road, covered in vegetables. The back of the driver's seat appeared to be lying across the boy's bent arm. Colin called to a group of workmen standing in the crowd. 'You men, could you please come and help us lift this cart off the little boy?' An older man stepped forward. 'We'll need some poles to lever it up Doc.' Turning to the other men he ordered, 'Charlie, you and your brothers run to the timber yard down the street, and bring back some stout poles or planks of wood, quick smart.'

'Yes Pa.' Charlie and his three brothers ran off down a side street.

While they were away, Iain used a bandage from Colin's bag to firmly bind an additional pad to the wound on the boy's leg. It wasn't long before the men arrived back, carrying two sturdy poles that were placed under the side of the cart, and lifted to slowly raise the side of the cart off the road. When the boy screamed, the men stopped lifting and looked at Colin. Scanning the street, Iain saw some wooden boxes scattered over the road. Giving one a push with his foot, he found it to be quite solid and heavy.

'Place two of these under the edge of the cart, and see if they hold.' With the side of the cart propped up on the boxes, he looked at Colin. 'I'm smaller than you Colin, and will try to wriggle under to get to the boy. Just keep those men ready to take up the weight if the boxes begin to break.' Taking off his coat, Iain lay flat on the road and began to wriggle under the cart, being careful not to touch the propped up vehicle above him, and trying to disregard the vegetables rolling and squashing under him. Once under the cart, he lay close to the boy, who stared at him with large frightened eyes. 'Hello Tommy, I'm Dr Campbell, and I'm going to help you get out of here. Where does it hurt most?'

Tommy stared at him for a moment, then sobbed 'I can't feel my arm. It was hurting, but it don't now.'

Iain called out, 'Lift the cart a fraction more, and I will try to free Tommy's arm.' As the cart above moved slightly, Iain gently grasped the trapped arm, and pulled it slowly towards him. Tommy didn't make a sound. 'He's free,' Iain called, then said to the shaking boy 'Do you think you can wriggle out now Tommy? I'll stay beside you.'

'I can't move.'

'Ok Tommy, can you roll onto your back, if I hold your arm?'

Slowly, with Iain's assistance, the young boy rolled onto his back, then lay panting from the effort. Iain placed his bleeding arm on his chest, then gently pushed the boy's feet around so that they were near the side of the cart.

'Can you see his feet Colin?' When he heard Colin's 'yes', Iain added, 'Please pull him out slowly.'

When Tommy's body began to slide through the vegetables, Iain supported the boy's head, while he was slowly pulled out from under the raised cart, then he too gratefully wriggled out into the sunshine. While Iain lay on the road, recovering from his efforts, Colin checked

Tommy, then bound his damaged arm to his chest, and supervised his placement in the waiting ambulance wagon that had just arrived to transport the three patients to the hospital.

Colin gave Iain a hand up. 'Are you alright man? That was a damned fine thing you did there, well done.'

'I don't think I'll be able to face cabbage for a long time!' Iain laughed as he put on his coat that had been handed to him. 'How are the other two patients?'

'They should be fine. Thanks to your quick action, young Billy Brown didn't lose too much blood. His mother has taken your handkerchief and cravat to scrub clean for you. And Shamus O'Toole is just happy that it isn't his drinking arm that is broken!'

The two men walked back towards the surgery. 'You know Iain, if you do decide to join my practice, these people will be flocking to see you after your efforts this morning. I might even be able to retire!'

Iain was impressed by the three storied, ivy covered, red brick house that was Colin Wilson's home and surgery. There was a small yard in front of the blue front door with a large brass lion doorknocker. Inside, the wide hall had several doors, opening into a receptionist's room and waiting room on one side, and the surgery and a store room on the other. Towards the back of the house, behind a dark green curtain, Colin explained was the dining room, a sitting room, and the kitchen, all the domain of his cook Mrs Stuart, and his housekeeper/receptionist Mrs Sullivan

Quickly Colin took Iain up to the next floor. 'You and your aunt could have rooms on this floor. Since my wife died a couple of years ago, I rattle around here by myself, while Mrs Sullivan, Mrs Stuart and a maid have rooms on the next floor.'

A middle aged woman, with her hair in two brown plaits coiled around her head, appeared at the head of the stairs. 'Talk of the devil, this is Mrs Sullivan herself.'

'Mrs Sullivan, this is Dr Campbell, who I have asked to join me in the practice.' Noticing her frown, he quickly added, 'Please don't take offence at his present grubby appearance my dear – he was already on the scene of the accident when I arrived, and he did a sterling job saving little Tommy Smith and Billy Brown, who owe their lives to his quick action. Unfortunately, as you can see by his clothes, Dr Campbell ran afoul of a load of cabbages!'

'Good morning Dr Campbell and welcome. Can I offer you two gentlemen a cup of tea before the waiting room fills up again?' 'Yes please Mrs Sullivan, but before you speak to Mrs Stuart, could you please ring Everton Manor, to ask Arthur Atkins to send someone to the surgery with a clean set of clothes for Dr Campbell?' Seeing her raised eyebrow, he quickly added. 'Dr Campbell is presently staying at Everton Manor, as a guest of Lady Mary.'

Iain was so impressed with the well-equipped surgery, he decided there and then to accept Colin's offer. Colin smiled broadly. 'We'll ask Gordon Lyons to draw up a partnership contract straight away, if you like Iain.'

'Don't you want a trial period, as we initially discussed Colin?'

'Not after your sterling efforts this morning Iain. Do I say 'welcome on board?'

'Yes, thank you Colin.' Iain shook Colin's outstretched hand. 'When do you want me to start?'

Colin laughed. 'I rather think you already have!'

CHAPTER 10

Near Lewes,
Sussex, England
Early October 1895

F our weeks following his accident, George Edwards was released
from hospital, with his injured leg still encased from ankle to thigh
in plaster, and with strict instructions to stay in bed for a further three
weeks. Although his wife had kept him informed on how Graham and
his two daughters were keeping the farm running in his absence, he
dearly wanted to be home to see for himself. Following the exhausting
journey home, lying on a mattress in a farm cart, George was too
exhausted to be embarrassed by being carried into the farm house by
a total stranger. Once he was comfortable in the bed that Graham had
helped the girls set up in the parlour, George looked at the sturdy young
man standing near the door, and frowned.

'You must be this Graham that I've been hearing so much about.'
He saw his wife glare at him. 'Thank you for what you've done while
I was in hospital. But now that I'm home, we can cope.'

Usually not one to stand up to her husband, Lucy Edwards startled
him (and herself) when she raised her voice to her husband. 'Haven't you
listened to a word the doctors have been telling you George Edwards?
You will not be leaving this house until that plaster has been removed,
and Dr Wilson says that you can go back to work.' When George was
about to speak, Lucy held up her hand. 'If you try to use that leg before
it is properly mended, you'll never walk properly again, and where will

that leave your family and farm, eh? Think about that before you dismiss Graham. If he hadn't arrived when he did, you would have lost your precious Bella and her heifer calf that day. He has calved down the rest of the cows, and the herd is milking really well, thanks to him, who by the way, hasn't had a day's wages since arriving.'

Graham stepped forward. 'I understand how frustrating it is to be laid up in bed Mr Edwards. I was injured earlier this year, and like you, found it hard to watch others doing what you feel you should be able to do. I don't want any payment. It has been a pleasure helping your wife and daughters keep your beautiful herd well fed and healthy, and I would be happy to keep doing so, with your guidance, until your leg has healed.'

'Thank you for what you have done young man, but I'm sure that my wife and daughters can carry on now that I'm home.'

'You're still not listening George! There is no way the girls and I can carry on without a man working on the farm. You bellowing orders from the house would be more of a hindrance than help. I'm proud of what the girls have done in your absence, but you would be the first to admit that there were few jobs outside that you have allowed them to participate in.'

'Yes but.'

'For crying out aloud George, listen to what I'm saying! We need Graham to keep working here, for as long as he is willing to do so. He's not trying to take over your beloved farm. In fact, he might be on his way back to Australia by the time you can work again.'

Having had her say, Lucy turned on her heel, and shooed everyone from the room, slamming the door behind her as she strode to the kitchen.

Bethany stared at her mother. 'Gosh Ma, I've never seen you get fired up like that before.'

Heather had collapsed laughing onto a chair. 'I don't think Pa has either!'

'I'm terribly sorry about that Graham. George is not usually like that. I'm sure he will come to his senses soon'

'Don't worry Mrs Edwards. As I said, I do understand, and I'm quite happy to keep helping as before, if you want me to. I wasn't anticipating receiving payment while I was in England, nor to be doing work that I love so much.' Graham headed for the kitchen door. 'It's time we milked the cows girls,'

'Wait a moment please Bethany?'

'Yes Ma, what do you want?'

'Bethany, are you beginning to have feelings for Graham?'

Shocked, Bethany blushed. 'No Ma, of course not. Why do you ask?'

'I saw the look on your face when Graham's probable return to Australia was mentioned. Please don't become too fond of him lass. It will just lead to heartbreak when he leaves to go home.'

Oh Ma, I can't help it. Graham is a wonderful man, who makes me feel that I can achieve anything I set my mind to. We work well together, and he is so easy and interesting to talk to.'

'Bethany, I like him too, and will be forever grateful for the work that he is doing for us. I would also love to see you settled with a family of your own, but I fear that if you let your feelings for him grow, you will suffer greatly when he leaves.'

Lucy gave her daughter a big hug. 'Off you go lass, the cows need milking. Just please heed my warning.'

When Bethany joined Graham in the barn, he had already started milking, and was sitting on a small three legged stool with his head pressed against the cow's side, watching the steady flow of milk streaming into the bucket between his knees as he squeezed the cow's teats. He looked up and smiled at Bethany, noting that she had been crying. 'Don't let your father upset you Beth, I'm sure we will come to an agreement, and I'll stay for as long as I'm needed.'

Seating herself beside the big brown and white cow in the next stall, Bethany sighed, and started milking. 'Thank you Graham. Pa is not usually so short tempered; I think he must still be in pain.'

'He's also concerned Beth. No good farmer is willing to admit that someone else can run their farm well, and he is also probably worried that he might not be able to carry on as before, when his leg has healed.' The two worked in companionable silence until they were each milking their last cow. 'Who is looking after your farm, while you are away Graham? Aren't you worried about what they're doing in your absence?'

'I've leased the farm to them Beth, so it is up to Bruce Scott how well they do. I know he is a good farmer, and will try to make the most of the property, treating it as his own. So, as you can see, the situation is somewhat different. Also, I haven't worked the farm myself for a number of years, and may not take it on again when I do return home.'

'What would you do instead Graham?'

'I've no idea Beth. It's been wonderful catching up with Mary and my Aunt Clara, but I need to settle down soon. I've been drifting around pretty much since I left the farm back in 1886'

'Do you have to return to Australia? Would you consider staying in England?' Graham looked at Bethany for a moment, then smiled. 'Maybe, if I had cause to. Now miss, we must get these cans of milk out to the cart, so that Toby can take them into Lewes for us in the morning.'

Mary had arranged with Bob Telford for Toby to stop at the Edward's farm each morning, to take their milk into Lewes with the Home Farm milk, then return the empty cans on the way home. This arrangement allowed Graham more time to carry out the work required to keep the farm in order. He had completed the ploughing that George Edwards had started, and had sown the crop planned for that field. He'd also spoken to Hugh about other crops that would benefit the herd. Now that Mr Edwards was home, Graham was hoping to be able to sit down and discuss this with him, and plan what other work he might be able to undertake.

Graham had thoroughly enjoyed working on farm again. He hadn't realised how much he'd missed it, especially working with the livestock, and often wondered how he could have been such a fool to allow Annette to convince him to sell the farm. He admitted that getting to know Bethany had added to his satisfaction, waking up each morning in his room in the barn, looking forward to the day's work ahead of him, and especially to the discussions they so readily entered into, about a wide range of topics. In fact, he was surprised how knowledgeable she was, considering that she had seen little life off the farm.

Wondering where these thoughts following the morning milking would lead, Graham whistled the two cattle dogs to him, and set off to walk around the boundary fences, to check for possible damage following the wild storm the previous night. He'd almost completed his check, and was following the hedge fence bounding the Lewes road, when he spied what looked like a bundle of old clothes under the thick bushes. As he walked past, one of the dogs growled and pushed his nose against the rags. To Graham's surprise, he heard a whimper from the bundle. Pushing the dog away, Graham dragged the rags out into the open, and to his horror, discovered a young girl wrapped in them. Her face was a blueish white, her eyes open and vacant, and he realised that she must have frozen to death during the night. Looking closer, he saw that she was clutching a bundle to her scrawny chest, which turned out to be a tiny baby, wrapped in a woollen shawl.

Shocked rigid at the sight, Graham stared at the baby for a moment, then picked it up. After quickly checking that the baby boy wasn't injured, he placed him inside his coat and shirt, and ran back to the house. Lucy and Heather, who were rolling out pastry on the kitchen table, looked up in shock when Graham barged into the kitchen. About to scold him for entering her kitchen while still wearing his outdoor coat and gumboots, Lucy gasped when he opened his coat and held out the baby.

'Glory be! Where did you find him Graham? Quickly, come over to the range to keep him warm, while Heather gets some dry towels and a blanket. Be quick lass.' While Lucy hugged the baby, Graham put his coat and boots near the back door, then re-entered the kitchen to answer Lucy. 'He was under the hedge, near the farm gate with a young lass, who I'm afraid died there during the night. I should go and bring her in, now that you can keep the young one warm.'

'Don't move her Graham. Ride into Lewes to ask Dr Wilson, or his new partner, to come here to see what we can do for this wee mite. Then tell the police where the girl is.'

'Shall do Mrs Edwards.' Graham grabbed his coat, and put his boots on again, then ran towards the stable, just as Bethany walked out of the cream room. 'What on earth's the matter Graham?'

'I have to go to Lewes Beth. I found a baby near the gate, and have to get a doctor for him. He's in the kitchen with your mother and Heather.'

Within a few minutes, Graham was cantering the horse that Mary had lent him out through the farm gate, and headed straight to the surgery where he was relieved to find both doctors at home. Quickly he explained the situation, and, thankful that Iain would leave for the farm immediately, he left to inform the police of the dead girl. Suspicious at first of a stranger telling him of a dead girl on the roadside out of the town, the desk sergeant began to question Graham as though he was a suspect. Exasperated, Graham snapped, 'Sergeant, I know nothing of the girl, nor where she came from. If you ring Longmire Hall, I'm sure that my sister Lady Mary Watson will vouch for me.'

He almost laughed at the instant change in attitude the mention of Mary's name brought about. 'I will have a constable accompany you back to the Edward's farm immediately sir. I apologise for being a bit brusque when you entered.' In fact, two policemen with a cart, accompanied Graham back to the farm. Putting the body in the cart, the policemen had a quick look around, then went to the farm house to check on the baby, and to speak to Doctor Campbell.

'By the look of him, he's only a day or two old constable.'

'That poor girl out there, looks awful young to be his mother Doc.'

'She might be his sister. Please take her to the surgery, so Dr Wilson and I can carry out a post-mortem to check if she might be his mother, and also to establish how, and why she died.'

Once the policemen left, Iain turned to Lucy. 'How is Mr Edwards adjusting to being confined to bed at home Mrs Edwards?' When Lucy frowned and sighed, Iain continued, 'Would you like me to have a quick chat to him while I check his cast?'

'If you would please, Doctor Campbell. He's like a bear with a sore head these days. I think he resents Graham doing the work that he can't.'

'Right, let's see if I can help, then we'll try to work out what to do with that wee lad there near the fire.' With that, Iain knocked on the parlour door and walked in, quietly shutting the door behind him.

'Good morning Mr Edwards, how's that leg feeling this morning?'

George looked up at the doctor standing near his bed, 'Good morning Dr Campbell, why are you here? And what's been going on in the kitchen, people coming and going, but nobody has been in to tell me anything?' After giving George a brief rundown of the situation,

Iain returned to the question of George's condition. 'To tell you the truth Doctor, I think I'll go crazy lying here all day and night with nothing to do.'

'Is your leg paining you Mr Edwards, or is it just the immobility that's the problem?'

'A bit of both. My leg itches something awful under the cast, which doesn't help my mood. Then, having nothing to do but lie here, and wait for people to come in and talk to me, is awfully frustrating, which then leads me to take it out on my family, and that chap that's helping out.'

'Do you read Mr Edwards? I noticed some magazines in the hall.'

'I like to read the farming articles, but since my accident, I haven't felt that we could afford to buy more.'

'Look, Mr Edwards...'

'Call me George please Dr Campbell. I keep thinking you're referring to my father when you call me Mr Edwards.

'Ok George, what I was going to say is, I could ask Sir Hugh Watson to lend you some reading material. He's well acquainted with your predicament, and has told me that he would be happy to help, in any way he can.'

George frowned. 'Why would the likes of him bother with small fry like me? I can't afford to employ his services as a farm consultant.'

Iain sat on the chair beside the bed. 'George, do you realise 'that chap that's helping out' is Sir Hugh's brother in law?'

'What! Nobody told me that. Lucy just said he was a farmer looking for work.'

'I know Graham well George, having travelled from Australia with him when he came over to see his sister Lady Mary. He had been seriously injured, and it was hoped that the long days of inactivity on the ship would help with his recovery. Thankfully he recovered well, and he's grateful to you and your wife for giving him the chance to work on your farm. So too is Lady Mary, who is pleased to see her brother so happy again. Graham told me that he has never seen a better herd of cows than the ones on your farm George.'

George was very proud of his herd. 'I bred them myself, every single cow.'

'Why don't you tell Graham that, and other things that you have done on your farm George. I know he wants to understand more about English farming practises. He's finding it quite different to his farm back in Australia.'

George sat back in surprise. 'He owns a farm in Australia? I thought he was just a farm labourer!'

'There are lot of things that you could learn from each other, if you'd just take the time to speak to him. Now, about that itching under the cast. Ask Graham to find you a thin piece of wood, a bit longer than the cast, and slip it down under the plaster, and gently scratch your leg. I stress, gently and not for too long, or you'll break the skin, and then you'll be much worse off. Right, I had best get this wee lad back to Lewes, and find someone to feed him. Think on what I've said Gordon. I'll see you again in a few days; this wasn't an official visit.'

'Thank you Dr Campbell. You've given me a lot to think about. I'll look forward to your next visit.'

When Iain re-entered the kitchen, Lucy looked at him, and he held up his hand with his fingers crossed. She laughed, and handed him a fresh cup of tea. 'So, what will happen to this young lad Dr Campbell?'

'I'll take him back to Lewes with me now. There a couple of ladies near the surgery who are happy to act as wet nurses until we can sort something more permanent for the wee thing. There's no way I would put him into an institution at his age.'

'I'm glad to hear that Doctor. They need love and care, not just the obligatory feed.'

When Iain rode off with the baby tucked under his jacket, Lucy went in to see Gordon. 'Would you like a cup of tea and some cake Gordon?' Expecting a grunt as reply, she was taken aback when Gordon smiled. 'Come here wench and give us a kiss.'

When she finally sat down on the chair, Gordon looked apologetic. 'I'm so sorry lass, for making life so hard for you and the girls. I'll try to be less irritable with you all. Where's Graham? Did you know that he's Lady Mary's brother, and that he owns his own farm in Australia?'

"He and Bethany are milking the cows at the moment. And yes, I did know of his relationship to Lady Mary, but not that he is a farm owner. Though why I didn't wonder why her brother was just a farm labourer, I don't know.'

'You've had a lot on your plate lately Lucy, so it's little wonder. If Lady Mary is his sister, do we need to call Graham 'sir' now?' Gordon chuckled for the first time in weeks. 'Imagine me saying, 'You can clean out the pigsty today, Sir Graham!'

Following Iain Campbell's discussion with George, the strained atmosphere in the Edwards household improved greatly. Before dinner George asked Lucy to send Graham in to see him. Wondering what the meeting was for, Graham hesitated in the doorway. 'Please come in and sit down Graham. I'd like to talk to you, but first of all, I'm sorry I've been so hard to get on with. Your friend, Dr Campbell has given me a lot to think about. Would you be prepared to shake hands, and start our acquaintance on a better footing?'

'I'd be glad to Mr Edwards.' Graham held out his hand, and the two shook hands. It wasn't long before they were in deep discussion about daily activities on the farm, and Lucy, preparing the evening meal, was surprised to hear her husband laugh several times.

Gordon was amazed to find that Graham knew the names of all the cows in the herd, and soon they were discussing the attributes of each cow. 'Like you Mr Edwards, Bella is my favourite cow, and I think she quite likes me. Kristy, on the other hand, is rather hard to handle and much prefers Bethany to milk her. We have had several altercations, most of which I'm thankful to say I came out on top!' Gordon laughed. 'I don't think she's ever recovered from a hard birth. She was an angry calf, and has carried a grudge ever since! If she wasn't such a good milker, I would have sold her. Each year I hope she has a bull calf, as I wouldn't like to keep a heifer from her.'

At Gordon's urging, Graham went out to ask Lucy if she would mind him taking a small table into Gordon's room, and eating his meal with him. Lucy couldn't believe what she was hearing, but showed Graham a table he could use, and followed him in to the room, with two meals on a tray.

'Did you know that Graham knows the names of all the cows, and can list which cows had heifer and bull calves this year Lucy? After supper, could you please bring me the herd book, so we can record the births?'

Eating her meal in the kitchen with her two daughters, Lucy sighed. 'What a relief girls. I don't know what Dr Campbell said to your father, but it seems to have worked. He's almost back to his old self.'

The next morning after milking Graham rode into Lewes to ask Iain if it would be possible to buy a wheelchair for Gordon. Iain said that he would look into it, so after a quick cup of tea, Graham returned to the farm. Everyone was surprised the next day when one of the Everton Manor grooms drove a cart into the farm yard, and lifted out a wheelchair, with an extension to support Gordon's plastered leg. He also relayed instructions to Graham, on how to correctly lift Gordon, and place him in the chair.

Now Gordon could sit in the kitchen, and eat his meals with the family, and if it was fine, Graham wheeled him across the yard to the barn, where he sat watching his cows being milked and fed. Gordon found Graham a willing listener to his plans for his herd and farm in general, and was happy to listen to Graham's comments and suggestions. Lucy was very content to sit knitting in the evenings, listening to the two men discuss the day's work plan for the next day, and often thought that this was what it might have been like, if one of their daughters had been a son.

Lucy was sure though, that the developing feelings between Bethany and Graham weren't those of a brother and sister. When she discussed the matter with George, he surprised her. 'I like the boy. I wish they could marry, and stay here on the farm.'

'I fear she will either have her heart broken when he goes back to Australia, or we will lose a daughter to the other side of the world.'

A week after Graham found the baby in the hedge, Mary was returning by coach from Lewes to Longmire Hall, and saw Graham working near the farmyard gate, clearing a blocked drain with a young lady who Mary assumed was the Edwards' elder daughter Bethany. Both workers were laughing as a large branch they pulled out of the ditch splattered them both with water and mud. Asking Robert to stop the coach at the gate, Mary alighted and called to her brother. 'Hello Graham, it's good to see you are enjoying your work.'

Graham looked up. 'Hi Sis, do you want to give us a hand?'

His companion gave him a horrified look, then tried to stay out of sight behind him. 'That can't be Lady Mary, can it Graham? I'm wet and filthy, and my hair has come down.'

'It suits you down Beth. But, yes that is the Countess herself, and by the looks of it, she's coming over to see us. Maybe she'll give us a hand after all!'

When Mary approached the duo, Graham laughed. 'I had best not give you a welcoming kiss Mary. Drain cleaning is a rather filthy job after a severe storm, as I'm sure you remember. Oh sorry, where are my manners? Pulling Bethany from behind him he continued, 'Bethany, may I introduce you to my sister, Lady Mary Evans Watson. Mary, this blushing beauty is Miss Bethany Edwards, my fellow drain cleaner.'

Mary could see that poor Bethany was mortified with this thoughtless introduction, so quickly took hold of Bethany's muddy hand, and smiled. 'It's a pleasure to meet you Bethany. I'm afraid my brother can be quite tactless at times. I remember him doing the same thing to me years ago, when he introduced me to the visiting vicar, just after I'd finished cleaning the pigsty!'

'Thank you Lady Mary, but I must look a fright. I'm sorry.'

'No, it's me who should say sorry Bethany. I shouldn't have asked Robert to stop the coach, when I knew that you would be splattered with mud. It's just that I haven't seen Graham for a while, and wanted to speak to him about our aunt's birthday.'

'That's right, its Aunt Clara's birthday soon, isn't it? I must get over to see her.'

'We're having a birthday dinner for her at Everton Manor next Saturday night Graham. Could you come if Robert picks you up after milking, and brings you back later? In fact, Bethany would you like to come with Graham?'

Watching Bethany's look of joy suddenly change to dismay, Mary quickly added, 'It will be a very informal dinner Bethany, as Aunt Clara can't stand what she calls 'the formal claptrap' that I sometimes have to put up with. I will just be wearing a skirt and blouse, so you don't have to think you have to dress up. For conventions sake, why not bring your younger sister as well.'

'That would be lovely thank you Lady Mary. I'm sure my parents would agree to me attending, if Heather goes too.'

'Wonderful, I look forward to seeing you all Saturday evening. If you could be finished your evening tasks by five o'clock, Robert will collect you all at five thirty.'

When Mary walked back to the coach and waved as Robert clicked the horses forward, Bethany turned to Graham. 'Your sister is a delightful person Graham. There are no airs and graces about her are there? Imagine her cleaning out a pigsty!'

'She's done it many a time, even over here. And she is an ace milker Beth. She could out milk me any day, and the cows loved her. I'm sorry I embarrassed you Beth, you look beautiful to me despite the mud, and I tend to forget that Mary is someone of status over here.'

'Do you really think I'm beautiful Graham?'

'I wouldn't say so if I didn't Beth. Do you think your parents will mind us going to Everton Manor, with Heather as a chaperone?'

'Let's go and find out, after we've cleaned up at the pump.'

Two days before Clara's birthday dinner, both Graham and Bethany had declared their feelings to each other, but were aware of the complications of their situation. Bethany decided to speak to her parents, so Graham rode over to Longmire Hall, hoping to speak to Mary. Hugh and Mary were both at home, and were happy to listen to Graham, when he poured out his feelings, and his uncertainty of continuing a relationship with Bethany.

'Do you love Bethany Graham?'

'I adore her Mary, that's the problem. I think it would break her heart to leave her family, if we married and moved back to Australia, and I couldn't do that to her.'

'Do you really have to go back to Australia Graham? What is there in Australia that you can't have here? Your family are all here now, and you could buy a farm nearby. It's not as though the farm in Victoria is just being looked after until your return. It is leased, and that could easily become a more permanent arrangement.'

Graham stared at his brother in-law for a moment, then slowly nodded his head. 'You're right Hugh. I would love to stay and farm here, especially if it meant I could marry my Beth. It would be wonderful to be near my family again too, and I could watch my nephews and nieces, and maybe others, grow up.'

'As a matter of fact Graham, the other day I heard that the farmer behind Gordon's farm is thinking of selling up soon. Maybe it would be worth your while to have a talk to him, if you're serious about settling nearby. Speak to Gordon too. He would know a lot about his neighbour's farm.'

That night after dinner, Graham sat with Gordon in his room. 'Mr Edwards, as you are aware, Bethany and I love each other very much. May we please have your blessing to marry? I plan to look for a farm nearby to purchase, as I've decided not to go back to Australia.'

'Of course you have my blessing lad. Bethany would never speak to me again if I refused! Do you have any particular area in mind?

'Hugh mentioned that Mr Wyatt next door, might be looking to sell up soon. What's his farm like Mr Campbell?'

'Old Harry? I haven't heard anything about him selling up, but then, I haven't been out and about for a few weeks. Well now, as you know, our back field adjoins his property. Harry's farm is about the same size as mine, has similar soil for most of it, but has some river flats and a few rolling slopes away from the river. He's done quite well on the family farm, but is getting on in years, and has no family to pass it on to. It would certainly be worth your while speaking to him Graham, if farming around here is what you truly want. I know Lucy and I would be thrilled to have you and Bethany as our neighbours.'

Bethany flew into his arms when Graham re-entered the kitchen. 'What did he say?'

'He said yes.' Graham swung Bethany around, then gave Lucy a hug. 'Do we have your blessing as well, Mrs Edwards?'

'Of course you do, you silly boy, even more so since Bethany told me that you plan to stay in England.'

CHAPTER 11

Near Lewes
Sussex, England
Late October 1895

The next day, Graham and Hugh rode into Harry Wyatt's farm yard, scattering chickens scratching in the dirt. The two storied stone farm house looked to be in good condition, although the window frames and door looked to be in need of fresh paint. As they dismounted, an elderly man with snowy white hair and beard, shuffled out of the barn, and shaded his eyes to look towards them. Hugh walked over, to shake the old man's hand.

'Good morning Mr Wyatt, how are you this morning?'

'Good morning Sir Hugh, was I expecting you this morning?'

'No Mr Wyatt, I've brought my brother in-law Graham Evans over to meet you.'

Graham shook hands with Mr Wyatt. 'Good morning Mr Wyatt. It's nice to meet you.'

'Brother in-law? Does that mean you are Lady Mary's brother? What's your title then?'

'I'm happy to be just plain Mr Evans, Mr Wyatt. When I was two, my widowed father married Lady Mary's mother, before Lady Mary was born. We grew up together on a dairy farm in Australia, but I had no idea of her aristocratic back ground and title until I arrived in England earlier this year.'

'The old man chuckled. 'Are you the chap what has been working on Gordon Edward's place next door? I reckon I've seen you in his back field. That were a bad business, that accident. He were lucky the place didn't go to rack and ruin, being laid up like that for so long.'

'Yes, Graham has been working for Gordon, and has enjoyed the English way of farming so much he wants to buy a farm here. Are you still planning to sell up Mr Wyatt, like you told me last week?'

'Aye Sir Hugh, if the right person comes along. I won't sell to just any Tom, Dick or Harry mind.'

'Mr Wyatt, I'm sure that Mr Edwards would give me a reference, if you asked him. He seems pleased with the work that I've been doing while he has been injured. Would it be possible to have a look around while we are here?'

Nodding his head, the elderly farmer turned and re-entered the barn. Hugh and Graham followed him, and found themselves in a large cow barn with twenty large red and white cows tied up in individual stalls. They were munching on grain in the feed bins in front of them, and the floor had recently been scrapped clean. Mr Wyatt explained as the three men slowly walked around the farm yard. 'Some of these girls come from Gordon's bull. Nice cows they be. Good temperament and easy to milk. My grandfather helped his father build this barn when he were a boy. The storage barn next door holds enough fodder for the winter months, and the stables will hold four horses. Pigsties for four sows and their litters over there, but my pigs spend a lot of time foraging outside. Keeps them healthier.'

Finally, they went into the kitchen, where Mr Wyatt pulled the kettle onto the hob, and set out three cups and saucers. The kitchen was clean, but old fashioned. 'There be four bedrooms upstairs, and a dining room and parlour downstairs with the kitchen and scullery. The laundry and privy are out back. There's also a workman's cottage near the stables, but it's been empty for a good while now.'

Seated at the table with their cups of tea in front of them, Graham looked at the elderly man. 'How big is your farm Mr Wyatt?'

'Forty acres Mr Evans, and I be asking £5,000.00 all up, herd included.'

Graham glanced at Hugh, who slightly inclined his head. 'I'm very interested in buying your farm Mr Wyatt, but could I please have a couple of days to discuss it with my family, and also to arrange for money to be transferred from my bank in Melbourne?' After a brief pause, Mr Wyatt nodded his head. 'Lady Mary and I will stand surety for Graham, Mr Wyatt. Thank you for your time. Would you like me to get Mr Lyons to draw up a bill of sale?'

Hugh turned to his brother in law as they rode back to the Edward's Farm. 'Well, what did you think of the place Graham?'

'I think it would be perfect Hugh. I'm sure that Bethany and her mother could do wonders in remodelling the kitchen, and probably the rest of the house. The farm buildings are sound, and won't need much change, and to get the herd, horses and plant included is more than I could have dreamt of.'

I agree Graham. I think the old boy is quite desperate to sell up. You might, over time, work the two farms together.'

It was decided, with Clara's blessing, to announce the engagement at her birthday dinner. George and Lucy were invited to attend as well as the girls, which sent Lucy into a flap about what to wear, until Bethany reminded her that Lady Mary did not want it to be a formal dinner.

The afternoon of the dinner, the cows were milked a little earlier, to allow Graham and Bethany time to get ready. On the dot of five thirty, Robert drove Mary's coach into the farm yard. Once Gordon had been lifted into the coach, and placed on one seat, Lucy and her daughters were handed in by Robert, and sat on the opposite seat. Lucy whispered to her husband, 'I felt like the queen, when I was handed up into the coach.'

With the wheelchair tied to the back of the coach, and Graham sitting beside Robert, the Edward's family were driven to Everton Manor. Mary and Clara were at the front steps to welcome the family, who were quite self-conscious, until Bill tumbled down the steps in his haste to meet the visitors, and landed in front of Gordon in his wheelchair, where a discussion was underway about the matter of getting Gordon and the chair up the steps to the front door.

Bill looked beseechingly at his mother. 'Oh, can I have a ride in that wheelychair please Mother?'

Gordon looked at Mary. 'Is this your son Lady Mary? I would be happy for him to sit on my lap, while I'm wheeled inside.'

'Why don't I push you and my son around to the back door, where there are no steps? Is that alright with you Mrs Edwards?'

'Lucy, please Sir Hugh. Yes, that would be fine, thank you.'

So, while Graham and the women entered through the front door with Mary and Clara, Hugh pushing the wheelchair and its two occupants, followed the coach around to the courtyard, where Bill pleaded to show Mr Edwards his pony. Finally, they entered through the back door, greeting Mrs Peters and the two maids as they went through the kitchen to the sitting room.

Lucy was fascinated, watching, and listening to the servants interact with the Countess. Slowly she began to relax as they waited in the sitting room, sipping sherry, while Dr Campbell and a number of people Lucy didn't know, who seemed to be on quite familiar terms with Lady Mary and Sir Hugh, arrived. Soon though, Lucy was chatting happily to Katherine Atkins and Bridgette Murphy about dress making, while Gordon was in a group of men with Hugh, discussing cattle breeding.

Clara attached herself to Heather, who was at a bit of a loss while Bethany and Graham were busy chatting to everyone. 'It's a bit overwhelming, isn't it Heather? I still find it hard to cope with, and I will be quite relieved to head back to the Dower House. Let me introduce you to my ward Ruth, who is about your age.'

By the time the guests were invited to enter the dining room, the Edward's family felt quite at ease. Following a delightful four course meal, a large iced cake with fifty candles was carried into the room, and placed in front of Clara. After a resounding rendition of 'Happy Birthday', Clara was invited to blow out the candles. This she achieved, with the aid of Ruby, Heather and Chloe.

When the cake was removed to be cut up, Mary stood up and tapped a spoon to her glass. 'May I have everyone's attention please?' To a quietened room she continued, 'It gives me great pleasure, in conjunction with Mr and Mrs Edwards, to announce the engagement of their daughter Bethany to my brother Graham.'

To loud applause, the embarrassed couple stood up, and Graham placed the ring they had bought earlier in the week, on Bethany's ring finger of her left hand.

All too soon, it was time to leave, and Robert drove the happy family home. On the way to the farm, he told Graham that Lady Mary wanted to see him the following day.

The next morning, once Graham and Bethany had finished the morning work, Graham rode over to Everton Manor to see Mary, wondering what she wanted to speak to him about. Before he could see her, his young nephew claimed him, and took him to the stables, where one of the cats had four tiny kittens.

'Could I keep these kittens, Uncle Graham?'

'That's really for your mother and father to decide Bill. Have you asked them yet?'

'No, not really. Can't you just say yes?'

'No, I'm afraid that's not the way it works Bill. If you don't think your parents will agree, you can't just go to other people, and ask them instead. Or worse still, if your parents have already said 'no'. By the look on your face, I'd say that's happened, hasn't it?'

Bill looked at the ground, and scuffed his feet, then defiantly looked up at his uncle. 'Mother just said I couldn't have one. But that didn't mean I couldn't have two, does it Uncle Graham?'

Graham swung Bill up onto his shoulders. 'I wouldn't use those bargaining tactics with your mother Bill. Wait until the kittens are a few weeks older, then maybe ask again for just one. They are too young to leave their mother at the moment, and she still has to feed them.' When they reached the back door, Graham put Bill down and he ran off into the house, while Graham went into the hall to ask Arthur where Mary was.

'She's in the study at the moment sir.'

'Thanks Arthur. I feel a bit like a schoolboy summonsed to the headmaster's office.'

'No need to Graham.' His sister appeared at the study doorway. 'Arthur, could we have some tea and cake please? Come in Graham, I'm not going to cane you!'

Following Mary into the study, the two siblings sat in front of the fire. 'Congratulations again on your engagement Graham. I was so pleased to be able to announce it for you and Bethany last night. Have you made any wedding plans yet?'

'Everything has come to a head so quickly Sis, we haven't planned past last night. Personally, I'd like to marry Beth as soon as we can, because working and living on the farm with the family is very difficult.'

'I can imagine Graham. You and Bethany need to sit down, and plan a date and church, though for proprieties sake, you shouldn't live at the farm with Bethany now, until you're married. Has Harry Wyatt decided on a sale date yet?'

'Once Charles Mee can arrange for the transfer of my money from Australia to my new bank account here, Gordon Lyons will draw up the sale documents. I know that Mr Wyatt would like to leave as soon as he can, now that he has agreed that I can buy his farm. I wish I could stay with him, and get to know his cows, while he is still there, but I can't milk both herds.'

'Graham, would you allow me to pay for the farm now, then you pay me back when your money arrives? Also, I know of a young couple who are looking for farm work, and could help out on both farms, while your future father in–law is still incapacitated.' Graham stood up and gave Mary a big hug. 'Thanks Sis, you've given me a lot to think about and to discuss with Beth. I'll let you know what we decide, as soon as I can.'

Mary heard him whistling like old times as he left the house.

CHAPTER 12

Scotland
Early November 1895

Iain Campbell was settling in well, working with Dr Wilson. He'd moved into one of the bedrooms upstairs, and had cleared the room next door for his aunt, who at present was convalescing at Everton Manor. She had been released from Lewes Hospital, on the condition that a nurse was employed to monitor her recovery.

Iain and Colin found that they had a lot in common, and when possible, chatted over breakfast and in the evenings, if they were both at home. Back in Australia, Iain had had little contact with other doctors in the practice where he'd worked in Melbourne, and was learning a lot from Colin. He soon discovered the highs and lows of home visits, both in the more salubrious and the poorer areas of Lewes, by day and at night, and was interested in learning how Colin coped with the issues he had to deal with. He was also finding his way to patients out in the country, driving the horse and covered buggy, although for the first week, a local lad was employed to drive. Much as he enjoyed the journeys in fine weather, Iain had been warned that it would be very different when winter set in.

One morning, Iain received a letter from Mr Roberts, his Scottish solicitor, requesting his attendance at his office as quickly as possible. Iain showed Colin the letter. 'You must leave today Iain. I can cope, so long as you don't decide to stay up in Scotland for too long.' Before he had time to think too much, Iain found himself on the train to

Edinburgh, which arrived in time for dinner at the hotel where he had booked a room. At nine o'clock the next morning he met with Mr Roberts in his office.

'Thank you for coming so promptly Iain. The urgency for a face to face meeting is due to your cousin Ross, who is claiming that you are an imposter, and are not really Robert Campbell's nephew. Although he's likely to be sentenced to a long spell in jail for his leadership of the thugs that have been terrorising the area of late, he's contesting your uncle's will.'

'But what's led him to do that now?'

'I don't know Iain, but he's denying that he ever had a cousin called Iain. His solicitor has given you a month to provide proof of your identity. Do you have your birth certificate with you in England?'

'I do have one, but it's in my father's desk in Australia. I'll have to have it sent to England.'

'That won't arrive in time, I'm afraid. Also, Ross is claiming that your aunt's removal from the workhouse was unlawful, and that his mother is an unreliable witness to say that you are her nephew. Do you have any other identifying documents in your possession?'

'Only my medical credentials, that I assume Ross will try to defame.'

Iain looked at Mr Roberts in despair, and noticed a photo of Mr Roberts with a lady and a small boy, on a shelf behind the desk. Struck by a sudden thought, Iain leant forward. 'My mother and Aunt Edie kept in regular contact over the years, sending family photos and presents for Christmas and birthdays. I know that my mother sent them a photo of my parents and me on my Graduation Day. Father and I looked very like the photos that we had of Uncle Robbie. I wonder if that photo, or anything else that might help prove who I am might be amongst the things stored in Mrs Douglas's spare room. I'll go to Roslin straight away to see her, as I do need to clear my uncle's things out for her.'

'They might do the trick, if you can find them Iain.' Mr Roberts stood up and shook Iain's hand. 'Good luck my boy. Bring back anything you think might be of use.'

Mrs Douglas was thrilled to see Iain later that morning, and invited him in for a cup of tea and a bite of lunch, before he started on his uncle's belongings. Sitting at the kitchen table, Iain told Mrs Douglas how well her friend Edith was progressing, and again thanked her for her help in her rescue.

He spent the afternoon sorting through the boxes in Mrs Douglas's spare room. The clothing, books, and medical instruments he re-boxed, intending to send them down to Lewes. Opening his uncle's medical bag, Iain found it to be fully equipped for an emergency medical visit so he decided to take it with him on his return to Lewes, to use for his future call outs.

Going through the personal possessions removed from his uncle's study, Iain found the graduation photo that he'd spoken about, plus many others of his family, and some of his aunt and uncle. It was noticeable that there were no photos of Ross. Probably Iain guessed, because he had left home before it became popular to have photos taken.

There was also a bundle of letters from his mother, dating back to 1859, not long after Iain's parents were married, detailing life in Australia, the birth of their son Iain in 1860, his childhood and education, plus his graduation as a doctor like his uncle. There appeared to be at least two letters every year, up to the last letter, expressing Lachlan's and her delight in Robert's invitation for his nephew Iain, to join him in his practice at Roslin. There was also Iain's hand written reply to his uncle, expressing his desire to join his uncle's practice, and his hope to be working with him well before Christmas of 1895.

Once arrangements were made for the boxes to be forwarded to London, Iain took his leave of Mrs Douglas, after issuing an invitation for her to visit his aunt in Lewes, once she was settled in Dr Wilson's house.

He took his uncle's medical bag, and the leather satchel full of photos and letters back to Edinburgh, hoping that this would be evidence enough to thwart Ross's claims. Iain was determined to fight Ross, not for his own benefit, but for his aunt, to allow her to have an independent income for the rest of her life.

Mr Roberts was elated to see the photos and letters, particularly Iain's handwritten letter to his uncle. 'I'll contact a handwriting expert to compare your writing with that letter immediately. I think this evidence will refute your cousin's claim totally. I hope you don't mind Iain, but yesterday I took the liberty to speak to the doctor who treated your aunt in hospital when she was first released from the workhouse, to verify her sanity. He's happy to send a written statement, confirming Mrs Campbell's sanity, and also he queried if her son's sanity has been assessed! We might just look into that, and fight fire with fire.'

Iain stayed in Edinburgh for three days, by which time Ross's claim had been dismissed entirely. Ross's reaction to the news was so violent, he was immediately put into a straightjacket, and taken to a padded cell, to await assessment to determine whether he should be sentenced to a mental asylum rather than jail.

Relieved to be back in Lewes, Iain went to Everton Manor to see his aunt, to inform her of the results of his visit to Edinburgh. While shocked at the prospect of her son's incarceration in an asylum, Edith was not totally surprised. As she said, he had become more and more irrational as he grew older, and his father had suspected that he may have been using opium or cocaine, since leaving home in his mid-teens.

Edith was steadily gaining weight, and feeling much more like her old self, now that the effects of the medications forcibly administered to her in the workhouse had finally worn off. While she enjoyed staying at Everton Manor to recuperate, and was very appreciative of all the care that she had been receiving, Edith was keen to move to her new home in Lewes, and to get back to a more normal routine.

When she arrived at the surgery, Edith was greeted by Mrs Sullivan, who took her straight up to her bedroom that had been re decorated with new curtains and wallpaper. As well as her bedroom, there was a bathroom across the hall for Iain's and her use. Once Edith had surveyed her fresh, spacious room with a large four poster bed, tallboy, wardrobe and two comfortable chairs beside the fireplace, Mrs Sullivan invited her to accompany her to the kitchen for a cup of tea. Passing the living room, and the dining room near the kitchen on the ground floor, Mrs Sullivan opened the doors. 'We hope that you and Dr Campbell will use these rooms with Dr Wilson. It will do him good to have company again, when he's not on call.'

Mrs Sullivan and Mrs Stuart the cook, had first met Edith when Iain showed her their proposed new home the day she left hospital. The housekeeper and cook had both liked the small Scotswoman on their first introduction, and were determined to help Edith settle into her new life as easily as possible. It wasn't long before the three women were on a first name basis, and Molly Sullivan and Edith were sitting at the kitchen table cutting up vegetables, while Susan Stuart prepared a leg of lamb, to roast for the evening meal.

'I gather from Dr Campbell, that you were your husband's receptionist Edith. Would you by any chance be interested in doing some of that for this surgery, when you have settled in?'

Susan laughed. 'Molly was roped into the job, when Dr Wilson's wife died, and was sort of stuck with it.'

'I wouldn't be sorry to give it up, especially now that there are more people living in the house.'

'If you are sure that I wouldn't be stepping on toes Molly, I would love to help. I've always been busy, until my husband died, and being idle now that I'm feeling better is hard to take.'

'It would be a pleasure to hand it over to you Edith. I'll help out if needed, like I give Susan a hand at times.'

'Do you like cooking Edith? I'm not one of those precious cooks, who won't let others in their kitchen, so anytime you feel like cooking, let me know, though I'm not the best at bookwork.'

'Thank you Susan, I do quite like cooking. I'll introduce you to some Scottish dishes one day. Maybe I could start with some shortbread.'

That night, Iain was pleased to see his aunt settling in so well, happily joining in the conversation, as the five of them enjoyed their dinner together in the dining room. After dinner, while Edith was in the kitchen, Molly asked Iain, 'To save Edith grief from hearing you constantly being referred to as Dr Campbell, would you mind if we called you Dr Iain, in the house at least?'

'I think that's a wonderful idea Molly, especially so soon after Uncle Robbie's passing.'

'What say you call me Dr Colin as well?'

'Wonderful, Dr Colin and Dr Iain you shall be!'

During the next couple of weeks, Edith eased into the receptionist role, making the front office her own space. The doctors and her two new friends kept an eye on her, to ensure that she didn't overexert herself. They were all thrilled, when Edith thrived, through once again doing the work that she had carried out for more than thirty years with her husband.

Chapter 13

Sussex, England
Early November 1895

Early one morning, before riding over to milk the herd next door, Graham stood in his new barn doorway, watching Harry stroking the cheek of one of Graham's new cows. 'I love you Rosie, you're the best cow in the world,' crooned Harry, unaware of Graham until he stepped into the barn. Startled, the young man stepped back and stuttered 'I-I-I love Rosie, M-Mr G-Graham.'

'I'm sorry I gave you a fright Harry.' Graham handed the young man an empty milking bucket. 'Rosie is a pretty special cow I agree, and I think she likes you too.' Both men began to milk their selected cows, and as Graham watched the white streams of milk flow into his bucket, he thought how sad it was that Harry's domineering father, Sir Gerald Knight, a local land owner, had almost ruined his youngest son's life.

Suffering from a young age with a slight hesitation in his speech, Harry's childhood had been tormented by his father's constant ridicule, and also physical punishment, leading to the development of a very pronounced stutter. He was victimised at school by his brothers and their friends, to the point that he stopped talking altogether. He found solace with the animals on his father's large property, and he spoke to them quite normally, providing no one was nearby.

Hettie, the young dairy maid, befriended the miserable boy, and after a while, he began to speak haltingly, then more confidently when they were alone together. Harry left school before he was sixteen, and worked on the farm as a labourer, until he was twenty one. When he informed his father in writing that he and Hettie wished to marry, his infuriated father dismissed Hettie on the spot, refused her a reference, and wouldn't pay the wages owed to her. He also spread word in the area, that she was an untrustworthy slut.

Harry was given such a thrashing, his brothers feared that their father might kill him. Eventually they managed to restrain him long enough for Harry to be taken out to the room above the stables that he had occupied for the past five years. It took many days before Harry could stand, and stagger painfully around his room. A week later, he managed leave his room, and stumble to an old shepherd's hut at the end of the property, where he and Hettie had sometimes met. He collapsed on to some old bedding in the corner of the hut, and knew nothing more, until he felt water dripping onto his face. Slowly regaining consciousness, he found a distraught Hettie leaning over him, crying.

The young couple stayed hidden in the hut, until Harry was strong enough to walk, with Hettie's help, to the nearest station, where they caught a train to Hettie's village. There, after consultation with Hettie's parents, the couple were married at the local Methodist church, and stayed with her parents. Unfortunately, Harry's father tracked them down, and convinced Hettie's parents that the young couple would be better off working again on his property.

Unbeknown to her parents, Sir Gerald took Harry and Hettie straight to the Lewes Workhouse, and had them admitted as a destitute couple. Poor Harry was unable to speak, and little notice was taken of Hettie's pleas for justice. Luckily for the young couple, the master was not at all happy with Sir Gerald's justification for committing his son and daughter in-law, so he mentioned them to Mary on her next visit to the workhouse. Immediately she asked to see Hettie, and soon had a full account of what had occurred.

Appalled, Mary asked for Harry to be sent up to the office, and was dismayed to find that a fortnight of incarceration in the men's quarters had turned Harry into a virtual physical wreck, who had to be carried into the office by two men. Seeing Hettie, Harry could only just lift his head, then he lay on the floor where he had been placed, crying as she held him in her arms.

Mary turned to the horrified master. 'Thank you for bringing this situation to my attention Mr Henderson. Mr and Mrs Knight will from now on be employed by me, and will reside at Longmire Hall, so please draw up their release papers immediately.' Turning to Hettie, Mary added, 'Hettie, please go down and ask the porter to let my coachman in, and bring him up to this office.' A few minutes later, Robert arrived in the office. 'Please take Mr Knight to the coach and make him comfortable Robert. Mrs Knight and I will follow, when we retrieve their clothes and paperwork.'

'Yes m'lady.' Robert stooped and picked Harry up, then carefully carried him down to the coach waiting outside the imposing walls, where he gently laid him on one of the seats, and placed a rug over him. 'There now lad, you just lie there. You're safe now that Lady Mary is involved, no matter what your father has to say.' Not long after, Mary and Hettie arrived, carrying a small bundle of clothes, and sat on the seat opposite Harry. Mary looked at the bewildered young man huddled under the rug. 'Try not to worry too much Harry. You're now officially one of my employees, so your father has no legal cause to drag you away. You and Hettie will be my guests at Longmire Hall, where my cook will take great delight in feeding you both with plenty of nutritious food. There's an empty cottage nearby waiting for new occupants, so once you feel able, you'll move in to your own home.'

Hettie was astounded. 'Oh, thank you so much Lady Mary.'

'Thank you m'lady,' mouthed Harry silently.

Harry and Hettie spent a month at Longmire Hall, recovering from their ordeal in the workhouse. While Hettie helped in the Hall, Harry slowly gained weight and confidence, spending time at the stables, where he loved being with the horses, and he also struck up a friendship with Robert. The two of them developed a sort of hand language, and were often seen with Robert chatting away as they worked, and Harry answering with his hands. Scruffy and Bill also befriended the silent man, and the three of them spent a lot of time together near the stables, and in the rear courtyard.

Following Mary's talk to Graham about the purchase of Wyatt's farm, she met with Harry and Hettie. 'Would you two like to work for my brother Graham? The workman's cottage will be repaired, and made ready for you to live in. But before Graham's wedding, you would stay in the house with him, and be in charge of the herd, while he keeps milking for Mr Gordon until he can get back to work.

For a moment even Hettie was speechless, then she saw Harry nodding his head vigorously. 'Oh Lady Mary, we would love to. We both love milking, and I've had a lot of experience making butter and cheese. Thank you so much for all you have done for us.'

'Having you both gainfully employed, and helping my brother on his new farm is thanks enough. When Graham and Bethany are married and living in the house, Graham wants you to stay on, and work with them. By the way Harry, have you heard from your father at all?' At first Harry looked at Hettie, then turned to Mary, shaking his head. 'N–No m–m'lady.'

'I must tell you Harry, your father has been spoken to by Judge Stephens, and has been warned that, should he or any of his agents have any further contact with either you or Hettie, an investigation into his mistreatment of you could very well end in a prison sentence.' A broad grin split Harry's face, then he kissed Mary's hand and said without hesitation, 'Thank you so much, m'lady.'

Mary chuckled. 'If you keep chatting to Bill, Scruffy and the other animals, we soon won't be able to shut you up!'

The sale of the farm took place within the week, Mr Wyatt keen to leave as quickly as possible once the decision had been made, and Mary had arranged for immediate payment. Graham moved into the house, while the wedding was being arranged, and Harry and Hettie had moved in as well. While Graham and Bethany continued to milk the Edward's herd, Harry and Hettie took over milking the new herd. Graham was thrilled with his new employees. Both Harry and Hettie were excellent milkers, gentle, but firm with the cows, and Harry soon knew the names of all of the new cows. Hettie was a skilled butter and cheese maker, and was soon using most of the milk, to make produce that was in great demand at the Lewes market. The pigs still had their skim milk, the result of the cream being separated from some of the milk.

Carrying two more buckets of milk to the dairy, Graham noticed that Hettie had arrived, to begin separating the milk and cream. 'Good morning Hettie. How are you this morning?'

'Good morning Mr Graham. I'm fine thank you. How is Harry this morning?'

'He told me that he loves the cows Hettie, and I'm sure he only stuttered because he got a shock when I walked in while he was talking to Rosie.'

'That's wonderful news Mr Graham. It shows that Harry's starting to feel safe with you. He loves all the cows, but Rosie is his favourite,' Hettie chuckled as she turned the separator handle.

'We've nearly finished milking Hettie. I'll send Harry in to help you, while I clean up in the barn.'

When Harry went into the dairy, Graham began to scrape, then sweep the barn floor, and put fresh feed in front of each cow.

CHAPTER 14

London, England
November 1895

Mary was in London to meet with some of her business managers before Christmas, and was delighted to be able to have lunch with her seventeen year old ward Jack, at the Savoy Hotel in the Strand, where he was currently serving his apprenticeship under Chef Auguste Escoffier.

Jack had always shown a passion for cooking, from the time nine years earlier when Mary rescued him and his brother Alfie when they had run away from the workhouse, after Jack had been whipped by the previous master. Whenever possible, he spent his spare time working in the kitchen at Longmire Hall with Mrs Smith, then later with Margaret Peters in the Everton Manor kitchen.

When Jack expressed his desire to leave school early to become a chef, Mary arranged for him to work in various hotel kitchens in London, to see if it was what he really wanted to do. While working in the Savoy Hotel kitchen, Jack came to the notice of the head chef, Auguste Escoffier, who asked if he would like to be apprenticed to him. Jack agreed with alacrity, as Auguste Escoffier was one of the top chefs in London, and had a reputation for running his kitchens in a much more professional way, than many of his rivals.

Throughout the meal, Jack regaled Mary with stories of his life as an apprentice chef, now that he had nearly completed his second year. While they were finishing their meal, Jack stared over Mary's shoulder, then suddenly stood up. Looking behind her, Mary saw the head chef walking towards their table, where he stopped, and bowed his head. 'Good afternoon, Your Ladyship. I trust that you enjoyed your luncheon?'

'Good afternoon Monsieur Escoffier. Thank you, the meal was delightful, and the Peach Melba was exquisite.'

'Thank you Your Ladyship. I created that dish for the Australian soprano Nellie Melba when she stayed at this hotel a couple of years ago. Jack tells me that you lived near Melbourne before coming to England, Lady Mary. Have you heard Nellie Melba sing?'

'My husband and I have attended two of her performances at Covent Garden, and I think her voice is divine. I must admit though, it made me feel quite homesick when she sang 'Home Sweet Home.'

'Yes indeed. Your Ladyship, I wish to ask your permission to take Jack with me next week, when my wife and I go to Paris. I would like Jack to attend some new classes, being held in the kitchens of the Palais Royal by some of the best chefs in France. He will reside at our chateau, and I will cover all costs.'

Mary glanced at Jack, who flashed her a broad smile, and a brief nod of his head. 'Thank you, monsieur. Jack has my permission to accompany you to France, to continue his training.'

'Merci, Your Ladyship. This is a chance for Jack to greatly enhance his learning.' Auguste Escoffier bowed to Mary, then quickly walked back to the kitchen.

'My goodness Mary. This will be the chance of a lifetime, to learn from so many well-known chefs from all over France. Thank you so much for agreeing to let me go.'

'Make the most of the chance Jack. I know that Monsieur Escoffier said that he will pay all your expenses, but I will ensure that there is money in your account, should you have need of independent means.'

When they stood up to leave, Jack gave Mary a big hug, regardless of the onlooking diners. He proudly escorted her out of the restaurant, then waited for her to board the cab the concierge had secured, before heading back to the kitchen.

Aboard the train to Lewes, Mary leant back against the padded seat, and thought how much her four wards had developed over the past years. Here was young Jack, the eight year old boy who she had found under a bush nine years ago, semi-conscious after being so cruelly whipped, heading over to France to develop his culinary skills.

Alfie, Jack's elder brother, had preferred to spend his spare time outside helping the gardeners. Although both boys had attended the Lewes Grammar School, neither had shown any desire to go on to university. Now nineteen, Alfie was employed by the Longmire Estate, to help manage the Everton Manor market garden, as well as the Longmire Village cooperative market garden, although he mainly worked at Everton Manor, where the bulk of the twenty acre property had been turned into a market garden, growing vegetables primarily for the London market.

A number of large glass houses had been constructed, and had initially been overseen by Alfie and Mick Murphy; although now that much of Mick's time was taken up by the construction business that he had developed, with Mary's backing, Alfie had taken over a more senior role in the management of the market garden.

Mick and his employees had renovated the old barn on the new Longmire land, and subdivided it into eight single bedrooms, with two bathrooms and a toilet, to be accommodation for the younger boys employed on the developing village cooperative market garden, and also at the mill. The farm house had been worked on to become the accommodation for four single girls, the housekeeper and her husband, and a cook, as well as the dining room and lounge area for the workers to relax in their spare time. A smaller version of this residential accommodation was built at Everton Manor, with a kitchen, dining room and separate staff accommodation included.

Mick's elder son, seventeen year old Ryan, was now employed as a labourer in the Everton Manor market garden. Ryan and Jack had become best friends while at school, and were still good friends. Ryan was happy to work on the estate, and stay living with his family in the Everton Manor Gatehouse, their home for the past seven years.

Twins Sally and Jane, Mary's other two wards, had been rescued from the streets of London when they were eight years old. Sally had been blinded when she was six, in the accident that had killed their mother. However, after a blow to her head, from a misguided snowball, thrown by Alfie after Christmas in 1888, her sight had been miraculously restored. She and Jane were now both in their second year of training at the Nightingale Training School, at St Thomas's Hospital in London.

Mary was very proud of all four children who she considered as her family. They all adored her, and were determined to make their own way in life, and not rely on Mary for their livelihood, as many envious school classmates had assumed. As yet, all four were unaware that Mary had spoken to Gordon Lyons about arranging for substantial trusts to be made for each of them.

CHAPTER 15

Early one foggy November morning, just as the sun was rising, twenty two year old Toby Atkins was nearing the outskirts of Lewes on his daily milk run with a cartload of full milk cans, when he heard a dog yelping, a man shouting, and a number of young boys jeering.

When he rounded a corner in the road, he could just make out a group of young boys, surrounding a man who was kneeling on the road, hugging a bundle to his chest. As the horse and cart drew closer, Toby realised that the boys were throwing stones at the man, as well as shouting insults at him.

To Toby's horror, a stone struck the man's forehead, and he fell to the ground, with blood streaming from the wound, then the boys moved closer, and began to kick him. Furiously, Toby urged Juno, his large black Shire horse forward, unclipping the coach whip that Bob Telford insisted he always took with him on his trips to Lewes.

The first the boys knew of Toby's arrival, was when one boy felt the end of the whip flick his cheek, and another the whip across his back. 'Get away from that man, before I give you all a good taste of my whip. What the heck are you playing at Max Hodge? Don't you realise that this man can bring charges against you for assault, and you could all end up in jail?'

The ring leader sneered, while holding his stinging cheek. 'If you hadn't interfered Atkins, he wouldn't have had the chance,'

Toby flicked the whip again, this time catching Max around his bare legs, and with a jerk of his wrist, he toppled the boy to the ground. Toby moved Juno to stand close to the prone boy. 'Best lie still Max, or Juno will step on you.' Seeing the boy's bulging pockets he added, 'Now, empty your pockets out onto the ground.'

Staring nervously up at the horse towering over him, the sullen boy slowly removed a grubby rag, some medals, and finally a bulging leather pouch from his pockets, and placed them on the ground. The rest of the boys had moved out of range of Toby's whip, and were about to pick up more stones. 'I wouldn't do that lads. I know all your names, and will happily report you to the police if you don't run home this instance.'

'What about Max?'

'Surely you don't need Max Hodge to take you home, do you? You won't survive long if you let him lead your little gang. Now get out of my sight.'

As the boys ran off, Max made to rise, and suffered another flick from the whip. 'I didn't say you could go Hodge.'

Toby noticed that the man was now sitting up, holding a handkerchief to his forehead, and still clutching his bundle.

'Are you alright sir? Can you get up?'

The man coughed. 'Aye lad, in a moment. Thank you for stopping.'

'Right Max, stand up slowly, and unless you want another taste of my whip, I suggest you head straight back to Lewes as fast as you can. I'll be following close behind, and if you're not at home by the time I deliver milk to you mother's shop, I'll go straight to the police.'

As Max's running footsteps disappeared into the distance, Toby limped over to help the man to his feet. As he did so, a yelp came from the bundle, which turned out to be a canvas sack.

'Do you have a dog in that sack sir?'

'Aye, those lads grabbed my poor little Rufus, after that boy you called Max, kicked him and broke his leg. Then they emptied my feed sack, and stuffed him into it, and were threatening to throw him into the river. Thank God you turned up when you did son, cause when I grabbed him back from them they started to pelt me with stones,

While the man was speaking, Toby noticed that he was missing the lower half of his right leg. 'Just sit for a moment sir, while I let Rufus out of that sack.' When Toby untied the cord at the top of the sack, a small brown and white dog crept out, and crawled into the man's arms, growling ferociously at Toby.

'That's enough Rufus, this man is our friend.' Taking Toby's hand, the man slowly moved it towards the wary dog, who after a couple of sniffs, gave Toby's fingers a lick. 'Good boy Rufus. My name sir, is Captain Blake Mitchell, recently a cavalry officer in India.'

'I'm Toby Atkins, sir. I'm an employee of Countess Mary Evans Watson. Please allow me to take you and Rufus to her house, which is nearby, to give you a chance to recover from your recent ordeal with those stupid boys, and to see if we can set poor Rufus's leg.' When Captain Mitchell nodded, Toby handed him the pouch and medals taken from Max. 'I take it these are yours sir.'

'Thank you Toby. Those scoundrels attacked me while I was asleep, and proceeded to rob me, trash my camp, and attempt to dispose of young Rufus. I don't know what they've done with my crutches. As you can see, I can't get far without them.'

'Why don't you let me help you and Rufus onto the cart Captain Mitchell, then I'll see what I can salvage from your camp, and try to find your crutches?'

Once Captain Mitchell was seated on the driver's seat of the cart, holding his dog, Toby went over to the remains of the camp, where he hurriedly collected all the articles he could find, and stowed them on the back of the cart beside the milk cans. The crutches had been thrown into a bush, one of them snapped in half.

Toby climbed up onto the cart, and sat beside his passenger. 'Captain Mitchell, I must go straight into Lewes, to deliver milk to the dairy and a couple of our customers, before we go to Everton Manor. I've some sandwiches and a bottle of tea in my bag, if you would like them. I'd hazard a guess that you haven't had breakfast yet.'

'Thanks Toby. A sandwich would be great.'

It wasn't long before Toby had delivered most of the full milk cans to the dairy and replaced them with the empty cans, then he stopped at a few shops that sold fresh milk to their customers. At Hodge's corner shop, Toby noticed a scowling Max at the upstairs window. Mrs Hodge looked unhappily at Toby. 'I gather Max has been in trouble again this morning Toby.'

'I'm afraid that Max and his cronies attacked this gentleman this morning at his campsite near town, and I'm sorry to say, I was forced to use my whip to make them disperse.'

'When Max told me that you hit him with your whip, I knew it would only have been if you had to Toby.' She looked towards the man sitting on the cart. 'I'm terribly sorry if my boy hurt you sir. I'll try to pay for any damages he caused.'

'Thank you Mrs Hodge, but there's no need to. My young friend here intervened before any great harm was done, though my little mate here might not agree.' Captain Mitchell pointed to Rufus hiding under his coat.

Mrs Hodge turned to a young girl standing behind her. 'Run into the kitchen and bring me the lamb shank Belinda. I was going to cut the meat off it to cook for your brother's tea, but I think this little dog might deserve it more.'

Rufus was delighted to receive the bone, and happily lay at Blake's feet, chewing at it while Toby drove on to Everton Manor with the last can of milk. When he pulled up at the back door, they were met by the cook Margaret Peters and Toby's sister in-law, housekeeper Helen Atkins. ''Where have you been Toby, we were worried that….?' Helen stopped mid-sentence, when she saw the strange man sitting beside Toby.

'Captain Mitchell, at you service Madam. This young man saved me and my dog from a gang of urchins earlier this morning, not far from here. He insisted that we came here with him to recover from our ordeal, and to sort through my belongings that were trashed.'

'Captain Mitchell's crutch was broken, and I was hoping that Mick might be able to fix it for him. Also, his little dog has been injured.'

Toby swung down off the cart, and gave Helen a kiss on the cheek. 'Are we too late for breakfast Mrs Peters?'

'It's never too late for you, Toby my lad!' Margaret ruffled Toby's hair. 'Please come in Captain Mitchell, and bring your dog with you.'

Margaret and Helen watched, as Toby carefully assisted the man down off the cart and handed him the unbroken crutch. He then gently picked up the little dog and his bone and they all went into the kitchen, while a groom took Juno and the cart to the stables.

Helen quickly bathed Captain Mitchell's forehead with some warm water and antiseptic, before neatly bandaging it, while Margaret prepared some breakfast for the two men. While this was being done, Toby checked the damage to Rufus's front leg. 'I think I'll be able to splint Rufus's leg after we've eaten, Captain Mitchell.'

Over a mug of tea, a bowl of porridge, then a plate of eggs, bacon, tomatoes and sausages and toast, Toby explained what had occurred on his way to Lewes.

At that moment, the kitchen door opened, and Mary walked in. Surprised to see a stranger sitting at the kitchen table, she paused near the door, and Toby hurriedly stood up. 'Good morning Lady Mary. May I introduce you to Captain Blake Mitchell?'

As Blake tried to stand, his crutch clattered to the floor. Walking to the table, Mary took hold of Blake's hand. 'Good morning Captain Mitchell. Please stay seated, and I'll join you for a cup of tea.'

Captain Mitchell then explained his circumstances. 'I'm on my way home, after being discharged from St Thomas's Hospital in London. I've spent the past two months there, since my return to England from India where my foot was damaged beyond repair in a cavalry skirmish, nearly six months ago. I don't remember much of those months in the army hospital, nor the sea journey home, and have been told that it was a miracle that I survived the first week, let alone the next four months before landing back in England.

My father has an estate near Eastbourne and I'm reluctantly making my way there, to hopefully recuperate.' Seeing the surprised looks on the faces of his audience he explained, 'My father is a hard task master, and a stickler for tradition. My oldest brother Ralph lives on the estate, only because he will one day inherit it and my father's title, while my other brother Alfred was forced into the church. As the third son, my designated role was to join the army.

I would have preferred to be an accountant, and was studying at Oxford when, unbeknown to me, my father purchased my commission

371

as a cavalry officer in the army. Within the week, I found myself on a ship sailing for India. Now that I'm a cripple, he wishes to have nothing more to do with me, but the doctors told him that I should return home to convalesce.'

'Are you by chance related to Viscount Mitchell, Captain Mitchell?'

'To my shame, he's my father, m'lady.'

'He is a bit of a tyrant isn't he?' Mary laughed. 'Our paths have crossed a number of times, and he can't abide having to acknowledge a lady with a higher ranking title!'

Toby explained, 'Captain Mitchell was telling us that he's not looking forward to returning home to recuperate from his injury m'lady.'

'Did I hear correctly that you rescued Captain Mitchell on your way to Lewes this morning Toby? Your prowess with the coach whip is being acclaimed already!'

Toby chuckled. 'Bob insists that I carry the whip with me on my daily milk run, m'lady. A couple of lucky flicks sent the pack of urchins running, then when I managed to trip up Max Hodge, Juno did the rest by standing over him in a most threatening way.'

'Still, well done Toby. I'm afraid it won't be long before young master Hodge comes up before me in court, for his increasingly aggressive transgressions. Now, Captain Mitchell, if you are in no great hurry to go home, may I offer you accommodation at Longmire Hall for your convalescence?'

'Thankyou Your Ladyship. I would be very grateful to accept your kind invitation.'

'I must warn you sir, I have a young son, who will be thrilled to have a soldier staying at the Hall.' Mary laughed as she stooped to gently pick up Rufus, who was sniffing her ankle.

'Toby, I think you and I should try to fix this little fellow's leg, before we head back to the Hall. Helen, will you please ring Polly to let Tom know that Toby will be late back. One of the grooms will take the milk cart back before the afternoon milking, then Toby and Captain Mitchell can accompany me in the coach.'

Blake Mitchell watched in awe as Rufus snuggled into the crook of Mary's arm as she and Toby headed for the stables, where the animal medical supplies were stored. Margaret laughed at the look on Blake's face. 'Both Lady Mary and Toby have a way with animals Captain Mitchell. I'm sure they'll have that little chap fixed in no time. Animals almost seem to be hypnotised by them.'

Sure enough, the stoic little dog barely whimpered while Mary gently massaged and stretched his broken leg, then he lay with his eyes shut when Toby deftly padded, then splinted the straightened limb.

Blake fell asleep during the coach trip back to Longmire Hall, and wasn't too proud to allow Robert and Toby to carry him into the sitting room, where he sat beside the fire, cuddling Rufus, while Polly arranged for a ground floor bedroom to be prepared for him. Following a wash, assisted by James, who Mary had asked to act as a valet for the Captain until a suitable man was employed, Blake slept through the afternoon, and felt much refreshed when he met Mary, Hugh and Bill in the sitting room before dinner.

As Mary had predicted, Bill was beside himself with excitement, at meeting a real live soldier. It mattered not that Blake was missing part of his leg, as Bill informed everyone, 'One of my toy soldiers is missing a leg too!'

Mary and Hugh were amazed how patient Blake was with their young son, who was bombarding him with questions of all descriptions, and how clearly he explained things, so that Bill didn't feel left out in the general conversation.

When Bill was finally taken up to bed by Nanny Roberts, Blake explained. 'I quickly learnt to be very concise and patient, when speaking and issuing orders to my men. Many of them had little education, and struggled to understand several of my fellow officers, who talked down to the soldiers, as though they were idiots.'

Blake paused. 'That young Toby is a very accomplished and self-assured young man, I must say.'

Hugh smiled. 'He's an absolute gem. Would you believe that seven years ago, Toby was a starving fifteen year old, living with his parents in a single room in a tenement at Bermondsey, close to the Thames River? Because of his club foot, the local boys would attack him when they saw him, to the point he became too terrified to leave the room. Luckily, his brother our butler at Everton Manor and I managed to rescue Toby and his parents, when they were evicted from their room. Lady Mary arranged for Toby to have some corrective work done on his foot, then he and his parents stayed at Everton Manor, until they recovered from their ordeal.

When his parents moved into a cottage in Lewes, to be nearer to their work, Toby went to work for Bob and Tess Telford on Home Farm and has lived with them now for nearly seven years. Bob, Tess and Toby now live in a smaller cottage on the farm, to allow their son Will, his wife Elin and their young son Bruce, to live in the farm house, as Will has taken over the management of the farm now, and employs Toby as a full time farm worker.'

'I noticed he has a pronounced limp. How does he manage the farm work?'

'Sheer determination, and an uncanny knack of finding different ways to complete a job satisfactorily. He has great self-belief in his ability to cope, and doesn't allow his club foot to control his life.'

Blake laughed. 'I must say, I would have thought twice to stand up to him when he showed his skill with that whip!'

'Toby's other forte is his compassion to animals, and his ability to communicate with them. A bit like my wife. She could pacify a dragon, if she needed to!'

Mary blushed. 'That's enough Hugh!' Poor Captain Mitchell must be wondering what he's come to. I think it's time we all retired for the night.'

CHAPTER 16

Longmire Estate,
Sussex, England
November 1895

The next morning, Iain Campbell called at Longmire Hall, to discuss with Mary the progress in finding a suitable doctor to run a medical centre in Longmire village. The village leaders had approached Mary to discuss the possibility of having a more permanent medical presence in the area, to cater for the growing population in and around the village. The six miles from Lewes was an issue in times of a medical emergency.

Early in Mary's first year at Longmire Hall, she had instigated a plan with Dr Wilson for either himself or his partner to run a fortnightly clinic at the village Church hall. Since then, under Mary's benefaction, the village had grown considerably, the number of houses having doubled. Mary had also had a row of twelve one bedroomed cottages built for single workers in the area.

The villagers now took great pride in their village, and were constantly looking for ways to enrich their community. Colin Wilson and Mary had been discussing the possibility of setting up a village medical centre for a few months before Iain's arrival. Now, Mick Murphy and his workers had nearly finished building the clinic and doctor's residence that Mary had committed to have built in the village for their new doctor, and Colin and Iain had agreed to look for a suitable rural doctor.

'Good news, Mary. Colin and I think we've found a suitable doctor for Longmire Village. Brian Heslop studied at The University of Glasgow School of Medicine, and has been working at St Thomas's in London for the past five years. His wife Christine is a St Thomas's qualified midwife, who has also been working in the South Bank area. They're both from the country, and would dearly love to move out of the city, and work together in a country practice.'

'That's great news Iain. I assume that you and Colin have interviewed them, and checked their credentials?'

'Yes we have. We've also spoken to their superiors at the hospital. Dr Heslop has shown great competency in diagnostic and clinical medicine, as well as becoming a capable surgeon. Christine Heslop is a much sort after midwife, and their superiors said they will be sad to lose them.'

'Elin Telford is a St Thomas's trained midwife. I wonder if they know each other.'

'They could well do. Mary, I would like to arrange a time for you to meet Dr Heslop and his wife.'

Mary thought for a moment. 'I'll be back at Longmire Hall next Wednesday Iain. Maybe I could see them mid-morning, if that's convenient. Then I could show them through the medical centre and house.'

As Iain was about to climb onto his buggy to return to Lewes, he saw Blake Mitchell sitting on a bench near the stables, holding his little brown and white dog. Walking over to him, he held out his hand. 'Good morning sir. I assume that you must be Lady Mary's guest, Captain Mitchell. I'm Dr Iain Campbell from Lewes.'

'Good morning Dr Campbell. Yes, Lady Mary has invited me to stay for a while, to regain my strength.'

Iain looked at the bandage around the man's head, and his dog's bandaged front leg. 'I heard that you and your little mate had an unfortunate encounter with master Hodge and his cronies yesterday. Word spreads fast amongst my patients!'

'Did they also tell you what a useless cripple I've become, unable to defend myself or my dog, from a group of young kids?' Blake stared at the ground.

'How do you feel this morning Captain Mitchell?' Iain sat down on the bench and held his hand out for Rufus to sniff.

'Apart from feeling useless do you mean?' Blake stared at Iain. 'To tell you the truth Doc, I have a splitting headache, and I think Rufus here is coping better with his broken leg than I am with my bad leg.'

'I wouldn't be surprised if you were concussed by that rock strike. Is your leg more painful this morning, than when you left London?' Blake nodded.

'Would you like me to give you a quick examination, to see why that might be?'

'I think that might be a good idea Doc, as I really don't feel too chipper this morning, despite Lady Mary's hospitality. I hadn't realised how helpless I've become. In hospital, the nurses did virtually everything for me. I would have dearly loved to have a bath yesterday, but even with the help of one of Lady Mary's grooms, it was all I could do to wash at the washbasin, and they had to set up a downstairs bedroom for me, because I can't climb stairs anymore.'

'Ok, let's go to your room, and I'll have a quick look at your wound. And don't worry about making work for Lady Mary's staff. Like her, they enjoy helping people in genuine need, and will do what they can for you quite cheerfully.'

'The servants I've met so far are unlike any I've dealt with before. They chatter and smile a lot, yet they've dealt with me very efficiently and politely.'

'Lady Mary runs her household like a business, with a staff of various abilities, who work together as a unified team. While everybody has a defined role, they all pitch in to help as needs be. As you saw yesterday, one of the grooms deputised as your valet, I'm sure quite happily, because Lady Mary asked him to.'

'Yes, James was very capable and quite cheerful in helping me. In fact, probably more so than my last batman.'

By this time, the two men and Rufus had entered Blake's bedroom, and Iain helped him out of his britches, then assisted him to lie on the bed. Carefully, Iain removed the bandage from the stump, to discover a large bruise near the knee, and several of the areas where stitches on the stump had been removed, oozing blood. Iain felt Blake flinch, when he gently touched the inflamed stump. 'When were you discharged from St Thomas's, Captain Mitchell?'

'Please call me Blake, doctor. It would be about two weeks ago I guess. When I left the hospital with my father, the doctors assumed that we would travel together to his estate near Eastbourne, as my father had agreed to take me home. However, when we left the hospital, he dumped me at the first boarding house showing a room vacant sign, paid a week's rent, and told me it was a pity I'd lived! As far as he is concerned, it is more preferable to have a dead hero in the family than a cripple!'

'Good grief, what sort of a cad would do that!'

'My father is a law unto himself, and nobody to my knowledge, has ever taken him to task. I was forced to sleep in the back shed, as I couldn't climb the stairs, and that's where I met Rufus. His master, the previous occupant of the upstairs room that I was meant to have, died a couple of days before I arrived and the landlady had thrown Rufus out onto the street. He'd been sleeping in the shed, and we've been looking after each other since that first night. After a couple of days, the landlady told me to leave, so I packed a swag, and Rufus and I left London, and have been on the road since then.

Until those boys attacked us, we were coping quite well, sometimes getting lifts on farm carts, and buying food on our way south. Each day I felt stronger, and was learning to cope with my disability. But those louts soon showed me how helpless I really am, and has me wondering if my father was right.'

'Now, you listen to me Blake. There are many men who have lost limbs, but still live happy beneficial lives. At the moment, you're concussed, and in shock following your ordeal, plus your wound has been aggravated by the boys kicking you. So far, you haven't been given the chance to find out what opportunities there are available for you, and I don't mean selling matches on a street corner! While you're at Longmire Hall, will you allow me to work with you, to look at options for a productive future?'

Looking at Iain sitting on the side of the bed, gently stroking Rufus who was cuddled up against him, Blake smiled. 'It looks like Rufus has made the decision for me, Dr Campbell. We'll give it a go.'

'Good. Earlier you mentioned your batman. Did he come back to England with you?'

'No, he was re-assigned to another officer in India, as they didn't think I would survive. Now that I can no longer serve in the army, I'm no longer entitled to a batman.'

'Would you be interested in having a full time valet, to help you Blake?'

'I'd certainly be interested doctor, but my financial situation is rather dire, now that both the army and my father have cast me adrift.'

'Would you mind if I spoke to Lady Mary about your situation?'

'I don't mind, but there's nothing she can do.'

'You certainly don't know our Countess Blake. When she's on a mission, she's as much a terrier as this little fellow snuggled up beside me!'

CHAPTER 17

Longmire Estate
Sussex, England
Mid November 1895

A week later, Mary was slowly walking through the rose garden with Blake, when a horse and buggy drew up in front of the Hall. By the time the young red headed man had handed down his female companion, Polly was at the bottom of the steps to greet them.

As Mary and Blake approached the front steps, Polly turned to Mary. 'Lady Mary, may I introduce Dr and Mrs Heslop. Dr and Mrs Heslop I present to you Lady Mary Evans-Watson, Countess of Longmire and Oakdale, and Captain Mitchell.'

After greeting Mary, Dr Heslop turned to Blake, and expressed his surprise at seeing him. 'I was under the impression that you had been released to convalesce at your father's estate near Eastbourne, Captain Mitchell.'

'There was a change of plans Dr Heslop. The Captain is now my guest, and will be convalescing here at Longmire Hall. I take it you know each other?'

'I was Captain Mitchell's surgeon at St Thomas's, Your Ladyship.'

'I see. And you were a nurse at the same hospital I gather, Mrs Heslop. Two of my girls are currently in their second year of nurse training at St Thomas's, and Elin Telford at Home Farm was a St Thomas's trained midwife.'

'Do you mean Elin Davies, Lady Mary? She and I did our training together. Unfortunately, we lost contact when matron sent her on a private secondment, while I was at home looking after my elderly parents.'

'Elin was assigned to me, to look after an orphaned baby who had come into my care, then she met her future husband, and came to live on Longmire Estate following their marriage several years ago.'

Mary turned to Blake. 'Please excuse me Blake. Dr and Mrs Heslop have come to discuss the medical centre in the village. I'll see you later in the day.'

She turned to her visitors, 'Shall we take your buggy to the village? It's about a mile away, so we can chat on the way.'

Polly and Blake watched the buggy drive around the house to the road to the village, then Polly stayed close to Blake as he used his crutches to balance, while he went up the steps, as Toby had shown him.

On the way to the village, Mary explained a little about the estate and the village, which was part of the estate. The young couple were surprised at the friendly, almost casual greetings called to the Countess as the buggy passed along the village street, and were delighted to see how tidy and well-kept the buildings were.

When Dr Heslop stopped the buggy in front of the medical centre, he stared at the large, newly constructed, two storied cottage with an annex attached to one side.

'Shall we have a look through the cottage and the clinic, before you make your decision doctor?'

The young couple were dumbfounded, as they walked through the dining room, large sunny sitting room, and spacious kitchen with a new gas stove, plus a coal range, scullery, and adjoining cook's room. Upstairs there were three bedrooms, a bathroom, and an indoor water closet. A sizable back garden extended from the back door and laundry, to a stable and carriage outbuilding that Mick Murphy was close to completing.

The annex, comprising of a reception area and patient waiting room, a consulting room, small surgery, and storeroom, had a front door to the street, plus a door into the house.

'This is beyond belief Lady Mary. We had no idea that these facilities would be offered to us if we took the job. I was envisaging working from a room in a small cottage that would still be a step up from the single room we currently rent near St Thomas's.'

'As I'm sure Dr Wilson has explained to you, you are both to be employees of the Lewes Clinic, working from Longmire village to treat the villagers and those living within approximately three miles of the village. Longmire Estate will supply the clinic and residence rent free for twelve months, to see how the venture works. We will also employ a cook/housekeeper and gardener/groom, as you will both be working. The groom will accompany you Christine, on any callouts outside the village, day and night.'

'Thank you m'lady. That was one aspect of Christine's job that I was concerned about. Whenever possible, the midwives from St Thomas's are accompanied on night visits by a porter.'

'The villagers are thrilled to have their own medical centre, and I'm sure that if you decide to accept the positions, you'll be welcomed by one and all. The majority of families will be able to pay for your services, but there are a few households who still struggle financially. I'll introduce you to the vicar's wife, who would be best to advise you of those struggling. The estate will cover their fees.'

Brian looked at his beaming wife. 'We would be thrilled to work here Your Ladyship, and can't wait to start.'

'That's wonderful news. Please let Colin and Iain know of your decision on your way back to London. You mentioned that you rent a single room. Do you have furniture to move, or would you like me to arrange for some furniture to be in place for your arrival?'

Christine looked shyly at Mary. 'A bed, table and some chairs would be wonderful please, m'lady. We have our own china, cutlery and some cooking utensils.'

'There's a lot of unused furniture stored at Longmire Hall that you are welcome to furnish your house with. Please feel free to have a look, before you return to London.'

By the time the young couple left the Hall, they couldn't believe their good fortune to not only have a substantial new residence to move to, but they had also been shown an abundant arrangement of furniture to choose from to furnish it. Mary happily agreed to have the articles chosen delivered to the house before their planned move, once their notice at St Thomas's had been served.

Later that week, a young man arrived at Longmire Hall to meet Mary, to discuss the possible position of valet to Blake Mitchell, following Mary's enquiries with her peers, managers, and friends. Lance Dixon, one of Mary's business managers, had informed Mary that his foreman's thirty two year old son Malcolm, was looking for a new valet position, preferably in the country, so she had requested they met for an interview at Longmire Hall.

Sitting in the study, Mary looked at the tall, sandy haired man standing in front of her desk. 'Please be seated Mr Cox, and tell me a little of yourself.'

Malcolm Cox sat on the edge of the chair facing Mary. 'I'm looking for a new valet position Lady Mary, as the gentleman I worked for died last month. I joined the army when I was sixteen, and was sent to South Africa in 1880, where I was assigned as batman to Colonel Duffy. When the Colonel returned to England four months later, I accompanied him, and remained as his batman until the Colonel retired from the army five years ago. I left the army soon after, and was employed as Colonel Duffy's valet, and we lived in his house in Paddington until his death last month.'

'You were with Colonel Duffy a long time Malcolm.'

'I really miss the old man, Lady Mary. Although he was my employer, the Colonel treated me as a friend, and we had many adventures together, both here in England and abroad. Unfortunately, earlier this year, he fell and broke his hip, and his health deteriorated very quickly, to the point where he was bed ridden for the last month of his life, and totally reliant on me for all his needs. Colonel Duffy's son and daughter visited him not long after he left the army, but I'm sure they never visited again, after he refused to pay his son's gambling debts.

However, they both arrived immediately on hearing of their father's death. His son James, assumed that he would inherit his father's estate, and was furious when he discovered that the Colonel had left his house, and the majority of his assets to me, with small bequests to his son and daughter. I was summarily dismissed, without references, and James refused to pay me the quarter's wage owing to me. He's also contesting the will, telling everyone that I duped his father into leaving me his house and money. So here I am, seeking a job, Lady Mary.'

Mary sat back in her chair and looked at Malcolm. 'We have a guest here at the Hall Malcolm, who requires the services of a valet. He was a Captain in the army in India, where he was wounded, and lost part of his leg. He's still convalescing, so will need a lot of attention to start with. If you're interested, I'll introduce you to Captain Mitchell, and you can discuss his needs. If you stay, you will initially be employed by the Longmire Estate, with accommodation, meals etc. included.'

'Thank you Lady Mary, I'd very much like to meet this Captain Mitchell.'

As Mary and Malcolm left the study, they met Polly in the corridor. 'Polly, please ask Captain Mitchell to meet us in the sitting room, and have some tea and cake sent in as well.'

When Blake arrived, Mary shared a pot of tea with the two men, then left them to become acquainted. After she'd spent some time up in the nursery, telling Bill and Patricia stories they loved of her adventures in Australia, Polly informed her that the two men were out in the garden.

Mary went out to meet Blake and Malcom. 'Thank you very much for your kind offer to employ Malcolm as my valet, while I'm your guest at Longmire Hall Lady Mary. We would both like to spend a few days together, to give Malcom a chance to ascertain my needs, and for me to get to know him better.' One very big thing in his favour already, is that young Rufus has claimed him as his own.'

Mary looked around for the little terrier, then noticed a bulge under Malcolm's jacket. When she laughed Rufus's head appeared, and he allowed her to pat him before snuggling back again.

'I think that would be a great idea. In fact, would you feel more at ease together if you both moved into the empty cottage near the stables? There is a room downstairs for you to sleep in Blake, and I know of a lady in the village who would love a job as your housekeeper/cook.'

Blake looked at Mary. 'Lady Mary, that's a most wonderful offer, but I can't impose further on your generosity, when I have no means to repay you.'

'Don't talk such nonsense Blake. You would be doing me a favour if you used the cottage, as it gives me a genuine reason to employ Gladys Hughes, who at the moment is desperately looking for work.'

'When you put it that way m'lady, I can do no more than graciously accept! Thank you.'

'The cottage kitchen will be stocked by Mrs Smith, so just let her know your requirements. Also, I think Rufus would be much happier in his own place, rather than having to keep out of Scruffy's territory!'

CHAPTER 18

Later that week, Blake and Malcolm were settled in the cottage, having decided that they were quite compatible. Blake found Malcolm to be a very competent valet, with the additional skill in caring for his medical needs, helping him physically when required, but leaving him to work out ways to cope as much as possible.

Gladys Hughes moved into their cottage, and proved herself to be a capable cook and a meticulous housekeeper. Rufus quickly learnt to wait at the back door to have his feet wiped before he entered the kitchen, where his bed was placed conveniently near the range, beside Gladys's rocking chair.

Brian and Christine Heslop were settling into the doctor's residence in the village, and had already run three days of clinics, and Christine had delivered two healthy babies, one in the village, the other late at night on a farm two miles from the village.

As Mary had assured them, their new groom had accompanied Christine, driving the buggy to the farm, as well as helping to keep the farmer occupied, while his wife gave birth to their first child, a strong healthy boy. Their new groom and housekeeper/cook were a middle-aged couple, who lived two doors from the clinic. Rupert Johnston had been a farm labourer, but quickly offered his services as the medical residence groom/gardener, when Mary asked his wife Daphne if she would consider employment as the new doctor's housekeeper/cook.

Dr Heslop had visited Blake to treat his leg, and to also discuss the possibility of having a prosthetic foot fitted. Brian told Blake that a number of his patients had been successfully fitted with prosthetics, made by Chas A Blatchford in London. Brian was pleased to see that in the short time Blake had been at Longmire Hall, he had a more positive outlook about his injury, and his future. This Brian attributed mainly to Malcolm's calm, but firm way of dealing with Blake.

Blake had noticed the way that Mary treated her staff, and decided to consider Malcolm more as a friend than a servant. Initially, he was surprised, but then delighted, with the easy way he and Malcolm now worked together. Malcolm was certainly happy not to have to conform to a rigid master/servant role. The two men were often seen walking slowly through the parkland around the Hall, discussing their army exploits.

Bill was also very pleased to have Blake living so near to the Hall. At first, Mary and Hugh were concerned that Bill's fascination with Blake would be annoying, but after a short discussion, where Blake expressed his delight in the small boy's happy personality and genuine joy in life, Mary's concerns were dispelled.

In the meantime, Mary contacted Richard Jones, the London private detective she had used in the past, to make enquiries about Colonel Duffy and his family, especially his son James. At Mary's directive, he interviewed many of Colonel Duffy's fellow officers, former employees, and long-time friends, who confirmed how much the Colonel liked, and depended on, his long serving batman/valet, and how conscientiously Malcolm had looked after the Colonel's needs. Colonel Duffy's doctor also confirmed how meticulously Malcolm had cared for the Colonel, when his health began to deteriorate, especially following his accident.

The solicitor who wrote the Colonel's last will, verified that the Colonel had been adamant that his young friend, who had served him faithfully for sixteen years, should be his major beneficiary, and was scathing of his son and daughter, with whom he'd had no contact for five years.

It wasn't long before Richard also obtained proof of a number of illegal activities that James was involved in, as well as additional statements from a number of people, who had witnessed James bragging about how he was enjoying swindling his father's lackey out of his bequest and wages.

Richard was sure that he had enough evidence for Malcom to have a valid case to put before the court, when James contested his father's will at the next court hearing.

Unaware of Mary's attendance at the court hearing in London, accompanied by many of these witnesses, and an eminent defence attorney, keen to secure Malcolm's legacy, James Duffy swaggered into the court room, joking with his friends accompanying him.

The smirk quickly disappeared from his face when the judge entered the court. Expecting the case to be held by a judge with whom he was on friendly terms, James was horrified to learn that his friend had been sent to preside at a County Court up north for a week, and that his replacement was a judge known to have little time for what he called 'family money squabbles'.

Malcolm's attorney took little time in convincing the judge of his client's entitlement to his bequest, and then submitted a counter charge of theft against James, for withholding Malcolm's wages, entered and signed by the Colonel in his wage's ledger. This charge, combined with the presented evidence of James's involvement in illegal activities, led him to be arrested, and taken away to the court cells, while a jubilant Malcolm left the courtroom confirmed as the Colonel's lawful beneficiary.

Following a quick lunch at a restaurant near the courthouse, Malcolm took Mary and Blake to his new house, a four storied terrace house in Sussex Place, Paddington, within easy walking distance to Paddington Station and Hyde Park. As the trio stood looking at the façade of the house, the front door opened and the butler stood on the front step. 'Welcome home Mr Malcolm. Congratulations on the successful ruling of your court case sir.'

'Thank you Higgins. My goodness, word travels quickly.'

'Connie sat in the back of the courtroom and ran back to tell us the wonderful news.'

'Higgins, this is Lady Mary Watson and Captain Mitchell. I wish to show them through the house.'

'Of course Mr Malcolm.' Higgins glanced at Blake's injured leg. 'Begging your pardon for asking, but will the Captain be requiring some assistance with the stairs?'

'That's alright Higgins, I'll assist Captain Mitchell if required.'

When they had looked around the ground floor and the back garden, Blake paused at the stairs. 'I think I'll wait in the sitting room Malcolm. You show Lady Mary the rest of your house.'

While they were away, Higgins entered the sitting room. 'Would you like some tea brought in while you are waiting Captain, or maybe something stronger?'

'A whisky would be wonderful, thankyou Higgins.'

Mary and Malcolm went through the numerous rooms on the next two floors, then up to the attics. 'So, will you come back to live here now Malcolm?'

'I haven't really had time to make any decisions yet Lady Mary. Until today, I couldn't believe that James would lose his claim to the house. Also, I enjoy working with Captain Mitchell, and we need to discuss whether he would like to live here.'

Mary looked thoughtfully at Malcolm. 'You do realise, that as you are now a man of considerable means Malcolm, you won't need to be employed as you are at present.'

'My solicitor told me the other day, that one of the Colonel's assets that James was so desperate to get his hands on, was the deeds to a small diamond mine that his father acquired when he first went to South Africa over twenty years ago. Apparently the Colonel was a very wealthy man. I can certainly afford to have a lift installed and employ others to assist Captain Mitchell if he lived here.'

They headed back towards the sitting room. 'Having a London base while Captain Mitchell is having his new prosthesis fitted would certainly be an advantage Malcolm. I guess you would just have to see how you both adjust to your new situation.'

While Blake and Malcolm returned to Longmire Hall, Mary stayed overnight at Everton Manor, in order to attend court in Lewes the next day. As she was leaving the courthouse mid-afternoon, a man who had been talking to Robert beside her coach, approached her and bowed.

'Lady Mary, could I please take a moment of your time to speak to you? I'm Captain Blake Mitchell's older brother Ralph.'

Mary could see a family resemblance to Blake. 'What can I do for you Mr Mitchell?'

'I've been told that my brother Blake is your guest at the moment Your Ladyship, and I'd like to speak to him.'

Mary studied at the man for a moment. 'Has your father sent you to look for your brother Mr Mitchell?'

'No Your Ladyship, he doesn't know I'm here. My brother Alfred and I only found out last week how abysmally our father treated our brother when he left hospital. We were both appalled when we heard, and I've come to speak with Blake, to see if there's anything we can do to help him.'

'Are you staying in Lewes for long Mr Mitchell?'

'I'll stay as long as it takes to find my brother Your Ladyship. A neighbour is keeping an eye on our property while I'm away.'

'I'll speak to Blake first, to hear what he wants to do, and I'll meet you here at the courthouse tomorrow morning at 9.00, Mr Mitchell.'

'Thank you Lady Mary. Please tell Blake that Alfred and I both want to help him, if we can.'

Early the next morning, Hugh and Blake arrived at Everton Manor, following Mary's telephone call to Longmire Hall the previous evening, and the three of them were driven to the courthouse where Blake's brother was waiting.

Mary noticed that, for a moment, Ralph stared in horror as his younger brother was helped from the carriage and handed his crutches, then he strode towards him and enfolded him in a big hug. Suddenly remembering the other two people accompanying his brother, Ralph released Blake and turned to Mary. 'I do apologise Lady Mary.'

'I quite understand your shock Mr Mitchell, if you haven't been informed of the extent of your brother's injury. May I introduce my husband Sir Hugh Watson to you?' The two men shook hands.

'Let's go into a room in the courtroom where you two can talk without interruption.' Once the two brothers were seated in the empty interview room, Mary and Hugh left them alone.

Blake looked suspiciously at his brother. 'Why do you want to see me now Ralph, and how did you find me?'

'Please forgive my apparent lack of concern for your welfare Blake. Alfred and I knew that you went to India last year, but whenever we enquired after you, father just told us he'd received no news. We'd no idea that you had been wounded, and were back in England, until last week.'

'I don't know how you can bear living on the estate with that tyrant Ralph.'

'Someone has to oversee the running of the estate Blake. Luckily, father has taken little interest in what goes on, and has been more interested in socialising with his cronies near home and in London. I spend as little time as possible in the house when father is at home, as his behaviour has become much more autocratic of late. Alfred only comes to see me, if he knows that father is staying at his club in London.'

Last week, father received a letter that threw him into an absolute rage, so much so I thought that he might have a seizure on the spot. He stormed off to his study and locked himself in, and I didn't see him for three days.'

'Was he trying to starve himself to death, or was he getting food sent in?'

'As you know Blake, father's whisky supplies are stored in a cupboard in his study, and he apparently just sat at his desk drinking. After a couple of days, Cook told me that father was going to the kitchen during the night and raiding the pantry. On the third night, one of the grooms and I waited up, and grabbed father when he entered the kitchen. He was filthy and extremely drunk, though not to the point of passing out. He put up quite a fight, until I punched him on the jaw and knocked him out. Before he recovered consciousness, we carried him out to the barn, and tied him to a chair and covered him with an old horse rug. I sent the groom to get the doctor, then I went into the study and found a screwed up letter in the wastepaper bin.

The letter was from father's club in London, informing him that he had been barred from entering the club for the foreseeable future, due to his dishonest, callous and unforgivable treatment of his heroic son

Captain Blake Mitchell, who had been severely wounded in the service of his Queen and country.'

'How in the world did the members of father's club know what he did to me?'

'Dr Heslop, the new doctor at Longmire Village, was one of the surgeons who treated you at St Thomas's Hospital. He informed the senior surgeon and matron of how father had dumped you in a boarding house, instead of taking you home as he'd promised to do to accelerate your discharge from St Thomas's. The head surgeon, an ex-army officer, is a member of the same club as father, and he was so infuriated at father's actions, he called a meeting of the board and they unanimously agreed to ban him.

Alfred's bishop gave him leave to help me look for you. We went to the club and spoke with the surgeon, who informed us that you were a guest of Lady Mary and Sir Hugh Watson at Longmire Hall. We've both been so worried about what might have happened to you, especially when we were told that you had been seriously wounded.'

'I've missed you and Alfred terribly Ralph, but have no intention of ever going back home again. At least not while father still lives there. As far as he's concerned, I should have died in India, and am a disgrace to the family for living with a missing foot!'

'At the moment, father is strapped to his bed in the Eastbourne Hospital Blake. He was so violent when he recovered consciousness, the doctor sedated him, and ordered that he's to remain strapped to his bed. He's recommended that father is to be committed to an asylum, if he survives this enraged flare-up.'

Ralph sat back and looked at his brother in contemplation. 'Look Blake, I'm sorry you lost your foot, but you're alive, and I love you, no matter how many feet you have! And I'm sure Alfred will feel the same. Please come back home, for a while at least, so that we can make up for the time you've been away.'

An hour later, Mary and Hugh arrived back, and the two brothers parted company, on the understanding that they would keep in touch.

Before he said goodbye to Mary and Hugh, Ralph turned to Hugh. 'I've heard a lot about the work you're doing with farmers in the area Sir Hugh. While my father is indisposed, could I please make an appointment to speak to you about the possibility of helping me to improve the productivity of our estate near Eastbourne?'

'Yes of course Ralph. Do you have the telephone connected?'

On Ralph's affirmative reply, Hugh wrote the telephone number in his note book. 'I'll contact you tomorrow evening Ralph, after I've consulted my appointment book.'

Blake was deep in thought for most of the coach trip back to Longmire Hall after lunch at Everton Manor, while Mary and Hugh quietly discussed Graham's upcoming wedding.

Graham and Bethany were married in the Longmire Village church on the third Saturday of November. What had been planned to be a quiet wedding, turned out to be quite a large affair, with many of the Gordon's neighbours attending, as well as most of the villagers and Mary's staff.

With the use of a cane, George was able to walk Bethany down the aisle to give her away, with Heather following as her bridesmaid. Hugh was Graham's best man, while Mary and Clara sat with the older children, proud as punch to see Graham so happy.

Following the wedding and reception at Longmire Hall, Graham and Bethany left for a three day honeymoon. Much to everyone's surprise, Mary and Hugh spent those three days working with George Edwards.

Each morning and afternoon, they rode from Everton Manor to the farm, where Mary milked the cows with George, while Hugh moved the milk churns, fed the cows and pigs, and cleaned out the pig sties and cow barns in the morning. While stunned at first, to have a Countess milking with him in his barn, George soon realised that Mary was an extremely skilful milker, who took real pleasure in milking each cow. Even Kristy was putty in her hands!

Harry and Hettie worked Graham's new farm, thrilled to be given the responsibility of looking after the farm while Graham was away.

CHAPTER 19

Malcom and Blake spent a lot of time discussing their reversed financial circumstances. Malcolm was keen to move back to London, but was reluctant to leave Blake without the assistance he still required at times. Blake looked on Malcolm more as a friend than his valet these days, and would like to keep the friendship going, but he dreaded the thought of living in London. He was willing to spend short periods visiting Malcolm, but could not come at committing to living there permanently, regardless of the alterations Malcolm was prepared to undertake to cater for Blake's disability.

During their deliberations, Dr Heslop visited Blake to inform him that an appointment with Chas A Blatchford, the prosthetics maker in London, had been made for him in a fortnight's time.

Dr Heslop explained 'The first appointment is for a discussion on your needs and expectations Blake, plus your measurements will be recorded. There will be need for subsequent visits for fittings and adjustments in the following month, then, if all goes well, you will be walking on two feet again.'

Malcolm was pleased to hear Blake's news. 'That's wonderful news Blake. Why don't you come to stay with me, and we can see if your view of London changes?'

'Thanks Malcolm, I will. I know you're keen to head back to London as soon as possible. I'm sure I can cope by myself with Mrs Hughes assistance, until I come to London for my appointments.'

When Malcolm left for London, Mary noticed that Blake still seemed to be unsure of his future. He and Rufus spent a lot of time out near the stables with the horses, so one day she joined them.

'You really miss riding, don't you Blake?'

'Oh, my word yes m'lady. I can get around with these crutches if I have to, but the thought of never being able to sit on a horse's back again is appalling.'

Mary looked at Blake for a moment. 'Once you become accustomed to your new prosthetic, you might be able to ride again Blake. Our estate supervisor, Adam Sinclair, who is currently up in Yorkshire, has a prosthetic lower leg, and he rides around the estate on his feisty mare on a daily basis.'

Noting Blake's sceptical look, she added, 'Robert had a special stirrup made, and that allows Adam's foot to come out unhindered if needed. Once Adam was confident that he wouldn't be dragged if he fell, there's been no stopping him.'

'I would certainly like to speak to this Adam when he comes back.'

'In the meantime, would you like to come for a ride with me, if we just walk around for a while? I'm sure, as an experienced horseman, you could quickly adjust your balance to riding bareback.'

After a moment's hesitation, Blake smiled. 'I'd very much like to give it a go m'lady.'

While Mary changed into her riding habit, James saddled Gem, then strapped a riding pad on one of the quieter horses. When she returned to the stables, James gave Blake a leg up, and he sat for a moment savouring being on a horse again. Mary stood beside him. 'While James leads Casper around the court yard I'll walk beside you Blake, until you get your balance.'

When Blake was ready ten minutes later, Mary mounted Gem, then James handed her the lead rope attached to Casper's bridle. The two horses left the courtyard walking side by side, then Mary and Blake spent the next half hour walking around the estate. When they returned to the stables, Blake was ecstatic. 'Oh, that was just magic Lady Mary.

Thank you so much. I can't wait 'til I can try riding in a saddle, and give the horse his head!'

'Blake, there is a way you could stay on a horse cantering and even galloping. Please don't be offended by my suggestion, but would you consider riding side-saddle?'

At first Blake was horrified at such an absurd suggestion, then it slowly dawned on him why Mary has asked such an unusual question. Although he was missing his right foot, he still had his knee and most of his shin, so he could hook that leg over the pommel, to help keep his balance on the saddle, instead of using both stirrups.

'I'll give it a go m'lady, if it offers me the chance to ride again. But I've not seen a side-saddle in the tack room.'

'Oh, that's not a problem Blake. A neighbour's mother has recently had to give up riding, and I'm sure he'd be happy to lend me her horse and side-saddle.' That evening Mary rang her neighbour, and arranged for James to collect the horse and saddle in the morning.

At first Blake was very self-conscious when he was lifted onto the saddle on a lovely bay mare. Robert and James carefully positioned Blake's injured leg around the pommel, and adjusted his left stirrup leather, before James again patiently led Blake around the courtyard. To save him further embarrassment, Mary asked Robert to accompany Blake on his first ride, while she went to visit Tess, and all the indoor staff remained inside.

An hour later, Blake swung into the kitchen on his crutches, gave Mrs Smith a big kiss on the cheek and hugged Sissy, who was cutting up vegetables for lunch.

'Oh, my word ladies, that was the most incredible experience. I thought I'd never be able to ride again. Lady Mary is an absolute genius, to make such an unconventional suggestion.'

Blushing, Mrs Smith laughed. 'Congratulations Captain Mitchell. Lady Mary never ceases to amaze us, with her ability to come up with unusual solutions, to solve all sorts of problems.'

'Was it very different riding side-saddle Captain Mitchell?' Sissy, ignored the glare from Mrs Smith.

'Do you know Sissy, once I adjusted my balance, I think I felt even more secure than I did on my cavalry saddle. And, I'm sure the joy of being able to ride again will by far outweigh the embarrassment of riding side-saddle.'

'Good for you Captain. Would you like a cup of tea?'

Blake was more controlled when he met Mary at lunch, but couldn't restrain from kissing her hand. 'Thank you so much for giving me my life back Lady Mary. If I can't ride with my new prosthesis, I will happily ride side-saddle in public. Who knows, I might start a new craze!'

Two days later, Mary and Blake rode over to Home Farm, with Scruffy and Rufus running with them. As Blake didn't have his crutches, both riders stayed in their saddles while they chatted to Bob, Tess and Toby. On the way back to the Hall, Mary took Blake past the water mill, where they stopped to let the horses have a pick of grass.

'Blake, are you still interested in being an accountant?'

'Yes m'lady. Once I get myself sorted out and settled somewhere, I think I'll seek work in the accountancy domain.'

'Would you consider remaining here, to take over as the bookkeeper at the Longmire flour mill?'

Mary continued as Blake looked at her in astonishment. 'The mill's current bookkeeper has recently informed me that he wishes to return to his hometown Whitby, to take over his father's accountancy firm. You could remain in your cottage, and I'm sure Gladys Hughes will gladly remain as your cook/housekeeper. I'll provide you with a cabriolet and horse, to travel to and from work each day, although I'm sure you'd rather ride on fine days, once you're walking without crutches.'

Finally, Blake managed to speak. 'You're too kind m'lady. I'd love to stay to work for you and repay your kindness.'

Blake was so busy thinking of Mary's offer, he didn't realise that they were entering the village, until people called out greetings to Mary and himself. As he rode past, he smiled at the villagers, who appeared oblivious to the fact that he was riding side-saddle, then laughed when the blacksmith called out 'Good day to you, Your Ladyship and Captain Mitchell. 'Tis great to see you up on a horse Captain. If you need a special stirrup made to suit your new boot, I'm your man.'

As they neared the Hall, Blake turned to Mary. 'I can't believe that not one of the villagers commented on my riding side-saddle, m'lady.'

Mary smiled. 'When you ride as well as you do Blake, it doesn't matter what sort of saddle you use. The villagers could see that you were sitting tall and enjoying yourself, and they were genuinely pleased to see you out and about.'

'When would you like me to start at the mill Lady Mary?'

'Clive Easton wants to leave as soon as possible, after he has shown his successor the books, lists of clients and suppliers, and other roles he carries out. You could spend the next couple of days working with Clive, then work until you travel to London for your initial appointment at Blatchford's in a bit over a week. While you're away, Sir Hugh and I will assist Jack Smedley with orders and deliveries.'

Blake smiled broadly. 'I'd like to do that m'lady. Can Rufus come to work with me?'

'Of course he can Blake, so long as he stays away from the machinery in the mill. He would be a real asset if he keeps the rats and mice away from the produce. Maybe he'll need to be put on the payroll as well!'

Jason, one of the new grooms, was assigned to drive Captain Mitchell to and from the mill each morning and afternoon until he was more mobile. So the next morning, feeling like a schoolboy carrying the packed lunch that Gladys prepared for him, Blake and Rufus arrived at the mill to be introduced to the miller Jack Smedley and Clive Easton.

It didn't take Blake long to get the gist of the mill's administration. He was pleased to see that his new office was built against the outside wall of the mill, with a sealed door leading into the mill, ensuring that the records and contents of his new office weren't covered in flour, as was the interior of the mill.

Jack Smedley and his wife Winnie lived in the house built beside the mill, and their sixteen year old apprentice Lucas lived with them. The mill had begun operations on the Longmire Estate six years ago, after being relocated from another area in West Sussex. Jack and his assistant Stephen, who had both worked the mill before its previous closure, had been employed by Mary, and worked together in the mill for the first four years, until Stephen married and left to work with his father in law.

Mary had met Lucas on one of her visits to the Lewes Workhouse soon after Stephen's departure, and had offered him an apprenticeship at the flour mill. Now Lucas, well into his second year of his apprenticeship, thoroughly enjoyed his work and was looked upon by Jack and Winnie as the son they'd never had.

On his first day at the mill, Winnie invited Blake to the house at lunch time for a cup of tea and to eat his lunch. Winnie forestalled Blake's inevitable question regarding Clive Easton's absence from the table. 'Clive likes to spend his lunch break's each day, rain, hail or shine fishing, ever hopeful of catching his dinner. I wonder if he will fish for his dinner in the harbour when he moves to Whitby.'

Satisfied that Blake had a good understanding of his new job, Clive left two days later and Blake settled into his new routine, revelling in being busy and working in his chosen field. Rufus was in his element, patrolling the storerooms holding the unmilled grain, and bags of milled flour and stock food, carrying out merciless attacks on any rodents seeking a free meal. Lucas was thrilled when Rufus showed his prowess as a hunter, because, until the little terrier's arrival, it had been Lucas's unpleasant job to try to keep the vermin population under control.

Blake travelled to London the day before his appointment, stayed the night at Malcolm's, then travelled straight back to Longmire Hall following his hour long appointment, where he was questioned at length about his life style and future plans, before he was measured for an appropriate prosthesis. Malcolm quite understood Blake's desire to return to his new job so quickly, and although sorry that his friend was not moving to London with him, Malcolm was relieved that Blake was showing a new confidence in his ability to look after himself. Blake's decision also freed Malcom to look into the numerous assets the Colonel had left him, some that could necessitate traveling away from London for possibly long periods of time.

Alfie, who had been in London to meet market stall holders who sold Everton Manor vegetables, met Blake at Paddington Station, and travelled back to Longmire Hall with him. During the journey home, Alfie explained why he'd been in London, and how he and Ryan Murphy were becoming more involved in the overseeing of the numerous workers now employed on the market garden, and also in the marketing of the produce.

'Who does the ordering, invoicing and wages for you Alfie?' Blake thought it might be interesting to speak with another administrator of the Countess's business ventures. He was surprised when nineteen year old Alfie replied, 'Ryan and I do most of that, Captain Mitchell.'

'If you don't mind me asking Alfie, where did you learn to be a bookkeeper?'

'Ryan and I went to accounting classes at school, and Lady Mary and Sir Hugh have been really helpful in showing us how to set up a good workable system for us to adhere to. Mr Lyons is always happy to help as well, if we have a problem.'

When Alfie was dropped off at Everton Manor, Mary boarded the coach to return to Longmire Hall after sitting for two days at the Lewes Court. Mary was delighted to hear Blake's enthusiastic response to her query about his appointment in London.

'After taking numerous measurements of both my legs, followed by a lengthy discussion on my lifestyle and future plans, the specialist said that he was sure they would be able to fashion a prosthesis that will allow me to live a normal, active life. They hope to have it ready for a fitting in a fortnight.'

A little later Blake turned to Mary. 'Lady Mary, thank you for asking Alfie to meet me at the station today. Travelling with luggage and crutches in a crowd is quite exhausting. He and I had a most interesting conversation on the train home, discussing his involvement in the running of the market garden. I found it incredible that he and Ryan have such responsible roles at their youthful stage of life.'

'Sir Hugh and I felt the same at first Blake, but have been delighted to see how well they are both coping with the added responsibility. Ryan has a flair for accounting, while Alfie's forte appears to be in marketing and negotiating deals with traders and merchants. The boys work well together, complementing each other's strengths and weaknesses.'

'How in the world does Alfie manage to deal with some of those London traders Lady Mary? Surely they must feel they can run rings around a youth not yet twenty.'

'Alfie started as an assistant to an experienced wholesaler for a couple of years, until one day Joe fell ill and Alfie finished the transactions solo. A number of market stall holders have told me that they like trading with Alfie, as he has proved himself to be an honest negotiator, who ensures that the goods he delivers are of the highest quality, and what was ordered. He also has an innate ability to engage with both men and women at the level in which they feel most comfortable, and has quickly developed a reputation of being a trustworthy supplier.'

'Would you mind if I had a chat to Ryan and Alfie about their bookkeeping Lady Mary? There are a few things I would like to change at the mill, and I wondered if we might be able to share ideas, and maybe incorporate similar practices where possible, to streamline and simplify the bookkeeping processes of each business.'

'I think that would be a good idea Blake. I'm sure the boys would appreciate a guiding hand at times.'

When the coach arrived at Longmire Hall, a frantic Rufus rushed up to Blake, who sat on the coach step and cuddled the wriggling terrier. Mary laughed. 'Rufus has well and truly adopted you as his master Blake. When you left for London, we had to lock him in a storeroom, to stop him following the coach. He only settled when Toby arrived on his milk round, and he has been with him until Toby was informed that we were on our way home from Everton Manor, and he brought him back to the Hall.'

'I missed my little mate too. When I get my new foot, we'll be able to go for long walks together.'

CHAPTER 20

Yorkshire, England
December 1895

Early in December, Mary and Hugh travelled by train to Yorkshire with Bill and Pat, to spend time with Hugh's parents at the Oakdale Estate before Christmas. They were accompanied by the nursery maid, who would look after the children when Mary and Hugh were busy.

Elizabeth, Hugh's mother, was thrilled to see her son and his family. She still found it hard to believe that her younger son was a Knight of the Realm, married to a Countess, and father to two young children

Two days after their arrival at Oakdale Estate, Mary and her brother in law Paul delivered two Hereford cows with calves at foot, to a farm near Hayton, a village a couple of miles south of Pocklington. On their return journey, after a quick lunch with the farmer and his wife, they noticed a small tree fallen across the road. As Paul slowed the horses pulling the empty cart, Mary saw a horse and rider emerge from the bushes to the side of the road in front of them.

To Mary's and Paul's horror, the masked rider pointed a pistol at them, while another masked man walked towards their cart. As the mounted man ordered 'Put your hands up,' Mary whispered, 'Keep a tight hold of the reins Paul.'

The rider pointed his pistol at Mary as the man on foot approached the cart. 'I know you're carrying the money from the sale of those cows, and I'm asking you to hand that and your jewellery to my friend, if you please Lady Mary.'

'The money is in my pocket. May I lower my arm to remove my purse?'

When the rider nodded his head, Mary put her hand into her skirt pocket, whispering, 'Sit back Paul.' Instead of a purse, she pulled out her revolver, and pointed it at the rider. Before he could react, Mary shot the pistol out of his hand. The second man, who was only a couple of yards from the cart, turned to see his partner thrown from his rearing horse. When he turned back towards Paul and Mary, he found himself staring at the gun pointed at his face.

'Don't even think of touching your pistol mister. Lie face down with your hands behind your head.' Quickly the man lay down. 'I'll hold the horses Paul, if you get down and collect their pistols.'

While Paul removed the pistol from the terrified man's waist band, Mary looked over to where the unseated rider was sitting on the ground, clutching his bloody hand. Once Paul had retrieved his pistol, Mary called to the man. 'Get up and walk slowly over here.'

The man refused. 'Your ear will bleed a lot more than your hand if you don't get up immediately.' Slowly he stood up, then still holding his hand walked towards the cart. While Mary kept her gun pointed at the men, Paul quickly bound their wrists with the rope used to restrain the cows in the cart, despite the howls of pain from the wounded man, whose hand had been wrapped in the sash he'd been wearing around his waist. They were then directed to get into the cattle crate on the back of the cart, where they were tied to either side.

Mary collected the men's horses and tied them to the back of the cart, then they set off for Pocklington, where the men were handed over to Paul's brother in-law Peter, who was the sergeant at the Pocklington Police Station.

After telling Peter what had occurred, and explaining how Mary had been given the revolver by her father when he was satisfied that she could use it correctly, Paul and Mary decided to stay at The Railway Inn, as it was getting dark. Paul rang his father to explain their situation, then he and Mary had supper in the hotel restaurant.

'I had no idea you had a gun Mary. Do you always carry it?'

'Not as often as I used to Paul. Mainly when I go out riding on the estate, though for some reason I felt I should take it today. I have special pockets made in my skirts, especially my riding habit, and still practice as often as I can, when out of earshot from the Hall.'

'I'm glad you warned me to hold the horses tight and to sit back. I think I got as much of a fright as those two men did. Would you really have shot the man if he hadn't stood up Mary?'

'I could easily have taken a piece out of his ear at that range, no worries Paul. But I'm glad I didn't have to. I don't like hurting people.'

The next morning, when Mary and Paul arrived back at the Oakdale Estate, Hugh hugged his wife tightly. 'I can't let you out of my sight for a minute, my love. How can I make you take things easier, now that we're expecting a new addition to our family?'

CHAPTER 21

Longmire Estate
January – April 1896

Following their return to Longmire Hall later that week Hugh insisted that Mary have an appointment with Dr Heslop, who was now the Longmire Hall doctor. When he'd completed his examination, Brian sat at his desk and waited for Mary to dress, then sit in the chair opposite.

'I can confirm that you are definitely pregnant Mary. What you may not realise is that you are carrying twins!'

Mary sat back with a gasp. 'Are you sure Brian? Aren't I too old to have twins?'

'I am pretty certain Mary – I could hear two strong foetal heat beats. As for too old, you will be what - 28 next month? That's not too old, when you are as fit and healthy as you are. However, to ensure the ongoing wellbeing of both yourself and you babies I'm going to insist that you cut back your workload and travelling. No more riding or travelling on rough roads in your coach. You should remain close to Longmire Hall or Everton Manor for the rest of your pregnancy and for as long as is required following your confinement.'

That evening, when Bill and Pat had gone to bed Mary informed Hugh of her unexpected news. He was delighted though, like Mary, was a little apprehensive about birthing twins. He agreed with Brian's stipulation that she cut back her workload, and was a little nonplussed with her ready agreement.

'My family means far more to me than my business and social commitments Hugh. I will appoint an executive manager who can work from an office in Lewes.'

'You could set up an office in the building that my company leases Mary. There are some rooms available if you decide to.' Hugh had recently opened a head office for his business in Lewes. His farm consulting enterprise had become so popular, he now employed five consultants who lived in Northern England, Cornwell, Wales, and the East and Central counties, while Hugh concentrated on the southern counties which allowed him to spend more time on or near the Longmire Estate, He was also heavily involved in trialling new varieties of wheat and other grains being grown on the new land near Longmire Village, measuring their yield and suitability for flour production and cattle feed.

After considerable thought, Mary employed Reginald Mason, the manager of a local brewery, to the position of executive manager, to assist her in the running of her numerous businesses. Mary had already employed Amy as her full time personal assistant. During the years the young maid had been employed at Longmire Hall, she'd impressed Mary with her amazing organisational ability, and within a few years Amy regularly accompanied Mary on her business and legal trips, acting as Mary's maid if required, but more importantly, as her personal assistant.

Now a confident twenty three year old, Amy lived in one of the three cottages at Longmire Hall. She ate most of her meals with the staff, and spent much of her time, when not working in Mary's study, in her own office in the cottage. Having the telephone connected at both Longmire Hall and Everton Manor, plus Amy's extreme competence in organising her legal, business, and social appointments, meant that Mary was able to slow down and rest during the remainder of her pregnancy.

To everyone's amazement and delight, five years following Patricia's birth, in early April Mary safely gave birth to two healthy babies, John Graham and Theresa (Tess) Clara. However, soon after their birth, it had become apparent that Mary wasn't producing enough milk to satisfy two young babies so Christine recommended that she should consider employing a wet nurse to help her feed the twins. Although initially shocked at the idea, Mary quickly agreed for the sake of her young babies

Three days after the birth Christine introduced Mary and Hugh to twenty two year old Elsie Logan, who Christine had attended earlier in the week when Elsie had gone into labour a month before the baby was due, following being told of her husband's death in a workplace accident. Regrettably, the baby boy died at birth. As Elsie no longer had access to an income, and was producing abundant milk, she agreed to Christine's suggestion to be a wet nurse. Little did Elsie realise that she would be offered such a position by a Countess. The twins immediately accepted Elsie, happily suckling from either their mother or Elsie. They enjoyed drinking at the same time, and weren't the least concerned who they drank from. Soon Mary and Elsie became accustomed to sitting together at feeding time, alternating the twins each feed.

Mary found Elsie to be a friendly, well-read young lady, whose father had been the local schoolmaster in Chorley, a town in Lancashire. Elsie had worked as his assistant until his sudden death when she was eighteen. She and her mother had to move out of the school house, and found lodgings in a boarding house, living on her father's savings for six months, then on Elsie's wages from her job as a shop assistant. One evening she arrived back at their lodgings to be informed that her mother was marrying the local publican, and that they were moving into the residence above the bar.

It only took a few months for Elsie's new step father to begin pestering her, and trying to enter her room at night. Her mother wouldn't believe her daughters accusations, so the next payday Elsie went to work carrying a bag of clothes that her mother thought was to be dropped off at the church, took all of her money from her bank account after work then went straight to the station, bought a ticket and boarded a train to London. On arrival at Euston Station Elsie bought another ticket to Brighton, where she lodged with a lady who ran a sea side hotel.

While working for her landlady Elsie met Stan Logan, a young builder renovating a nearby hotel, and after a six month courtship, at the age of twenty one she and Stan married and moved to Lewes, where Stan's employer was based. They lived in a house next to the builder's yard, and were overjoyed when they learnt that Elsie was pregnant. Sadly, a month before the baby was due Stan and another builder were killed when the roof they were working on collapsed. Christine had been visiting the medical clinic in Lewes when Dr Wilson had asked her to attend Elsie when she went into premature labour.

By the end of August young John and Tess were both healthy, happy five month old babies, having more than doubled their weight since birth, and already beginning to eat solids. They loved being put on a rug on the floor, and were beginning to roll over and could sit up with support. Mary was sure that they recognised different people who entered the nursery.

Nanny Roberts had been considering retiring once Pat started school, as Bill now slept in his own room near Mary and Hugh, and Pat, although still sleeping in the nursery, was having most of her meals with her parents and Bill downstairs. With the unexpected announcement of Mary's pregnancy, Nanny Robert's tenure in the Longmire Hall nursery was extended, and when Elsie arrived to help feed the twins she was employed as Nanny's assistant. Elsie was allocated a bedroom next to the nursery, and when not feeding the babies, she helped Nanny Roberts look after the twins day and night, while a woman from the village was paid to launder all of the twins clothing and napkins.

Both John and Tess loved being outside when the sun was shining so Elsie often took them up the long drive or out to the stables in the double pram that Hugh had brought back from London, usually accompanied by Scruffy and Mac while Bill and Pat were at school.

Each morning before Mary and Elsie fed the twins, Nanny Roberts woke Pat and dressed her ready for breakfast, and a maid took a small glass of warm milk up to Bill. After a quick wash, he dressed himself in the clothes that Elsie had laid out for him the night before, then he went down to the breakfast room to join his parents and Pat.

Elsie soon learnt the names of all the staff, indoor and out and she also met Captain Mitchell who was the accountant at the Longmire flour mill. Elsie had first seen him from the window of the nursery when he left his cottage to walk to the stables with his little Jack Russell running beside him. She knew that he had a prosthetic foot and was amazed that he only had a slight limp and rode his horse to and from work, unless the weather was too inclement. When they first met, he had ridden back to the Hall for a meeting with Lady Mary, and Elsie was at the stables with the twins, letting them see and hear the horses from their pram.

Captain Mitchell handed his horse's reins to the groom. 'I'll be returning to the mill after my meeting with her ladyship James. Please unsaddle Kira and put her in a stall, until I return.'

He turned to Elsie. 'Good morning. I am Captain Blake Mitchell. I gather you are Elsie Logan, the assistant Nanny.'

'Good morning Captain Mitchell. Yes I'm Elsie Logan. I'm sure you have met Master John and Miss Tess.' Blake looked in the pram and smiled at the twins.' Oh yes, we have met many times. They are certainly growing. How are you settling in?'

'Well thank you. Lady Mary has made me feel very welcome and Nanny Roberts is very encouraging.

CHAPTER 22

Longmire Village
Sussex, England
September 1896

Jeff Williams stretched his arms above his head as he stood in the early morning sunshine, thinking how lucky he was to be the Longmire Village blacksmith. Although he and his wife Cathy had only been in the village for the past five years, they'd been made welcome and had many new friends. As his eyes adjusted to the gloom when he opened the front door to the smithy, he noticed what looked like a bundle of rags behind the forge. On closer examination, he realised it was a young child huddled in the corner, staring up at him with terrified eyes.

'Please don't hit me mister. I aint took nothing. I just wanted to get warm.'

Squatting down in front of the frightened child Jeff stared at the grubby, tearstained face. 'I won't hurt you lad. Why are you hiding in my smithy?' To his consternation the boy burst into tears. 'I was so cold last night I crawled through a gap in the side gate. I was going to leave before the sun came up, but I fell asleep.' Jeff noted the tattered, threadbare shirt and shorts the boy wore, and thought how cold the past night had been.

'Where have you come from lad?'

The boy peered at Jeff suspiciously. 'You won't call the police will you mister?'

'Not if you tell me the truth.'

'I jumped off a milk cart last night.'

'What's your name son?'

'Noel.'

'Noel what?'

'Don't know. Just Noel.'

'Well Noel. What say we go into my house where it's warm, and my wife will give you something to eat.'

Cathy was astounded when her husband ushered a young, scrawny, blond headed urchin into the kitchen, putting his finger to his lips as she was about to query the boy's presence. 'Noel, this is my wife Cathy. Noel was in the smithy trying to get warm Cath. Will you please give him something to eat, and make him a warm drink while I hunt up a jumper for him to wear?'

'There are some old clothes up in the attic Jeff.'

Cathy smiled at the young lad before her, then held out her arms. 'Come here you poor little mite, and give Cathy a hug.' To her surprise, Noel ran to her and snuggled close when she wrapped her arms around his trembling shoulders. As the boy sobbed against her, she moved slowly towards the chair near the range and sat down, lifting him on to her lap.

Jeff came back into the kitchen holding a navy blue jumper. 'This will be too big Noel, but it will keep you warm. I'll get some twine to tie around your waist, to keep it off the ground.'

'Would you mind bringing in the bath while I get him something to eat and drink Jeff? A bath is definitely required before he puts on that jumper.'

When Noel grabbed the bread and dripping that Cathy put in front of him, and tried to stuff it all into his mouth she held his hand. 'There's no need to gobble it all at once Noel. There's plenty more here, but you shouldn't eat too much, or you'll be sick.' Noel stared at Cathy, then hung his head. 'I is awful hungry.' Cathy hugged the sobbing boy. 'Trust me Noel. I'll give you small amounts to eat during the day to help your stomach get used to having food in it again. Now drink your milk, then we'll give you a warm bath.

While Noel finished his breakfast, Jeff brought in the tin bath from the laundry and poured in hot water from the kettle, before cooling it with water brought in from the pump. 'I have to get out to the smithy now Cath. I've three of the Estates horses to be shod first thing this morning.'

'Out you go Love. Noel and I will be fine, won't we Noel?'

Noel looked up from where he was enjoying lying in the warm water, and nodded his head. As Cathy washed the young boy's back she was horrified to see how emaciated he was. His arms and legs were like matchsticks, and his body was skeletal. There was also a large suppurating sore on his upper arm.

'How old are you Noel?'

'Mam told me I's seven.'

'Did you have a birthday party?'

'What's that?'

'When people meet to remember the day you were born.'

'Don't know when I were born. Mam told me it were when a special boy were born.'

'Would that be Christmas Day Noel?'

'I think that's the big word Mam told me.'

'Right Noel, let's get you dried, then I think you could do with a sleep.' When she saw the worried look on the young boy's face she added 'I'll be right here in the kitchen when you wake up Noel.'

'Will you take me to the workouse then?'

'Do you want to go to the workhouse Noel?'

Noel shrank back from her. 'No, not a good place. I run away.'

'Noel, please believe that Jeff and I will do our best to make sure that you don't go to the workhouse. Let's tuck you up in bed for a sleep, then I'll give you some more food to eat.' Cathy carried the sleepy lad up to her bedroom and he was asleep before his head touched the pillow. Leaving the door open, she went into the spare bedroom and made up the bed, then went back down to the kitchen to wash the dishes, then make some bread. While she kneaded the dough, Cathy thought how little Noel seemed to know, and wondered whether it was because he was slow, or whether he just hadn't had the chance to learn the basic vocabulary that she thought a seven year old should know.

Two hours later she heard a sound on the stairs and looked up when Noel entered the kitchen. He smiled with relief when he saw her, then walked around the table to hug her. 'You didn't leave me.'

'No Noel, I told you I'd be here when you woke up, and here I am. Now sit at the table and I'll get you some more food.' Soon a small bowl of porridge, milk and honey was placed in front of the delighted boy. 'Oh yum, my bestest food!'

'Eat it slowly Noel, then you'll enjoy it even more.' Cathy wiped a tear from her eye as she watched the young boy savour every mouthful of porridge, then scrape as much as he could from the empty bowl. 'You can have some more at lunch if you wish.'

'It was so yummy. Thank you.'

'Where did you live before you came here Noel?'

'Da worked on a farm, but Mam and I had to leave when he was dead. Some nasty men told Mam they would come for her the night after they put Da in the ground. She was frightened, so we left home after she tied some things in a sheet. Mam and I walked lots of days and nights looking for food and places to sleep.' Noel stopped talking for a moment and looked at the floor. Then he looked back at Cathy and there were tears in his eyes. 'When we came to a big town she cried a lot, and told me we had to go to the workouse. But after we slept in an empty shed she was real cold in the morning, and wouldn't wake up. I ran away when some men came and put her in a cart.'

Cathy wrapped her arms around the sobbing boy and held him tightly until he calmed down. 'Did you have other children to play with at the farm Noel?'

'No, we lived in a hut in the trees. It wasn't big like this. The roof was just above Da's head. Mam and Da slept on a bed near the back wall and I slept near the fire.'

'Do you know where the farm is, or the name of the farmer your father worked for?'

'Da called him the old bastard, but Mam called him Squire Brown. Mam and I walked away from the trees in the dark. When it was light, we were out where you could see a long way all around you. I was scared, but Mam said it was alright, and that it was good to be able to see so far without trees.'

When Jeff came into the kitchen for lunch, Noel sat at the table watching him eat the large sandwich Cathy placed in front of him. 'How are you feeling Noel? You look a lot warmer now, and I gather you like my Cathy's porridge.'

'I am warm and I slept in a bed like my Mam and Da slept in. Did you put shoes on the horses?'

'Yes I did, and I also made some more shoes for the horses coming this afternoon. Would you like to see them being shod, if Cathy has time to bring you into the smithy?'

'Oh yes please. I like horses.'

Cathy placed a smaller sandwich in front of Noel saying 'Remember Noel, if you eat this slowly and chew each mouthful, you won't feel as hungry. Also, I'll give you a glass of milk when you finish eating.'

Jeff and Cathy smiled at each other as they watched Noel try to eat slowly. While he drank his milk, Cathy walked with Jeff to the door. 'Jeff, Noel has a badly infected wound on his arm. Would you have time to ask Christine to come to see him?'

Jeff leant down and kissed the top of Cathy's head. 'Yes I will, my darling, but don't get too attached to him before we find out more about him.'

Not long after Jeff left the kitchen there was a knock on the back door. Noel looked startled and was about to run upstairs when Cathy grabbed his arm. 'Don't be afraid Noel. No one in this village will hurt you.' When she opened the door, she smiled at her visitor. 'Christine, thank you for coming so quickly. Please come in.'

Christine Heslop, the wife of the village doctor, followed Cathy into the kitchen and removed her headscarf. 'How are you Cathy? Jeff mentioned you had a small dilemma you'd like to discuss.'

Cathy pulled Noel out from behind her skirt. 'This is my small dilemma Christine. Noel, this is Mrs Heslop. She's a nurse, and I'd like her to look at the sore on your arm.' Noel looked at Mrs Heslop, then at Cathy who smiled, then nodded her head. Christine knelt down in front of Noel and held out her hand. Shyly he put his hand in hers and said 'Hello Mrs Heslop.'

'Hello Noel, I gather you've come to stay with Jeff and Cathy, and have been walking for a long time. How did you hurt your arm?'

'A big rat bit me! I yelled and it let go and ran off.'

Christine looked carefully at the inflamed sore on the boy's upper left arm, noting the large yellow pustule and the redness of the skin surrounding the bite. 'That looks quite sore Noel. Do you mind if I touch your arm near the bite?'

Noel bit his lip and looked at Cathy. 'Will you hold my hand Cathy?'

Cathy stood with one arm around Noel's shaking shoulders, and gave him her other hand to grip, while Christine gently touched his arm a number of times, each time nearer to the wound, until she felt the boy flinch.

'You're certainly a brave boy Noel. I'm sure that's quite painful.' Noel nodded, then bit his lip again. 'Will you have to cut my arm off now?'

'Good heavens, no. What gave you that idea Noel?'

'A boy in the street told me rat bites go rotten, and my arm will have to be chopped off.'

'Was this after your mother was taken away Noel?'

'Yes. I got scared and ran away when he told me that.'

'Well Noel, my husband is a doctor, and I'm sure that he will help your arm get better, if you come with me to see him.'

'Can Cathy come with me?'

Christine looked at Cathy. 'Could we go now please Christine, before Jeff comes in for his dinner?'

'Yes, let's go now. We live just up the street Noel.'

Dr Brian Heslop, the village doctor looked up in surprise when Christine, Cathy and Noel entered the consulting room in the annex attached to the side of the doctor's residence. 'Hello Brian. This young man is Noel, and he's staying with Cathy and Jeff. Noel, this is Dr Heslop.'

Brian looked at the emaciated boy hiding behind Cathy's skirt. Slowly he walked close to Cathy, then bent down and said softly 'Hello Noel, it's nice to meet you.'

'Hello. Will you stop my arm coming off please?'

Brian looked up at Cathy in surprise. 'Noel has an infected rat bite on his arm Dr Heslop.'

'Okay, let's take your jumper off and have a look Noel. Tell me if your arm hurts too much when I examine it.' After a quick examination Brian handed Noel a piece of toffee to suck. Brian sat down on the floor beside Noel, after popping a small piece of toffee into his own mouth. 'I can tell that you're a brave boy Noel, but do you think you would be brave enough to let me take away that yucky yellow part?'

'Would that make my arm better?'

'I will certainly try my hardest to make it better for you.'

'Will it hurt?'

'You'll be asleep Noel, so won't feel anything. When you wake up, it will be sore like it is at the moment, but will get better quickly.'

Brian stood up and faced Cathy. 'That wound needs to be cleaned up as soon as possible Cathy, before the infection spreads. I'd like to use a few drops of chloroform to put Noel to sleep, so I can cut some of that infection out without him feeling anything. Is Noel a relative of yours so you can give me permission to operate on him?'

'Jeff and I only found him this morning Dr Heslop. His father and mother both died recently, and he has no idea where they lived before he and his mother were forced to leave their home. It appears they'd been walking for a number of days and nights – a seven year old has little concept of time. His mother was heading for the Workhouse in Lewes when she died, and he's terrified of going there.'

'If that wound isn't treated quickly he might soon join his parents Cathy. If I declare he's a homeless orphan, would you and Jeff be happy to look after him while he recovers, and we can make some inquiries as to his origin?'

'Certainly we would Dr Heslop. I've only known him since Jeff found him in the smithy early this morning, but already I have a fondness for the poor little mite, and would dearly love to help him grow into a healthy, well fed young lad.'

'Right, let's see if we can convince this young lad to allow us to put a mask over his face without too much fuss.'

Cathy sat Noel on her lap. 'Noel, Mrs Heslop needs to put a piece of cloth over your nose and mouth for a short time. It will smell a bit funny and will make you feel sleepy. Will you let her do that if I cuddle you tightly?'

'Will it hurt Cathy?'

'No my little love. It will just smell a bit different. And when you wake up, I'll be here with you.' Noel looked frightened, but nodded his head.

Christine stood next to Cathy and showed Noel the cloth mask she would put over his face. 'Can you count to ten Noel?'

'Noel shook his head. 'I can count to three.'

'That's fine. When I say 'go' you count to three with me, then we'll start from one again.'

Christine gently placed the mask over Noel's mouth and nose, then Dr Heslop immediately placed two drops of chloroform on it. 'Go. One, two, three, one, two...' By the time Christine reached three Noel was asleep. Quickly she removed the mask, then picked Noel up and placed him on the table in the surgery, while Dr Heslop tied on his apron and washed his hands. Christine washed the skin around the wound with warm water and carbolic soap, then Brian used a sharp knife to lance the pustule, releasing a surprising amount of pus that Christine quickly cleaned away. Within a short time, the wound was swabbed with carbolic acid, then Christine bound it with a calico bandage. By the time she began gathering the bowls and instruments Brian had used, Noel began to stir.

Beckoning to Cathy, who had been sitting away from the table, Brian whispered 'Hold his hand Cathy and talk quietly to him, so that he hears your voice as he wakes up. His arm will be sore, but try to take his mind off it by talking about something he likes, until he's fully awake.'

'Hello Noel. This is Cathy here holding your hand. In a little while I'll take you home, and you can sleep in your new bed. Jeff has been busy this afternoon shoeing horses from a farm nearby and...'

Noel opened his eyes and stared at her. 'What happened to me? My mouth tastes yucky and I feel funny.'

'Yes my little darling, you have just woken up after Dr Heslop cleaned the wound on your arm.'

Noel's eyes widened in alarm. 'He didn't.' 'No Noel he didn't cut your arm off. It's bandaged up and will be sore for a while, then will get better.'

'Oh yes, it is sore.'

'Well, you be a brave little soldier and I'll take you home.'

'I'll call Rupert Johnston, our gardener to carry him home for you Cathy.'

'That's alright Dr Heslop. I can carry him as he doesn't weigh much at the moment, and it isn't far.'

After placing the jumper over Noel's head Cathy stood up with him in her arms, and Brian walked to the door with her. 'Here is some laudanum to help him sleep for the next couple of days Cathy. He can have a small amount of food before he goes to sleep tonight. Christine will call in tomorrow to check his wound, and will put a new dressing on it, but please contact me at any time if Noel develops a fever, or you are worried about him. In the meantime, I'll make some discreet enquires about Noel's mother and possible family.'

CHAPTER 23

Longmire Village
Sussex, England
September- October 1896

For the next couple of days Noel slept most of the time under the influence of the small amount of laudanum that Dr Heslop had prescribed for him. Christine visited twice a day to check his wound, and was able to calm Cathy's concern. On the third morning Noel woke up, and unsteadily walked down the stairs to the kitchen, where Cathy was cooking some porridge. She nearly dropped the saucepan when Noel said 'I need to go to the privy.'

'Oh, my little lad, I'll take you out, but put my shawl around your shoulders first.' When they returned to the kitchen Noel sat at the table and watched Cathy at the stove. 'I'm really hungry. Can I please have some porridge?'

'Apart from feeling hungry, how do you feel Noel? And how is your arm?'

Noel looked at the bandage on his arm. 'It's not as sore now. I just feel hungry.'

Cathy placed a bowl of porridge in front of Noel, then after sprinkling some sugar, and pouring some milk into the bowl, she handed Noel a spoon. 'There you are my lad. Wrap yourself around that.'

Noel looked up at her and smiled. 'You say some funny things, but I like it. Can I call you Cathy?'

'Of course you can Noel.' Cathy placed her hand on Noel's forehead and was pleased that it no longer felt hot. Hopefully, her young charge was on the mend. When he finished his breakfast, Noel carried his bowl and glass into the scullery, then they went up to his room to dress him in some warm clothes.

Following Noel's surgery, the villagers soon became aware of his presence at the blacksmith's residence, and women with young boys offered Cathy clothes for the young lad currently in her charge. He now had some warm trousers, shirts, a jumper, and a warm jacket. When he first saw himself in the long mirror in Cathy's bedroom he stared at his image, then turned to Cathy. 'Is this what other boys in the village wear Cathy? Boys I saw in the town had clothes like my old clothes.' Cathy frowned, remembering the pitifully thin, dirty clothes Noel had arrived in. 'These clothes will keep you much warmer Noel, and I'll wash them often so they stay clean. We'll get you some boots as soon as we can.'

Brian called in to see Cathy the next day to check Noel's arm, but more so to inform her of the results of his enquires re Noel's family. When Noel went out to be with Jeff in the smithy, Brian sat at the kitchen table and accepted a cup of tea and some cake.

'I spoke to both Dr Wilson and Dr Campbell about Noel and his mother Cathy, and they had a list of the recent arrivals of dead women at the morgue. There was one unidentified lady brought in about three weeks ago, who appears to have died of starvation in a derelict building in Lewes. The only thing in her pocket was this little bear.' Brian sat a small knitted black bear on the table. 'Could we take this out to see if Noel recognises it?' When Noel saw the little bear in Brian's hand he began to cry. 'Where did you find Sooty? Mam said she would look after him for me, but the men took him away with her.' Brian handed Noel the bear, and the small boy hugged him to his chest. 'Your mother died during the night Noel, and she was taken to the hospital morgue. Thankfully the attendants found Sooty in her pocket. Now we know it was definitely your mother they buried. What was her name?'

'I called her Mam. Da called her Jean.'

'What did your Mam call your Da?'

'Ken.'

'Do you have any brothers or sisters Noel? Or aunts and uncles or grandparents?'

'I don't know. I never saw anyone at the farm.'

The next day James, a groom at Longmire Hall, arrived at the smithy, with a large pot of beef broth and a basket of vegetables. 'Good morning Cathy. When Mrs Smith heard about your new young lad she made some broth for you to, as she said 'put some meat on his bones!' And Sam picked these vegetables for you this morning. Her Ladyship is away at the moment, but she told Polly on the telephone that she is looking forward to meeting Noel.'

As Noel regained his strength he ventured outside with Cathy, and was introduced to the grocer and butcher when they went into their shops. He also met ladies who stopped to chat to Cathy, and began to lose his shyness at meeting other people.

One day he was sitting in the sunshine at the front of the smithy watching Jeff hammering a ploughshare when a large grey dog came running down the street towards him. Thinking it was a wolf, Noel gave a shriek and ran into the smithy, then heard a lady call 'Scruffy, sit!' When Noel hesitantly peeked around the door frame he saw a pretty lady riding a grey horse stop in front of the smithy and dismount. Jeff came to the doorway and touched his cap. 'Good morning Lady Mary. Sorry I couldn't come out immediately; I had to cool the metal I was working on. Cathy's in the kitchen.'

'Thanks Jeff.' Mary handed him Gem's reins. 'I think your young lad thought Scruffy was a wolf. I'll just allay his fears, then I'll go in to see Cathy'

She smiled at Noel. 'Hello Noel, my name is Mary. I'm sorry Scruffy scared you. Would you like to come out to make friends with him?'

Slowly Noel edged out through the door, keeping an eye on the dog sitting beside Mary. 'Would you like him to lie down, so he doesn't look so big?' Noel nodded. 'Lie down Scruffy.' When the big dog lay down and looked at Noel with what looked like a grin on his face Noel was happy to go over to where the lady stood. 'Hold my hand, and we'll both bend down to let Scruffy smell your hand. I promise he won't bite you.' Noel giggled when Scruffy licked his fingers, then rolled onto his back to let them tickle his tummy. 'You're his friend now Noel, and he won't hurt you, although he might accidently hit you with his tail when he's excited!'

Cathy came hurrying out, having heard Noel's shriek. 'Oh, hello Mary. Is Noel alright?'

'He's fine Cathy. He got a fright when he first saw Scruffy, but he seems to be fine with him now.' The three adults looked over to where Noel and Scruffy were sitting cuddled together near the gate.

'He's a bonnie lad m'lady. Both Cathy and I are becoming very fond of him, and I think he likes being with us.'

'He couldn't find a better couple to live with Jeff. Now, I'll let you get on with your work, and go in for a chat with Cathy. Are you coming in with us Noel?'

Noel jumped up and took Mary's offered hand. 'Can Scruffy come in too Mary?'

'Yes Noel, he loves visiting Cathy.'

Most of Mary's tenants called her Lady Mary or m'lady, but a few like Cathy and Tess Telford at Home Farm now called her Mary in private. Mary and Cathy had developed a close friendship since she and Jeff had arrived in the village to take over the smithy, after the previous blacksmith hurt his back and retired to Brighton.

Mary sat at the table, watching Noel and Scruffy rolling around together on the floor, while Cathy poured hot water into the teapot. 'Noel seems a lovely little lad Cathy, though he looks like he's suffered some hard times in his young life.'

'He's adorable Mary, and Jeff and I would love to have him as our son if we could.'

Mary knew that Cathy and Jeff would dearly love to have children, but after five years of marriage none had eventuated. As a married woman now with four young children, Mary felt very sorry for her friend. 'Where does he come from Cathy? I've just been told that Jeff found him hiding in the smithy.'

'His story is rather vague as you can imagine for someone so young. He says he's seven, but he's much smaller than your Bill.'

'By the looks of young Noel, he's been lacking adequate food for some time, which could have impeded his growth.'

'From what he's told us he lived with his parents on a farm until his father died, and he and his mother took a number of days and nights to walk to Lewes. She died before they reached the Workhouse, and unbeknown to Toby, Noel hid on the milk cart and jumped off when he stopped in the village when Toby was heading home to Home Farm.'

'So you've no idea where he's from.'

No. He doesn't appear to have had much contact with anyone other than his parents, who lived in a hut in a forest, and I'm beginning to suspect that they weren't very educated. He doesn't know his surname, but he said his parents were called Ken and Jean. He can only count to three, and he sits in one spot for ages, just watching what's going on, which makes me wonder if he had to stay put when his mother worked.'

'Would you like me to contact a detective I know well to make some discreet inquiries Cathy? Hugh could also ask his clients when he travels around the district.'

'I guess we should try to find out if he has family anywhere. In the meantime, I'll try to feed him up, and look after him as best I can.'

'Have you thought of sending him to school? He's small enough to start in the beginner's class, and it would do him good to meet with other children.'

'I will when he has a bit more energy. Plus, I'll have to go to Lewes to get him some boots. The ladies here were wonderful letting me have some clothes for him, but he needs footwear that fits.'

'I have to go to Lewes for court tomorrow morning Cathy. You and Noel could come with me if you'd like.'

'That would be wonderful thanks Mary. I'll prepare Jeff's lunch before we leave.'

CHAPTER 24

Longmire Village
October 1896

The next morning, James collected Cathy and Noel in Mary's coach, and Noel sat in wonder looking out of the windows as the two black horses trotted back towards Longmire Hall to collect Mary, who was standing near the front door, holding hands with a young boy and smaller girl.

That's Master Bill and Miss Pat Noel, two of Lady Mary's children.' When the coach stopped at the steps Mary bent down and kissed each child, then a tall lady took their hands and led them into the house as their mother went down the front steps. A young groom opened the coach door for her, and she thanked him as he shut the door behind her.

'Good morning Cathy and Noel. How are you both this morning?'

'Good morning Mary. We're both well thank you. Say good morning to Lady Mary, Noel.'

Noel, who couldn't believe the size of the building they had just driven up to looked at Mary with his eyes and mouth wide open in wonder. 'Do you live here Mary? Does Scruffy live here too?'

'Yes, we both live here Noel. Bill, the little boy who was on the steps with me, wants you to come and visit him soon.'

Noel turned to Cathy. 'Can I do that please Cathy? Then I could see Scruffy too.'

'Yes you can Noel, when the time comes.'

When Noel turned to look out of the window Mary smiled 'Scruffy has certainly made a friend with your young man Cathy. I have court this morning, but we can have lunch together before we come home. Will that give you long enough to do your shopping?'

'Plenty of time I should think Mary. Jeff is flat out at the moment, and people are paying him regularly, but I had better not spend all of his profits!'

'Has he considered putting on an apprentice?'

'Yes, he's spoken about it, but so far hasn't gone any further.'

'I know of a couple of likely lads if he's interested Cathy.'

Aware of Mary's position on the Board of Governors of the Lewes Workhouse, Cathy was pretty sure that was where the boys would come from, and was grateful to her friend for not mentioning the Workhouse in front of Noel. 'Thanks Mary, I'll let him know when I get home.'

When James stopped the coach at the Courthouse, the young groom jumped down from where he was seated beside James, and opened the door. When Mary alighted, she looked up at James. 'You can take the coach to Everton Hall for the morning James, then return here for us at two o'clock.'

'Certainly m'lady. Come on up Jake and we'll see if Mrs Peters has a cup of tea and some cake for us.'

As the coach moved away, Mary slipped half a crown into Cathy's hand. 'Buy yourself and Noel a hot drink and some cake before you set off on your shopping Cathy. If we meet here at midday, we can have some lunch before heading home.'

Cathy kept a firm hold of Noel's hand as they walked through the town to the market. There she found a pair of sturdy, well-fitting boots and some woollen socks for Noel, plus some long shorts and a warm coat with plenty of room for him to grow into. Noel was bemused with the whole shopping process, but tolerated it when Cathy promised him a cream bun when they'd finished.

While they sat in the teashop, Noel devouring his cream bun and Cathy drinking her cup of tea, the small lad watched the people walking along the street outside. When he swallowed the last mouthful of his bun he pointed to the street. 'I was really scared of all those people when I was here by myself Cathy. I like it much better in the village.'

'I can't say I like the crowds much myself Noel. I only come here if I have to buy something special, like your boots and coat.'

'Da had boots for work, but I've never had boots on my feet before. Do I wear them all the time?'

'No Noel, I'll buy you some soft slippers to wear in the house, like Jeff does in the evenings.'

Noel fell asleep during lunch, so Mary asked the waiter to put some food in a box for him to eat on the trip home. She and Cathy enjoyed a meal of steak and kidney pie and vegetables, followed by a bread and butter pudding before they went out to where the coach was waiting.

A month after Noel's arrival in the village Cathy and Noel had a meeting with the village school headmaster to discuss Noel's enrolment at the school. Angus Dowell was a relatively young man to be the headmaster of the school, but he appeared to be having great success in teaching the village children, and they loved going to school. An additional classroom had been built to cater for the growing number of students, the younger students being taught by Angus's wife Amanda.

After speaking to Cathy for a while, he sat on the floor beside Noel, who was busy drawing on a piece of paper that he'd been given. Looking at the drawing, he was astounded to see a picture of a hut amongst some large trees, with a lady standing crying in the doorway, way above the standard expected of a seven year old.

'What are you drawing Noel?'

'Mam at our home, before we had to leave.'

'Who taught you to draw?'

'Da learned me how to draw. He made sticks pointy so I could draw on the floor while Mam worked.'

'Do you know any letters or numbers Noel?'

Noel looked puzzled until Angus opened a book with writing and numbers on the front page.'

'I've not seen those before.'

'What about books with pictures?'

Noel pointed to the book. 'Is that a book?' Angus looked at Cathy and raised an eyebrow. 'Yes Noel, that's a book. We use books to learn things we need to know.'

'Will you learn me those things?'

'I will start to teach you those things, if you come to school next week Noel. If I give you some paper to take home, would you like to draw me some more pictures?'

'Yes please. I like drawing.'

Cathy had no need to fear that Noel was a slow learner. Within a month, he could count to ten and was able to copy the letters of the alphabet written on his slate each day, and he could soon spell his name. His drawing ability seemed to develop each day, especially when Mr Dowell gave him some out of school instruction on basic shapes and perspective, something he'd never dreamt to be teaching to such a young child.

Noel loved going to school, and soon made friends with the other boys, especially Bill. Although a bright child, Bill was not the most attentive student, but when he became friends with Noel, he actually enjoyed assisting his new friend with his letters and numbers, until Noel's reading was on a par with his. Then they helped each other, although Bill couldn't draw to save himself!'

It wasn't long before Bill asked Mary if she would teach Noel to ride one of the ponies. With Jeff and Cathy's consent, Mary and Robert, the Longmire head groom, taught Noel to ride, and soon he and Bill were seen riding together around the Longmire Hall grounds, accompanied by a patient groom.

Early in October Hugh informed Mary that he had heard of a farmer near Holtye, about twenty five miles north of Lewes, who was locally known as Squire Brown. She contacted her detective friend Richard Jones in London, who went to Holtye to see if he could find any information about Noel's parents.

It turned out that Noel's surname was Collins. His parents were Irish migrants, who had migrated to England when both their families had been decimated by the potato famine, leaving them with no known living relatives. Ken was employed as a woodcutter on 'Squire Brown's' property, while his wife Jean did all the washing and mending for the main house. Ken had been killed when a London friend of 'Squire Brown' mistook the unfortunate woodcutter for a deer!

The shooting hadn't been reported to the authorities, and the body was buried immediately after the incident. When asked had Mr Collins wages or any recompense been paid to his wife, Mr Brown initially became quite uneasy, then he explained that he couldn't pay her because Mrs Collins and her young son had disappeared soon after her husband's burial.

Further investigation revealed that the Squire had encouraged some of his men to molest the widow and make sure that she didn't report the incident. As she was illiterate and rarely spoke to others on the farm, he felt sure that he could conceal the death of his employee.

With Mary's consent, Richard spoke to a friend in the legal service in London about the case, and was advised that although it was illegal to not report the death, it would be difficult to press a case of murder against the man who had fired the fatal shot. However, he did indicate that it might be worthwhile alluding to the Squire that if some form of reimbursement was paid to Ken's family, in the form of a donation towards their living costs, the case might be brought to a close.

Hence £12, the quarter's wage the farmer owed to Ken Collins, plus a bank draught of £100, a donation from an unknown benevolent patron, was sent to Gordon Lyons, who promptly opened a trust fund for Noel.

CHAPTER 25

Mary buttoned her jacket as she walked from her bedroom to the children's' nursery. Margaret Roberts turned from plaiting Pat's hair. 'Good morning m'lady. I shan't be a moment.'

'Good morning Nanny Roberts. Good morning my darlings.'

Seven year old Bill walked over from where he'd been standing near the fireplace. 'Good morning Mother. Can I go down now to see Mrs Smith before breakfast?'

'Yes Bill, but don't pester her if she's busy. Pat and I will soon join you in the breakfast room.'

As Bill shot out of the nursery Margaret laughed. 'I'm not sure what he's up to m'lady, but he's been like a caged lion pacing around, waiting for you.'

'No doubt we'll find out soon enough. He has Mrs Smith wrapped around his little finger, so he's sure to get whatever he's after. We'll go down for breakfast in a moment my darling. I'll just say good morning to those two scamps in the bathroom.'

Bill was waiting in the breakfast room when Mary and Pat arrived. The children quickly ate the porridge Mary placed in front of them, then some toast and jam, while Mary drank a cup of tea.

'Mrs Smith gave me some big red plums to take to school Mother. I swap them with Noel for one of Mrs William's yummy pasties.'

Mary knew that Cathy had lived in Penzance until she married Grant. Her father had been a pastry cook and taught her to make Cornish Pasties with meat and vegetables in one end and jam in the other. Whenever she baked some for Grant's lunches, she made smaller ones for Noel.

'Maybe you should ask Mrs Smith to make some for you.'

'I asked her one day, but she said that only someone from Cornwell could make them like Mrs Williams does.' Mary smiled at her cook's adroit method of deflecting Bill's request.

Once they'd finished their breakfast, the two children kissed Mary goodbye, raced upstairs to clean their teeth, then they grabbed their school satchels and ran out the backdoor to where a groom waited with the covered governess cart used to take them to school when it was wet.

Relaxing after their departure, Mary helped herself to some of the hot food steaming under silver covers on the sideboard, and poured herself a cup of coffee. While she was eating, Amy came into the breakfast room.

'Good morning m'lady.'

'Good morning Amy. Help yourself to a cup of coffee and join me.' Mary knew that Amy would have eaten her breakfast earlier with the staff, but was pleased that she was willing to sit with her for a cup of coffee. Although Amy was quite comfortable to eat her meals with Mary when they were away from the estate on business, she preferred to have her meals with the staff when at the Hall.

Mary was well aware of the strange position that Amy was now in, having been a maid at the Hall for a number of years until her promotion to become Mary's personal assistant, making her neither a 'servant' nor a member of the family. However, Amy appeared to be coping with the awkward situation very well, loving her elevation to having a cottage to live in, but also retaining the friendship of her previous workmates.

'I spoke to Reginald Mason on the telephone yesterday afternoon m'lady. He would be happy to meet you in Lewes at 11am tomorrow, if possible. Also, Jack rang and said he'd ring you tonight.'

'Thank you Amy. I'll be in the study soon.'

That night while waiting for Hugh to come home, Mary sat in front of the fire in the study staring into the flames, and she thought how dramatically her life had changed since she had followed her dying mother's wishes, and sailed to England, to discover that she was the heiress of a high ranking aristocratic family. As the new Countess of two large English estates, Mary was an extremely wealthy young lady.

Unused to the way of the British aristocracy, and much to the consternation of her peers, she had stamped her own style in dealing with the patrician life that she was fated to live. Used to a hard life on the small family farm in Australia, she had been determined to use her wealth and position to improve the lives of her tenants and servants, who, when she arrived were very oppressed and demoralised, thanks mainly to her uncle's greed and total disregard for the welfare of those living on the estates,

Her tenants couldn't believe how lucky they were to now have such a benevolent landlady, and now took great pride in their village since Mary had initiated the long overdue repairs to the rundown buildings that she'd inherited. She'd restored the rents to their previous agreed rate and repaid the extra money that her uncle had demanded be paid. Businesses flourished as the tenants took pride in their work, and word spread around the district of their fair trading practises.

Mary often visited the village and chatted freely with the villagers, and she knew those who were struggling. Those in genuine need would often find a basket of groceries at their back door, or some of the younger villagers were paid by her ladyship to clear a garden or mend a broken fitting. The few not willing to help themselves didn't stay in the village for long.

Now she had a loving husband and four beautiful children plus tenants and staff who loved and revered her.

Since Mary's involvement as a Lewes Workhouse Guardian not long after her arrival in England, the many changes she'd initiated were gradually proving that just because a child came from a poor family, it didn't mean that they were incapable of living a worthwhile life if given the chance. Once the children were regularly fed nourishing food, and began attending a well-run school with dedicated teachers, many had confounded the doubters, and were now qualified and working in numerous professions.

Several of the older girls were studying nursing in London, and of those who went into service many did so as trained housekeepers or cooks. A couple of boys were currently studying to become doctors, and many businesses were seeking the Lewes Workhouse students who studied in modern accounting practices, and both boys and girls were employed as teacher's assistants in the district. Several boys were now employed by Mary's shipping company, both in the office with Charles Brown and as seamen on the ships.

Last year, Mary had bought a struggling local cartage business, and had utilised the vehicles to cart fresh vegetables from the Everton Manor market garden to the Lewes station for the London markets and to local customers. Several men from the workhouse were employed as drivers, while others worked at the stables and yard to care for the horses and vehicles. Three extra carts had been purchased and a depot and stables were opened in Longmire village to work for the mill, transporting wheat to the mill and ground flour to Lewes for distribution to London and local businesses.

As with the children at the warehouse, the adults were given the opportunity to attend classes, both to improve their literacy and numeracy, and to develop new skills in various trades. The health of most of the adults was improving with the more nourishing food they were receiving, and the better conditions they were living in. The women still did the washing and cleaning, and some helped in the kitchen, but the jobs were rostered, and the hours were reduced to allow for the tuition many undertook.

Parents were allowed to see their children regularly, and husbands and wives were given the opportunity to meet for some meals together.

Many of Mary's peers had scorned the changes that she was instigating, predicting an uprising of the illiterate, ne'er-do-wells. Of course, there were some malcontents amongst both the men and women, but those who made no attempt to conform were soon moved to more traditionally run institutions. Recently Mary had been approached by the administrators of some other regional Workhouses, to discuss the changes initiated at Lewes Workhouse.

Mary hoped that her mother would have been proud of what she had accomplished in her past ten years as a Countess.